SWEET TWISTED PINE

Lori R. Hodges

outskirts
press

Outskirts Press, Inc.
http://www.outskirtspress.com

Paperback ISBN: 978-1-9772-1635-9
Hardback ISBN: 978-1-9772-1636-6

1

THE JOURNEY

OCTOBER 1882

I stared out the train window as passengers boarded in Cheyenne, Wyoming, trying to keep my mind from replaying nightmarish images. Images of my sister and where she might be. Images detailing what may have happened to her. It was the final leg of my journey, and the beauty of the landscape was the only thing keeping me sane. Whenever anxiety built in my chest, I'd focus out my window and concentrate on the vast landscape. Almost there.

I knew that the longer it took me to get to Colorado, the less chance I had of finding Lucy. I had never been this far west, and had no idea what my options would be once I arrived in Fort Collins. For the first time in my life, I had no answers. I tugged at the tightness of my starched collar and fidgeted in my seat.

From my pocket, I pulled out the short message left for me in Philadelphia. When the patrolman had shown up on my doorstep, in the middle of the night, asking me to identify a body found in an alley, I'd never thought the note and the body would be connected to the disappearance of my sister. I unfolded the missive and stared at the lines on the page before me.

An elderly man boarded the train. He didn't move well, and his knees popped when he sat down across from me. His face softened with a smile. "Good afternoon, sir," he said pleasantly, taking off his hat. He wore an impeccable dark blue suit and tie and a constant smile upon his face.

"Pleased to meet you, sir," I said with a slight nod of my head. "Michael Mullen."

"Leo Biehler, sir." He spoke with a bit of a chuckle in his voice and a twinkle in his eye as he shook my hand. I was pleased to have him seated near me, as I craved a bit of the sophistication I'd left back home.

Another voice jarred me from my reflections, and I looked up to see a tall woman in her late twenties yell at a man and push him with her bag as she boarded the train. Although her hair was pulled back into a bun, several dusty brown strands had come loose and hung in damp tendrils around her face. She was filthy. Her face was smudged with dirt, and her soiled clothes made her look as if she had rolled around in the mud and filth outside. Surprisingly, however, the dress she wore was of the finest quality.

As she walked down the aisle, a man made a crude comment to her and then grabbed her backside firmly with his left hand. I sprang up and moved to intervene, unable to accept such conduct, but I stopped abruptly when I saw her silently and swiftly pull a knife out of her skirt and hold it between the man's legs. "If you value your manhood," she warned ruthlessly, "you'll take your grimy hands off me, you plug-ugly son of a bitch!"

The man jerked his hand away and apologized for his

behavior. The woman retracted her knife with a smile and continued along the aisle as if nothing happened. I sat back down, my mouth agape, and continued to stare as she came toward me. I had never seen a woman act like that.

"What are you staring at?" she shouted, standing in front of me.

"Pardon me, ma'am." I quickly averted me eyes and turned my attention to the paper in my hand, hoping she'd keep moving through the compartment.

Instead of moving on, however, she shoved her bag under a seat and sat down across from me, next to Mr. Biehler. Dust from her clothes wafted around the area and into the air. I quickly folded the note and placed it in the inner pocket of my jacket, close to my heart. I tried to keep my eyes focused elsewhere but found myself watching her surreptitiously. She was not as horrible as I had first imagined. In fact, her face would be quite lovely if she washed it.

"Good afternoon to you, ma'am," Mr. Biehler said pleasantly, tipping his hat in her direction.

The two entered into a pleasant conversation. As we traveled, I learned that she lived in Colorado and had just spent several weeks in Wyoming on family business. While she was pleasant toward Mr. Biehler, she continued to remain quite cold with me. Whenever I'd attempt to add something to the conversation, or when Mr. Biehler asked me a question, she looked away with annoyance. Perfect, I thought. Let them talk. Better him than me.

I glanced up occasionally from my book at the people around me and decided that perhaps she had good reason to treat me with such distaste. After what happened when she boarded the train, with the rude man and his unwelcome groping, I understood why she would avoid the attentions of a younger man. This was a very different world than the one I had known in Philadelphia. The farther west we traveled, the more severe the people seemed. I wondered what my fellow professors would think of such a place.

I glanced once more at the woman as she talked to Mr. Biehler. Personal cleanliness isn't too important out here either, I thought, returning my gaze to the book in my lap.

Mr. Biehler remained pleasant and chatty throughout our train travel. He said he was traveling to Denver, Colorado, to visit his daughter, which gave me hope that he might help me once we arrived. As soon as the offensive woman headed to the dining car, I decided to ask him about Fort Collins. I knew he had spent several months in Colorado when his daughter first moved out West.

"What brings you to Colorado, Mr. Mullen?" he asked before I had a chance to question him.

"My little sister," I said softly. I hadn't spoken to anyone about her since I'd left Philadelphia, and it felt a little strange doing so. Actually, I was desperate to find someone to confide in, someone who could help me.

"Does she live out here?"

"No, not exactly," I said hesitantly, clearing my throat. "Actually, I live in Philadelphia with my sister, Lucy. She ... um ... disappeared, over a week ago." I studied Mr. Biehler's face closely as I continued, hoping to find even one small answer to my mountain of questions. "I've received information that leads me to believe she's been taken out West. I'm trying to get to a ranch in northern Colorado, owned by the Donnelly family, where an old friend of my father's lives. Do you know anything about the area?"

"I don't really know much. Denver is the only place I have traveled in Colorado." He paused and then asked in a softer tone, "Why do you believe your sister is in Colorado?"

I hesitated, not knowing how much to tell. But I also

knew my time was limited, and I needed to get information. "About a week ago, I found out a man was in my neighborhood asking questions about my family. Then my sister caught him following her. You have to understand my sister. Nothing, not even an act of God, could stop my sister from going where she wanted to go, so we agreed to have Arthur, an old family friend, escort her on her daily outings to the hospital where she volunteered." I smiled. My family had employed Arthur after he'd sailed from Ireland to America with my father. He'd watched Lucy and me grow up, and we trusted him. "You must understand that Arthur is a huge man in both height and build, so it is unlikely that anyone would approach him, let alone cause trouble around him."

Mr. Biehler leaned forward as I continued my tale.

"I went to work at the university as I did every day, but I remained troubled. Lucy means more to me than anyone in this world. I went for a walk and tried to get information about the man from some of the merchants on Market and Chestnut streets, but I found out nothing. When I returned home that evening, Arthur said he'd dropped Lucy off at a friend's. He promised to pick her up the next morning, so I didn't worry too much."

I paused in my story, remembering the anxiety I'd felt when Arthur awakened me late in the night and insisted that I come downstairs. Clearing my thoughts, I continued. "A patrolman stood at my front door late that night. He was investigating a murder in an alley a few blocks from where Lucy was staying. Convinced that it was Lucy, I grabbed the officer by his shoulders and almost committed bodily harm when he refused to give me any information. He took me by carriage down Broad Street to Bainbridge, where he led me down a dark alley. They'd covered the body with a dark wool blanket, and the sergeant leaned over it with a lantern in his hand. He motioned me forward and continued to stare hard into my eyes. When he didn't speak, I felt more like a suspect than a possible witness."

"Who did you find under the blanket?"

"A stranger," I said, louder than I intended. I lowered my voice a little to keep others from overhearing. "I crouched down next to the sergeant and stared at the corpse. He clearly hadn't been there but a few hours at the most." I remembered seeing a knife protruding from the man's abdomen ... and the large amount of dark blood that pooled beneath him. His face was a dreadful gray with a deep shade of blue lining his lips. His glassy eyes stared blankly into the night.

Mr. Biehler seemed relieved and intrigued at the same time. "Why did they pull you out of bed to identify someone you had never met?"

"I asked the sergeant the same question, but he refused to answer. When I told the sergeant I had never seen the gentleman before, he pulled a note out of the dead man's pocket and handed it to me. As you can imagine, I was rather shocked to see my name written on the outside."

Mr. Biehler shifted in his seat.

"The note was short but contained all I needed to know. A man who wants something from my family took Lucy. After reading my father's journals, I believe he took her to Lone Tree, Colorado."

As the disagreeable woman returned and sat down, Mr. Biehler and I moved apart. Unable to continue further, I pulled out one of the journals from my bag and attempted to read.

Mr. Biehler leaned forward again and tapped me on the knee. "If you have trouble finding information once you arrive," he whispered, "your best bet is to go to the taverns and ask the owners about the ranch you're looking for. If anyone can help you find the Donnelly ranch, it'd be them."

"Thank you, sir," I said, trying to smile. "I'll do that when I get to town."

Glancing at the woman, I saw that her look of disdain had changed to one of wonder as she stared at my face. She kept her eyes on me as I excused myself, stood, and walked past her. I wondered about her expression while I continued toward the dining car for refreshment.

I was scheduled to arrive in Fort Collins late that night. I couldn't wait to get off that train. I spent the remainder of the daylight hours staring out the window at the passing scenery. Fatigue settled in, and I drifted off to sleep after the darkness swallowed the landscape. I had slept for only a few hours at a time since the beginning of my journey, caught between fear, hunger, and a constant ache in my heart. My body finally gave in, however, and I slept deeply with my head against the window.

————((◉))————

I woke to find people passing through the aisle with their belongings in tow. Most of the passengers had already exited the train, so I grabbed my bags, picked up my father's journals, and left the train. It had been ten long days of travel, and I could think of nothing better than placing my feet on solid ground to work the kinks out of my legs.

As I followed the crowd through the station, I saw Mr. Biehler just ahead of me, ambling slowly, as if each step caused him pain. He had been one of the only civilized people I had met on my journey, and I remained grateful for his attention and kindness. I hurried to catch up to him and wish him a good journey before he reboarded the train heading to Denver. However, as I was about to call to him to get his attention, I stumbled over something and lurched forward, landing flat on my face in the dirt. The fall took my breath away. The only thing I injured, however, was my pride, so I scrambled to my feet and dusted myself off.

"Watch where you're going, you daft fool!" the woman from the train yelled. Her heavy bag was the obstacle I had tripped over, and her belongings were scattered across the ground.

"Excuse me, ma'am, but could you not holler at me?" I wiped dirt from my clothes, feeling filthy and more than ready for a hot bath.

"Oh, it's you." There was a distinct change in her demeanor. She made no further comment and almost looked sorry about the incident. She bent down and grabbed her various belongings that had scattered during the accident, shoving them into her bag.

I had grown increasingly tired of this woman and her disdain. I bowed, turned on my heel, and walked away without saying another word.

As it was too late to check in at the telegraph office, I headed toward the first tavern I could find. After the long hours of sitting, I needed to stretch my legs. I entered the ramshackle tavern and stood at the bar to order. I spoke with the barkeep, who offered to rent me a room for the night.

"Excuse me," I then asked the man. "Would you know a man named Joseph Donnelly?"

"I did know Joseph," he said, wiping the bar, "but he died over a year ago."

"Oh." I slumped over the wood bar. He'd been my only hope when coming to Fort Collins.

"Pat Donnelly, his oldest, runs the Lazy D now," he added. My spirits brightened, and I leaned closer. With a rush of anxiety and excitement, I asked, "Will you tell me how I can find their ranch?"

"Sure," he said, handing me a cup of ale and dumping a plate of steaming buffalo stew in front of me. "They live several miles east of Lone Tree, a little over a day's ride from here." He looked over my shoulder at the patrons and excused himself.

I drank deeply. The heavenly cold ale slid down my throat and settled into my stomach. I raised chunks of buffalo steak into my mouth and savored every bite, but what I really craved was the solitude of a private room and the comfort of a soft mattress.

While finishing my dinner and a second mug of ale, I glanced around the tavern, getting a better look at the people around me. The patrons were mostly rough-looking men. Dirt and sawdust covered the floor. The gaudily dressed women in the tavern were much too friendly for my comfort. One heavyset woman interpreted my stare and gaping jaw as an invitation to approach me.

"Welcome, honey. How'd ya like some company?" She ran her fingers through my hair and hoisted her enormous breasts in my face.

"I beg your pardon, ma'am." I flinched from her touch and moved away. "I do not wish for ... uh ... company. I'd thank you to let go of me."

Someone standing behind me laughed, and I tilted my head to find the unfortunate woman from the train. She stood with crossed arms, laughing at me as I struggled to get free.

"You've been whipped," she told the woman as she stepped forward. "This one isn't for you."

The woman became indignant. "You should have tol' me ya had a sweetheart, honey," she said. "I wouldn't have bothered." She stalked off and found a new target to molest.

I could not believe I had found myself in the company of that woman once again. I took a huge gulp from my ale. As I prepared to pay my bill, she reached out and grabbed my arm.

"Would you mind talking with me for a moment?" Her laughter at my misfortune had vanished, and she unexpectedly looked quite sincere.

I yanked my arm away but didn't try to escape. My conduct didn't seem to disturb her, and she settled next to me at the bar. She ordered a couple of new drinks and we sat in silence for a few minutes.

"How can I be of service to you, ma'am?" I asked with an edge to my voice.

"You know," she said with a smile, "even when you are fuming mad, you're the most polite individual I've ever met." She looked me over and chuckled. "It's plain bothersome." She returned to her drink.

I sighed heavily and stood. "If there is nothing I can do for you, then please excuse me. It's late and I must get some rest." I placed my hat on my head and turned to leave, hoping to escape.

"I heard you're looking for the Donnelly Ranch," she said. "Mr. Biehler told me you need some help."

Glaring at her from a few feet away, I said, "He would not speak to you about such a personal matter."

"Actually," she said, looking away from my stare, "I heard you talking, and I asked Mr. Biehler about it later." She continued drinking her ale as I approached and reluctantly resumed my place next to her.

"Don't blame him," she added. "He wanted to help, and I initiated the conversation."

"Why did you do such a thing?"

"Because I can take you to the Donnelly ranch," she said matter-of-factly.

Dazed, I stared at her. The last thing I wanted was to spend more time with this repugnant woman. She had been rude and unpleasant throughout our acquaintance, and I was too tired to play games or attempt civility.

"Why would I want to go with you when you have done nothing but scowl at me since I first met you?"

The busy barkeep returned and smiled, only now seeming to notice that the woman was sitting next to me. "Oh, wonderful," he said, smacking my arm. "I see you've found one of the Donnelly clan. Your luck's gettin' better!"

I turned to stare at the woman sitting next to me.

"You have a problem with staring, you know that?" She turned her head away and took another sip of her drink.

"Your name is ... Donnelly?" I knew my jaw was gaping, but I found myself unable to correct the situation.

"Sarah Donnelly," she said, lifting her cup, "at your service."

"Are you related to Joseph Donnelly?"

"He was my pa," she said, turning toward me again. "And if I didn't know better, your father was Thomas Mullen."

"You knew my father?" I took a deep breath and swallowed hard. I knew my face had paled, and I felt dizzy.

Her face suddenly softened, and she looked at me with kindness and concern. "Yes," she said softly, "I knew him well—he was a good man." I merely nodded, unable to speak. "I realized on the train that you're his son, and I know my brother, Pat, will help you find your sister."

"But—"

"Quit staring at me." Everything she'd said shocked me so much that I'd temporarily lost my ability to function, and that included the act of blinking.

After watching me for a long moment and realizing I wasn't going to look away, she sighed and continued. "Like I said, I heard you talk with Mr. Biehler, and you said something about your sister, Lucy. That's when I realized who you are."

She placed her money on the bar, stood, and thanked the man for the drink. "Do you want me to take you there?"

I couldn't believe what I heard. The person who seemed least likely to help me had given me a way to find my sister. My head spun from the ale and lack of sleep. I stood silently, looking down at my mug on the bar. Miss Donnelly remained standing, waiting with her arms crossed.

After several moments of silence, she finally spoke. "Look," she said brusquely, "it doesn't matter to me one way or the other. If you decide you want my help, it'll be a long day of hard riding." She looked me up and down as if deciding I could not remain on a horse that long.

I straightened my shoulders and tried to look dignified. "I can ride a horse, ma'am." The truth was, I hadn't spent much time riding since my mother's death. We had no reason to ride in the city when everything was within walking distance, and we took long-distance trips in the carriage.

"Good," she said, taking a step away. "Meet me here tomorrow morning at sunup. I'd like to get an early start." She turned as if to walk away but looked back at me. "I didn't ask if you *needed* my help; I asked if you *wanted* it. God forbid a man *need* a woman for anything." She smiled and left the tavern.

I was still for quite some time, thinking that Sarah Donnelly was the most infuriating woman I had ever met.

2

THE PAWN

I awoke at daybreak, my body stiff and sore from lying on a worn mattress. I realized I had no choice but to go with Miss Donnelly. Perhaps her brother held the key to Lucy's disappearance. I needed to check the telegraph office before leaving town, so I packed my belongings and prepared to leave. When I had finally retired to my room the night before, I hadn't found the comfortable room with privacy and the soft mattress I'd hoped for. Instead, I shared a small, dank room with four other gentlemen. I spent the night listening to their snores and smelling the rank stench of dirty bodies and filthy clothes.

Before continuing my journey, I insisted on washing. I had never felt so grimy, and the reek from my roommates lingered on my skin even after their departure. I discovered a washbasin down the hall and requested water from a maid. While I waited, I glanced in the mirror at my rumpled clothing and disheveled hair. I couldn't have looked worse.

When the water arrived, I thanked the maid and washed my face and hands. A tub would have been nicer, but I did the best I could to freshen up. Rubbing my hands across my jaw, I noticed a beard beginning to show. I smoothed back my hair and tied it with a black ribbon. There was nothing I could do about my clothing. I straightened my jacket and pressed my hands down my wrinkled pants before proceeding downstairs.

Outside, I headed for the telegraph office. Arthur had promised to send word if anything changed during my travels, and with any luck, I would be able purchase a train ticket back home and leave this godforsaken place.

I found a wire waiting for me, but after reading it, I felt heartsick. I shuffled down the boardwalk, back toward the tavern, slowly rereading the telegram. Lucy was still missing.

———◦《◉》◦———

I scanned the tavern, almost looking past Sarah Donnelly, who sat at a table in the corner of the room. A tavern employee had just handed her a plate of eggs, meat, and potatoes. She'd obviously bathed and changed her clothes. No longer covered in grime, her face had a fresh, youthful look. She wore her hair, the color of light whiskey, pulled back into a tidy braid down her back. The difference in her appearance astounded me.

I approached the table and reluctantly sat opposite her. Appearances aside, I was still not incredibly pleased to be spending more time with this woman who obviously hated men. She had offered to help, however, and she was agreeable to Mr. Biehler, so I knew her demeanor could not be completely unpleasant. Besides, I knew she was the best hope I had of finding the answers I needed. I hadn't had a plan when coming to Colorado, so I figured I'd have to take what I could get, even if that meant a constant battle of wills with this peculiar woman.

She watched me with a smirk on her face as she ate. The waitress came by and quickly dropped a second plate on the table. Eggs, meat, and potatoes were clearly the only items on the menu at that hour.

"Good morning, Miss Donnelly." I tried to sound pleasant. "Did you sleep well?"

"Yes, thank you." The tension between us seemed to diminish a little as we ate breakfast.

"Miss Donnelly, may I ask you a question?"

"Certainly."

"How do you plan to get to your ranch?"

"My horse, of course." She laughed at the obvious absurdity of the question.

I sighed. "What I meant to say is that I do not have a horse. If I'm to follow you, I'll need to purchase one. Could you please tell me where I might find someone to sell me what I need for the trip?" My annoyance with Miss Donnelly had returned, but I tried to keep it under the surface. The day was going to be exceedingly long if we continued to argue.

"I already thought of that." She pushed her plate away. "I know a man at the end of town who can get you what you need." She cleared her throat, leaned forward, and motioned me closer.

"What is it?"

"When we get there, let me do the talking." She spoke quietly. "He'll gouge you if he knows you're from out East."

"I don't think it's right to have a woman complete my business transactions. Will he not look down on that as well?"

"Not if you remain outside while I talk to him alone." She smiled broadly.

"I don't know —"

She slammed her cup onto the table. Coffee splashed over my plate. "Look, if we're going to spend any time together, you have to adjust your thinking. You need me to take you to my ranch. The only way to get there is on horseback. Therefore, take my advice or get back on that train and go back to the city where you belong!"

The woman I'd met on the train reappeared in Miss Donnelly's eyes. She was stubborn, bitter, and incredibly intolerant. How could she go from being an agreeable, lovely woman to this hellion?

I waited for her to calm down before I finally nodded. "All right, Miss Donnelly, I'll do as you ask." I still felt it improper, but I was unwilling to antagonize her further.

Miss Donnelly jumped to her feet, obviously ready to be on her way. I hastily ate a few more bites of my meal, set some money on the table, grabbed my hat and bags, and followed her outside. She did not speak on our way through town, and keeping up with her fast pace, I was too preoccupied to do so. She moved with confidence and purpose, in her element.

She wore a loose-fitting tan shirt tucked into a long brown skirt, a thick leather belt around her waist. She had replaced her feminine bonnet with a floppy leather hat for riding. It was easy to tell where she belonged and was most comfortable. I found her incredibly intriguing.

The atmosphere of the town had changed from the night before. Hundreds of people were up and about, taking care of their daily business. Horses, carriages, and people were all fighting for a way through clogged streets. I moved through the disorderly traffic carefully, for the roads were not well cared for and holes appeared everywhere. Dust hung in the air, clinging to everything.

Fort Collins was actually much larger than I'd imagined,

and many of the people were noticeably sophisticated. Unlike in Philadelphia, the obviously wealthy mingled in the streets with the poor. Status didn't appear to be much of an issue in this Western town. I looked up at the buildings, all similarly built of wood and faded from the sun. Their hanging signs advertised their wares.

Still looking up and lost in thought when Miss Donnelly halted in the road, I ran directly into the back of her. She flew forward, stumbling and almost falling to the ground. I latched on to her arm to stabilize us both, catching her before she fell. She swung around and reeled out of my grasp with both fists clenched.

I raised both hands in surrender as her arm lifted to strike me. In the fighting stance she held before coming to her senses, I recognized a look of fear in her glare. Once she realized it was me, she lowered her arms and flashed an exasperated look.

"You really need to watch where you're going, Michael." She straightened her skirt.

Her casual tone surprised me, as did her use of my first name. I had no time to object however, because she continued to lecture me as she walked.

"You're going to injure or kill someone, probably yourself, if you don't start paying attention. Things are different here than in the city."

"I apologize. I'll try to do better in the future." I didn't appreciate her tone or attitude, but I had to admit she was right.

"Never mind all that. We're here." She swung around and put her palm up, pointing her finger in my face. "You stay outside."

To my left was a large livery stable with a corral and several horses. As she headed inside, I stood close to the rail and thought about the next leg of my journey. I'd never made an extended journey on horseback. The thought made me nervous, although I didn't want Miss Donnelly to see my apprehension. She already had enough doubts about my abilities, without my admitting my ignorance where horses were concerned.

Raised voices inside the stable drew me closer. Sarah, obviously upset about something, was becoming increasingly agitated. Forgetting the agreement I'd made not an hour before, I opened the door and entered. I straightened and squared my shoulders, not knowing what to expect.

"Miss Donnelly?" I said as I approached. "Is everything all right?"

She had backed a short, bald man into a corner. Her face was a deep shade of red, and she jabbed a finger at his chest. I assumed he was the owner of the livery.

"Miss Donnelly?" I said again, louder this time.

She swung round to face me with a frown, her breathing heavy. The little man slid along the wall to make his escape, but Sarah turned back around.

"Can I assist you in any way?" I asked, trying to calm her by placing a hand on her shoulder.

Lucy was the only other woman who had ever shown me that kind of temper, and the familiarity sent pain to my heart. Lucy I could calm, but Sarah was still a mystery.

"No, you can't help me!" She shoved my arm away and pointed at the man. "This imbecile claims someone stole my horse!" She had a murderous glare in her eyes.

"I told you, Sarah, I wasn't here when it happened. Billy was in charge of the stables when the horses were taken."

"That's no excuse, you idiot!" she snapped.

The man looked to me for support. "I'll give you a horse to replace the other animal, but you'll have to pay for the other, as well as a rig to go with it."

She rushed toward the man with renewed hatred, her eyes widened maddeningly. "Do not assume you can handle my business with this man." I tried to keep her from reaching for the man's throat. "It was *my* horse that was stolen! You will deal with *me*!"

"Sir." I spoke calmly. "If you have business to settle with Miss Donnelly, I suggest you address her instead of me."

The man's eyes became unusually round as I spoke. By his manner toward her, I assumed the man had previous knowledge of Miss Donnelly.

She stared at me briefly, and then her face softened. The stable master continued to discuss the business of the horses, and eventually, she relented. She let out a long sigh and smoothed her skirt. The fury left her eyes, but her unpleasant attitude remained.

"Now, Horace, what do you plan to do about this?"

"Like I said, I give you any horse you fancy to replace yours." His tone held finality.

"Like *I* said," she began, "I'll take the horse I like, and you'll also supply me with a rig and a horse for my friend here."

"Absolutely not." He folded his arms.

"You'll do as I suggest, Horace, or I'll announce to everyone in town what you did in Loveland two years ago." She squared off with the small man and mimicked his body language by crossing her arms and glaring at him.

I didn't think Horace's eyes could get any bigger, but they did. He sputtered and moaned, apparently unable to complete a sentence. Sarah Donnelly had obviously closed the argument for good. He lowered his head and paced up and down the dirt floor with his hands in his pockets. He finally looked up and moved toward Sarah. "I'll give you a rig and a horse, as well as your own rig, but I ain't givin' you another horse for nothin'."

19

"You're barkin' at a knot, Horace." She smiled.

I had no idea what she meant by that comment, but he obviously did. I was perfectly willing to buy my own horse, but I remained silent.

"Oh, Sarah, you're killin' me!" He threw up his arms in resignation. "Fine … take 'em. But don't think I'll give you a bargain again, ya hear? I'll remember this—don't think I won't!"

Even though Horace was upset about the arrangement, I believe he was even more relieved to have us finally out of his stable and on our way. He saddled my horse and assisted me in securing my bags before he left and returned to the safety of the stable. He didn't quit muttering under his breath the entire time.

It wasn't until he was finally out of sight that Sarah looked at me and smiled widely. She came over to my horse to make sure everything was secure for travel. I tried to look as if I knew what I was doing as I finished placing the last of my belongings into the saddlebags.

Sarah bent and tightened my saddle straps. I leaned down at the same moment she stood up, and her forehead struck my mouth. Blood flowed down my chin from my split lip. I whirled around, held my hand to my mouth, and tried to walk off the searing pain in my jaw.

"Christ, Michael." Sarah rubbed her head. "Have you always been this clumsy?"

"No," I said with frustration. "As a matter of fact, most would say I'm quite graceful." I pulled a handkerchief from my pocket and pressed it firmly to my mouth to staunch the bleeding.

"Graceful, huh?" She glanced at me, shook her head, and turned toward her horse. Clearly, she had nothing more to say.

The bleeding slowed with the pressure from my handkerchief. I blotted it a few more times and then looked over at Sarah. My reservations about riding had vanished until I saw her swiftly swing up into her saddle. Suddenly, nervousness surged back into my body. As I prepared to mount, Sarah's close observation didn't help.

"Ginger's the perfect horse for you."

The chestnut mare was beautiful, with its black mane and tail. Sarah grinned at me. Obviously, she thought Ginger would show patience with inept horsemanship. She looked as if nothing would bother her.

I placed my foot in the stirrup and held on tightly to the horn to pull myself onto Ginger's back. Safely mounted, I sighed with relief at my success. Then I noticed the reins still hanging from the bridle. Leaning forward to reach for them, I promptly fell off the horse. If there was any place I did not belong, it was in Colorado ... under a horse.

3

THE FIRE WITHIN

The movement of the horse soothed me as we silently rode out of the town and into the deep valley. Pine trees, wildflowers, and long green grass covered the entire area. I had never seen so much untouched land before. Enormous mountains jutted up from the plains to the west. As we followed a river through a large valley, I absorbed the peace as the sun's rays warmed my back.

"Miss Donnelly, can I ask you a question?" I asked, breaking the silence.

"Only if you call me Sarah." She turned and smiled at me.

"Excuse me?"

"I understand you feel you must remain proper and polite at all costs, and that you have a code of conduct to follow, but Miss Donnelly is much too formal if we're going to spend time together. I called your father Thomas, and I'd like to be able to call you Mike."

"As you wish … Sarah," I said uneasily, "but I'd prefer Michael, not Mike."

"Okay, what'd you want to ask me?"

"What is so wrong with people from the city? You have

made assumptions about me because of where I'm from, and I'd like to know why."

"Here's a question for you," she said, frowning. "What could possibly be good in the city? All I see are men who claim to have respect for women, and claim to have manners, but then they lie and cheat at the snap of the fingers. At least out here, I know what to expect."

Her reasoning didn't make much sense since I'd seen a man grope her publicly, but I kept the thought to myself. "Is that why you treated me as if I had wronged you in some way when I met you on the train? There are good and evil people everywhere, Miss ... uh ... Sarah. The city is not the only haven for criminals."

"I know there's evil everywhere. Sorry to place the blame of an entire city on your shoulders. I was out of sorts when we met. I dealt with men of your status in Wyoming." She waved her arm up and down, indicating my clothing and appearance.

"Did you offer to be my guide only because of my father?"

"I was in a foul mood when I boarded the train, and I didn't wish to visit with another so-called gentleman." She whirled her hand in the air in obvious contempt, and then she leaned toward me in her saddle, raising her eyebrows. "I didn't know at the time that you were the son of Thomas, a truly proper gentleman."

"You obviously liked my father very much."

"Yes." She glanced at me and then quickly turned away. "He was the best of men."

"Then is it so hard to imagine that I may be a good man as well?"

"Easy, Michael. We wouldn't want you to fall off your horse again."

I scowled at her, no longer expecting an answer.

She turned her horse in front of mine and stopped. "I'm sorry. I'll try to forget that you're from the city I hate and remember that you are the son of one of my favorite men."

We smiled briefly at each other and continued down the valley.

"Your father is one reason, but there are others as well." She gave me a wistful grin. "When I heard you and Mr. Biehler talking, I realized you had good reasons for your travel. I could also tell that you didn't have any idea what you were doing."

"I beg your pardon!" I automatically straightened myself in the saddle. I understood the importance of remaining on my horse, especially at that point in the conversation.

"I don't mean to offend you." She laughed. "I only meant that it's obvious you're a greenhorn, but I honestly didn't believe you'd let me help. Most men would never allow a woman to lead them."

"You really don't like men, do you?" I bit my tongue, having promised myself that I wouldn't purposely start an argument. However, it seemed unavoidable.

After several minutes, Sarah sniggered softly. She saw me watching her and slapped her thigh before she burst into a hearty laugh that included a snort or two.

"What's so amusing?" I was unable to contain a faint smile.

"When you told Horace he'd have to do business with me, I thought he'd drop dead right there."

"You have never met my sister." I smiled. "She could tear a man to pieces with a hard look in his direction."

"I'd love to meet her," she said sadly. "I've heard so much about her." Remembering my sister's spirit and beautiful kindness erased my smile. Sarah must have noticed the sadness cross my face, for she lowered her head. "I'm sorry. I wasn't thinking."

"Don't worry about it." I shrugged. "It is rather nice to be able to talk to someone about her. I miss her very much."

"I could see it in your eyes," she said quietly.

"What?" I asked with curiosity.

"On the train, I could see and feel your need to find your sister. I couldn't just leave without offering to help."

"Whatever your reasons, thank you." I tipped my hat. "I wouldn't ordinarily admit it, but you have already saved me. I don't know what I'm doing out here." I couldn't lie. She already had me figured out.

The horses moved forward at a healthy pace, Sarah and I riding side by side.

I cleared my throat, changing the subject. "Since we're being so honest with each other, I am curious about the man at the stables. What did he do in Loveland?"

"I don't have a clue." She didn't succeed in hiding her hilarity for long. She snorted and clapped a hand over her mouth as her laughter bubbled forth.

"Honestly, you can tell me. I won't mention it to anyone." Her laughter made me smile as I waited for her to control herself.

"I'm serious." She wiped moisture from her eyes. "My brother Pat told me to mention Loveland if Horace ever gave me a hard time, but he wouldn't tell me why. Actually, I'm just as curious as you are—especially after seeing my uncle's face. That was priceless!"

"Uncle?"

"Horace is my father's brother."

"But ... how ... I don't understand."

"He's my uncle, Michael." She looked at me as if I were dense.

"Then why did you want me to wait outside if he's family?"

"Because, unlike my father, Horace is a cheat and a liar. He would've taken you for everything." She looked me in the face and continued. "Why do you think he tried to finish our conversation with you? He knew I wouldn't budge, so he thought if he turned to you, he could squeeze you for more."

"I see." The humor of the situation finally sunk in. "I am glad to be of assistance, ma'am." I smiled and tipped my hat once again.

"I cannot wait to tell my brother … Horace … backed into a corner." She laughed again. "He'll just die!"

<hr>

We settled into casual conversation while riding throughout the day, discussing the area and our families. I told her about my life in Philadelphia. I felt displaced being so far from everyone I knew as family. That led me to think about Lucy again. The last time I'd spent time with her, we were getting ready for one of my aunt Olivia's dinner parties, just one night before her disappearance. That was when it all began—the night I met the strange man in the parlor. The man Lucy recognized as the one who had been following her. By the time I raced into the parlor, however, he had disappeared.

"What's your sister like?" Sarah's question broke into my troubled thoughts.

"She has one of the brightest minds of any woman I've known, and she constantly seeks further insight into the world. Lucy loves a good debate and stands up for injustice without a moment's hesitation." I laughed aloud, thinking of her fiery nature. "She gave one man a very thorough tongue-lashing at my aunt's last dinner party. I thought my aunt would explode with mortification."

"What was the argument about?"

"Politics, as always. My sister takes on causes with great passion. She is only twenty-two, but she believes there is no problem that doesn't have an answer." I paused, trying to erase the images of what could have happened to her. "She sees goodness in everyone."

"I like her already. She sounds just like your pa."

I looked at Sarah to see obvious sadness etched across her face. Eventually, the story would have to come out. But what would Sarah think about my father once she knew the truth?

"From what I know, a woman tricked my sister into entering a dark alley after she left her friend's house. Once there, two men grabbed her. Stubborn Lucy! What on earth was she thinking walking home that night?"

"She's an independent woman. I understand her need for freedom."

I looked at her sharply. "I asked her not to! She knew a man was following her, and she promised to stay at her friend's until the next morning, when Arthur was scheduled to pick her up." I took a few deep breaths, trying to calm my emotions. "She has always been very headstrong. When her friend's family got into an argument, she decided to come home. Instead of using a carriage like a normal person, she insisted on walking home just as she always did. Don't you see? Her routine is what got her in trouble. They knew she'd be coming, and they used it against her."

"What do they want?"

"All I know for certain is that my father took something from a man named Turner, and now he wants it back."

Sarah looked startled, and her head snapped around to face me. "Did you say Turner?"

"Yes. Do you know him?"

"I did," she said quickly, looking behind us and then all around. "But he's dead, Michael. He cannot hurt your family now."

I reined in my mare. Sarah stopped as well.

Reaching into the inner pocket of my jacket, I pulled out the note the police had found on the dead man and handed it to Sarah.

I stole from you as yer pa stole from me. Give back what's mine or yer sister is dead.

J. Turner

"This is a mistake." Sarah shoved the note back at me, as if the mere touch of it scorched her hand. "Turner is dead. He's been dead over a year."

"There is no mistake. My sister is missing, and this note was left on a body in the alley where she was taken. Explain that."

Her brow furrowed, and the color in her face vanished. She looked confused and deeply disturbed. I noticed as we rode farther into the valley that she continually looked behind her and scanned the landscape. She was scared.

"What did Turner do, Sarah?"

"I need to get you to my brother Pat. He'll know what to do."

She pulled a pistol from one of the bags near her left leg and secured it to her belt. She was silent for quite some time, but the troubled look on her face remained, and she quickened the pace of the horses.

It wasn't until over an hour later, when Sarah noticed

me squirming in my saddle, that she relented. We stopped the horses.

I shrugged. "It's just that I haven't been on a horse this much since ... well ... ever."

"If you spend enough time here, your legs will get used to riding."

"In another few hours, I fear my legs will fall off." I rubbed the back of my thigh, attempting to get circulation to return.

Sarah reined in her horse and dismounted. "We'll give the horses a bit of a rest and then continue on." She obviously felt sorry for me.

"God bless you!" I followed her lead. The tension from our initial meeting had faded into the vast landscape surrounding us.

After walking for some time, we mounted the horses again and rode swiftly along the trail. There wasn't time to talk throughout the afternoon, as Sarah set a fast pace.

As the sun set behind the mountains, we stopped by a bend in the river to allow the horses to drink and rest, while we set up camp for the night. Every muscle in my body ached. Moving slowly, I swung my leg over the saddle and slid to the ground. My muscles screamed as I attempted to straighten my bowed legs and walk normally.

Absentmindedly, I rubbed my backside, which had lost all sensation several hours before. Sarah chuckled, and I looked over my shoulder to find her with the horses, watching me. I hastily removed my hands and approached her. "This really is glorious country."

"Walking will take the sting out of your ass." Before I could reply, she waved me over to where she'd built a fire, instructing me in various outdoor tasks, such as setting up camp and getting the horses settled for the night. Even the things I already knew, I allowed her to teach me without interruption. I felt very much like a child, but I appreciated her assistance and patience as I glimpsed her way of life.

Once we accomplished everything for the night, and while Sarah cooked dinner, I slipped down to the river to take a much-needed bath. The quick wash at the tavern had in no way sufficed, and the river called me since I'd first set eyes upon it. I walked several yards downstream to have a little privacy and then stripped to nothing. I experienced the odd, but not unpleasant, sensation of being naked in the wild. I felt free from my troubles for a few moments.

The water chilled my skin as I entered the stream, but I became accustomed to the temperature quickly. The current flowed slowly, so I turned onto my back and floated without danger. The breeze, noisy with the sounds of animals and insects, blew through the trees, while a full moon rose in the east, causing everything to have a slight blue glow. I experienced a moment of peace I hadn't sensed in over a month. I lingered in the water for as long as I could before drying myself with the towel I'd brought and then quickly dressing.

I returned to camp to find Sarah standing over the fire, stirring a pot of soup. While we ate in silence, the tension began to creep back into my shoulders at the thought of sleeping next to Sarah, alone, in the woods. I had overlooked the impropriety of the two of us alone together, but now we were planning on sleeping within a few feet of one another. As each moment passed, my apprehension grew.

Sarah, on the other hand, seemed completely at ease. She finished eating and set up her bedroll near the fire without hesitation. She placed her pistol under her blanket. I had to keep reminding myself of my situation and the new set of rules before me. In Philadelphia, this would have been highly unacceptable.

"Are you certain you are comfortable with me sleeping near you?" I asked.

"Michael." She lowered her shoulders and sighed heavily. "We both need the warmth from the fire, and there are animals and people in these woods. It's better together ... for safety reasons."

As an afterthought, or possibly to ease my tension, Sarah took her knife from her dress and pointed it in my direction. "Come anywhere near me in the middle of the night, innocent or otherwise, and I will slit your throat."

I had forgotten that she carried a knife hidden in her skirt. The pleasantness of the afternoon made me overlook my first impression of Sarah as a ruthless and disagreeable woman. I understood now why she acted the way she did—and why she carried the knife. She obviously trusted me, however, and I felt honored.

"I would expect nothing less, Miss Donnelly." I bowed deeply.

After rolling out my bedroll, I settled on my side and pulled my blanket over my broad shoulders while staring at the fire. The blanket didn't completely cover my six-foot frame, but it would do.

I'd never imagined I would get this far in my journey. I was lucky. Now if only I could get to Pat Donnelly and find the man who took Lucy ...

4

HORSES AND OTHER DELIGHTFUL CREATURES

I woke with my heart racing, and I jumped hastily to my feet. I expected the nightmares as a part of my nightly routine, but each step along my journey made the dreams more disturbing. This last one left me with an image of my sister I had never seen. The joyful expression that usually covered her beautiful face had been replaced by a scared, bloody complexion, and her hair was filthy and tangled in knots. I experienced an overwhelming sense of fear that Lucy's time had run out.

The sun barely lit the sky, but my nightmare lingered, making me feel anxious and alone. Even my aching bones didn't disturb me as I packed up camp and got the horses ready. The fire still smoldered, indicating that Sarah had tended it throughout the night. I managed to get the fire going again and had water boiling in a small kettle before Sarah woke. Her smile and the twinkle in her eyes showed her surprise at seeing me up and managing the camp, but she said nothing. Instead, she grabbed a towel, wrapped her blanket around her shoulders, and headed toward the river.

I had breakfast ready and the camp packed by the time she returned from bathing. Other than checking her horse to ensure that I'd saddled it correctly, she followed my lead and didn't argue when I insisted on a quick departure.

The sun's rays warmed the air, and the heat was giving me a headache. I could think of nothing but bringing my sister back home. She counted on me. I tried to picture her laughing and smiling, but the image of that horrible blood-stained face always resurfaced.

By midmorning, sweat collected at my temples from the increasing heat, and my stress had caused a horrible head-ache. Sarah insisted on stopping frequently to allow the horses to rest and drink from the stream. At each stop, my irritation grew. I tried to hurry her along, but she refused to listen, which led to awkward silences and tense conversation throughout the morning.

When we stopped just before dinner, I found the shade of the woods too inviting to pass up. Sarah warned me against going into the woods without a gun, but I stubbornly dismissed her with a wave over my shoulder as I left camp.

"Fine, be a fool!" she yelled as I disappeared into the woods. "But don't come running to me when you get into trouble!"

I knew I only had a few moments to spare, but I needed time to think without the sun beating on my face. I ate my sandwich slowly as I walked through the woods. The trees were enormous, and the smell of pine needles filled the air.

I couldn't understand how the peace and cheer I'd felt in the river the night before could vanish so quickly. In a way, it would have been better to remain miserable, instead of having a welcome moment of peace and seeing it disappear again. The constant headache and pounding behind my eyelids made the sun's intensity unbearable. To make matters worse, I'd been rude and unpleasant to Sarah all day.

I turned to go back and speak with her when I accidentally

stepped on a branch, lost my balance, and reached for the closest thing I could find to keep from falling. Unfortunately, this caused me to hit a large, extremely unpleasant porcupine. Clearly seeing me as a threat, the beast decided to unleash its wrath upon my body, embedding quills into my right arm and side. I felt as if I had been stabbed with several hot pokers, but I had no time to think about the pain. I jumped to my feet and ran as fast I could through the trees.

I must have hollered—or, more likely, screamed like a little girl—because Sarah rode her horse into the woods with her pistol drawn. She had a frightened look on her face, which quickly changed to irritation when she caught sight of me.

"You are a stubborn, arrogant man!" Sarah yelled as she looked around the forest and shoved her gun back into her belt. "Why can't you listen to what you're told?"

In no mood to hear a lecture, I waved her away and walked toward the river. I didn't know how many quills had actually struck me until I felt the moisture on my arm and looked down to see my sleeve blotted with blood and stuck to my body. I stumbled slightly when I saw the large quills sticking from my side.

Sarah started to ride past me toward Ginger but slowed when she realized what had actually happened. Her scowl disappeared, replaced by a look of great concern. "Michael, you're hurt!" She swiftly jumped off her horse and walked toward me.

"I know," I said sharply, continuing toward the river. "I'll take care of it." I looked down at the stab wounds again and knew I was the fool Sarah thought me to be. She followed me, but I never turned around to acknowledge her. My face grew red, and I couldn't make eye contact with her. I shook my head in frustration over my foolishness.

I tried to strip off my mangled shirt, but the quills kept the material firmly attached to my body. Every small movement sent a jolt of sharp pain up my arm and into my shoulder. I counted at least fifteen quills in my arm and several more near my ribs. I couldn't believe how bad something that small could hurt. Light-headed, I washed the blood away and tried to pull out the first quill. No matter what I tried, however, it wouldn't budge. It held on dearly to the tissues beneath my skin. I tried again and again, but the quill just wouldn't move. I sat clumsily on the bank of the river, laid my head against a tree, and tried to steady my swimming head and erratic emotions.

Sarah came up behind me. "Do you need help?"

"No, just leave me alone for a few minutes," I replied crossly. The memory of her scolding me was still vivid in my mind. I felt horribly foolish, but I couldn't bear to hear any more lectures.

"What's the matter with you?"

"What's the matter?" I repeated, turning to glare at her. "I'm sitting out here in the middle of nowhere. My sister is missing. God knows where. She could be in Philadelphia, or any other town, for all I know. Never in my life have I been helpless, but right now I am utterly and completely ... lost."

I stood, wobbling slightly before turning to look at her. "I am in a land where I do not belong, with a woman who detests me and cannot wait to see me fall on my face again so that she can laugh at my awkwardness. And a beast just attacked me!" I turned on my heel and took as deep a breath as I could, blowing it out as I stumbled away.

Sarah had remained silent during my rant, staring at me with a look of pain on her face. Why did I keep lashing out at the one person who could help me? It wasn't her fault that I kept making mistakes.

After walking only a few hundred feet, I turned back to find Sarah only a few feet behind me. Trying not to act too surprised, I finally looked her in the eye.

"I want to apologize for my horrendous behavior." I looked back at the ground and held my arm away from my right side, keeping it from striking the sharp quills near my ribs. "I was unforgivably rude."

"You don't have to apologize to me for expressing how you feel. Besides, there's truth in the things you said. I've been very hard on you since we met, and not always for good reason." She stood with her hand behind her back and her head tilted to one side, closely examining me.

"That's no excuse for my unbearable behavior," I protested. "I just don't know who I am anymore." I sat on a log carefully, aware that several sharp objects still protruded from my side.

"I do," she said clearly. "You are a brother who dearly loves his sister, and you want nothing more than to keep her safe. You're in a hard position, Michael, and I realize I haven't made it any easier."

"Thank you, but you've given me more than I hoped to find when I traveled to Colorado. No matter how it may seem, I do in fact appreciate your kindness."

She smiled and turned toward the horses.

"Sarah?"

"Yes?" She hesitated but didn't turn around.

I looked down at my arm and my side. "Could you please help me get these horrible things out of my body?"

"Of course." She started walking again. "Let me get a few things from my bag."

She returned a few moments later with a bundle in her hands and handed me a large bottle. "It's whiskey. This is going to be painful so start drinking."

"I'm really not much of a drinker," I replied. "Are you certain this is necessary?"

To prove her point, she grabbed one of the quills and wiggled it forcefully, making me growl in pain. With a scowl, I yanked the bottle from her hand and took an enormous swig, choking on the rough spirit, grimacing at the taste. I had tried whiskey once before in my life, and now I understood why I had not done so again. It felt as if it were scorching every inch of my throat as it made its way down to my stomach.

"I told you to drink it, Michael—not inhale it." Sarah forced me to lower the bottle. She removed her knife and began cutting away the cloth of my shirt. "Do you know anything about porcupine quills?"

"Only that it feels like being stabbed." I laughed and lifted the bottle to take another drink.

"It'll take some time to remove them all."

"Aren't they just like big splinters that can be pulled out?"

"Not exactly," she said. "I can remove them, but the ends of the quills have barbs that catch on the skin, causing them to hold in place. Sometimes it takes quite a bit of effort to remove them."

With that thought, I took another drink. With each swallow, I grew accustomed to the taste of the liquor and the way it made me feel.

She quickly cut the end off each quill to remove any pressure and to allow for easier removal. "There's another problem." She paused. "Some of the quills may be too deep to get out. We may have to leave them until we get to town and visit the doctor."

"Lovely," I murmured.

Removal of the first few quills caused me to shout nasty

expletives into the woods, but it seemed that the longer Sarah worked, the less I felt the pain.

"The reason I was so dreadful this morning—ouch!—was because I had a horrible dream about my sister last night. So much time has passed."

She twisted her face into a frown as she pulled on another quill. "I figured something had happened."

"I just couldn't get her frightened face out of my mind. I should've told you sooner, but my head has been so muddled." I looked down at my arm and grimaced as she pulled on another quill. "Obviously, I haven't been thinking clearly."

"Quit being so hard on yourself." Triumphant, she held a stubborn quill up in the air. "If it'd make you feel better, I was like a fish out of water in the city. I could tell you some frightful stories of my adventures if you like."

"No, that's all right." I smiled but was immediately yelping again in pain. I looked at my bruised and bleeding arm before glancing back at Sarah. "I don't believe my body will ever forgive me for this abuse."

It took over an hour to complete her work, with small pauses every now and then to allow me to relax. She told me there were at least three that would need to be removed in town, but all the others came out clean.

By the time she finished, I realized that the pain had kept me from feeling the full effects of the alcohol, but now that I no longer felt pain, I no longer felt my fingers, my lips, or even my teeth.

Sarah heated water in the kettle and dumped the contents of a small bag into the boiling water. She took the whiskey from my hands and used it to clean the wounds. I flinched but remained steady, learning my lesson for the day about trusting Sarah. The wounds still seeped blood, but much less than before. She tore a section off my mangled shirt and soaked it in the mixture she was brewing in the kettle. She then wrapped the wet bandage around my upper arm several times.

"What are you putting on my arm?" I slurred.

"It's dried horsetail I picked up on my trip. It's good for healing wounds and helps stop bleeding." She finished wrapping the poultice with a dry bandage before repeating the procedure with my ribs.

"You are a handy woman to have around, ya know?" My head swam slightly, and my vision blurred.

"Do you think you feel all right to keep riding?"

"Yesh, of coursh," I attempted to stand. The feeling of all the alcohol swept through my bloodstream, causing me to lose my balance and fall.

"No, I don't think so." She sat next to me.

I briefly rested my head in her lap with a sigh of contentment. I looked up at her and examined her face closely. "To be honest, I really din't like you much when I first met you. But now I know I made a mishtake."

"That's great." She shook her head. "Why don't you rest a bit?" Sarah had obviously dealt with men in my condition before, for she merely patted my head, shoved it off her lap, and got up to tend the camp. She had apparently given up on finishing our journey to Lone Tree that day.

I attempted to sit, managing only to rest on one elbow. "I am shorry you had to tend the fire lasht night."

Sarah smiled and waved her hand in dismissal. She'd found me a horse, taught me to cook, tended the fire, tended my wounds, and dismissed it all with a wave of her hand. Incredible.

"Michael, you'll feel better after a good rest," she said, concentrating on her business. "I laid out your bedroll so you can lie down."

"You're an angel." I crawled to the blankets and rolled up into a ball. It took approximately two seconds for me to pass out completely.

⊸⊸⫸《◉》⫷⊶⊶

A short while later, I opened my eyes to find Sarah finishing supper preparations. While remaining on my side near the fire, I quietly watched her work. Efficient and graceful, she moved from one place to the other, finishing her work and unpacking her bags.

She paused and turned, her gaze fixed on the horizon. I heard the horses a few minutes later, riding fast in the direction of our fire. I tried to stand, but dizziness kept me kneeling on the ground. I felt useless. Sarah grabbed the pistol from her belt and threw the rifle in my direction. I steadied myself on the ground and fumbled with the rifle until I had it in position.

As soon as the riders got close enough, three men dismounted and headed purposefully toward the fire. Sarah's face changed. The worry lines disappeared, and she smiled broadly, clapping her hands together. Clearly recognizing the three figures, she put her pistol away and ran in their direction.

She embraced the tallest of the three, still laughing with joy. The two other men hugged her tightly as well, lifting her off her feet, twirling her in the air.

"I'm so glad to see you," she said to them all. "What are you doing here?"

"The real question is what are *you* doin' here?" the tall man asked, looking Sarah over. He seemed extremely upset to find Sarah there, but he had yet to notice my presence in the shadows. "You told us you wouldn't be arriving for another few days. We were on our way to town, to meet you when you got off the train."

"What's the matter with you, Pat? You haven't met me at the train since I was seventeen."

"Things are happening in Lone Tree," he said, with an edge to his voice. "I couldn't risk your travelin' alone."

One of the other men noticed me kneeling on the ground with the rifle in my hands. "Well, what do we have here, Sarah?" Moving slowly forward, he took out his pistol and pointed it in my direction. Instinctively, I raised the rifle.

"Put that away, Tommy!" Sarah said. "This is Mr. Mullen's son, Michael." She looked at the men closely and lowered her voice. "His sister has disappeared, and he came with me, hoping we could help him."

The biggest of the three men hastily looked around and instinctively placed his hand on the pistol resting low on his hip. "Sarah, we need to hightail it outta here." He took hold of her arm.

"Tell me what's going on." She attempted to remove her arm from his firm grasp.

Tommy came closer, forcing me to stagger upright when he grabbed the rifle from my hands and threw it into the shadows. "I wouldn't try nothin'; yer so drunk that you couldn't hit the ground with your hat in three throws." To prove his point, he pushed his pistol against my chest and watched me stagger back.

"Put the gun down, Tommy!" Sarah hurried to her brother's side and smacked him upside the head.

The three of them looked me over for a long while before finally putting their pistols away; then they stepped aside and returned to their horses.

"Sorry about that, Michael." Sarah moved closer as the men stepped away. "These three ruffians are my brothers."

I tried to walk a few steps but then realized I weaved slightly, so I stopped. I did my best to sober up, as this was no way to make a first impression with three large men who weren't the least bit pleased to see me traveling alone with their sister. Instead of attempting to walk again, I stood as straight as possible and lifted my hand toward the man standing closest to me.

"Hello, I'm Michael Mullen." I smiled uneasily. "I am pleased to meet you." It was gratifying to hear the words come out of my mouth correctly.

"Good to meet ya," Tommy said, slapping his gloves on his thighs and tucking them into his belt. He shook my hand firmly. Pain shot through my arm with his hearty handshake, and I grimaced. "Why, you're the spittin' image of your pa, Mike. Did you know I was named after him? Good man, your pa."

"Thank you, but my name is not Mike; it's Michael."

"Meet my brothers, Mike," Tommy continued. "This here's Pat. He's the old coot in the family, and this bag o' bones is my half-pint little brother, Will."

Choosing not to make the mistake of shaking hands again, I merely nodded to both gentlemen.

"What do you mean half-pint, you horse's ass!" Will exclaimed indignantly. Tommy dodged a slap in the face from his brother, while managing to hit Will squarely in the gut. He doubled over and wheezed slightly, and Tommy sat, looking incredibly amused. Pat's glare put an immediate end to their antics.

"I'd rather be addressed as Michael," I said weakly, straightening my shoulders.

"Well, ain't you the dandy?" Tommy said, standing again

and moving in front of me. With his head tilted slightly and his lips twitching upward, he looked intently into my eyes. "What're you kickin' about?"

"You're a bit sensitive, ain't ya?" chimed in Will, after recovering from the blow his brother had given him. "He's one o' them sensitive city types."

"Actually," Sarah interrupted, "Michael had a bit of an accident today, and I made the mistake of giving him too much whiskey." She looked at me and shrugged. "He isn't quite himself right now."

Her speech embarrassed me, along with the fact that I couldn't drink alcohol without making a damn fool of myself. I turned around and headed back to the fire, listening to the quiet chuckling behind me. I sat on a rock and listened to their conversation. It was going to be an awfully long evening.

"Sarah, we can't stay here," Pat said again. "We need to pack up your things and head out."

"We can't leave now," she replied. "Michael's injured and unable to ride."

"Son of a bitch!" Pat grasped Sarah's shoulders and leaned down to make sure they were eye to eye. "Turner didn't die. He's back in the area and lookin' for a fight." Pat hastily glanced around. "He's causin' trouble, and I feel like a sittin' duck out here in the open."

Just the mention of the man named Turner caused Sarah's face to pale and her voice to tremble. "That explains a few things, I suppose."

"What do you mean?" Pat asked, studying his sister.

"When I attempted to board the train in Wyoming, two men grabbed me from behind," she replied. Pat's expression was murderous. He took a quick step closer to Sarah and clenched his fists until his knuckles turned white.

"I know what you're thinking, but I was able to fend for myself, just as you taught me. I thought I heard one of them mention Turner, but I figured it was just my imagination. But then, Michael —"

"Turner's alive and meaner than ever. We need to get you to safety."

"But, Pat," she said, motioning in my direction, "you need to talk to Michael."

"We can talk on the trail. Now let's git." He looked toward the fire, where Tommy and Will continued to argue with one another, and then he swore under his breath when he saw my bandages.

Turner was alive, and Pat knew how to find him. Although tired, and probably pale too, I attempted to hide the lingering effects of the alcohol. If a man his size and appearance was nervous about being out in the open, I knew something was horribly wrong.

"I'll ride," I told him steadily. "Just let me get my things, and we can be on our way." When I turned around, I swayed slightly but managed to remain on my feet, heading in the direction of my bedroll.

Pat growled deeply and let out a string of obscenities. He kicked a rock and faced Sarah again. "Fine, we'll stay here till dawn and keep watch through the night." He leaned down to look Sarah in the face, pointing a finger at her. "You are not to go anywhere alone, ya hear?"

Sarah's brothers seemed much more subdued after settling their things for the night, and they all kept busy around camp as they prepared supper. I noticed Pat scowling at me occasionally. I couldn't blame him; because of me, his sister and brothers were in danger. I stared at the yellow-orange flames dancing in the fire. Embers cracked and sizzled in the otherwise quiet evening.

Pat thrust a metal cup full of stew in front of my face and handed me a spoon, startling me out of my trance. Before I could say thank you, he turned around and returned to the fire. He didn't seem to want to have anything to do with me, but he continued to watch me across the fire.

As the stew slid down my throat and into my stomach, I felt human again. The side effect, of course, was realizing my predicament. This journey had been rather unsettling, and I knew it had much more to do with just my sister's disappearance. Extremely out of place in this wild land, where nothing I did turned out as I expected, I wished only to get my old rhythm back—for Lucy's sake, if not my own.

Looking at Pat, I never would've guessed he was Sarah's brother. The man looked like worn leather, aged over forty years. His face, rugged and scarred, held pain and misery. But when he looked at his sister, I saw kindness and a gentle nature. I knew from looking at the sadness in his eyes and the way he moved his body that he had seen many rough days.

Tommy looked much like his older brother, minus the leathery face. He had long brown hair, tied back with a strip of leather. He looked to be about my age, his attitude carefree and enjoyable.

Both Tommy and Pat were large men, and I hoped I would never have to come up against either of them in a fight. While Pat shared my height and Tommy was just an inch or two shorter, they were both composed of solid muscle, with only a hint of softness around the edges.

Will, on the other hand, had a tall, lanky frame. He lacked the broad shoulders of his two older brothers, but he shared their muscular physique from working outside every day. Will had the face of a child, full of innocence and mischief at the same time. He also had long hair but wore it free, tucked behind his ears. It blew around his face in the breeze, seemingly without him taking notice. The firelight glinted off the sun-bleached strands.

Looking into Will's blue eyes and his innocent features, I thought again of Lucy. Glancing back toward the fire, the sadness returned. Not only because of the long journey ahead—or the strange men around the fire, who didn't seem to like me. But because of the number of things that could've happened to Lucy.

Sarah moved happily around the campfire, obviously relieved to have her brothers near. I remained uneasy, however, as they continued to watch me with suspicion.

I looked up from my empty cup to find Pat standing in front of me again. "If you're done eatin', take a walk with me?" Pat said, more as an order than a request. He walked away before I could respond.

I stood up and hesitantly followed Pat away from camp. The moment had come. He'd tell me about Turner, and I would finally understand why she was taken. Or he'd give me a good talking-to for traveling with his sister. I only hoped Pat would wait to hear my story before gutting me like a pig.

When we were a good distance from camp, Pat stopped and looked up at the sky. He didn't say anything for a long time. Perhaps he hadn't made up his mind to kill me just yet, and I didn't want to give him a reason now. On the other hand, he could've been going over all the different ways to kill a man without getting caught. Either way, I decided it would be best not to speak.

While waiting, I looked at my surroundings. I'd grown accustomed to the dark after being away from the light of the fire. I could see the outline of the mountains to the west and the miles of rolling hills in between. The last traces of wildflowers covered the ground. Never in my life could I have imagined the vast magnificence of the prairie. I had heard many stories, of course, but they all consisted of savages, wild beasts, and treachery. Instead, I found the land beautifully untouched and the air crisp and clean. I understood why so many people had left the East in search of a new life far away. I also understood why my father often talked of this place with love in his eyes.

Pat shuffled next to me, which brought me out of my thoughts. "How long have you been travelin', Mike?"

"A couple of weeks or so. I lost track of the days some time ago."

"My sister said Turner left a note," he said quietly. "Tell me about it."

Relief dripped from my shoulders, and the tension lifted away when I realized that he might have the answers I had been waiting for. I began my story on the night before my sister's disappearance in Philadelphia. I left nothing out, knowing Pat could best help if he knew every detail. The man before me had a younger sister as well. Having seen the love between them, I was sure Pat would search the ends of the earth for Sarah if she were in trouble.

"What does she look like?"

"She's small, thin, and about five feet two. She has long blond hair that she often wears on top of her head in braids. She's only twenty years old." My voice caught, and I cleared my throat. "Sarah offered to lead me to your ranch in hopes that you would have some information that might help me."

After a long pause, he mumbled, "I understand." Pat drifted back into silence again, moving a few steps away and stooping toward the ground. After a few minutes of contemplation, he stood. "You'd better get some shut-eye, Mike. Tomorrow's gonna be a long day."

"What about you?"

"My brothers and I will keep a watch on the camp tonight." Heading back to camp, Pat had his head hung low. He frequently scanned the horizon as if expecting someone or something. We walked in complete silence.

I no longer felt so alone. That had to be enough for now. Fatigue settled in, and all I could think of was placing one foot in front of the other until I reached my bedroll near the fire.

When we returned, Will and Tommy were sitting close together, quietly talking. Pat went peacefully around the fire to where Sarah sat. He leaned down and kissed her softly on the head. Sarah looked up into his dark eyes and smiled warmly. The gesture touched me, and I knew immediately that Pat would help me after all.

I sat down next to Sarah, grimacing as I felt one of the remaining quills move under my skin. Tommy and Will were in one of their many debates about the ways of the world, in which they obviously never agreed. I realized that Will was the sensitive brother, Pat was the caretaker, and Tommy was the clown. I watched as they battled one another.

Finally, Pat left the fire and moved Sarah's blanket across the fire from mine. His lack of trust may have seemed offensive to others, but I could easily understand his protectiveness. After all, I would do the same with Lucy if our situations were reversed.

As I lay by the fire that night, I remembered every detail of what had gotten me there. I looked back over at Sarah, sitting silently by the fire, and remembered again all the things she had done to help me. I needed to start lending more of a hand. I needed to learn to hold my own in this wild country.

5

AN ENTIRELY NEW LIGHT

I decided to leave the warmth of the fire and walk in the woods to clear my thoughts before trying to sleep. The evening air remained calm and clear, with the moon rising high over the trees. It lit the land in a beautiful shade of blue, while a cool breeze rolled over the hills. The fresh, clean air felt soft on my face as I took a long, deep breath.

I entered a copse of trees that led me to an open meadow surrounded by enormous pines. The grass was tall and lush, with no hint that winter was just around the corner. A strange peace settled inside my chest. Never in my life had I seen a place so beautiful and full of promise. Within the circle of trees surrounding the meadow, several twisted and wove through each other, as if finding mates and wanting to be closer. Two trees in particular wove around one another so tightly that they looked to be one. I closed my eyes and breathed in the peace of the night and the beauty of the meadow with the twisted trees.

"Are you all right, Michael?" Sarah asked as she appeared from the shadows.

"As well as I can be, I suppose."

Sarah stood just a few feet away, the glow of the moon

lighting her face and hair. My first impression of Sarah had been entirely wrong. While tough when needed, she also possessed great kindness. Her features were strong but delicate, and her fiery spirit touched my soul. With the moon creating a shining glow around her face, illuminating her brown curls, she was quite lovely.

She moved closer, until she stood about a foot away, and placed her hand flat on my chest, near my heart. Her touch was warm and gentle. Intuitively, I lifted my uninjured arm and placed my hand on hers, wrapping my fingers around her palm. Instead of moving away, she squeezed my hand lightly with acceptance.

"I'm sorry about everything you've had to go through these past couple of weeks, Michael. I know it must be difficult."

"Thank you."

"Is there anything I can do to help?"

My mind raced with thoughts of all the things she could do to make me feel better, to make my bones stop aching and send relaxation swiftly throughout my muscles to ease their pain. "You have already done so much," I replied instead, quelling my impure thoughts. "I cannot tell you how grateful I am."

"You aren't alone anymore. My family will do whatever we can to help."

She stood only a few inches from me, and our hands remained intertwined just below my left shoulder. Without thinking, I leaned down and kissed her gently and briefly on the lips. Energy soared through me, causing my lips to tingle. Realizing that I may have just ruined the trust we had started to form, and that I may have betrayed her kindness in some way, I took a quick step back and let go of Sarah's hand.

"I'm sorry. I should not have—"

Before I could finish my sentence, Sarah took two steps forward, wrapped her hand around the back of my neck, and put her mouth to mine. Without further hesitation, I pulled her tight against my body. She smelled of wood smoke and wildflowers, and her lips tasted of sweet herbs.

After several minutes, I slowly loosened my grip and dropped my arms. Sarah pulled her head away slightly to look into my eyes. She raised a hand and gently placed it upon my cheek, moving her thumb lightly over my lips, while looking at me and smiling warmly.

"Mike?"

Instead of hearing Sarah's husky accent, a deep, masculine voice intruded into our conversation. I pulled my head away and took a long look at Sarah's face. She continued to gaze at me with a beautiful smile and slightly flushed cheeks. I glanced around the area to see if her brothers had found us together, but I could see nothing. I glanced back at Sarah just before she brushed my hair from my face and patted my cheek firmly.

"Wake up, Mike," she said quietly, again in a masculine voice.

"What—"

"Mike!" the male voice said again. Opening my eyes, I found Sarah gone. I was lying on my side near the fire, bundled up tightly in my blanket. A tingling sensation lingered throughout my limbs, and my lips felt faintly numb. Loneliness crept into my body as I realized that my paradise had been but a dream and my closeness with Sarah faded.

As the blurring of my vision cleared, I blinked to find Pat and Tommy sitting close by, watching me. I felt stiff and incredibly sore. I had slept on my left arm, so it wasn't ready to work quite yet, and my right side ached, feeling much worse than it had the day before. A terrible thought jolted me into full consciousness. I squeezed my eyes closed and quickly prayed: Oh, please, please, God, tell me I didn't say Sarah's name in my sleep!

"Well, mornin', Mike," Tommy said cheerfully. "Havin' a bit of a dream, were ya?" I remained silent, not knowing how to interpret his statement. "I have strange dreams all the time too." He chuckled casually. "Sometimes Will or Pat wake me 'cause I'm makin' such a racket. You should pay attention to those dreams. They're usually trying to tell ya somethin'."

I opened one eye, convinced that even though I may have said something in my dream, it hadn't alarmed the men around the fire. Deeply relieved, I knew they hadn't read my thoughts about their only sister—and where did those thoughts come from, anyway? Sarah and I had been butting heads since the moment we first met, and she obviously hated all men except her brothers. But then again, she was kind and gentle when she tended my wounds. She was a contradiction I couldn't seem to figure out.

"Would you like some vittles, Mike?" Tommy asked.

I grimaced slightly at the new name but didn't bother to correct him. My head throbbed at my temples, and the smell of the food made me nauseous. "No, thank you." I rose to my feet, wobbling slightly and looked around quickly, breathing a sigh of relief when I didn't see Sarah anywhere. "Can I help in any way?"

"Nah, we're set," Tommy looked at me closely with a grin on his face. "Anyhow, you looked like you needed the rest."

He looked clean-shaven and well rested, as did Pat. The outdoors seemed to suit them. I, on the other hand, must have looked rather gruesome, as I got a wary look from Pat and a raise of the eyebrows from Tommy.

Sarah came back from the woods, with Will at her side,

and sat down next to me near the fire. I felt slightly uneasy in her presence, due to the intimacy of my dream, and found it difficult to look her in the eye. The burn of a flush crept up my neck, making me feel like a schoolboy caught ogling the teacher.

Sarah handed me a plate of food with a warm smile. I still felt a little queasy, but I took the offering from her hand and attempted a few small bites.

"Relax, Michael," she said, leaning closer. "I can feel your tension from here."

My eyes widened, and I jumped as she placed her hand on my arm. I took a deep breath and tried to calm my rattled nerves.

"Don't worry," she said softly. "If your sister's here, we'll find her."

Lucy. A pang of guilt rapidly swept over me. Preoccupied with my dream, I hadn't even thought of my sister. Feeling awful again, the sorrow from the last few weeks returned, making knots form in my stomach as I thought of the day ahead. My sister could be found today. But what if she wasn't in Colorado? What if something horrible had happened? What if—

"How about you let me change your bandage?" Sarah came closer but would not look me directly in the eye. Her hands trembled slightly.

"It can wait." I quickly stuffed food into my mouth.

"No, it can't. Don't be so stubborn. I've prepared more dried horsetail, and it's boiling on the fire. The poultice is ready, so take off your shirt."

I looked up at her brothers, who were busy cleaning the camp. Pat glanced my way and nodded, as if to say I had better do as she asked. Reluctantly, I stripped off my shirt and Sarah took my arm in her hands.

"The wounds look good, Michael." She poked my ribs and examined my arm closer. "I see no signs of infection, and the bleeding has stopped completely." She sat up and smiled with satisfaction before continuing to dress the wound.

The poultice did seem to be working. The swelling remained, but the wound looked much better—slightly red but no longer looking angry along the puncture marks. I watched her closely as she cleaned my wounds and rebandaged them with a clean cloth. Her skin was pale, and her eyes still would not meet mine. It was intriguing to see her tongue rest against her upper lip while she worked, completely intent on what she was doing.

Finished with the bandage, she helped me pull my shirt back on and button it. Pat, Will, and Tommy came to sit by the fire, each with a strange, unpleasant look on his face. Sarah sat back down beside me with the same look on her face. She glanced briefly at Pat and then lowered her gaze to the ground near the fire. Something was definitely wrong.

Why couldn't my pleasant feelings last for more than a few seconds? Just a brief moment of peace—that's all I asked for.

"Mike," Pat began, "we need to talk."

"What is it?"

"We talked about your situation last night. Like I said, I knew your pa." He gestured with his hand toward his brothers and his sister. "We all did. He was good to our family."

I nodded silently, waiting for him to continue.

"About ten years ago, your pa started visiting us regularly, often stayin' at the ranch." I could see the frown deepen on his face as he contemplated his next sentence. "Did you know our pa?"

"No, not exactly," I replied. "I remember my father

talking about your ranch, and I recently read of him in his journals."

"You mentioned that one of the men in Philadelphia had a limp, correct?" Pat asked after remaining silent for some time. Unlike Sarah, Pat's eyes bored into mine with an intensity rarely seen in others.

"Yes, the few people who saw him mentioned a considerable limp and a scar on his face."

"We know the man." Pat frowned again.

I jumped to my feet. "Why didn't you tell me last night? Who is he? Why are we still sitting here?" I yelled the last sentence.

Pat stood slowly, pulled out his pistol, and started checking the chamber. I wasn't certain if it was purposeful, but his actions stopped me in my tracks. I ceased talking. "I felt it'd be better to wait till mornin' to talk to you about it," he said calmly, "after you had a good night's rest."

Sarah glared at her brother and raised her arm to quiet him. "I'm sorry, Michael. By the time we put everything together, you were sleeping. We didn't feel it best … given your condition."

"What is that supposed to mean?" I was instantly angry again.

Pat sat back down, looking exhausted. "I'm the one who asked her not to tell you last night. I figured the only thing it'd do would keep you from sleepin', and you needed your rest for today."

The anger subsided, leaving me with a multitude of questions. All the people sitting around me had known my father in a world I never knew existed. He loved the West, and they had the chance to see that side of him. I wasn't given that opportunity.

After the pause in conversation, Tommy picked up where

Pat had left off. "There are two men in town who are damn near connected at the hip. One sounds like the man you saw in your parlor the night before Lucy disappeared. His real name is R. J. Booker. The other man walks with a limp; he has since he was a youngster. I don't know his full name, but he goes by Blake. It's more than just a coincidence that they both disappeared a few weeks before your sister disappeared ... and the same time Turner returned to the area."

"So these men work for Turner." I began to understand the bits of conversation I had heard throughout the night and morning.

"R. J. and Blake are a part of his gang, and either of them would do damn near anything for a price. If Turner wants to hurt your kin, he'll be willin' to do whatever it takes." I noticed again that Tommy and Will glanced at Pat when mentioning retribution. Something passed between the brothers in the moment Will and Tommy stared at each other.

I followed their gaze to Pat, who sat stone-faced, glaring into the fire. A muscle in his jaw twitched, and his hands were clenched tightly. Whatever had happened with Turner had deeply affected the eldest Donnelly.

"What's your plan?" I asked, clearing my throat.

"First," Tommy said, "we'll stop in town on our way to the Lazy D. Some folks there might be able to answer some questions."

"What are we waiting for, then?"

Pat didn't hesitate. He nodded and stood to pack up camp. Tommy and Will started moving as well. They extinguished the fire and cleaned the plates before heading out. Sarah readied her horse and came up to me before we set off again.

"I truly am sorry about everything." Sarah laid her hand

on my good arm. A small electric shock ran through me at her touch. I couldn't understand how everything had changed overnight. I found that I saw her in an entirely new light.

"How about we just call it even and forget about it." After all, I'd arrived safely because of Sarah, and by some odd coincidence, her decision probably brought me closer to my sister.

I rode close to Pat, and we talked more about the men who could've taken my sister. I tried to avoid riding near Sarah because of the new tension that existed when near her. She seemed preoccupied anyway, so Pat and I concentrated on developing a strategy for finding my sister.

"Pat, why is your family so willing to get involved? This could be quite dangerous."

"Your pa was a good man, Mike. He was kind to everyone he met." Pat looked away suddenly, and I saw something shut down inside him. "I owe him a debt that cannot be repaid."

I had a difficult time listening to his account of my father. After reading his journals, which I'd found while searching for Lucy, it became evident how little I really knew about him. I'd known the businessman who was well versed in city politics, the society gentleman who never missed the chance to shine, and the loving father who would read to us late at night when we were young.

While scanning the journals, I recognized the kind and generous man who often longed to be with family while away, the man who loved his wife dearly. He spent most of his time building a large house several miles from the Donnelly ranch. His greatest hope was to finish the house so that my mother could move west and hopefully recover from her illness.

Upon finishing my reading on the train, however, my vision of the man had changed dramatically. I'd found several entries about a strange woman, which made my heart quicken and my palms sweat. My father's last journal spoke almost exclusively about a woman named Maggie, who lived at the Donnelly ranch.

April 2, 1877
Colorado

Maggie showed me around the hills behind the ranch yesterday. They are packed with large pine trees and a ground covered with a thick layer of needles and branches. We camped out under the stars last evening, while talking late into the morning. She never tires of the woods or the animals that scurry around in the pine and mulch. I have never met a woman so suited for life out West, and I admire her courage for living this life. She has become so important to me, and I miss her dearly when I must leave to go home.

Unable to comprehend my father's relationship with this woman, I'd forced myself to read slowly, even though I fervently wished to rip through the pages to find out more about Maggie.

The more I read, the more I became convinced that my father had been unfaithful to my mother. I could find no additional letters from my mother hidden in the pages, which gave me no reference concerning her knowledge of Maggie. Why did he spend so much time with her instead of being home with my mother, who was ill?

I didn't find any explicit truth that my father had been unfaithful, but no matter how many times I read over the pages,

I could find no other conclusion that made sense. His journals did not contain any intimate accounts of their time together, but then again, these were surely not things my father would put down on paper. After my mother's death, his journals devoted most of their time to the Donnelly ranch ... especially Maggie.

At first, I shrugged the feelings off as a terrible misunderstanding; however, the doubts kept creeping back into my head, haunting me throughout my trip. The part that was so distressing, that made a cold chill run down my spine, was that my mother was at home sick while my father was away. I thought I had finally put those feelings behind me after my father's death, but the pain and anger I felt only reinforced their existence. The thought of him having a relationship with that woman while my mother was slowly dying made my blood boil. What if Lucy's disappearance was because of my father's relationship with Maggie?

Jarred from my reflections by a loud whinny from my horse, I closed my eyes tightly and willed the horrible thoughts away. Pat's family had spent more time with my father than I did during his final years. I was certain they had the answers I sought.

"I cared for your pa," Pat continued, "and I'd help you find Lucy because of that alone, but this goes much deeper than that." The darkness in Pat's eyes from the night before returned, and I realized that he not only wanted to help, but that he and I were connected somehow. The frown deepened across his face, and he became silent and pensive for several minutes. Something I had said, or asked, had clearly upset him, causing him to shut down. I longed to press the matter further, to understand him, but thought better of it when I looked at his face. It held anger, and in his eyes, I could see profound sadness.

I let it lie. When ready, Pat would explain the connection

the two of us had with the men who took Lucy—and perhaps relieve my fears about my father.

"Why don't you ride with Will and Tommy for a bit and tell them everything you told me last night," Pat suggested.

I rode alongside Will and Tommy for over an hour, sharing the events in Philadelphia and telling them what I knew about the two men who took my sister. We traveled a good distance in that time, crossing the valley and heading into the trees that would lead to Lone Tree.

"There's somethin' you should know, Mike," said Tommy. "There were about twenty men who rode along with a man named Jack Turner; they called him Black Jack because his soul is dark as night."

On the other side of Tommy, Will leaned closer to me. "It sure ain't because he's good at cards, Mike. He's a very evil man." A shiver ran down my spine at the thought of the possible link between this man and my sister.

"He used to come in and out of the area, scarin' the hell outta the merchants and townspeople," Tommy continued. "He'd take and do anything he wanted, and there wasn't nothin' anyone could do about it. When someone did come up against him, Turner found his vengeance on him, as well as the rest of his kin."

"Doesn't the law do anything about it?"

"For a long time, no one could prove Turner was tied to any crime, even though everyone knew he was guilty. The old town marshal was a member of his gang and paid to keep quiet. Since we heard about Turner's death, a new town marshal was appointed, but with Turner's return to Lone Tree, he skedaddled outta the area, with nothin' but the clothes on his back. Good riddance, I say. He was a worthless human being. The problem is that now the town remains without the presence of the law."

As we came over the rise, Lone Tree came into sight several miles away. It looked like a speck on the landscape, but my pulse quickened. I itched to reach our destination. Pat separated from the rest of us and rode ahead at a fast pace. When I dug my heels into Ginger's sides to follow, Tommy forestalled my progress. Instead, we continued at a brisk pace but allowed Pat to scout out the area before our arrival.

Tommy continued. "Several months ago, we got word from what we thought was a reliable source that Turner had been killed in Central City. We heard nothin' from his brother, and many of his gang left the area, so we started thinkin' we could finally live in peace. Things have been mighty nice lately, but just before we came upon you and Sarah, we learned that Turner's alive and back in Lone Tree."

"Where's he been all this time?" I had a hard time controlling Ginger. She must have sensed my tension, and she was fighting the restraint on her reins.

"Don't know, but he's definitely not dead—and he's already startin' trouble in town. He tore up the general store, and his men beat a whore half to death at Belle's place." He gave Will a look of disgust as he continued. "We think he must've paid off the doctor in Central City to report his death. Hell, he looked close to death after he'd been shot, so no one doubted hearin' he'd been put in the ground."

"What about his brother?"

"Don't know that neither," he said with a shrug. "Haven't seen him in damn near a year. He and Turner are very different men, but brothers just the same."

"What could Turner possibly have to do with my father?"

Tommy and Will looked at each other for a long

moment. "All I can tell you is that he went through an awful lot of trouble to find you and your kin. I'd be careful if I were you."

Tommy slowed as he talked his horse through a thin spot in the trail. When it widened again, I moved Ginger alongside his horse, and Will positioned himself next to me. Once we maneuvered our mounts down the last ridge, it would be flat ground the rest of the way to town.

"How do you know all this?" I asked impatiently.

"We went up against his gang before, Mike," Tommy said quietly in explanation, after seeing my puzzled expression. "There's nothin' our family wants more than to see Jack Turner hang, along with his men." The anger in his voice shocked me. Whatever had happened had been deeply personal, and I finally understood why they were so eager to help.

"That's why we met you along the trail," Will chimed in. "We didn't want Sarah to be travelin' alone with Turner in the area. We weren't expecting her for another few days. When we saw you last night, we were on our way to meet her when she got off the train. But Sarah, who never sticks with her original plans, left the city before she was supposed to and beat us to Fort Collins."

"If we would've known about Sarah's early arrival," Tommy said, "we would've met her at the station and made sure she got right back on the train outta town." He looked at his sister thoughtfully, with palpable anxiety. "She shouldn't be here right now."

Sarah merely continued to watch the town as it got closer.

"Well, I am definitely lucky to have met up with all of you last night. I really had no idea who I'd be dealing with once I arrived in Colorado."

"It pleased me to find her travelin' with you, Mike. It isn't safe right now for her to be travelin' alone."

Tommy's grateful tone and honest words touched me. He trusted me to protect Sarah, even though he knew nothing about me.

6

LONE TREE, COLORADO

We entered Lone Tree just after dinnertime. We'd decided to wait until we arrived in town to eat, giving us an opportunity to ask around about Jack Turner. The nervous stomach I had endured during breakfast returned, and my breathing quickened at the thought of coming one step closer to finding out what had happened to my sister.

The town was much smaller than Fort Collins. It had a small group of buildings, including a mercantile, livery stable, post office, two hotels, a rundown schoolhouse, an abandoned jail, and two saloons.

"The first thing we need to do, Mike, is get you some new duds." Tommy glanced at his brother and winked before continuing. "Ya stick out like a sore thumb."

I had noticed that my clothes weren't exactly appropriate for horseback riding or any hard work of any kind. My thin breeches were close to tatters, and I would've welcomed something to protect my backside while riding. The best shirt I had for outdoor weather had been destroyed when the porcupine punctured it a few dozen times, and it was now merely useful for bandages.

Before we left the horses, I noticed the Donnelly men taking several firearms from their saddlebags and securing them to their bodies. They each carried no fewer than four guns, two in plain sight and the others either hidden in their boots or secured to their backs. Will even strapped a large knife in a leather sheath to his thigh. I felt a bit naked amongst them and realized that the danger was much worse than they'd let on.

As we walked down the street, I heard someone bellow at Tommy from an upstairs balcony.

"Well, hello, Belle," Tommy said with a mischievous grin. "How might you be doin' today?"

"Tommy Donnelly, if you don't look up to no good," she said in a husky feminine voice. "After you cause whatever trouble you're thinkin' about causing, come over for a drink and tell me all about it."

Tommy tipped his hat and bowed with a flourish. "You, my darlin', have got yourself a deal." He continued to move down the street, but there was a distinct swagger in each step that hadn't been there before, and he grinned like a fool.

It astonished me to see the beautiful redhead leaning against a railing of a second-story balcony. She wore a tasteful silk gown of deep green and black, and her red hair flowed around her head in glorious curls. I would've expected to see someone like her in my aunt's parlor back home, sipping tea and discussing the latest scandal, not hanging over a balcony of a large brothel in Colorado.

When I finally pried my eyes away from Belle's figure, I noticed Sarah standing in front of me with her arms across her chest, shaking her head in disgust. "Typical."

I had returned to the unbearable man she met on the train. Great.

Sarah turned without another word and stalked across the street to the saloon, with Tommy at her side. Will herded me to the local doctor's house, so that he could properly look at my wounds. The remaining quills shifted and moved under my skin as I walked, and I couldn't wait to get them out, even if it meant the pain I knew would follow.

Doc Boylen's house was located at the far end of Main Street—close enough to be convenient but far enough to stay clear of any trouble caused by the men in town. It had a large sitting room on the main level, along with an office and surgery in the back. A short, middle-aged man greeted us as we entered and introduced himself as the doctor. Despite his frail appearance, he made it known from his direct questioning and no-nonsense manner that he could certainly hold his own against the cowboys in the area. He had a certain air of authority, much like a grade school teacher who'd scared the daylights out of me on a regular basis.

Will found great joy in retelling my story about the evil porcupine that maimed me in the woods. He made it so overly dramatic that even I laughed by the time he finished. Will and the doc were obviously longtime friends, most likely from a kinship born of the doc's treatment for injuries Will undoubtedly sustained as a troublemaking boy.

While Doc prepared his equipment, he spoke to Will about the trouble that had started in town since Turner's unexpected arrival. The damage to the mercantile was extensive, and Will promised Doc we would stop by and visit with Mr. Baker, the owner, and perhaps buy some clothes and other supplies to help him.

"What about the woman at Belle's?" Will asked.

Doc lifted his gaze from the examination of my wounds and shook his head with regret. "It isn't good. She's taken a room at the Franklin Hotel until she's fully recovered. You know Ms. Mabel can't stand to see the poor girl cast aside in the condition she's in, regardless of how she chose to make her money."

Doc returned to his work, gathering supplies and placing a table of sharp instruments, knifelike in appearance, near my arm. I swallowed hard but remained silent. Without further consent, he unwrapped the bandage and poked around until he found the area he wanted. Although his attention seemed to be completely focused on my punctures, he continued his conversation with Will while he cut away the skin and removed the quills.

"Besides Turner's presence, there are a number of new men in town, gathering supplies for what looks like a long trip. Horses have been stolen from the livery stable, and the jail's been invaded since the marshal disappeared."

It seemed insane to me that the people of that small town would allow such cruelty to occur without fighting back. They allowed their belongings to be taken and their livestock to be killed. They all seemed to live in fear but continued business as if their lives weren't threatened on a daily basis.

Though I knew little of Turner, I knew enough. He obviously thought he could do anything without punishment. I'd never been a fighter, but I would never sit idly by and allow his wrath to continue if I were a citizen of Lone Tree. Regardless of his strength or ruthlessness, if anything had happened to Lucy, Turner's days would be numbered.

By the time I left the doctor, all the quills had been removed. I'd received a few stitches in the worst wounds, and a clean bandage had been wrapped around my arm and my side. They'd fed me whiskey again while cutting away the quills, but I had learned my lesson from the night before and taken it slowly. I managed to remain on my feet when we left the office.

Will's next errand was to set me up with new clothing for the remainder of my stay in Colorado. As promised, he headed toward the ravaged mercantile in the center of town. "The most important thing you need is new boots," he said, leading me down the street. "You won't have time for custom boots to be fitted, but we can find a pair that meets your needs. It'll help you with your ridin'. You seem a bit ... *uneasy* in the saddle." He chuckled and nudged me in the side with an elbow, making me wince as he hit my newly tended wounds. Even though he was several years younger, I felt like a child as he winked at me and laughed at my inadequacies. He truly was Sarah's brother.

"Next, we'll get you some new trousers and a few new shirts." He moved with purpose, and although he continued to laugh and talk as he ushered me down the street, he scanned his surroundings and remained aware of everyone we passed. "Mr. Baker owns the mercantile, and he'll set you up. You'll need wool trousers, as winter is settin' in."

I hadn't thought much about the upcoming winter ... or what it would mean if I didn't find Lucy right away. I had assumed that I'd find her quickly and take her home to safety. Will made me realize, however, that I needed to be prepared for anything.

In the mercantile, I could've sworn a tornado had devastated the area. All the shelves had been stripped and dumped into piles, and grain and flour covered the floor. Mr. Baker looked nervous when he heard the door open, but he immediately calmed when he saw Will. He was busy restocking the shelves while his wife swept the floor. It was evident from the looks on both their faces that more had been lost than food and a few supplies. Their livelihood had been threatened, and they looked somewhat desperate.

"Hello, Mr. Baker." Will remained cheerful amongst the

chaos. "This here is an old family friend. Do you remember Thomas Mullen? Well, this is his son, Mike." Will's easy manner and cheerful attitude seemed to lighten the mood and ease the couple's worries, even if for just a few moments. "As you can tell, he is in *dire* need of your masterful assistance. Just look at him ... ain't he a *mess*?"

Mr. and Mrs. Baker looked at one another and laughed quietly. "Of course we can help this poor, unfortunate gentleman, Will." Mr. Baker visibly brightened. "What do you need, exactly?"

Will never missed a beat. "I'd say just about everything." He moved around the store, naming several things that he needed immediately for our travels. He also mentioned various items that would help me survive in Colorado. I endured the torture to my ego as a small gift to the Bakers, who looked like kind people needing a small break. I even joined in on the fun during several long-winded rants from Will about my inadequacies—and how a tool, such as a shovel, was just what I needed.

Mr. Baker took great delight in outfitting me with appropriate clothes for my journey. He had to scrounge in the back to find suitable items, but when he returned, he had a mound of clothes that might do the trick. As Mrs. Baker helped me root through the clothes and the boots, Will and Mr. Baker talked to each other about what had happened in town, and to their store. Unlike Doc Boylen, however, Mr. Baker was much more tight-lipped about Turner. He was on edge and prepared for the worst, which for him, was to pack up and move from the town he had lived in since before it was first considered a town.

By the time we were finished, the Bakers had me decked out in a comfortable flannel shirt, wool pants, a slicker, boots, and a bandana for my neck. I truly looked like the cowboys I had read about as a child. The new boots were awkward at first, causing me to stumble a few times on the wood floor, but I soon got the hang of them. The heels made me an inch or two taller than normal, and I towered over every head in the store. With the new height, the footwear gave me a fresh sense of confidence, even as I tripped out the door, Will following.

"You look as if you were born here, Michael." Sarah leaned against the railing along the boardwalk, watching me. A man of considerable size stood near her, silent but ever-present. "This is Red; he's the foreman at our ranch."

We shook hands quickly, but neither of us spoke.

Sarah rubbed her chin and looked me over, circling my body. "You're missing something."

I glanced down at my new clothes, looking for anything that could be missing. I felt utterly complete in my new garments. When my eyes returned to Sarah, I noticed the hat in her hands. It was a high-quality Stetson made of jet-black felt.

"Pat wanted to make sure you had a proper hat for riding." She removed my old city hat and placed the new one on my head. Surprisingly, it fit like a charm. I couldn't tell if I liked it because of the quality workmanship or because Sarah had placed it on my head.

"This is wonderful."

"Pat and Tommy are at Pate's Place. How did everything go at Doc's?" She had already taken my right arm, examining it closely while talking. She looked me in the eye and quickly glared at Will. "I see he was quite liberal with the whiskey."

"Don't blame me!" he cried. "He wanted to refuse the whiskey, but he started drinkin' it when Doc had to slice open his side to dig out a quill. It was a deep one, it was, and Doc had to twist and dig with all his might."

Bile rose up in my throat, and my face must have turned various shades of green, because Sarah hastily sat me down on a bench outside the mercantile. She forced my head down between my knees and continued to berate her brother about my condition.

"You know," she then said softly to me, "you really shouldn't drink."

"I do believe I told you that the first time *you* gave me whiskey." I pulled my head up and glared at her incredulously.

"How much did you two give him?"

"I'd say just about enough." Will chuckled and slapped me heartily on the back, making me lose my balance on the bench.

Sarah rolled her eyes and then took me by the arm and yanked me up. "We need to eat and get moving again." We started to walk quickly toward the tavern.

"You know," I said, looking down at her, "it's not so bad this time. At least I can still walk." She glared at me, effectively silencing me, and led us into Pate's Place.

Tommy and Pat both whooped and hollered upon our entrance to the tavern, indicating their approval of my new attire. It would take a great deal of time to get used to their casual attitude in public. I could imagine the stares I'd get from people at the Social Art Club if I ever tried to whistle at someone entering a room. And Sarah, sitting amongst the men in a tavern ... well, it would be impossible.

The tavern consisted of one large room with a bar that ran along the wall and several tables scattered throughout the room. A stairway was in the back, near the kitchen, leading to the owner's personal rooms. The owner stood behind the bar, filling glasses. He was a large, muscular man with a kind face.

As I sat down and the noise cleared, I heard several

men at the bar make comments as they looked at Sarah. I couldn't understand what was said, but Tommy obviously did. He stood slowly with a clenched jaw and sauntered over to the men.

There were three of them sitting side by side. Each had a body like a steam engine, hard and solid. Tommy approached the biggest man without hesitation.

"Did I hear you correct?" he asked slowly, his tone casual.

"I dunno." The man spit tobacco on the ground at Tommy's feet. "What'd ya hear?" His size became more apparent when he stood to face Tommy.

"Did you make a comment about that woman sittin' over yonder?" Tommy gestured toward his sister. Sarah shook her head and rested it in her hands. She had obviously been through this before.

"What if I did?" the man asked.

The other two men now stood to face Tommy as well. My nervous stomach took a tumble as I foresaw a battle in the not-so-distant future.

The owner shook his finger in Tommy's face. "I don't want no trouble in here, Tommy. I'm sure they don't mean nothin' by what they said."

"I believe she deserves an apology." Tommy ignored the saloon owner's plea for peace.

"And what're ya gonna do if I don't?" The man was an inch from Tommy's face, with his friends flanking both sides.

"I'm warnin' you." The owner grabbed a large stick from behind the bar. "You men take this argument outside, or I'll end it right here!"

Pat stood up, took his hat, and grasped Sarah by the arm. They left the tavern. Will leaned over the table in my direction and waved me toward the door. I followed them.

"What's going on?" I asked as soon as we were outside. I was able to see the confrontation through the window of the saloon, and I felt certain that Tommy was about to come to blows with the men at the bar. "Why are we out here, while Tommy is in there with those men?"

"Tommy has a *special* way of dealin' with sons o' bitches like them." Pat sat casually on a bench next to Sarah, watching the street. Will remained standing, but he didn't seem upset either. He leaned against the railing across from Pat and carefully examined each person who passed.

I remained near the window, tension seeping through every pore. My heart raced at the thought of Tommy alone in the tavern and the fight about to begin. I looked back and forth, from Pat and Sarah talking casually, to Will, and back to the window, through which I could see Tommy inside the tavern.

"I wouldn't stand there if I were you," Will said offhandedly.

Immediately, I moved away from the window and closer to Will. I heard an enormous thud and a grunt inside the tavern, followed by Tommy's voice, lecturing the men on the proper way to address a woman. In between each remark, more pounding and crashing occurred. Several patrons quickly exited the tavern and made it down the boardwalk.

I paced up and down while running my fingers through my hair. I occasionally glanced at Pat, Sarah, and Will, who still showed no emotion about what occurred. A final crash inside and a chair flying through the window sent me to the door without thinking. I entered the tavern to find several chairs broken or overturned and a table on its side. The owner remained behind the bar, cleaning the surface with a rag as if a fight hadn't just occurred all around him. He cursed under his breath, however, and was obviously upset about Tommy wrecking his tavern. All the other patrons had disappeared.

The man who had insulted Sarah was in a corner of the tavern, beaten, bruised, and probably unconscious. The other two, obviously giving up the fight, ran toward the exit. They flew past me without a second glance, each carrying the markings and reminders of their "quarrel" with Tommy. Tommy stood next to the bar, a few minor scratches on his face and a tear in his shirt. He adjusted his hat, took a long drink, and placed a large amount of money on the bar before moving toward the door. The owner's expression perked up immediately when he saw the payment Tommy left for the damages he caused. Tommy tipped his hat, smiled, and winked at me as he slowly left the tavern.

I'd never seen such a thing in my life. I followed him, watching him with a gaping jaw. Sarah and Pat remained silent, but Will smacked me on the shoulder and laughed at me as he passed.

"You really didn't think we'd abandon our brother if we doubted his abilities, did you? It's best if we just leave him to his business."

"Can he teach me that?" I asked stupidly.

Will laughed again and rested his elbow on my good shoulder. "Well, it's an unusual talent, Mike, but we'll see what we can do."

7

THE TRUTH ABOUT SAVAGES

It wasn't until we were on our way again that I realized we hadn't eaten. My stomach growled loudly, and my head pounded as we rode out of town, making me feel sick. I couldn't wait for the day when I'd feel normal again.

Pat rode silently beside me until the town disappeared behind the foothills. A deep scowl and worry lines appeared along his forehead as he rode in contemplation. After a long hour of silent riding, he led his horse closer to mine.

"Some merchants noticed R. J. and Blake in town a few days ago," he said. "They stopped for a bit before ridin' away again."

"Did they have Lucy?" I knew that either answer would be an unpleasant one.

"I asked around, but no one's seen her." Pat must have seen the look of dread cross my face, because he quickly explained that it wouldn't make sense for them to bring her into town, as it would raise too much suspicion. It was likely that they kept her somewhere on the outskirts of Lone Tree while they took care of business. "They didn't linger as they normally do," he explained, "meaning they had to get back on the trail."

"So they may still have her?"

"It makes sense after what happened to Sarah."

At the mention of what had happened to Sarah while in the city, I reflexively tightened the reins, stopping Ginger. I took a deep breath and eased up on the reins to get her moving again.

"You think Sarah was also grabbed by someone involved with this Turner man?"

Pat nodded slowly, frowning again. A sense of panic swept over me. Sarah had been grabbed just as Lucy had been.

"Do you know where R. J. and Blake were headed after leaving town?"

"No." He spoke more softly. "I think they took her because of Turner. If so, they'll be takin' her to him, but no one seems to know where he is. He's been gone for a long time."

"I heard." My voice cracked slightly.

"Don't worry, Mike." He nudged my shoulder. "I have some friends that may be able to help us find 'em. They're the ones who told me Turner was alive, and they've been keepin' an eye out around Lone Tree. Don't give up."

A few hours later, we stopped along a creek to allow the horses to rest. I noticed a wonderful difference with my new clothes. Riding didn't chafe so much, and I was able to balance in my stirrups better with my new boots. The five of us walked in the field, talking, while the horses drank from the stream. Pat explained that he planned to split from the rest of us to meet with his friends briefly, and then he'd meet us at the ranch, where we could rest and further develop a plan.

As I went with them over a hill, I set eyes upon three men coming our way on horseback. "Indians!" I quickly dropped to the ground onto my stomach. Visions of scalpings and arrows flying into my chest kept my head pressed hard against the grass and dirt.

Pat, undisturbed by my proclamation, kept walking forward, past my prone form and over the hill. "I know," he said, "they're the ones I told you about. This'll save me a trip to their homestead."

Tommy and Will followed their brother but hesitated when they got to my body. "We need to hunt you up somethin' you can use as a backbone. Till then, don't worry. We'll protect you." Tommy patted me on the back and watched the dust scatter in the air; then he grabbed my jacket and pulled me to a standing position. "Will you be needin' another new set of drawers?" The brothers howled with laughter as they followed Pat.

I straightened my clothes and dusted myself off, slapping my hat against my trousers as I moved hesitantly in the direction of the strangers. Before arriving, I squared my shoulders and attempted to look as fierce as possible. One look at the tallest of the men and I knew it didn't matter.

As I met up with Pat and his brothers, Will leaned over. "You're more skittish than a long-tailed cat in a room full o' rockin' chairs." He grinned and smacked me on the back. I grimaced slightly at the jarring of my arm, which Will always seemed to hit.

"You could have told me." I removed the last of the dirt from my clothes.

"Now what fun would that be?"

I decided to concentrate on our new visitors. A feeling of awe swept over me. All my preconceived notions of Indians on the frontier instantly fell to pieces as I took in the vision before me. The men had notably dark skin, with beads and feathers hanging from their long black, braided hair. But instead of being outfitted in nothing but a strip of leather, they were dressed much like the Donnelly brothers. The main difference was that each was wrapped in an animal hide for warmth. They also rode bareback on horses that seemed exceptionally strong and gallant. The animals had been well cared for and were unusually calm and quiet. When they dismounted, I noticed that the men carried various weapons, such as rifles, knives, and the dreaded bows and arrows.

For several minutes, Pat and Tommy had a conversation with them in a foreign tongue. I knew it had to do with my situation because they frequently glanced in my direction.

"Come meet our friends," Pat said, waving me closer to the men standing near him.

"This is Little Bird." He gestured toward the tallest of the three men, who had a friendly face and a warm smile.

"I've been told you like to be called Mike." He held out his hand with a broad smile. "Good to meet you." He spoke perfect English, which was another surprise.

I looked at Tommy suspiciously. "I take it I have you to thank for that?" He merely shrugged and walked away, but I could see his shoulders shake with laughter as he returned to our horses.

Pat introduced me to the other men as well. One was named Running Deer, obviously the youngest of the three, and the other was named Two Dogs. They had a small homestead in the mountains, and they'd lived in the area all their lives. Many of their people had been forced into the agency and placed on reservations throughout the West, but their family had remained hidden peacefully in the mountains until the soldiers focused their attention elsewhere. Now, several years later, each man had grown up free amongst the settlers who moved into the area. Pat's family had known them for as long as he could remember, and they were obviously cherished friends amongst the Donnelly clan.

Pat told me his friends always kept an eye out on what was going on around Lone Tree. They told him that even though they hadn't seen him, they knew Turner was back in the area. Several members of his old gang had gotten together in town a week before, gathering supplies, along with several other men who were strangers to the area.

"Was Lucy with them?" I interrupted, unable to wait.

"They didn't see a woman with them."

I must have looked disappointed, because Little Bird took a step forward and placed his hand on my shoulder. "Don't worry, friend." He smiled warmly and patted my shoulder.

"After several days in town, all the men rode away, scattered in several directions," Pat continued. "There was no way to follow, but soon they all returned to town for another load."

"What about R. J. and Blake?"

"They must've ridden into town while the men were in the woods."

"How are we ever going to find Lucy?" I mumbled under my breath, pacing back and forth.

"We will, Mike." Pat grasped my left arm tightly. "You've got to trust me."

After several more minutes of consultation, they all decided that the best course of action would be to continue toward the Donnelly ranch to gather men and then set out the next morning. Reluctantly, I agreed.

We rode into the Lazy D Ranch just before supper. Tommy assured me that one of the ranch hands would take care of Ginger and make sure she was properly bedded for the night, so I left my belongings and followed Pat.

In the large house, I felt a sudden feeling of home. In the middle of all the wild country and men, the Donnelly homestead was decorated the same as that of any society gentleman's. The parlor, lavishly adorned with tapestries and mahogany wood furniture, featured a grand piano in the corner, with several sheets of music waiting to be played.

We walked through the main floor after Pat introduced me to May, his housekeeper. She was a short, round woman with nothing but smiles for everyone she met. While Pat went into Mr. Donnelly's private study, May ushered me into the dining hall for supper. Pat joined me several minutes later, and the cook swept through, announcing that supper would be ready in no time. I learned that his name was Gustave, and he had been with the Donnelly family for over fifteen years. He was a short, stocky gentleman with silver hair.

When he found out I was the son of Thomas Mullen, he took an involuntary step backward. He seemed to assess me for a few minutes, and then he held out his hand and smiled warmly. "It's grand to meet you." He pumped my arm up and down enthusiastically.

"I am pleased to meet you as well, sir." I bowed slightly.

"Oh, we'll have none of that, lad," he said, waving off my formalities. "You can call me Gus. I've known your pa for many years, and from our conversations, I know you well enough too." He ushered me into a chair and patted my shoulder gently, as if I were his son. "You look like you could use some food in your belly and a good night's rest." He turned and hurried back toward the kitchen to prepare for the extra people at supper.

The remainder of the Donnellys entered the room. Three young children ran into the house just as everyone sat down, pouncing on Pat, yelling and laughing. He took the youngest girl, about three years old, by her waist and hoisted her onto his lap. He wrapped his arm around her as she settled comfortably and nestled close to his chest.

The tension in Pat's eyes vanished the minute his children entered the room. They were loud, and they all talked at once, smiling and laughing. The closeness of the family warmed me.

"These are my kids." His oldest son, Eddie, was twelve, and strong and tall like his father. There was no doubt he'd follow in the family tradition of ranching. The middle child was a beautiful nine-year-old girl named Laura. She had long brown hair, bright brown eyes, and dimples in her cheeks when she smiled. She instantly reminded me of Sarah. In the course of just a few minutes, she managed to tell me how ridiculous it was that a porcupine had quilled me, because "everyone knows you don't go near one." Pat tried to quiet her, giving gave her a look of disapproval, but I enjoyed her spirit.

The little girl in Pat's lap had long blond hair hanging in ringlets all around her head, and everyone called her Bittie. Unlike her sister, she kept her face hidden in Pat's shirt, afraid to look or talk to me. I'd learned through Sarah that Pat's wife had died a few years earlier, leaving him to raise the children on the ranch.

After supper, Sarah led me outside and down a long path toward a row of cabins near the stable and corral. I wouldn't be able to see the ranch fully until the next day, as darkness had already settled across the landscape.

The largest cabin in the row had a long porch with a bench and a rocking chair outside. Sarah showed me inside.

The entire cabin was lit with several lanterns, and a fire burned in the stove in the corner of the sitting room. My private bedroom was stylishly decorated, with clean blankets covering the bed and warm water waiting in the water basin.

I noticed a second bedroom with fresh flowers and the bed made. I could tell that this room was meant for Lucy when she returned, and I was exceedingly grateful for the kind thought.

I turned to Sarah. "Thank you. This is absolutely perfect."

"We thought you might like some privacy after so many days of travel. One of the boys brought all your belongings in from outside and set them next to the bed, and you'll be able to find anything else you need if you talk to May at the main house."

"I cannot thank you enough." I continued to look around my temporary home.

"I'll let you get some sleep."

I followed Sarah to the hall and watched as she slowly closed the door behind her.

———— ‹‹◉›› ————

Waking at sunrise, I quickly dressed and met Gus and May as I entered the main house for breakfast. Even though my cabin had a small kitchen, I had nothing to cook and no way to get supplies. They seemed excited about my presence at the ranch and the chance for us to talk. The three of us sat alone in the large room, chatting about the Donnellys and the time my father spent at the ranch.

Gus found it hysterical that I fell off my horse and ran into one of the small beasts in the forest. It seemed my father was just as out of place when he first traveled this way, but I learned that he easily adjusted to the different way of life and became a regular fixture at the ranch. Gus reminded me of Arthur. It must have been due to the strong Irish accent because they looked nothing alike. But they were also both comfortable and incredibly easy to talk to, and each of them had an adoptive family, which they'd protect with their lives.

May had lived with the Donnellys for several years as well. She was first hired to help take care of Mr. Donnelly's children, and she stayed on as the housekeeper. May and Gus argued constantly, but a deep understanding plainly existed between the two, for they showed obvious affection.

"We'll have everything ready in a few hours," Pat said, walking into the dining hall with Sarah and Laura. He sat next to me at the table and waited for the others to leave or occupy themselves elsewhere before leaning toward me and looking me straight in the eye.

"Mike," he said in a low voice, for us alone, "you're new to the West, and new to this type of fight. You've also been travelin' for some time and must be weary. I don't think it's best for you come with us. I don't know when we'll return ... or what type of trouble we'll see along the way. I promise to bring Lucy back ..."

I stood and took a few steps backward. "You're trying to talk me out of going to find my sister?"

"No, no. I'm just lettin' you know that my brothers and I can find Turner and your sister. You don't have to go." He stood slowly.

"That is where you're wrong." I raised my head defiantly. "This is something I most definitely *have* to do. I will be going with you."

He looked at me searchingly for a moment and then

nodded. "Okay. We'll ride first into town and then head up into the mountains."

"How do you know where to go?" I hoped Pat had some plan.

"We don't. Get ready for some hard ridin'." He turned and walked away.

"Is there anything I can do to help?" I tried to get his attention before he was out of earshot.

"No. Just get your things and have your horse ready to ride just after dinner," Pat hollered back. "I left some gear in your cabin. Sarah will show you around." He went up the stairs without looking back.

Back in my cabin, I found several more sets of traveling clothes waiting for me, along with new saddlebags to pack them in. In addition, several guns were laid out on the bed, including different versions of the Colt army revolver and the Winchester rifle.

"Pat wanted you to choose your own gun," Sarah said from behind me, entering the cabin. She shrugged. "He has several in the house that my pa once used, and some he's collected over the years."

Her comment, and the assortment of guns, helped me to understand Pat's reluctance to have me go along. He expected bloodshed and remained unsure of my ability to handle myself—or my ability to kill if necessary. I placed a hand on my stomach, trying to ignore the turmoil within. I could do this. I had to do this.

"I want to show you something before it's time to leave." Sarah gestured outside and turned to leave. I took one last look at the guns lying on my bed and followed her.

The Lazy D Ranch was situated in a small valley, surrounded by aspen and pine trees, with a gentle river flowing near the main house. The mountains towered over the ranch in three directions, their peaks already covered with snow. Winter was just around the corner.

The large house faced the only path leading to the ranch, and all the outbuildings lined the south side. There were at least seven small cabins and a large bunkhouse in which the ranch hands stayed while employed by Pat. In the center of it all stood a large circular corral, with the nearby stable capable of holding over forty horses.

Many of the ranch hands had left for the winter, trying to find work until the spring roundup. Sarah told me that Red, the foreman, had graciously given up the cabin upon hearing about my dilemma. It was the only one with two bedchambers, a kitchen, and a sitting room. The others all consisted of several small bunks, a table, and a woodstove.

It would take months to explore fully the vast wilderness surrounding their homestead. Paths led in every direction, some toward the river and others into the woods. Sarah led me down a long, wide path that led to the sound of water. After walking in silence for several minutes, hearing nothing but the music of the forest and river, Sarah stopped and clasped her hands together near her waist, waiting. I passed her on the trail and then glanced back over my left shoulder to study her face.

"You don't have to go, Michael."

"You sound just like your brother." I offered a slight grin.

"He's only worried for you."

"I know, but this is something I have to do. I cannot allow Pat and your brothers to go to a fight, *my* fight, while I remain safely here."

"Pat would be going even if it weren't for your sister. This is his fight too."

"I know that there is history between Turner and Pat. I've seen it in his eyes."

Sarah nodded slowly in agreement, gesturing me to follow her up the path along the river. We walked quite a distance, until we came to a clearing in the woods. The area reminded me of the dream I'd had near the campfire, of the hidden meadow near the twisted trees.

She stopped at the top of a hill and sadly looked down the other side. I followed her gaze to the lonely remnants of a large log building, only partially standing, charred from a great fire.

"What happened?" It was impossible to look away. The forest seemed unusually silent.

"This is where your father built his dream home for your mother."

As I looked at the gloomy remains of the homestead my father had worked so hard to complete, I noticed that the forest seemed unusually silent. All that stood was one log wall, along with the hearth of stone. The outline of the building was clearly visible, making it easy to see his original plans for bedchambers and the sitting room.

"When was the fire?"

Sarah turned away suddenly and looked toward the river. "This is where Pat's wife, Lilly, died," she said in return. "Pat couldn't bear the pain of losing her. When he was able to return to the ranch, he burned the cabin to the ground." A tear slid down her cheek, which she quickly wiped away before turning to face me again. "Your father died before Pat let his sorrow destroy this place, so he never saw its destruction. I'm sorry it was burned before you could see it yourself."

"It's all right, Sarah." I took her hand. "It's not your fault."

"Pat understands what you're going through," she said abruptly. "Turner killed Lilly."

"But why—"

"Listen, Michael. Pat won't speak of it, so you mustn't bring it up to him. He'll just get angry and shut down. He never speaks of Lilly." Sarah turned and began walking back down the path to the house. "He almost died when he fought Turner the first time, and after what has happened to your sister, I just don't know how this will all end."

I caught up to her and gently turned her toward me. Her eyes were filled with pain and damp with tears. Her hands were shaking. I looked up with my brows knit, forcing myself not to take hold of her hands.

"You're shaking."

"Yes. I'm frightened." She folded her arms across her chest to hide her tremors. "I'm frightened for my brothers, especially Pat. He's been fighting for so long. I just wish it all would end. But my brothers would be going to this fight regardless of you … or me."

8

THE LAZY D

I left the small ranch cabin and went to the stable, where everyone was preparing to leave. I had chosen a small pistol of my father's that I had brought from home, to carry in my belt, and a Winchester rifle Pat loaned me. This I secured to the saddle. I had fired guns before, but I felt uneasy about doing it now. If I fired them this time, it would be at a living, breathing soul, who would be firing at me as well. Could I take another man's life ... or risk losing my own?

Ginger was saddled and ready to go when I reached the others. Most of the men looked at me warily, knowing I wasn't from the area, but Pat's stern glare kept them from saying anything. As I settled into the saddle, I was surprised to find Sarah nearby on her horse.

"What are you doing?"

"What does it look like I'm doing? I'm riding with you."

"You cannot go with us." I looked over at her brothers in complete disbelief that they would allow her to follow. The thought of Sarah in the midst of a gunfight quickened my pulse and made me feel nauseated. But they were all busy finishing preparations, apparently unconcerned about Sarah.

"I really don't think you can tell me what I can and cannot do." She glared at me and pushed her horse into a walk with her heels. I hastily nudged Ginger to catch up.

"Sarah, this isn't right."

"Would you relax, for goodness' sake?" She rolled her eyes. "I'm only going as far as town, and then I'm staying there with Red until you return." I let out an audible sigh of frustration mingled with relief.

It took much less time to get back to town than it had to reach the ranch from there, as a new energy drove us forward. I no longer felt pain while riding, and I had forgotten the wounds to my right arm and ribs. I rode with Pat at the front of the group, and he urged us forward at an impossible pace.

When we reached Lone Tree, Tommy and I split from the rest of the group to gather additional supplies for our trip. The streets were much quieter than the day before, and the tension in the air was palpable. There were no children playing on the boardwalks, and the people's faces were stern and wary of those around them. When a group of riders approached, those who were in the streets quickly sought the safety of the indoors. Tommy stopped in his tracks and stiffened, telling me that the riders were all part of Jack Turner's old gang.

As soon as we saw them, we deviated from our original plans and headed toward Pate's Place, where we met Pat and the rest of the men from the ranch. It was evident that they had already learned about the arrival of Turner's men, for Pat sat brooding in the corner with a severe frown, and Sarah had the familiar look of anxiety in her eyes.

Since Turner remained absent, Pat planned to take a few men, along with his brothers and me, up into the mountains to find his hideout. He knew Turner's moves well after so many years with the man, but he expressed disappointment at never finding him where he thought he would be. After Pat explained his plan in harsh words, I sat stunned.

"You cannot just go up there and shoot everyone." There had to be some semblance of order in the town. "If we find out where he is, we must contact the law."

Pat leaned over, placed his elbows on the table, and glared at me. "There is no law in Lone Tree. The town marshal left weeks ago. If he were still around, he wouldn't help us get Turner. He was a no-good cold-footed bastard." Pat leaned back in his chair again and crossed his arms over his chest. "Don't ever forget that these men are your enemy and won't hesitate to put a bullet into your head if given the chance." Pat picked up his glass of whiskey and swiftly drank the last of it, immediately pouring another.

Before I could argue, the doors of the tavern swung open and crashed against the wall, making the owner spill a drink on the bar and curse severely. A man staggered in, looking pale and incredibly ill, and sat down clumsily on a stool near the end of the bar, demanding whiskey. He seemed young, just a bit older than Lucy, but his face was haggard and filled with pain. His eyes were red-rimmed and miserable, and he mumbled to himself while ordering a bottle—not a glass—of whiskey.

We all watched him with fascination as his emotions waxed and waned between sorrow, when he hunched his shoulders over the bar, and anger, when he slammed his bottle down on the wood top and stormed toward the door, merely to return and start the cycle all over again. After several minutes of watching his torment, I excused myself from Pat and Sarah and sat down next to the young man at the bar.

"Is there something I can help you with, sir?" I asked quietly.

"You can leave me be." His tone was sharp, but his eyes never left the bottle in his hands. Streaks from tears dried on his cheeks left clean trails along his dirty face. Sitting so close to him also made his fury and anxiety much more clear.

"I would like to help, if you would allow me."

Two of Turner's men, whom we had seen in town earlier, entered the tavern and quickly approached the young man. Each grabbed an arm and turned him toward the swinging doors. He attempted to yank his arms from their grasp and struggle to get away, but he was no match for their combined strength.

It is hard to describe what went through my mind as I stood and blocked their way. I felt a kinship to the young man, whose face was so filled with pain. Too much trouble had been caused to the people of Lone Tree. I had no choice but to intervene.

Chairs crashed to the ground as people stood and quickly moved out of the way. Pat and his brothers stood as well. Sarah continued to watch me from the back of the room, with ranch hands on each side of her. Instead of grabbing a stick this time, the owner of the tavern leaned down behind the bar and picked up a large rifle, placing it squarely on the bar, in plain sight of everyone in the room.

I addressed the two strangers while blocking their exit. "Let go of this man."

"This ain't your business," one of the men said, tightening his grip on the young man's arm. "Step aside or you'll wish you had."

Several patrons escaped out the front of the tavern. Boots scraped across the rough floor around me as those who remained surrounded us. Pat and Tommy appeared on both sides of me, raising their guns to the two outlaws' heads.

"I bet mine'll die before yours." Tommy said to his brother as he cocked his pistol.

"You're on." Pat's stony expression made it evident that he would relish the task.

Thoroughly unprepared, the two men dropped the young man to the floor and slowly stepped aside. Pat jerked his head toward the door, and two of his men left the room without a word. I helped the man up from the floor and offered him a seat at the table in the corner.

Pat immediately took control of the conversation. "Who are you … and what are you doin' with Turner's men?"

The young man wrapped his fingers around the bottle of whiskey sitting on the table and tilted it to his lips to take a large swig. Pat grabbed the bottle mid-gulp and removed it from the man's hands before he could drink himself into oblivion. He scowled at Pat for a moment and then bowed his head to stare at the tabletop.

"Are you part of Turner's gang?"

"I wish Turner were dead," the man said in a low raspy voice. "He … he killed John, my brother." His hands were shaking, and the sadness deepened in his eyes.

I put a hand on the man's shoulder as a small gesture of friendship. "What's your name?"

"James."

"My name is Michael Mullen, and these are my friends, Pat, Will, and Tommy Donnelly."

James looked up from the table for the first time, staring directly at Pat, who sat across from him. "You're Patrick Donnelly?" A faint glimmer of hope shone in his eyes.

"I don't know you, do I, son?" Pat obviously was not ready to trust James or anyone associated with Turner.

"My pa is Daniel Morgan. He told my brother and me that if ever we needed anything, we should try to find you."

"I know Daniel. He was a friend of my pa's and a well respected rancher." Pat leaned forward in his chair and studied James's face closely. Apparently satisfied that he was not there to cause us harm, Pat took down his guard a notch and relaxed in his seat. "What do those men want with you?"

James closed his eyes and sighed heavily, running his hands through his hair. "Jack Turner weaseled his way into our lives about a year ago, and he managed to get my pa so much in debt that we were gonna lose our ranch. Turner agreed to let my brother and me pay off that debt by workin' for him." James watched as Pat's neck turned red and the muscle in his jaw twitched.

"M-my pa didn't want us to have nothin' to do with Turner, but we had no other choice. I've been ridin' with Turner's men, b-but I never actually met Turner until l-last night."

"So you know where he is?"

"Yes." His eyes cleared, and he straightened in his chair. "At least I did. He's been stayin' in an abandoned homestead high up in the hills."

Pat continued to look at James suspiciously. "Why should we believe you? I don't know anything about you other than that you claim to be Daniel's kin, and that you've been a member of Turner's gang."

James slammed his fist on the table. "I told you! I'm not part of his gang. He killed my brother!"

"Easy, son," said Pat. "I meant no harm, but I just can't go trustin' every man who tells me he knows how to find Turner. That kind of trust can get a man killed."

"I know about your past," James said. "I've seen what that bastard is capable of, and he's got to be stopped. Please ... I'm telling you the truth. I need to make sure he pays for what he done to John." James ran his hand across his face but watched Pat closely for an answer.

"I'll figure a way to help you if you tell us how to get to the cabin."

"I'll do whatever you want." The weariness and guilt started to fade from his face, replaced by the relief of future revenge and freedom from the grasp of Jack Turner.

"Was there a woman with him?" My question caused Pat to look back up at James. "A small woman with long blond hair?"

"Yes," he said quietly, looking down again, "but ..."

"What?"

"He ... he killed her."

Sarah stood slowly and came around the table, placing her hand protectively on my shoulder.

"What did you say?" It was impossible to comprehend fully what I had heard. James looked closely at me and then looked away, remaining silent, along with many of the other men.

After receiving no answer, the fury inside me overflowed, and before anyone could stop me, I had my hands tightly latched around the man's neck, squeezing forcefully as I threw him onto the table.

"What did you just say!"

It took three men to remove my hands from around James's neck, leaving him lying on the table, coughing and gasping for breath. While Tommy and Will held me back, trying to control me, Pat approached James again and raised him to his feet. He kept his hand fiercely wrapped around James's upper arm, holding him close.

"What makes you say he killed her!" I demanded. The room began to spin.

"Turner came into the cabin and went to the room where

the woman was held. She must've said somethin' to him, 'cause a few minutes later he lost what little mind he had left and began beatin' the life outta her." James said the last part quietly, watching me warily. "I'm sorry, but she's dead."

"Lucy's ... *dead*?" If I hadn't had a man on each side of me, my knees probably would have buckled. As it was, though, Tommy and Will continued to hold me by my arms. Sarah was close, but she didn't try to touch me again or intervene in the conversation. Tears formed in her eyes and she held her hand to her mouth. Time slowed to a halt around me as the young man's words sank into my soul.

I shook off the men holding my arms and slowly stepped backward, turning and leaving the saloon. The power returned to my legs, but I still didn't have the capacity to think clearly. I headed quickly away from the tavern, suddenly desperate for air. After stumbling a good distance away, I ducked between two buildings, knelt down, and vomited in the alley.

I remained seated for several minutes, unable to get my body to move. I thought about what James had said and couldn't make myself believe it was true. Lucy and I had been close all of our lives, and I had always known when she was hurt or sad, without being near her. I just couldn't imagine that she had been killed without my knowing it. I remembered my dream about her, however, and realized it could've been a sign, telling me her horrible fate. But James hadn't actually seen her die. He said she couldn't have survived. Confused, I stood and began walking.

No matter what scenario I came up with, I always returned to the thought that this was a mistake. What if I didn't go after her ... and she was still alive? That question was all I needed to move one foot more rapidly in front of the other, quickly returning to the saloon.

The Donnellys were all standing outside, watching me as I approached. Sarah was the first to move forward. She held out her hand and grasped my arm. I placed my hand shakily over hers and squeezed firmly.

"I need to find that cabin." I was addressing Pat, knowing he would make the decision for all the Donnelly brothers.

"Michael, you don't have to—"

"Lucy may still be alive, Pat," I interrupted. I stood tall and strong, and my voice was confident. Sarah and her brothers all had pity in their eyes as they glanced around at each other.

"Michael—"

I cut him off again. "We cannot give up on her now. If she's at that cabin, then I'm going there." One by one, I made eye contact with each of them. "I am going with or without you." When catching Pat's eye, I locked my gaze with his, knowing that he saw how serious I was, and that my decision would not be altered. Slowly, but decidedly, he nodded his head.

"We can't go up to that cabin and start shooting," I said, bringing us back to our earlier conversation. "If Lucy is up there, she'll be right in the middle of the gun battle. We need a different plan."

"If you knew for a fact that Lucy was dead, would you feel differently?" I could see it in Pat's eyes as he spoke. He was already convinced that Lucy had been killed.

"My sister is alive," I said sternly. "I refuse to accept anything else until I see her for myself."

"We'll do what we can, Mike. But if anything goes wrong, I can't promise that gunfire won't end this fight."

"As long as Lucy is safe, you do whatever you have to do."

Tommy and Will left to gather the horses and gear, while

Pat, Sarah, and I returned to James, who waited in the tavern. He had been given food and water while I was gone, but his fork stopped close to his mouth when he saw me enter the room. All hesitancy gone, I confidently approached the man and sat next to him.

"When did you first see my sister?"

"I don't even know if we are talkin' about the same woman."

"What was her name?"

He gulped. "Lucy."

The pain at first hearing she might be dead ripped through me again as I heard her name, but I shook it off the best I could. I had to know what happened.

"Lucy is my sister," I said through clenched teeth. "Now tell me what happened."

James took another swig of whiskey. "John and I met up with R. J. along the trail, and we were tasked with helpin' to take her to Turner's hideout. As soon as we figured out what was happenin', we knew we had to get her out of there."

"Was she doing okay? Was she well?"

"At that point, yeah." He tried to grab the bottle again, but I removed it before he could grasp the top and placed it as far from him as possible. Pat and Will sat down at the table next to us, while Tommy remained at the bar, watching the door with a few of the men from the ranch.

"Knowing we couldn't just take her and run, we tried to stay close and protect her. You see, the men made her skittish with their sneers and their filthy talk. They tried to frighten her every chance they got, but John and I kept them from doin' any real harm. When we finally arrived at the hideout, Lucy was shoved into one of the rooms in the back and left alone. Blake or John came in every now and again to give her vittles, but otherwise she was forgotten."

"Where was Turner?" Pat asked.

"He didn't show up right away. While we waited for him, John and I came up with a plan, but before we could do anything, Lucy disappeared."

"What do you mean she disappeared?" I rubbed my temples and tried to concentrate. I didn't want to miss anything that would be useful later.

"She hightailed it outta there when we weren't lookin'. The men were playin' cards and were drinkin'. They got lazy, which is why John and I were thinkin' about doin' somethin'. Two men got into a fight and when it was all over, the room Lucy had been in was empty. It took us all night to find her."

"Why didn't you help her when you found her?" Pat clenched his jaw, and his eyes bored into the young man. "I reckon you had the perfect chance to get her away."

James's eyes widened, and he held his hand out in front of him. "We would've, but we didn't find her. Blake did. And before we could stop him, he knocked her out."

"How?"

Obviously reluctant to share the details in front of me, James stopped talking again.

"Listen." My tone was harsh, and I slammed my hand down on the table. "If I am going to find my sister and those who have caused her harm, I need to know the truth. Spit. It. Out."

"Blake struck her on the head with the butt of his pistol. She learned the hard way not to cross Blake when he's mad. By the time we arrived back at the cabin, she was pretty banged up. John talked to Lucy when he came in to give her water, and he convinced her we'd help. We just needed time for a new plan. But then Turner showed up."

Frustrated with the man I had once felt sorry for, I stood abruptly, causing the chair to crash against the floor. "How the hell did you help her? You just watched as she was tormented by Turner's men and let Blake beat her senseless. Now you're telling me you just watched Turner kill her. What kind of man does that?"

Tears sprung into the young man's eyes again, and he shook his head back and forth. "My brother died tryin' to save your sister, so don't talk to me about what we should've done!" It was the first time he had shown real anger toward me.

"Enough of this. Tell us how to get to that cabin." Pat stood and glowered over him.

"I'll take you there," he said shakily. "I want to see that bastard dead as much anyone."

"How can I trust you? You're one of the men who killed my sister."

He stood and backed up several feet. "My brother and I were tryin' to get her out of there! Why won't you hear me?"

I went forward as the man backed around the table away from me. Pat impeded James's progress, however, when he approached him from the other side. Backing up against the wall, we trapped James between the two of us.

"Please believe me," he said, looking me in the eye. "The only reason we stayed with his gang so long was because our pa owed Turner money. As soon as we saw the woman, we knew we couldn't stay."

I didn't listen to a word he said. My anger toward the man turned to disgust. He'd watched Jack Turner abuse my sister, and he didn't lift a hand to help.

Pat, feeding off my anger, placed his large hand around the man's throat. "If we take you, and I see you make a move I don't like, I won't hesitate to put you in the ground. Understand?"

James nodded anxiously and then slid across the wall, out of Pat's grasp. Pat turned and left the tavern. I followed him but stopped and turned at the door. "Finish eating—we leave in two minutes." Not waiting for an answer, I left the tavern and walked over to Ginger.

Tommy, Will, and Sarah talked quietly as I prepared to leave. When Pat went past them, Sarah stopped him with her arm. "Pat, Michael isn't thinking," I heard her say as I adjusted my saddle. "Something has snapped inside him since he heard about his sister. You can't let him go like this."

Pat took a deep breath and glanced in my direction while checking his supplies. "He's better off this way. He's more prepared for a fight than he was earlier this mornin'. If we tried to stop him now, he'd just go on his own. Besides, Turner's alive and needs to be stopped. He's not gettin' away with murder again." He motioned everyone into action, and all riders were ready to leave within minutes.

Before leaving, Sarah hugged each of her brothers and spoke to them quickly. I could tell she was reluctant to leave them. When she got to Pat, she placed her hand on his cheek and told him to come home soon. Sarah turned toward my horse and moved slowly toward me.

She took my hand. "Be careful, Michael," she said, trying to get me to look her in the eye. "Promise me."

I stared at her and tried to smile. "I'll do what I can. Will you be all right in town?"

"Red is going to stay with me now that Turner's men are here. Don't worry about me; just take care of yourself." With one more squeeze of my hand, she let go and watched us ride out of town.

9

LUCY

The trail was narrow and rugged, slowing our pace considerably. Overhanging branches and downed tree stumps littered the path, causing us to move single file through the woods. The air chilled considerably, and our group quieted as we rode farther up the mountain.

Just as the sun began to set, we found the small chinked log cabin nestled snug within the trees. Only a few men were outside watching the cabin, but they were all heavily armed. We stayed out of hearing distance, watching the cabin while Pat assessed the situation. I wouldn't allow any plan that included drawing Turner and his men closer to the cabin. We needed to remove as many men as possible to enable us to get inside. The men decided to wait until dark and try to catch them by surprise. We hoped they'd run or ride down the path, where Pat's other men would be able to intercept their descent. Pat made it clear that no mercy was to be given to any man found with Turner. He looked closely at James as he spoke, waiting for James to nod in agreement.

Pat, James, and Tommy crept down through the trees, toward the back of the cabin. Without a sound, Pat approached a man from behind and knocked him uncon-scious. Pat's face held no expression as he lowered the man to the ground and moved forward. Tommy and James came from the other side of the cabin as quietly as Pat did. They disabled their man with a few quick punches. I watched and waited for my chance to reach the cabin.

On Pat's signal, the remaining men came out of the woods on horseback. One of the few remaining guards heard the horses approaching and shot blindly into the trees. Gunfire rained over the men surrounding the area. One man dropped with the first shots from the woods. The other three scattered when they saw the horses coming. All hell broke loose.

A man came out of the cabin, but he was shot before he was able to mount his horse. Will Donnelly and the other men on horseback galloped across the woods, each aiming for a single man. I heard gunshots. My heart pounded in my ears, and my forehead was damp with sweat. Men shout-ed from all around. My eyes focused. My only goal was to reach the cabin.

When close enough, I checked my father's pistol and made sure I was ready for anyone I might find inside. My hands shook. My stomach churned. But I ignored my body's protest as I walked through the door.

The cabin felt eerily quiet compared to the shouts and noise from outside. I kept my gun in front of me in my right hand as I searched the sitting room for anyone who might have stayed to fight. The room was rustic, with a table by one window. Cards were scattered around the top, along with other assorted items that could fetch a price. My heartbeat quickened as I saw the large bloodstain on the wood floor in the middle of the room. Even though the cabin was ut-terly silent, the feeling in the air reminded me of our house when my mother had died—a stillness, along with the smell of lingering illness and death. The sensation caused a shiver to run up my spine as I rushed toward the room near the bloodstain.

A door creaked closed. I hurried toward the back room. With my pistol ready, I flung open the door and scanned the room. Except for a small bed in the corner, it was empty. My palms were so wet with sweat that I thought the gun might slip from my hand. My shirt was damp against my skin. There was a ringing in my ears as I left the room and went back toward the other room in the cabin.

My hands trembled as I wrapped my fingers around the knob, turned it, and stepped inside. The first thing I noticed was a disheveled bed with blood on the blankets. Everywhere I turned, I saw streaks of blood and broken furniture.

As I turned to leave, a small form on the floor caught my attention. She was naked and rolled up into a ball in the corner behind the door. I wasn't sure it was Lucy at first, as her hair was matted, dark with blood, and her face hidden. I remembered the feeling I had when I came into the cabin, as well as the smell of death. All air escaped my lungs in a quick moan as I dropped my gun and ran to her side. I picked up her head, rested it on my knee, and brushed the hair from her face. And there, under all the blood, grime and bruising, was my little sister, Lucy.

I wrapped my arms around her and squeezed tightly, holding her close. She was cold as ice, and her skin was extremely pale. When I moved her arm, which hung at an unnatural angle, I thought I heard a faint but distinct moan. Believing again that my mind was playing tricks on me, I pulled away and stared at her face. Seconds later, a slight twitch of pain ran across her cheek, and her lips moved. I quickly let go and fumbled my hands to reach her neck and feel for a pulse. Although it was weak, her heart was beating. She was alive.

I put her face close to mine. Her breathing was unusually shallow, but all that mattered was that she was breathing. I looked around at the state of the room and imagined the torture Lucy must have endured there. I grabbed a blanket from the bed and wrapped it tightly around her body; then I picked her up and headed out the door.

"Well, well, if it isn't Mr. Mullen," I heard from behind me. Before I could turn around, I felt the cold metal of a gun smack against my temple, causing me to fall to my knees near the large bloodstain in the main room. I still held Lucy's frail body firmly in my arms, and I concentrated on staying focused in order to keep her safe. I stumbled back to my feet just before a fist drove into my jaw. Miraculously, I was able to remain standing, but I reeled away from the man attacking me, shaking my head to get my eyes to work again.

Knowing I couldn't possibly defend myself while holding Lucy, I reluctantly set her down on the couch against the wall. I turned around slowly and froze, taken aback by his size and appearance. The man was large, with a pistol in his right hand near his waist. I immediately noticed the horrific scar that ran down his face. Blake was as ugly as they'd said, but his eyes held more meanness than I could have imagined in one man.

I glanced hastily around the cabin again, saw no one else, and then reached down for my gun, which I realized I'd left in the other room. Looking down at Lucy's bloody face, fear of being shot or dying had never entered my mind. I'd felt nothing but searing fury. Lucy's ordeal was over, and I would do whatever it took to ensure that she got home safely.

Blake obviously felt he had the upper hand, and he stood smiling in the entrance to the hallway. He looked at Lucy closely, his smile widening, and then his gaze locked with mine. "She's a fine piece, ain't she?" He was baiting me. "It looks as if Turner had a bit of fun with her."

"Where is Turner?" I clenched my fists and my teeth.

"Gone," he said with a shrug. "It don't matter, though."

"What do you mean?"

"When he comes back … you'll be dead." He raised his pistol slightly and slowly circled me. I moved around him, never allowing him to get behind me. I kept my eyes focused sharply on Blake, waiting for the slightest movement.

"As for the little girl there," he said, looking at Lucy, "I reckon Turner can get a good price for her in town if she lives. There's always room for one more whore."

I could feel my heart snap as I thought of my little sister being sold like a cheap piece of luggage. Fury rose up inside me. I shouted and lunged for the man. After two steps, I heard a crack, followed by a loud explosion, causing me to fall backward. Halting to look at the bullet wound to my right shoulder, I felt the world slow once more.

Seconds later, I heard another shot and looked up to see Blake standing still as the pistol dropped from his hand. His eyes held a blank, dull gaze, with the absence of smugness that I had seen so vividly. Blood oozed slowly through the man's pale blue button-down shirt, just below his left collarbone. He slowly fell to his knees and collapsed face forward onto the wood floor, his blood pooling where a stain already existed.

I cautiously turned around to look into the face of Will Donnelly filling the doorway. He held a gun in his left hand. One corner of Will's mouth curved upward, and he shrugged.

"I never did like that man." He quickly looked around the cabin before entering. "We need to go."

Without hesitation, he moved toward Lucy to carry her. I stood up quickly and held my left arm out. "Don't!" I managed to get to my feet and thrust myself between Lucy's injured form and Will.

"Michael," he said softly, using my full name for the first time. "If I thought you could carry her, I wouldn't stop you." He held both arms out, palms up, to show he meant no harm. The arm I was holding out in front of me dropped as he spoke. I knew that Will wasn't the enemy, but I didn't want anyone to harm Lucy again.

"You can't carry her with that wound to your shoulder."

I looked down at my right arm and noticed for the first time that my sleeve was drenched in blood. I knew I had been shot, but I hadn't felt pain and had forgotten about the wound when Will arrived. I tried to lift my arm but was unable to.

"Let me help you," he said again. "We need to leave, and I can carry Lucy ... if you'll let me." His voice was calm and reassuring.

I looked back down at Lucy for a moment and then nodded toward Will. "Be careful of her left arm," I said, my voice cracking. "It's badly broken."

He nodded in acknowledgement and then slowly walked around me, not taking his eyes off mine. I realized I was still standing between them, and he was clearly hesitant that I may try to intervene if he came closer. I took several steps backward as Will moved forward, gently picking Lucy up in his arms.

"I won't let anything happen to her—I promise." He looked me directly in the eye as he walked toward the door.

As we exited the cabin, I saw another body lying near

the door. Walking toward the horses, the sinister feeling of the cabin washed away in the crisp, clean night air. The men who had accompanied us were outside on their horses. James had been shot in the leg, but he insisted that his wound would be fine until we returned to town. A few others had minor scratches and scrapes, but they all felt okay to ride. The remaining few members of Turner's gang who had run when the gunfight started had been killed in their attempted escape into the woods. Pat was certain that R. J. had been there, but no one knew where he went, or if he had made it out of the woods. Turner was nowhere to be found.

Tommy and Pat approached us as we walked toward the group. Pat was furious that Turner had escaped him again, but one look at my blood-drenched shirt and the bundle held in Will's arms and his expression changed to one of concern.

"Is that Lucy?" Pat asked hesitantly, focusing his gaze on me.

I nodded, no longer able to speak.

"Is she okay?"

I stared up at him with pain in my eyes, causing Pat to look back down.

"She's alive, Pat, but it's bad," Will said firmly. "We need to get her to Doc quickly."

His comment seemed to spin everything back into motion. Pat quickly untied Will's horse and led it to him, as the other men turned to go. Will passed Lucy to Pat momentarily while he mounted his horse, and then Pat lifted Lucy to the front of the saddle, where Will cradled her tightly.

"I won't let anything happen to her," he said, looking down at me as he nudged his horse forward. Confident that Lucy was in good hands, I turned toward my own horse.

Tommy and Pat whispered to each other for several moments before Pat headed quickly into the cabin. As he stepped off the porch and moved toward his horse, I noticed that he had tucked my father's pistol into his belt. Tommy approached me with a shirt balled up in his hands. He shoved the cloth under my own shirt and pressed hard on the wound.

"Keep this pressed against your shoulder," he said firmly. "I'll help lead you down." He helped me into the saddle and then rode next to me to keep me from falling. Unlike the wound from the quills, the gunshot had left my right arm completely disabled.

When we reached the other men farther down the path, we were told that R. J. had gotten away, and that no one had seen Turner. Pat sent a few of the men back to the ranch with instructions as we rode back toward town. I stayed close to Tommy and Will, never taking my eyes off Lucy. Tommy talked to me most of the time, about anything and everything, clearly in an attempt to occupy my mind.

"Where are we going?" I asked with a raspy voice as town came into sight.

"I've been wantin' to talk to you about that," Tommy said, riding closer. "There's a place we can take Lucy, where she'll get the best care possible in town without anyone knowin' she's there."

"Good, what's the problem?" I could see the hesitation on Tommy's face and knew there was more he did not want to tell me.

"The thing is," he continued, "I don't think you'll like goin' there."

"You said it's the best place for her ... to get the best care?"

He nodded. "She'll be safe and hidden."

"Then it doesn't matter what I think, does it?" I asked, looking at him.

He shrugged and let out a deep sigh. "I guess not."

Pat separated from the group as soon as town came into sight, riding quickly to get Sarah and Red from the hotel. We headed toward the rear of several buildings lining Main Street. The three of them soon met up with us at the back entrance to one of the establishments. I saw the grim smile and sullen look on Sarah's face and knew that she had been told about Lucy. When she saw me, she tried to change her expression and smile warmly, but the illusion didn't quite reach the sorrow in her eyes.

Red helped James into the building so his leg could be treated. Will was helped from his horse, and he carried Lucy toward the door. Since I'd relinquished Lucy's care to Will at the cabin, he'd clearly made it his personal responsibility to take care of her, not allowing others to share the burden of carrying her. Without waiting for Pat and Tommy to stop their conversation, Sarah held open the door as Will entered the building, and then she followed him up the stairs.

"Did you tell him?" I overheard Pat ask Tommy as we reached the door.

"I tried," he said with a shrug.

"Christ, Tommy!" Pat looked up toward the heavens as if asking for patience and then slapped his hat against his thigh. I listened with only one ear as I hurried after them to get to Lucy. Pat put an arm up to stop me.

"What's going on?" I was annoyed and tried to push past them.

"Do you know where we are?"

"Tommy told me this was the best place for Lucy," I said, suddenly suspicious. "Where are we?"

Pat looked at his brother in disgust and then looked back

to me. "Tommy should've told you before," he said. "This is Belle's place."

"What!" I hollered, pushing against Pat. Due to his size and my crippled arm, I made little progress. "How dare you bring my sister to a brothel? Can't you see what she's been through?"

"I reckon I do." He leaned closer. "Tommy was right. This is the best place for her right now."

"What about Doc?" I asked in irritation.

"We can't take Lucy there if we hope to keep her safe and hidden," Pat said, lowering his voice. "Besides, we've already sent for Doc. He's supposed to be at a homestead about five miles outside of town, but I'm sure he'll be here as soon as he can."

"But ... how ...?"

The fire went out of my protest, but doubt still lined my brow. Pat stopped struggling with me. "If it makes you feel better, the madam of this place is a healer. As you can imagine, she's had to use her skills over the years. Until Doc can get here, Belle will know what to do. She and Sarah will take good care of Lucy."

"*Belle* is the madam of this place?" I asked with surprise.

"Yes." Pat stopped suddenly and gave me a curious look. "Do you know her?"

"I ... we met with Tommy ... I haven't ... never mind." Lucy's condition had me so muddled that I couldn't seem to manage a complete sentence without stumbling over my words. I grabbed Pat's arm again. "Promise me that we'll leave here before Lucy is able to understand where we are. I don't want her to wake up in this ... atmosphere."

Other than the fact that I was offended at the thought of Lucy being in such a place, I knew the abuse that she had endured. I wouldn't allow her to feel that pain again by seeing or hearing the women around her.

"Don't worry. We're goin' in the back way, straight to Belle's personal rooms. Lucy won't know where we are." Pat moved again toward the stairs and ushered me forward. I followed him up a long, narrow stairway to the second floor, leading to a room at the end of the hall. Lucy had been laid out on the bed, still wrapped in the blanket I'd found at the cabin. Will was waiting by the door.

Belle and Sarah went quietly into the room. Sarah had a bowl of water, and Belle had several clean cloths and soap. Sarah touched me on the shoulder and asked me to leave the room so they could wash Lucy and get her ready for the doctor's arrival. I knew what that would entail and hesitated before consenting to leave. They would have to scrub Lucy's body vigorously to remove all the dried blood and dirt accumulated from the days she'd been captive. Sarah was right about washing Lucy as soon as possible, however. Besides being covered in filth, she wouldn't feel the pain so much in her current condition.

I knelt by the bed and took Lucy's hand in mine, careful not to cause her any undue pain. It was difficult to tell what was dirt and what was bruising because her fair skin was now dark with blood and debris. I kissed the back of her hand softly and brushed her hair out of her eyes. She hadn't moved at all since our arrival, and she made no sound when I kissed her and squeezed her hand. I slowly got to my feet, let go of Lucy's hand, and walked out of the room, without looking at Sarah.

Just as Sarah and Belle finished, the doc headed up the stairs and down the hall. After knocking softly, he entered the room with me close behind him. I was uncomfortable with his being alone with Lucy after everything that had happened. Sarah seemed to read my mind, for she offered to remain in the room while the doctor examined Lucy.

She told me a short while later that the doctor first assessed Lucy's heart, lungs, and head for obvious life threats. It was difficult to tell if Lucy's state of unconsciousness was from the prolonged use of alcohol and drugs to keep her from fighting, or from the injuries sustained to her head.

He'd placed Lucy's arm in a splint to keep it aligned while it healed. As for the lacerations all over her body, some he decided to stitch, while others he left alone. He gave Sarah several instructions as he moved from one injury to another, and he cautioned her against using further sedatives for pain control, as he was worried about her head injury and wanted her to wake.

After covering Lucy with warm blankets, he left the room and ushered everyone away from the door to keep from disturbing her. He told me that Lucy's condition was serious, and that she would need a quiet place to rest, where she could hopefully recover. He urged us to remove her from the brothel, as the noise might disturb her. Even though I didn't like the idea of moving her again, I readily agreed. The last place I wanted Lucy to be when she woke up was in a brothel surrounded by men propositioning women.

Pat suggested taking her back to the ranch first thing in the morning, before dawn, where she would get peace and quiet, plus anything else she might need. Doc agreed, saying he would come to the ranch in a few days to check on her condition.

Before he left, he glanced at my blood-soaked shirt and stepped toward me. "I should take a look at your arm, sir."

"No, thank you. It'll be all right." I took a step backward, guarding my right arm against my chest as if the mere mention of examining it would cause pain. "James needs you to tend to his leg; he is down the hall."

"I think you should let me have a look at your arm before I leave," he said.

"No." I went back into the room where Lucy slept and closed the door. I moved a chair next to the bed and covered her with one more blanket that was folded on the dresser. I watched Lucy closely for the few remaining hours of darkness, trying to soothe her when she moaned or cried out in her sleep.

Red had arranged a wagon for the ride home, and he had it waiting outside before first light. It was outfitted with a large straw mattress and several pillows in the back to make the ride as comfortable as possible for Lucy. Will carried her out the back door of the house and set her gently down on the soft improvised bed.

James took Tommy's advice and followed the rest of us to the ranch. Doc had stitched his leg, and James insisted on riding his own horse. The bullet hadn't hit the bone, so his leg was still functional. His only complaint was a slight amount of pain, but he kept silent after watching Will bring Lucy outside.

Sarah rode with Lucy in the back of the wagon, while Tommy drove the horses up front, as we carefully began the long journey back to the Donnelly homestead. I wasn't up to riding the horse, so I sat next to Tommy in the wagon, while Will followed on horseback, and Red rode ahead to prepare the ranch for our arrival. The rest of the men flanked the wagon on all sides, keeping a lookout for trouble along the way.

Pat had disappeared during the night, with no word of his plans. Tommy told me he was most likely continuing the search for Turner—alone. He had been furious to find that Turner was not at the cabin, and he was unwilling to let him slip out of his reach again.

While I felt relief upon finding Lucy alive, it was quickly replaced by a new fear when I realized her rescue had in no way removed her from danger. I was incredibly nervous about her fragile condition. She had been close to death when we found her, and I couldn't yet tell if the treatment she'd received had improved matters. I desperately wanted to stay close to her, but I knew Sarah would take good care of her.

As soon as we arrived, one of the ranch hands met us outside. James was led to the bunkhouse, where he would stay while his leg healed. Pat had told him that he'd have a job for him and would speak to his father about John's death and the situation with Turner.

The cabin was ready for Lucy's arrival. Red stood next to Will as we spoke, and without asking, he went to the wagon, picked up Lucy, and carried her into the cabin. She looked incredibly small and frail lying quietly in Red's arms. For his strong build and rough exterior, he was extremely gentle as he laid her on the clean bed.

Sarah entered behind me. "I need to prepare Lucy for bed, if you all wouldn't mind leaving us alone a bit. I need to tend her wounds and get her warm." She held a thick featherbed and several blankets. I hesitated slightly while looking at Lucy's supine form, but I slowly walked out the door.

I waited on the bench outside the cabin until Sarah finally opened the door and stepped onto the porch. She looked extremely tired, walking as if it caused her pain. She rubbed the back of her neck with one hand, holding a bowl of dirty rags with the other. I stood facing her, not able to find words to describe my appreciation for her attendance to Lucy. I lightly placed my hand on her arm and squeezed while looking into her eyes, which seemed to convey my thoughts.

"She's awake, Michael," she said quietly, "but I'd let her

rest." She smiled wearily and then told me I could go back in. I let go of her arm and quietly entered the cabin, shutting the door behind me.

Even though there were two bedchambers in the small cabin, I couldn't bring myself to leave Lucy's side. Red had already tended the fire, which kept us both warm throughout the day. I continued to sit by Lucy's bed, holding her hand, well past the time when she finally drifted back into sleep. It was much more from exhaustion than anything else, as her slumber was in no way restful. She whimpered and moaned frequently, with only moments of peace in between.

Sitting vigil over Lucy, after I was sure I wouldn't wake her, I slowly and silently let the tears come. I wept from weeks of worry, frustration, anger and sorrow all rolled together. I wept for the innocence lost at that torture chamber in the woods. And I wept thinking about what the future would bring.

At suppertime, Sarah knocked lightly on the cabin door and entered with a tray of tea and food. She knew I had gone several days with little sleep, but she also knew I wouldn't be willing to leave my sister's side. She knelt by the bed and handed me a cup, which I took with shaking hands.

"I have to get her home," I said softly, a slight crack in my voice.

"She cannot travel like this," Sarah whispered. "She needs time to heal."

"I don't believe she'll be able to heal ... not after this." I gestured toward my sister's frail condition on the bed and then looked away. The tears returned to my eyes, and I couldn't bring myself to look back at Sarah.

"If Lucy is anything like you or your father, then I know she has the strength to get through this." She placed her hand on my knee. "Give her time," she pleaded.

I kept my head turned away without answering her. After several minutes, she stood up, set the tray on the table, and left the room, closing the door silently behind her. I could tell that she was frustrated that she could not help me, just as I could not help my sister. We both needed time to heal, and neither of us would be traveling anytime soon.

10

A TIME FOR HEALING

After Lucy finally faded into a deep sleep, I stood and left the cabin. I didn't want to be gone when she awoke, but I needed a quiet moment alone in the cool night air. Outside, snowflakes gently drifted down over the countryside, blanketing the ground with a cool white glow, hiding the last traces of fall. Sarah and Tommy sat on the porch of the cabin, clearly waiting for me. Tommy looked ready to kill someone, while Sarah had a look of concern etched on her face.

She stood as soon as I closed the door and stepped onto the porch. "Michael, please let me take a look at your shoulder and clean the wound."

The wound had already gone too long without care, so I merely nodded and sat on the bench. Tommy continued to slowly rock in the chair next to me.

As soon as she removed the makeshift bandage, Sarah took a step back, crossed her arms in front of her, and shook her head. "Michael, how could you let it get this bad? You haven't kept the wound clean, and some of your stitches from the porcupine have reopened."

Ignoring Sarah's scolding, I inched closer to Tommy. "What happened to Pat?"

"He went to find Turner."

"Alone?"

Tommy glared at me and nodded.

"Why wouldn't he take someone with him?"

Tommy jumped to his feet and paced the length of the porch. "You'd think he would, the stubborn ass!" He kicked the railing and then sat heavily on the steps, deflated. "Pat's tryin' to take care of everything alone, like he always has. I wish I knew where he was so I could kick his ass."

"I'm sorry, Tommy."

"I reckon he'll be gone for a while." Tommy stared out at the ranch, as if searching for something. He answered my occasional question but didn't really give me any new information.

The cryptic answers and lack of attention irritated me. When would the Donnellys tell me what they knew about Turner and his gang? I couldn't protect anyone if I didn't know what I was up against.

I'd been worrying so much about Lucy that I had hardly felt the pain in my shoulder. The bullet had entered through my chest just under the collarbone and exited the back of my shoulder, barely missing my lung. With Sarah poking and prodding the wound while she changed the bandage, I could feel sharp stabs shoot from my shoulder to my elbow. The pain was an instant reminder of everything that had occurred over the last several weeks, and my irritation quickly turned to anger.

I yanked my arm away and allowed it to drop like dead weight next to me. "Would you please stop fussing over me, woman?" The outburst was a surprise, and I regretted it as soon as I uttered the words. Making matters worse, Sarah's eyes filled with tears and she quickly looked away.

"Sarah, I'm—"

She threw my shirt at me and smacked me on the head before storming away. I tried to get up to follow her, but Tommy grasped my arm and forced me to sit.

"You'd better let her be," he said. "She'll be in no mood to talk to you for a bit."

As I watched Sarah cross the field toward the main house, Pat's oldest girl, Laura, approached the cabin with slightly limp wildflowers in her hand. She held them out so I could take the beautiful posy. "I picked these yesterday and wanted to give them to Lucy," she said. "They might make her feel better."

"Thank you, Laura," I said softly, feeling incredibly foolish. Everyone in the Donnelly family had bent over backward to help Lucy and me. Even Laura cared enough to send wishes for Lucy's welfare, and she had never met her.

"I shouldn't have said that to Sarah." I watched Laura leave the porch and skip down the path. "She was only trying to help me."

"Well, you ain't lyin', Mike." Tommy shook his head. "Ya sure know how to stir up a hornet's nest ... Whew!"

Tommy was never one to hide his true feelings, and I had learned that he always told the truth, whether I wanted to hear it or not.

Why did I lash out at Sarah whenever I felt lousy? She only wanted to help, and I knew she was just as worried about Lucy as I was. All the soreness, bruising, and pain seemed to intensify as I thought about my situation. Lucy shouldn't have been taken. Sarah never should've been saddled with me in the first place. I felt wretched.

"You'd better have somethin' real nice to say when you do try talkin' to her again." Tommy stood and placed his working gloves on his hands. "You're lucky you merely got a smack on the head. She could scare the skin off a rattler ...

believe me." He had a wry grin on his face when he spoke, as if remembering something from the past. Tommy shook his head again. "You've got balls, I'll give ya that!"

———————

Lucy rarely woke during the first few weeks at the ranch, and I seldom left the cabin, continuing my vigil by her bedside. When I did leave, I noticed that one of Sarah's brothers, most often Will, would come and sit in the rocking chair on the porch. I had never asked any of the family to watch over her in my absence, but I was glad to know someone would be there when I was not.

The physical reminders of her captivity started to fade. Doc had come and gone, removing the stitches and assessing her badly broken arm. Only the bruises on her face looked worse after several days. Although the swelling had receded, the bruises deepened into purple and brown along the left side of her face. The multiple bruises all over her body would be gone in another few weeks, but the emotional scars might remain forever.

As I sponged the lacerations slowly healing on her arms and face, pity and hatred for the man who had done this to her tangled in my heart. I dipped the piece of cotton cloth in the salted water, squeezed it in my fist, and then gently dabbed her face.

Sarah came in twice a day to check on Lucy and to help wash the wounds Lucy didn't want me to see. She had forgiven my rude behavior after I'd apologized, and she seemed to have forgotten the incident completely. In return, I consented to having Doc Boylen look at my arm again so he could clean and bandage the wound.

For the first few days, I feared Lucy no longer had any fight left in her body. The fiery spirit that had defined her since childhood had vanished with the abuse she had endured.

"Please talk to me, Lucy."

She shook her head and looked away.

"This is the third night you've woken screaming." I moved my chair closer to her bed. "You shake every time you hear a loud noise, and you haven't even tried to get out of bed. I know you're hurting. You need to talk to someone about it."

A tear escaped her eyelashes and traveled down her cheek. She tried to smile, but her lips shook and she turned away again.

"Would it help to talk to someone else, maybe Sarah?"

She reached out and grabbed my hand. "Please ... just leave me." She let go and rolled on her side, away from me.

"I'm not going to give up on you." When her breathing changed and I knew she was sleeping, I left the room. "That bastard will pay for what he's done," I growled.

I tried to make plans to get Lucy home to Philadelphia, but there was no way to tell how long it would be before she was fit to travel such a long distance, and winter was closing in quickly. Instead, I turned to the one thing I knew Lucy would enjoy. I visited Mr. Donnelly's study, picked out several books, and took them back to the cabin. While my arm healed, I spent my days reading to Lucy. She'd lie in bed listening, and I'd occasionally glimpse the old light shine in her eyes when I read one of her favorite stories.

After a while, I began telling her stories about the Donnelly family and my experiences blundering in the dark when I'd traveled with them. I caught her smiling when I told her about falling off my horse in front of Sarah.

One morning as I came back from the main house with food, I noticed James sitting on a chair outside the bunkhouse. He looked up at me warily before raising his arm and tipping his hat. I still hadn't come to terms with my feelings about James and his brother, and wouldn't until I knew what actually happened at Turner's cabin. I didn't gesture back. Instead, I turned my head and continued walking.

While averting my gaze from the bunkhouse, several other ranch hands came into my line of sight. Actually, they seemed to be everywhere. Instead of engaging in their typical ranch work, most were heavily armed, riding from one point to the other, always looking into the distance. For the first time, I'd allowed myself to notice the atmosphere of the ranch. Tension permeated the air. The ranch expected a fight.

Will sat at his usual place by the cabin door.

I walked up the steps to the porch, sat on the top step, and watched the men guarding the cabin. "How safe are we? Is the ranch in danger with Lucy and me here?"

Will lounged on the bench with a piece of whittling cedar in one hand and a Barlow knife in the other. He looked up from his whittling. "We killed some of Turner's men, and until Lucy talks, we won't know why he took her in the first place. Besides that, R. J. got away, so I'm sure it's only a matter of time before he comes after us." He spoke in a matter-of-fact tone, without the slightest hint of fear or worry. "We have some time, though," he continued. "Winter's comin', and it'll be damn near impossible to get to the ranch without leaving tracks."

We sat for a few minutes in silence. "Do you think Pat is all right?"

"I reckon Pat is doin' what he has to do." Will looked back down at the small piece of wood he had been chipping. He hadn't answered my question, but I figured it was all I could expect.

I stood to go inside and paused by the door. "Thank you for watching over my sister."

"Lucy's a strong woman," Will said unexpectedly. "I've seen a lot less done to a woman, and they'd just curl up and die. Lucy's a fighter." He turned his attention back to his whittling. Not knowing how to respond, I entered the cabin and closed the door.

I settled into the chair in my own room and thought about what Will had said. Lucy's strength had improved, but the darkness that surrounded her remained. I had tried all I could to help ease her suffering, but I had run out of ideas. It seemed the more her physical wounds healed, the worse she felt emotionally. Instead of each day getting easier, her pain increased. After my attempts to soothe her failed, I'd retire to my own room in despair.

Unable to think of another way to help Lucy, I left the cabin first thing one morning in search of Sarah. I found her behind the house, taking down dry laundry before inclement weather moved in.

"Sarah?" I removed a giant sheet so she could see me.

"Hello, Michael," she said cheerfully, then frowned when she noticed my troubled face. "Is something wrong? Is Lucy all right?"

"Do you have a few moments to talk with me?" I kept my head low.

"Of course." She stepped away from the empty laundry line and placed the clothes basket inside the back door. We moved slowly along the path, never leaving sight of the ranch.

"I wanted to ask your advice ... about Lucy," I said.

"What's going on? Does she need to see Doc?"

"No, it's not that." I shook my head. "I think her physical wounds are healing well. It's ... it's something else." I told Sarah how my relationship with Lucy had been getting progressively worse over the last several days. "It seems that everything I do or say hurts her. When I try to talk to her about it, she shuts down or starts to cry. I don't want to cause her pain. I don't know what to do." I ran my fingers through my hair slowly, releasing a long breath.

Lucy's hesitance to speak troubled me, but I'd watched her with Sarah, and I knew things were different between them. Even though Lucy had not known Sarah long, she talked to her rather freely, without the pain I had often seen on her face. Now that Lucy had someone she could confide in, my heart filled with gratitude toward Sarah.

"Do you want me to try to talk to her about what's bothering her?" she asked softly.

"She trusts you, Sarah. She needs to start talking about what happened."

"I could try, but there are things she may not discuss, no matter who she talks to."

We both turned at the sound of horses coming up the path. Pat was among the men riding toward us. He looked as if he had been through hell, and he needed help dismounting when they arrived at the stable. Sarah ran to him and embraced him tightly. He looked weary, but a small smile formed on his lips when he hugged his sister. She helped support him as he walked toward the house and his kids. He acknowledged me with a nod and disappeared through the door.

11

SIX MOONS

The next night, Sarah and Lucy wanted to have supper at the cabin alone, so I joined the rest of the family at the main house for the night. As I stepped into the main house, Pat came down the stairs, followed by his children, who were talking excitedly behind him. After shaving and bathing, he looked much better than the day before. He smiled wearily at me but continued to joke around with his children, waving at me to join them in the dining room. The long, hard days of travel still showed in the lines on his face, and disappointment lingered in his eyes.

I found James sitting at the dining room table with the Donnelly family. Pat greeted James warmly with a pat on the shoulder. It seemed he had come to terms with his feelings toward the young man and his association with Turner. I, on the other hand, felt like slamming the man's head against the table. James shifted in his seat when he saw me. He stared blankly at his plate and gripped his fork, but he barely touched the food.

"How's your leg healin', James?" Pat said kindly.

"It's not troublin' me much these days," the man replied, rubbing his thigh and glancing in my direction. "Actually, I'm feelin' good enough to be on my way soon. I'm sure my pa needs help at the ranch."

Pat's eyes went from mine to James and back again. He took a bite of food and set his fork on his plate. "I wanted to let you know I stopped by your ranch on my way home, and I spoke with your pa." Pat glanced at his children and saw that they were messing with their meals and not paying much attention. He lowered his voice before continuing. "I told him about John. I also told him about what you and your brother were willin' to do for us."

James's smile shook as he nodded. I looked back down at my plate but sensed that Pat's words were meant for me more than James.

"Well, then, I'll be on my way, as soon as I'm able," James said.

"Actually, Daniel's made some decisions that may change your mind a bit." Pat leaned back in his chair. My head popped up from eating, and I stared at him long and hard. James was a daily reminder of the filth my sister had encountered while with Turner. The last thing I wanted was for James to remain at the Lazy D. I had warmed to the idea of the man leaving the area, especially before Lucy saw him at the ranch.

"It seems Daniel's been thinkin' about makin' some changes for quite a while." Pat wiped his mouth and set the napkin on the table. "Now that there's trouble back in town, and after hearing about John, Daniel wants a change."

"What are you sayin'?" James's good leg started to tap up and down in a fast rhythm.

"Daniel's decided to fill the marshal's position in town. He's already taken on the duties. For the first time in many years, there's real law in Lone Tree. He even has a reward out for Turner." Both James and I leaned forward in our chairs.

"I didn't take kindly to the idea of Daniel putting himself out there as a target, but after listenin' to the man, I was sold. Your pa was a born lawman."

The only noise that could be heard was the ticking of the clock on the wall.

"You're kiddin', right?" James said in disbelief, pulling everyone out of the trance. "My pa can't be the law in Lone Tree."

"Why the hell not?" Pat said in an amused voice. "He is a might bit better than the last five marshals we've had."

"What about my pa's ranch?" James asked.

"I wouldn't fret about it. He's got enough help at the ranch to keep it going," Pat replied, "and I agreed to help whenever needed. Talk to your pa and I'm sure you'll see what I mean."

James's mouth opened, but no sound came out, only a slight rush of air. Pat seemed more relaxed than when he'd first come downstairs, and he had a strange grin on his face when he looked in my direction. Tommy and Will walked through the door, arguing as usual, but they quieted before they settled at the table.

"That brings me to your notion of leavin' the ranch," Pat said, ignoring James's stunned expression and my puzzled one. "As I see it, you have a choice. Your pa wants to talk to you about helpin' him in town. He can't do it alone, especially with new townspeople comin' in and out."

"You mean he wants me to be his deputy?" James asked. It was the first time since I'd met James that there was a slight glimmer in his eyes.

"You can stay here, go back to your ranch, or meet your pa in town. Daniel wants to leave the decision to you. Your pa is stayin' at the Franklin Hotel until he can build a small house behind the jail."

James sighed heavily and nodded. He put his napkin down and got up from the table. "Pardon me. I have some thinkin' to do." He turned and walked out of the dining room and out the front door.

Ten minutes later, James came back up to the main house, walking much quicker than when he had left. His small bag was packed and waiting for him. With a shake of his head, he grabbed it and walked outside, where his horse had been saddled for the trip. We followed him outside and waited on the porch.

"You knew all along?" he asked with surprise.

"I had a feelin'." Pat handed him a package. "Gus wanted you to finish your supper. Say hello to your pa, and if you need anything, send someone to the Lazy D, and we'll do what we can. Four of my men will travel with you to town in case you run into trouble."

James tipped his hat and wasted no time in securing his belongings and mounting his horse. Before leaving the ranch, I saw him take one last look at the cabin where Lucy continued her recovery. He nodded once in my direction before turning his horse and nudging him into a fast trot toward town, with Pat's men close behind him.

I'd just turned around to go back inside when I saw Sarah standing near the cabin stairs, talking to one of the ranch hands. He was tall and blond, slightly younger than Sarah. That, and the fact that Sarah smiled and laughed when he talked, made me want to hog-tie the man and watch Ginger drag him across the ranch. The tight feeling in my chest startled me, and I tried to rub it away with my knuckles. I had never felt such strong dislike toward a man I had never met before. Then again, I had never met a woman quite like Sarah.

They were just talking, for heaven's sake. I took one last

look at Sarah's smile and the way the man leaned close, and I had to turn around before I made the unsound decision to separate the two, forcefully if necessary. Sarah's laughter rang in my ears as I turned to go back inside.

I heard riders coming toward the ranch and turned to see Pat and his brothers watching the horizon. Even from a distance, I could tell they were Indians. The colors they wore gave them away, along with the lack of headwear. Since no one from the ranch escorted them, I also knew that they must be the friends of Pat's that we had met along the trail.

Little Bird rode at the front, followed by Running Deer and Two Dogs, who flanked a short, older Indian woman. She and her white horse traveled as one, with grace and pride. She wore her hair free, blowing over her shoulders and down her back. Other than a string of beads near her right temple, her salt-and-pepper hair was unadorned.

The Donnelly brothers stepped off the porch and quickly went down the path to meet their friends. Sarah abandoned her admirer and ran down the path toward the riders. I had never been so glad to see strangers in my life, if for no other reason than removing Sarah from the young man gazing into her shining gray eyes.

While Will, Sarah, and Tommy greeted Little Bird and his brothers, Pat went directly to the older woman, who swung off her horse to greet him. As I drew closer, I sensed a connection between Pat and the woman—an admiration that existed between the two. He treated her with the gentlest touch, and his eyes were filled with warmth as he smiled down at her and took her hands.

Without a word, Pat and the woman headed away from the other visitors. Little Bird and the others removed their belongings from their horses before heading toward the back of the house.

We sat on logs near a fire pit, catching up on the problems in town and the lives of their visitors. I found out that the woman who had traveled to the ranch with Little Bird was his mother, Six Moons. Pat had stayed at their homestead for several months, and he and the old woman had become as close as family. I learned that Six Moons always sensed when something was bothering Pat, much like his own mother had. She'd come to the ranch to talk to Pat about his endless search for Turner.

"A few of Turner's men are still stirring up trouble in Lone Tree," Little Bird informed us, "but most of them left when Daniel took over as marshal."

"They'll be back," Tommy said quietly.

"Yes, my friend, they will." Little Bird traded tobacco with Tommy. "I only hope they come soon so that we can end this once and for all."

When we returned to the front of the house a few hours later, I noticed Six Moons standing alone in the field, staring at the cabin where Lucy and I slept. Following her gaze, I observed Lucy standing, for the first time, by the window. My breath stopped in my throat as the two of them stared at one another for several minutes. Lucy was inches from the glass windowpane, with a bright smile on her face—a smile I never thought I'd see again.

Behind me, the door opened, and all three of Pat's children bounded out of the house and down the porch steps. Laura held little Bittie's hand as they crossed the field toward Six Moons. As soon as the three were close enough, Six Moons removed her gaze from Lucy and knelt down to greet the enthusiastic hollering from the three young ones. She reached into her pouch in front of her deerskin dress and pulled out gifts for each of them, laughing as they all jumped up and down with excitement. When I looked back toward the cabin, Lucy was gone from the window.

———◦((◦))◦———

Later that night, just as I started to nod off next to the fire back in my cabin, a soft knock sounded at the door. I silently stood and went outside, closing the door behind me, and found Pat and Tommy standing on the porch.

"Michael, Sarah asked us to come here tonight," Pat said, watching me closely.

"Yes?"

"Well, we know that Doc looked at Lucy and treated her wounds, but we'd like to try somethin' else." Pat took off his hat and held it with both hands.

"What do you mean?" I asked, shifting my weight uneasily. After Tommy's suggestion of a brothel, I could only imagine what other plans he might have.

Tommy looked toward the lawn, and following his gaze, I saw Sarah standing in the dark. Standing by her side was Six Moons, dressed in her deerskin outfit, with beads, feathers, and fringe hanging from her sleeves. She held a bundle wrapped in leather close to her chest.

"The doctor has done everything that can be done," I said, shaking my head. "Please tell your friends thank you, but there is nothing they can do." I started to go back into the cabin, but Pat grabbed my arm to stop me.

"I know you're used to a different life," he said, "but we wouldn't have sent for her unless we felt she could help. There are things that can be done other than bandaging wounds and splinting an arm. She needs help, and Six Moons can give it to her. At least hear us out."

I sighed loudly, glancing at Pat and then back to the area where Six Moons stood. She didn't seem offended by my protests but merely stood like a statue. I remembered the look on my sister's face as she'd watched Six Moons earlier that afternoon. I also remembered how intrigued my sister had always been by the Western natives.

"What are you suggesting?"

"I was once in bad shape, Mike," Pat said. "Six Moons took me in and healed my wounds, along with my spirit. Most doctors would've given up, but she never did. Six Moons is a wise woman and a healer."

"I don't want to cause Lucy any more pain, Pat." I shook my head. "She barely speaks and trembles at the sight of men on the ranch."

"Give it a chance." His tone held a note of pleading. "Aren't you even willin' to try?"

Could Six Moons really hold the answer to what troubled Lucy? If so, how could I deny her help?

I took one more look at the woman holding the bundle in her arms and finally consented. "I'll leave it up to Lucy, but if she seems distressed at any time, it ends."

Pat smiled and motioned for Sarah and Six Moons to come to the cabin. Six Moons walked up the steps and stopped in front of me. She placed a hand over my heart and smiled warmly, and then she turned and entered the cabin alone. I'd intended to be inside while Six Moons was with Lucy, but her gesture stopped me.

Before the door closed, I saw Lucy standing in the sitting room, fully dressed and waiting. As far as I knew, she hadn't been told to expect a visitor, but you'd never have guessed from her appearance. She seemed pleased when Six Moons entered and closed the door behind her. I slumped onto the bench and waited.

Close to an hour later, I heard voices at the door. "Michael seems to be a fine man," I heard Six Moons say. "Trust him to understand."

The door opened quietly, and Six Moons stepped outside the cabin, followed closely by Lucy. The peaceful look on her face was all I needed to know that the visit went well. It was also the first time Lucy had stepped outside, obviously reluctant to see the night end.

"I will return if you need me." Six Moons patted Lucy's hand.

"But how do I reach you?" Lucy asked quietly.

Six Moons merely squeezed Lucy's hand. She walked past me without saying a word but patted me on the cheek and smiled warmly when she looked in my eyes. She moved slowly down the steps and into the darkness, her family flanking her on each side.

Sarah hadn't said anything to me while Six Moons was inside, and she stood on the porch and waited for her brothers to leave before she did. "I'm sorry, Michael," she whispered. "I knew she might be able to help, but I wanted Pat's advice first."

"I'm not upset, Sarah," I said with a smile. "You've been a good friend to my sister, and I'm sure you did the right thing." I paused before going inside. "What do you think I should do now?"

She shrugged. "We'll just have to wait and see."

Several days after Six Moons and her family left the ranch, I came home to find Sarah and Lucy talking quietly in her room. Not wishing to disturb them, I put my hat on and went back outside.

Sarah did not linger inside. She followed close behind me. "Will you walk with me, Michael?" Her face was drawn, and I could tell she'd been crying.

"What's wrong?" I asked anxiously.

"Just come for a walk with me, would you?" she asked, taking my arm and leading me down a nearby path.

"I can tell something's the matter," I insisted. "Please tell me what's going on."

"Lucy wanted me to speak with you tonight." She kept her head down and her eyes averted. "She just told me what happened to her while she was held at that horrible cabin—everything that happened to her. She understands your need to know but is unable to tell you herself. She asked me to relate her story to you."

I had wanted to know what had happened to Lucy since the day I found that she was missing, but I had no idea if I'd be able to hear what I knew in my heart to be true. The condition in which I found Lucy, and the blood that covered her body, spoke more than any words. Not knowing everything, however, left too many unanswered questions about why she was taken and if Turner would return for more.

We walked in silence until I found a large downed tree just off the path. I brushed snow from it and sat down heavily.

"I don't think things will be right between you and Lucy until you know everything." Sarah sat next to me and took her handkerchief from her pocket. "She said the two of you have always shared everything, and I believe it's eating away at her that she can't talk to you about this."

I sighed deeply and slowly. "If this is what Lucy wants, I suppose you should tell me."

12

THE LOSS OF INNOCENCE

"Yer as stupid as the day is long, Blake," R. J. said. "I got the brains so trust me to use 'em. I brought laudanum and whiskey to keep her sleepin'. Now she's bleedin' all over, and it'll be damn near impossible to get her on the train!" R. J. paced up and down.

Their partner, who had been listening in silence to the argument, stepped forward. "You never mentioned nothin' about takin' her with us," he said as he stared at R. J. "I was told we were only gonna rob her."

R. J. turned toward the man with hatred in his eyes. He gripped the man's shoulder and led him down the alley. He leaned in close as if to tell him a secret but swiftly drew a large knife he'd had in a sheath on his belt and stabbed him. The man looked down to find the blade jammed to the hilt in his chest. R. J. kept his arm on the man's shoulder and looked him straight in the eye. "You couldn't expect us to tell you everything ... now could ya?"

He let go, and the man fell to the ground, landing flat on his back. He made a few brief gurgling noises in his throat before his last breath exhaled from his lungs. His dead eyes stared blankly into the night.

R. J.'s calm face remained unchanged as he moved over to where Lucy lay on the ground. He wrapped his fingers around her necklace and yanked forcefully, breaking the chain. He slid the locket into a folded paper before returning to the corpse and stuffing it in the pocket of the dead man's jacket. He stood and brushed off his hands and checked his clothes to make sure they didn't have blood on them.

"We gotta go," he told his friend as he went to Lucy and looked her over.

"What are we gonna do?" Blake kneeled next to R. J. on the ground.

"Clean her up. Find somethin' to wipe the blood from her head, and then we need to get to the tracks."

"Can't we take the train tomorrow?" Blake took the handkerchief from Lucy's dress and wiped the blood from the gash on her head.

"No, you idiot, we can't wait!" he shouted. "We have to go ... now!" R. J. pointed at the corpse while glaring at Blake.

"Stop hollerin'!" Blake said. "Ya wanna wake the entire town?" He glared at R. J. before hoisting Lucy up and following him out of the alley through an opening leading down the street. They lurked in the shadows of the city as they half carried, half dragged her toward the station, trying not to raise attention. Luckily, it was late, and most people were sleeping.

Before entering the station, R. J. took a flask from his jacket, opened it, and took a few large swigs. He then handed the bottle to Blake. "Drink some, but don't take too much. We'll need it for her." He took the flask from Blake and lightly slapped Lucy's cheeks to get her attention. Blake supported her with his arms as R. J. forced her to take several drinks from the flask. Lucy coughed and choked down the liquor. He then poured some of the alcohol on her dress, making her reek of whiskey. Once satisfied, R. J. covered Lucy's head with her shawl and headed into the station to board the train.

"Excuse me, sir." A railroad worker quickly approached them. "Do you require assistance for this woman? I could call for a physician."

"Oh, you know women," he replied hastily. "They just can't hold their drink. I warned her this'd happen." The man merely smirked knowingly and returned to his duties.

They took the last train that evening. During their days of travel, R. J. continued to force whiskey down Lucy's throat and feed her laudanum to keep her from crying out. Most people ignored them or, at most, paused and shook their heads at the sorry state of the inebriated woman.

R. J. gave Lucy less medicine and whiskey, allowing her to gain her bearings and assess her situation during the last few days of travel. In Fort Collins, they met up with at least ten other men, all with hard, unfriendly faces. A few looked Lucy over with desire, but no one talked to her after forcing her into a wagon and heading out of town. Four men were inside the covered wagon, along with Lucy, making sure she would not try to escape, while several more rode alongside them as they headed deep into the woods.

The men inside the wagon taunted Lucy endlessly during their journey about what they would do to her if given the opportunity, but no one harmed her. No matter what they said they would do, none acted on it. It seemed they were too afraid of the wrath of their employer, who had given them instructions to bring her to him unharmed.

Lucy tried to drown out their voices by humming softly and concentrating on how she could possibly get free. She was in an unknown land, in clothing no way suited for the oncoming cold weather, and if she did escape, she had no way of knowing if her path would lead to safety or certain death.

She couldn't see anything of their route into the woods, as they had covered every opening with hides and blankets before leaving town. Once they were deep in the woods, they finally removed many of the coverings, which only revealed a thick layer of trees and brush, making it impossible to see what lay ahead.

The fear in Lucy's soul became almost more than she could bear. She had been calm and cooperative, waiting for a chance to escape. Now, however, everything she knew vanished quickly behind her, as they traveled deeper into the trees. She didn't know anything about life in the West, or the dangers she faced. So far, the only man who truly frightened her was Blake. He had a mean streak, and no matter how many times R. J. told him to leave Lucy alone, he tormented her with his insane eyes and ugly words. He also hit Lucy without the slightest provocation whenever R. J. wasn't looking.

She had maintained a belief in the back of her mind that she would escape her captors, but now she wasn't so sure. All civilization had vanished. Lucy wept silently at the thought that she would never go home again and never see the family she dearly loved.

The wagon finally came to a stop at the narrowing of the trail, and men loaded the extra horses with supplies, while two others guarded Lucy. One of her guards was a young man about her age. She noticed he was one of a few kind faces, but he rarely looked in her direction or addressed her directly. While listening to the conversations around her, she found out his name was John. When the other men made advances toward Lucy or tried to frighten her with remarks about the indecencies they would inflict upon her if they were alone, John attempted to get them to focus on something else.

Although he tried to protect Lucy from harm, John said little to her. When he did, his words were just as stern as the rest. He had a job to do, and if he showed any weakness, he'd be in danger as well. James was taller and broader than his older brother was, but Lucy saw the same innocence etched on his kind face.

Lucy could find no allies amongst the others in the group. They were all older men who thought of her as property to do with as they pleased. Lucy knew there was only one thing keeping the men from abusing her terribly ... and that was a man named Jack Turner. These were his men, and he had sent them to bring her to him. Every time she heard his name mentioned, she could feel their fear. Jack Turner had not yet arrived, which left Lucy with many unanswered questions and fears of her own.

The men finished loading the supplies and readied the horses before they returned their attention to Lucy. They forced her from the wagon and placed her in front of John on his horse.

"If she tries anything, shoot her in the leg," R. J. said through a clenched jaw as he looked up at John. "She needs to be alive when we get there." He handed John a length of rope. "Tie her hands."

John tightened the rope around her wrists and secured it to the saddle horn just before setting out with the other men. They were only able to ride single file up the rugged, narrow trail. Several men rode in front and behind John's horse, ready for any possible encounter.

The group rode in silence throughout the afternoon, occasionally stopping to rest or to water the horses. Lucy couldn't remember the last time she had eaten, and her head continued to swim from the whiskey. Weariness and fatigue settled in as they continued to travel, causing her to finally give in and rest her head back against John's shoulder to sleep.

A few hours later, Lucy woke when John tugged the rope loose from her wrists. He lowered her to the ground, where R. J. grasped her arm tightly and jerked her away. His grip was intense, causing pain to shoot up her arm.

The long sleep had allowed her to clear the fog in her mind and look at things in a new way. She saw the rugged cabin set within the thick stand of trees. It tilted to one side slightly and was made of chinked logs, with smoke coming out of a pipe in the roof. The main room had several chairs and a table near the window, with a couch and a stove along the remaining walls. Several animal hides hung along the walls, along with other hunting trophies, such as horns, hoofs, and the head of a large elk.

Her thoughts of escape dwindled as they set her in a back room with a small window that didn't open and only one door leading to the main room, where at least a dozen men remained. Lucy listened quietly through the door and realized they were talking about Jack Turner again. The only men who seemed dedicated to Turner were R. J. and Blake. The others followed him with only one thing in mind: money. Turner had promised them all a huge payoff after delivering Lucy to the small cabin in Colorado.

After a time, Lucy heard a heated argument outside her small room. She crawled to one side and cracked opened the door. Several men had already passed out on the floor and couch, snoring heavily, while four men sat at the table, arguing over the current hand of poker.

"Just admit you cheated."

"I had four aces, you son of a bitch. Pay up!"

"How can you have four aces when I have one in my hand?"

The man threw his cards across the table. All four men stood. The man who cheated pulled his weapon, causing a standoff in the cabin. Men woke, and yelling filled the room. Not a single eye was on Lucy's door. It was her only chance.

She slowly opened the door farther and slid out of her room, making sure no one was watching. All eyes were on the two men throwing punches, and the men cheered as each punch made contact. She was out of sight within seconds and managed to slide down the hall into a dark room in the corner of the cabin. She had no means of lighting a candle or match, and she could tell from the darkness that there was no window. She slid down onto her knees and crawled hastily around the room, trying desperately to find anything that might help her. A stick, a knife, a gun. Anything.

As she swept her hands around the darkness, she hit her knee upon something metal. When her fingers wrapped around it, she realized it was a handle coming from the wood-planked floor. She traced her fingers around the area and found a crease that formed a square in the floor.

She suddenly heard a shot from the other room. The loud explosion took her off guard and caused fear to run through every bone in her body. She heard chairs being broken and furniture being thrown. Her shaky hands fumbled toward the handle and pulled on it briskly. A gust of cold air entered the room as she lifted the trapdoor. Without hesitation, Lucy lowered herself into the space and the ground below, crawling under the cabin. The gunshot brought everyone to the main room and into the scuffle currently going on inside the cabin.

The thought of freedom was all that remained in Lucy's

head as she sprinted from the cabin into the dark woods. She didn't know where she was or how to get to safety, but she knew she had to get away. Her skirt ripped on branches, and her arms and face were scraped raw with abrasions as she frantically darted down the mountain.

Lucy heard the charge of men tearing outside. She quickened her pace when she realized they knew she was gone. She ran deeper and deeper into the woods, trying to get as far from the trail as possible.

She ran with the sound of horses behind her, getting closer as the men came from every direction in search of her. Knowing that she couldn't outrun them, she finally found a small outcropping to duck under, and she moved the branches to hide her small form. She tucked her skirt as close to her body as possible to make sure it wouldn't give her away. She huddled into a ball and listened as the horses thundered by her.

The heat wore off quickly, and the cold air chilled her body to the core. Even after the noise subsided, she refused to move. She waited until late into the night, after the silence had continued for several hours, before she finally poked her head out of her hiding place. The air was much colder out in the open, but Lucy knew she couldn't stay hidden forever.

Her feet and hands were freezing, causing movement to be difficult, but Lucy stumbled as briskly as possible down the mountain. Besides being cold, she was exhausted and hungry. Her greatest hope was to find someone to help her before she was discovered.

Just before dawn, as the sun lit the sky in a pale orange glow, Lucy found a small river. Even though the sun had not yet warmed the cold night air, the water was too inviting to pass up. She knelt near the shore and scooped up several handfuls, placing them to her mouth. She splashed the water over her face and hands to wash them, attempting to wake her tired body.

Hearing the crunch of pine needles behind her, she stood and whirled around in time to see a pistol come down upon her head, causing her to lose consciousness. When she woke, her hands were bound again, and Blake was leaning over her, screaming in her face.

"Ya try another stunt like that again, ya filthy bitch, and I'll gladly start cuttin' pieces off your body, startin' with your feet so ya can't run no more. Can you hear me, you sorry excuse for a woman?" He finished his rant by kicking her in the stomach, causing her to roll up into a ball as she frantically tried to catch her breath.

Instead of tying Lucy on a horse, Blake tied his rope to the saddle and made Lucy walk behind him as he rode uphill back to the cabin. Lucy fell several times, but Blake just continued to ride, oblivious of her shouts of pain or the rope dragging her until she was able to stand again.

As he continued up the mountain, more men arrived, hearing him yell and curse. Without delay, two of them dismounted and quickly cut the rope that held Lucy.

The rest of the men looked tired and irritated, but they said nothing. Eventually, John picked Lucy up and placed her on his horse, settling himself behind her.

"That was a fool notion, girl," he said quietly, so the others couldn't hear him. "Do you have any idea about the men you're dealin' with? Are you trying to get yourself killed?"

"I would rather freeze to death in the wild than wait to be killed by them." A tear rolled down her cheek.

He remained quiet for a few moments and then looked at Blake, who had finally stopped ranting and was quietly riding in front of them. "Whatever you do, stay away from

Blake," he said. "That man has a temper like none I've ever had the misfortune to see, and you've pushed him right over the edge."

"My only desire in this world is to stay away from Blake," she said softly.

"Why are you here?" she asked finally. "Why are you helping them?"

"I don't have a choice," he whispered, after checking to make sure nobody was paying attention to them. "My pa owes Turner a big debt, so my brother and I agreed to work it off in trade. Things ain't been so bad over the last few months. There've been lots of plans and moving equipment, but that's all. It weren't till I saw you come off the train that I realized what was goin' on. James and I talked and agreed we can't continue to work for the likes of him." He paused again and looked around. "We stayed because of you."

Lucy looked up at John with tears still in her eyes. "Because of me?"

"We can't just leave you here with these men," he said, "but we don't rightly know what to do next."

"Thank you," she whispered, openly crying now.

"Don't thank me yet," he said, removing a handkerchief and handing it to over. "Like I said, we don't have a plan. Blake isn't well, and who knows what's goin' through his mind." He looked around again quickly, but the other men seemed lost in their own thoughts and unaware of their conversation.

"Just do me a favor and sit tight. Don't cause no more trouble until we can figure a way to get you out of here. Okay?" He looked down at her and waited.

She silently nodded and rested her head against his shoulder. Feeling she could trust him, she decided to remain quiet and cooperative from that point forward.

They arrived at the cabin later that evening, and with the exception of her attempted escape, she remained in the small room for several more days without being allowed outside. Sometimes R. J. or one of the other men would bring in food, a chamber pot, or newspapers, but other than that, Lucy remained alone.

She hadn't seen John or James since arriving back at the cabin, but she could sometimes hear their voices outside, so she knew they remained amongst the other men. Blake was as evil as ever, once striking Lucy over the head with a pot when she thanked him for her food. He had to be removed from her forcefully by the other men, and he hadn't been allowed back in her room. The blow caused Lucy to experience debilitating headaches. As evil as he seemed, the men were much more skittish about how Turner would react to Lucy's injuries.

Lucy heard the door to the cabin open, followed by several footsteps and many men talking and laughing. Her tension eased a bit until she heard two large, heavy boots continue to move slowly across the floor toward her room. She didn't want to open her eyes, as the motion was bound to cause searing pain to shoot through her head. On the other hand, she wanted to be prepared for what insult might come next.

The door flung open unexpectedly, forcing Lucy to open one eye. Moving her head was still difficult, but she managed to turn enough to see a large man darkening the doorway, swaying slightly. As soon as she realized that the man was not someone she had seen before, her eyes sprang open, and she sat bolt upright in bed. Blinding pain shot through her skull. She fell back and clutched her forehead.

He stood still by the door for several moments and then entered the room, roughly closing the door. Lucy opened one eye and waited for the room to stop spinning before trying the other.

"What do you want?" she said loudly, gathering up the blankets and holding them close as if they could protect her.

The man sauntered into the room, set a bottle of whiskey on the table, and sat down. "First, I'd like to apologize for Blake's behavior. I can assure you I will rectify the situation as soon as we are done here."

Lucy sat up slowly, never taking her eyes off the man's face. He wasn't a clean man. He reeked of stale whiskey, body odor, and rotten teeth, making Lucy feel nauseated. His face was hardened and scarred, and he had a few days' growth of beard. His black hair was slicked back messily, but he kept running his hands through it to smooth it to his head, and he had straightened his filthy clothes and buttoned his shirt to his neck.

He was very calm and sat quietly for several minutes with a strange smile on his face. He poured two glasses and slid one toward Lucy's side of the table. All his motions were slow and deliberate.

Hesitantly, she moved to the edge of the bed, sat up, and leaned over to take the cup. There was something strange about this man, causing a prickling sensation at the back of her neck. Although he smiled at her, something in his dark blue eyes made her cringe.

"Who are you?"

"Oh, I'm sorry. I assumed you knew." He stood and bowed with a flourish. "Jack Turner, at yer service."

Lucy's eyes widened, and she began to shake uncontrollably.

She remembered the stories the men told about Jack and the horrible things they claimed he had done. Trying to remain calm, she lifted the glass to her lips and slowly sipped the golden liquid. She didn't want the whiskey, never wanted whiskey again, but she felt the less she antagonized him, the better, so she remained quiet.

Seeing the uneasiness of her grip and the shaking glass, Turner's grin widened, and he chuckled under his breath. After swigging two full cups and pouring a third, he leaned back in his chair and closed his eyes.

"So tell me about yer beau, Lucy. His name is Mr. Westley, I'm told."

"You didn't bring me all the way out here to talk about my social life, did you?" She spoke quietly and measured every movement the man made. "Is all this about Mr. Westley?"

"Oh, I just thought you'd want to talk about home a bit, is all. I'm sure you miss yer kin—yer aunt and yer brother, Michael. They must be worried sick." There was a gleam in his eyes.

"Just tell me what you want from me so I can go home!" Lucy's temper rose at his obvious pleasure over her circumstances.

"Well, now, I like a woman who gets right down to business." He poured another glass, downed it in one swallow, and leaned close to her. "I think you and I will do just fine."

Lucy mentally weighed her chances of making it to the door, or possibly outside. She looked at the man and then back at the door.

"So tell me," he said, startling her, "how's Maggie?"

She turned her eyes from the door to find him staring at her. "Maggie?" she said, confused. She tried to think back but couldn't remember hearing that name. "I'm sorry, but I don't know a Maggie."

Without warning, he smacked her hard across the face, causing her to spill whiskey all over the bed. She placed her hand across her cheek and sat up as tears of pain gathered in her eyes.

"Sorry 'bout that, sugar, but I don't like bein' lied to." His rage seemed to disappear as quickly as it came, and he sat back in his chair and closed his eyes again. "How've the last years been without yer pa?"

"What do you know about my father?" Lucy said apprehensively, wary about his sudden change in conversation.

"Lots … probably more'n you."

"I doubt that, sir." Lucy's anger rose again as she recovered from the slap across the face.

"Sir, is it? Well, then, if'n you know so much about him, tell me how he died."

Lucy could tell he was baiting her, but she had no choice but to answer. "He died of an infection after being injured at work."

"You're a might bit right, I reckon," he said with a deep laugh.

"What do you mean by that?"

"Yer pa did die of an infection, but he weren't workin' at the time." A spiteful grin formed on his lips as he leaned forward and took another drink.

"How do you know about my father's death?" Lucy knew she was treading on unsafe ground, but she needed to know what all this had to do with her father.

"Because I shot that son of a bitch." He reached down to take his gun from his belt. He placed it firmly on the table in front of her. "He died of an infection, all right—from a bullet shot from this here gun. Yer pa was a stubborn fool, though. I shot him four times, but the old bugger just kept on livin'."

"But why?" New sadness showed in Lucy's eyes at the thought of her father dying such a horrible death.

"He got involved in my business. Now, how about we talk about Maggie?"

"If I could help you, I would," Lucy said, bracing for the worst. "But I don't know what you're talking about. Please let me go."

His face turned a deep red with barely controlled rage, but he didn't strike out at her again. "It worked out fer the best, though—yer father's dyin', I mean. Instead of killin' him instantly, he died a long, slow, painful death. Have you ever seen a man die?"

Realizing that Turner would never let her go, Lucy leapt out of her chair and sprang toward the door. The weakness from days of captivity and dizziness from the wound to her head slowed her escape, however. Just as she opened the door to the sitting room and noticed several men sitting in chairs, Turner grabbed her by the arm, yanking her back into the room. He swung her around and threw her into a nearby wall, causing her to collapse onto the floor.

"If you'd just cooperate, all this would end."

Lucy slowly staggered to her feet with one arm on the wall, bracing her from falling. Turner came toward her, took her by the arm again, and led her to the center of the room. He stepped close to her and looked down into her pain-filled eyes. "Don't make me hurt you, little one."

No longer feeling fear, Lucy clenched her fists and let her anger get away from her. "Go to hell!" She faced him and spat directly in his eye.

Turner backed up a few steps and wiped the spit from his face. Fury and hatred filled his eyes, and his skin turned almost purple in rage. He swiftly raised his right leg and forcefully kicked Lucy in the abdomen, causing her to fall backward and land outside the room. The men in the sitting room stood up in unison and jumped hastily out of the way as Turner came through the door. He yelled at everyone to leave the cabin. He grabbed Lucy by the hair and was about to drag her back into the room when John spoke up.

"Turner, you've gone too far." He looked at Lucy on the floor and then up at Turner. "This isn't necessary."

Turner turned around, drew his gun from his belt with his right hand, and without hesitation, shot John in the head, killing him instantly.

A cry rang out in the room as James watched in shock as his brother fell to the ground, lying motionless against the wood. The men still inside the cabin ran outside before he could turn his wrath on them. They grabbed James by the arms and forcefully pulled him out of the cabin before he had time to go after Turner.

Turner adjusted his grip on Lucy's hair and finished dragging her into the room, without ever looking back.

"Please," she begged, trying to crawl away.

"I don't think so," he said, throwing her on the bed. He reached down and unbuckled his belt. "Since you can't be civilized, I'll have to find another way for you to talk."

She tried to make it to the door again, but with little success. He picked her up and threw her against the table. Lucy felt her left arm crack during the initial impact against the hard wood as she fell. She cradled her arm and rolled up into a ball underneath the table. Her solitude didn't last long, however, as Turner kneeled on the floor and snatched her leg, dragging her into the open.

"Yer like a wild horse ... that must be broken," he said, pinning her arms to her sides.

"Let go of me!" Lucy screamed.

"I will if you tell me where Maggie is."

"I don't know Maggie!"

He moved quickly now, shifting his weight over her, pressing her to the floor. With days of very little food, followed by physical abuse, Lucy knew she didn't have the strength to fight him, but she continued to struggle for her life. She kicked and screamed with every ounce of power she could find. She was able to get her working arm free, allowing her the chance to rake her nails across his face. Turner hissed in pain but didn't budge—his force only grew.

He took both her arms and placed them above her head, holding them with one hand, while ripping off the front of her dress, including her corset, exposing her bare breasts. His weight was far too much for her, making Lucy's struggle much more difficult. She felt Turner's knee wedge itself in between her legs and force them apart, as he continued to fondle her breasts and hold her down.

In one last effort, Lucy turned her head and bit down hard on Turner's arm. He instinctively let go of her arms when the pain first hit him, allowing Lucy to move her body away. When he restrained her again, Lucy managed to punch him in the nose, making it bleed.

In retaliation, Turner slapped her across the face and slammed her head against the floorboard. Lucy's vision blurred again, and she almost blacked out.

He grabbed a knife from his trousers and cut recklessly away at the rest of her dress, leaving it in shreds beneath her naked body. Several of the slashes to the fabric pierced her skin as well, leaving her badly bleeding.

"Don't worry, I won't kill you." Turner pulled down his trousers and forcefully separated Lucy's legs again, this time holding the knife against her throat. "I'll just make you wish you were dead."

The fight was gone from Lucy, however, and she sank in and out of consciousness. Lucy welcomed the darkness after that, hoping never to wake again.

13

A GLIMPSE OF HOPE

Pat was already at work, repairing a wagon by the stable, when I left my cabin the next morning. I straightened my shoulders and approached him. "Good morning." I hadn't slept much the night before, after hearing about what Turner had done to Lucy, but my mind was clear for the first time in weeks. "Could you spare a few moments?"

"Will told me you were skittish about the men guardin' the ranch," he said, sliding back under the wagon with a mallet in his hand. "Don't worry, though. We'll keep an eye out for trouble."

"I appreciate that," I said, in between a series of blows hitting the bottom of the wagon, "but that isn't what I meant."

"Oh, well, what do ya need?" He finally stopped and crawled out from under the wagon.

"I want to know if you, and your brothers, could show me a few things about ranching and the work you do."

"You want to learn how to be a cowboy?" He laughed, and I couldn't tell if it was from pleasure that I wanted to learn his trade or mere amusement of the thought of my trying to rope cattle.

"Yes, I'd like that very much."

"It takes more than a few months to learn how to work a ranch," Pat said, unable to hide the grin that spread across his face. "For some, it takes years of workin' before learning what's needed ... especially someone such as yourself." Pat looked me up and down for a second and then returned to his work on the wagon. It leaned to one side and looked like the wheel had broken. "You've lived in a city all your life, Mike. That makes you a tenderfoot."

"I'm not expecting to become an expert at what you have spent a lifetime accomplishing. I just want to be useful and learn a little about your way of life. As you said, it is terribly foreign to me, and I'd like to change that. Lucy and I have lived off your generosity for far too long, and I'd like to find a way to pay back your kindness."

"Don't worry about that. Your pa's already paid that debt."

I studied his face for a long moment. The laughter was gone from his eyes, and his smile had evaporated. Pat never ceased to speak well of my father. In every situation, he illustrated how deeply he felt for him and the close connection they'd had. I'd asked him once about his relationship with my father, but he merely said he knew him well, and that my father had helped the Donnelly family through extremely difficult times.

I remained quiet, thinking, and Pat finally looked up from his work. "As far as you learnin' the ranchin' business," he said, standing and placing a hand on my shoulder, "I reckon we could show you a thing or two."

"Thank you."

"Swear to me," he continued, "that you will not, under any circumstances, try something with one of our horses or cattle without us teachin' you first. I can't afford to have you snap your neck trying to break a new mustang or herd cattle."

"Of course," I said, remembering the day I'd watched a tough leathery cowboy get thrown from a horse they called Satan. I had no plans to commit suicide by getting into a corral with a wild beast such as that.

"There's one more thing, Pat." I waited until I had his full attention before continuing.

"What is it?"

"In addition to learning how to work the ranch ..."

"Yes?"

"Would you and your brothers teach me how to fight?"

He looked confused as he leaned in close and studied my face. "I saw you with James, Mike." He raised his eyebrows. "You already know how to fight."

"I'd like to learn more." I thought back to the day when Blake came after me in Turner's cabin. Even if it weren't for the fact that I was carrying Lucy, I wouldn't have had a chance with him one-on-one. "I want to be prepared for anything and fight like you and your brothers." I grabbed several ropes lying on the ground and followed Pat as he stepped into the corral.

"You want to learn how to fight dirty is what you're sayin'? To be ready in case Turner comes after your family again?"

"No. I mean, yes. But I also want to be prepared to find him before he has the chance to come here." I grabbed Pat's shoulder and turned him to face me. "I plan to find him ... and then I plan to kill him."

I felt the tension build in Pat's shoulder and saw the telltale muscle jump along his jaw. "You what?"

"I've done a lot of thinking about my future and the future of my sister. Neither of us will be free until that man is dead. I plan to find Turner and kill him. But I cannot do it alone. As you said, I'm a tenderfoot and new to the West. I'm asking for your help."

He looked around to see who was in the area and then motioned for me to follow him into the stable. He asked the man inside to leave us alone for a few moments. When he left, Pat closed the door and went to the back, where he kept his tools. Part of me was convinced he would try to talk me out of my decided course of action, but the other part knew he wanted Turner dead as much as I did.

"Sarah told me what happened to Lucy," Pat said. "Do you honestly believe I'd let the man go after all he's done? But it ain't that easy, Mike." The shadow that I had often seen on Pat's face passed over his eyes as he spoke of Turner, and he clenched his teeth in anger as he slammed his fist on the worktable. "Turner always seems to be one step ahead of us whenever we go after him, but we'll get him. This time, I will make damn sure I see his corpse before returning home."

"So you'll help me?"

"You aren't hearin' me, Mike. Once winter breaks, I'll search the ends of the earth till I know Turner's dead." Pat's voice was like steel, causing a tremor to run up my spine. His eyes were on fire, and I could see the past etched inside the darkness of his pupils. "You aren't ready, and you don't know the area. You'll slow us down."

"No." I shook my head. "I have to go."

"Red will need extra hands," he said, taking a different tact. "I'd also feel better havin' you here to watch over Sarah and the kids. I swear I won't let him slip past me again."

"I need to do this, Pat." I planted my feet firmly in his path. "I'll go with or without your help, but I'd have a better chance with you and your brothers on my side."

After a few moments, and a short staring contest, he finally cursed under his breath and nodded. I still didn't know what had passed between Turner and Pat, but I knew that if anyone could understand the pain I felt upon seeing my sister in that bloodstained cabin, it would be Pat.

"There's one more thing," I said, clenching and releasing my nervous hands.

"Shit, Mike. Whatever it is, consider it done."

"If I am going to go after this man, I need to know more about him." I cleared my throat and lowered my voice close to a whisper so others wouldn't hear my question. "I still don't know why my sister was taken, and I get the feeling that you and your brothers know more than you have told me."

Pat's face lost all hint of pleasantness, and a deep frown outlined his mouth. I continued anyway.

"Lucy was taken because of a woman named Maggie—"

Pat almost broke my arm when he grabbed it and yanked me toward his face. "Who told you about Maggie?"

"Lucy said that Turner kept asking where a woman named Maggie was hiding. He obviously thinks my sister knows her. If you could just tell me —"

"That woman can't help you. Don't mention her again!"

"Pat—"

"I'm not messin' with you, Mike," he said, still gripping my arm with the strength of an iron manacle. "I don't want to hear that name again! Drop it."

"Lucy and I are in danger, and I don't understand why!"

Pat let go of my arm and stepped away. He didn't say anything for several minutes. Then his shoulders went up and down with a long sigh, and he turned around. "I'll tell you everything you want to know after we find Turner, but not before. Don't mention her name again."

My frustration kicked up several notches. Everywhere I turned, I found secrets and unanswered questions. And then there was my father and his relationship with Maggie. My suspicions about them were confirmed by everyone's reaction to her name. The more they kept secrets, the more curious—and angry—I became.

Pat put his arm around my shoulders to lead me out of the stable. "I know your life's been turned inside out, but I need you to trust me. If I thought it'd help, I'd answer all your questions. But for now, all you need to worry about is Turner."

I realized that the conversation was not getting me anywhere, so I resigned myself to the fact that I'd have to wait to get the answers I so desperately needed.

"If you still want my help, meet me here first thing in the mornin'," Pat said when we reached the main house. "I'll work on it." All signs of his earlier anger, and our conversation about Maggie, were gone as if the confrontation had never occurred.

"But it is morning," I said, looking up at the sky.

He turned to face me before going up the steps and into the house. He smirked when he saw my face. "When I say early, I'm talkin' just before sunrise, and you'd better be ready to work."

"Got it. Thanks, Pat." I turned and slapped my hands together. Our tense conversation had not squelched my excitement to begin working again. Perhaps the Donnelly men would open up to me once I proved my worth. I'd watched everyone working on the ranch, and I knew the days were long and hard. I also knew that winter was the slow time for the ranch, making it hard to imagine their lives during the roundups and the summer.

I returned to the cabin and noticed that Lucy was still in

bed. We hadn't spoken since Sarah told me about her time with Turner. Her entire future had been changed in those dreadful minutes.

The anger I felt toward my father also returned, quickly transforming into rage for his part in what had happened. The more I thought of him, the more I felt he was a liar and a man without honor. I resented all his time away from home, but even worse was the fact that my sweet sister was punished for something he had done. There was no forgiving my father for Lucy's current misery.

I went to my room and made sure I had work clothes ready and waiting in the cabin, along with my father's gun and the others that Pat had given me when I first arrived at the ranch. Then I sat down at my desk near the window and removed several pieces of paper from the drawer. It was long overdue, but I finally felt comfortable enough with Lucy's progress to write home. I didn't mention the full details of Lucy's capture to my aunt. I merely mentioned that she had been injured, and that she needed time to recover. The Donnelly family was more than willing to allow us to stay at the ranch until we both felt up to traveling again.

The one piece of information I wished to obtain right away included the current intentions of Lucy's suitor, Mr. Westley. They had become notably close over the last several months, and I had expected a proposal before Lucy's capture. Not being able to communicate with my aunt had kept me from learning how Mr. Westley had reacted to Lucy's disappearance.

Her future was quite dependent upon that young man, and I didn't feel I could make further arrangements without knowing what was in store for Lucy back home in Philadelphia. Would he still want her after all that had happened? Would she still want him?

I rubbed the tension from my temples and tried to concentrate on finishing my letters instead of the never-ending questions that swarmed inside my head.

Hearing Lucy move around the living room, I went to join her, unable to put it off any longer. She stood unsteadily from a chair when her eyes met mine, and she walked toward me with an arm outstretched. Both of us were crying by the time I wrapped my arms around her, moving carefully to avoid jostling her injured arm.

We stood there for several minutes, without speaking a word, allowing weeks of frustration and anxiety to escape from our bodies. Finally, I pulled away to remove a handkerchief from my pocket. I led Lucy to the couch and sat next to her while I dabbed her face with the cloth.

"I'm so sorry, Michael," she said through her tears. "I am so sorry about giving you a hard time when you were protective of me, about leaving the Haag residence without an escort as I promised, and for leading you to the middle of nowhere to find me." Her crying intensified, and she lowered her face into her hands. "Can you ever forgive me?"

Astonished at the realization that she had been holding in all that guilt for so many days, I reached down and placed my hand under her chin to lift her head. "None of this is your fault."

She shook her head and let the tears fall down her cheeks. "It is, Michael."

"I don't want to ever see you lower your head to anyone again," I said sternly. A pain burned in my heart as I realized how hard Lucy's future would be. I raised my handkerchief and dabbed at her wet cheeks. "None of this is your fault. You need to understand that."

"But, Michael—"

"I mean it, Lucy," I interrupted. "Neither of us is to blame.

It tortured me to think that I didn't protect you enough in Philadelphia, but neither of us could have predicted the events that led us here. We didn't know about our father's history ... or the fact that someone was looking for us. You are not to blame for living as you always have."

"I should have done more," she cried, shaking her head. "I failed, and men died because of me."

Suddenly angry, I placed both my hands on her cheeks to make sure she could see my face and not look away. "You did nothing wrong. What happened to you was a terrible thing, but you are not at fault. Do you understand?"

I stared into Lucy's eyes and waited silently for acknowledgement. She tried to look away and shake her head, but I didn't want to go another day knowing she felt that kind of guilt. Finally, Lucy wiped her tears and gave me a slight nod. A shaky smile formed on her lips as she wiped away the last bit of moisture on her cheeks. She looked up at me and nodded again.

I released my hold on her, and we went to sit at the table, which Lucy had set for lunch. I reached over and grabbed a piece of bread.

"Michael," Lucy muttered, "I need some time."

"I know. We have to spend the winter here anyway. It will allow you to get your strength back." And it would allow me to figure out what to do next.

"That isn't what I mean," she said, staring out the window. "You need to start living your life again, without constantly worrying about my every need."

I shook my head and started to interrupt, but she held up a hand to stop me. "There are some things I must learn to face alone, and I need the time to sort them out in my head. When I was left alone in that room, lying on the floor, I wished desperately for death to come and take me away.

I was freezing and in pain, and I just hoped that my end would come soon. Then you came and brought me back."

Her hands shook as she lifted the teakettle and poured us each a cup. "I was angry for a while that my wish to die had been ignored, and I was angry with you for bringing me back to life." She glanced at me and offered a sad, sweet smile before looking back out the window with tears in her eyes. Knowing she wished for death added another layer of hatred to fuel my growing desire to find Turner. Only the worst sort of pain could take away my sister's will to live.

"I understand now why I was saved and why I was given a chance at life," she continued. "He took something from me, something I will never have the chance to get back, but he didn't destroy me. I'm alive, and I don't plan to waste my life."

She brushed her tears away and looked back into my eyes; she looked more at peace than before. "I'm glad you found me and brought me back. Life is worth living, and that's why I don't want to see you waste one more minute in this cabin, waiting for me to get better." She patted my cheek gently. "You don't look so good these days."

Laughing at the broken pair we had become, I took her hand in mine. "Well, then you will be pleased to hear that Pat has agreed to teach me the ranching business." I relayed what had happened that morning—and the fact that Pat was willing to teach my how to fight as well as ranch. I did not tell her, however, about my desire to find Turner. I wasn't really lying to Lucy, but I still felt a pang of guilt at not telling her the whole truth. But she had been through so much, and I didn't want her to have another reason to worry about me.

"From this point forward," I continued, "I will be gone before you wake in the morning, and I'll most likely be asleep before I hit my bed. Have you seen the work that goes on at this ranch?"

"I'm happy to hear that, Michael. You have never been an idle man. This will give you the chance to get back to a normal life and give me the time I need to figure things out."

⸻※⸻

I decided to explore the ranch further before I needed to start working. The fresh, cold air helped clear the fog in my head. I thought of my other life in Philadelphia: the elegance of the city and its people; the familiar sounds of trolley cars and carriages on the roads; and the memories of my family, career, and friends left behind. On the other hand, when I thought of going back home after all Lucy and I had been through, I couldn't imagine returning to the life I had lived for so many years.

While out walking, I noticed Sarah working outside near the stable. It seemed impossible to believe I had ever seen her as plain or ill mannered. Sarah's beauty was obvious. I couldn't decide whether it was the way her hair rested on her graceful neck or her smile in the sunlight. She had a mind like no one I had ever met, allowing us to talk for hours about anything and everything. I remembered those first days together and the judgments I'd made about her lifestyle. Now, however, I admired her courage and way of life greatly. I thought about my injuries and remembered her gentle touch on my arm when she helped mend it. I never seemed to get my fill of listening to her or watching her, and I felt empty whenever we parted.

I finally had to admit that I had become deeply infatuated with Sarah Donnelly. Along with her compassion and warmth,

Sarah had an inner strength and spirit that flowed through her and into those around her. She was a welcome friend for Lucy, who needed that strength more than ever before.

I caught her eye as I passed the house, and I waved uncomfortably. My stomach filled with butterflies when her face crinkled into a lovely smile. After seeing me, she stopped working and strolled in my direction.

"Good afternoon, Michael," she said. "How is Lucy today?"

"She seems better."

She joined me in my walk away from the cabin, toward the river and down the path we had traveled several weeks earlier. A gentle dusting of snow covered the ground, creating the illusion of walking on clouds.

When we arrived at a secluded spot where a downed tree provided a resting point, we each dusted off a spot and took a seat. Sarah remained silent, but she glanced over at my face several times as if waiting for me to say something.

"Did I tell you I was a professor at Pennsylvania University?" I finally asked.

"Lucy told me," she replied. "It was quite a surprise."

I could imagine her version of my life, and I laughed aloud. "What did you think—that I was a bored, spoiled aristocrat, spending each day finding new ways to amuse myself and spend my wealth?"

"Very funny, Michael," she replied, shoving me off the log. "I just never imagined you as a teacher."

"It's true that our family is wealthy, but my parents expected more from Lucy and me. She volunteered at the hospital, and I taught literature and philosophy." I got up, dusted off my pants, and sat back down beside her.

"No wonder I'm no match when it comes to debating with you."

"You're more of a match than I have found in a long time." Large white flakes of snow began to fall gently, some catching in her hair as they fell toward the earth. Her cheeks were red from the cold, and her eyes glowed in the winter light.

"When Lucy disappeared, I took a leave of absence. One of the letters I just wrote home was to officially resign my position."

"Why would you do that?" She turned and placed her hand on my arm. Her eyes seemed troubled.

"I cannot expect them to hold my position forever, Sarah, and I'm still uncertain about when we will go home … if we go home." I placed my hands back in my pockets. "If Lucy and I return home, I can always try for another position, but I'm no longer certain about returning to the city." I remembered again the pain in Lucy's eyes as she spoke of her past, and I knew that going home might not be possible. "It seems that we are displaced, Lucy and I."

Sarah was silent, but I could feel her grasp tighten on my arm. From what I knew about Sarah, she was used to being able to fix things that were broken, and I could see the wheels turning in her head as she tried to find the right solution for Lucy and me.

"Don't worry so much," I said, nudging her out of her thoughts. "We'll figure out something."

The river was covered with the gleam of newly formed ice, but water could be heard rushing beneath it. I took a long breath, inhaling the cold air. There was nothing quite like the smell of winter.

"I spoke to Pat this morning, and Lucy and I will be staying for the winter. My arm is healing well. I can now work for our room and board."

"That sounds great, Michael." Her brilliant smile returned. "I know Pat will be pleased."

"I plan to learn everything I can about this place, this town, the people, and this way of life." I waved my arm around the ranch and the forest that lined it, taking it all in. "I wasn't entirely wrong when I described my life as a bored aristocrat. I worked, but I also had a full social schedule, thanks to my aunt, and I was quite bored in that world. The only time I felt truly comfortable was when I taught or spent time alone in my library. I failed my family by becoming lazy in life, by taking everything for granted."

"I don't see how you have failed, Michael." She shifted next to me, and I felt her leg touch mine. "You are a wonderful brother to Lucy."

"All my life, I have lived in peace," I replied. "My life was profoundly different in Philadelphia. It had structure and stability. I was confident in my abilities as a man, and my biggest worry was being late to the opera." Sarah didn't speak, but a small grin formed across her lips. "I was also confident that I would always be able to protect my family."

I took a breath and swallowed. "Then I leave Philadelphia, and the first thing I do when I get off the train is fall flat on my face in the dirt." My smile broadened at the memory of Sarah standing over me and hollering as I lay sprawled out on the station floor. "I haven't done one thing right since I came to Colorado. My thinking has been muddled and unclear, and I have felt insecure and awkward. I never doubted my instincts until I arrived here, but now I no longer trust myself." I ran my fingers through my hair in frustration.

"You trusted me, when you had no reason to," Sarah pointed out. "That has to count for something."

"I don't think I can take credit for that. To tell you the truth, it wasn't trust that led me to follow you—it was desperation. When you offered to help, I really had no other option." I looked down at the ground and shuffled the snow with my feet. "I hope you aren't offended."

"Of course not," she said, laughing. "After all, I really was quite awful to you then."

"Well, you had your reasons, as I have had mine. Besides, you have more than made up for it ... you and your family." The sun's rays had reached the horizon, and a multitude of colors illuminated the mountains. Large clouds added to this effect, creating purples, pinks, and oranges throughout the sky. The breeze began to cool as night approached and the winter air closed in.

"I've been walking around in a cloud, Sarah," I said, resuming my story, "and I'm tired of it. The last few days of silence have allowed me to think clearly again. For the first time in a long time, I feel ready for the future—whatever it may bring."

"So what do you see in your future?" she asked after a few minutes.

"I honestly don't know," I said. "I think I'll just take it one day at a time." She smiled at me with obvious approval, making my face flame with heat. I smiled back, looking down to see my hand resting on her thigh. Jerking it away as if her leg were on fire, I bound to my feet. I could feel the slight flush on my face turn to a bright crimson as I realized how close I had been sitting to her, and how intimate our conversation had been. I had never shared that much with anyone but Lucy, and I suddenly felt extremely foolish. I looked around as if something were going to materialize to save me from my embarrassment. When nothing appeared, I quickly turned back toward Sarah, flushed and fidgeting.

"I'm sorry ... um ... sorry to keep you. I need to ... uh ... check on ... something. Please excuse me." I started hastily back down the path. Since I was young, I had found that a fast getaway was the cure for any embarrassing encounter.

Sarah's loud laughter followed me. My continual rules of proper conduct and my sense of propriety clearly remained amusing to Sarah. I'm sure she'd never met a man so worried about offending a woman.

I passed Will when he came from the stream, leading his horse. He nodded, and I slowed my walking when I realized he stopped to talk to Sarah, who was just around a bend in the path. I couldn't help eavesdropping.

"Is Michael gonna be okay?" he asked her.

"I think he's going to manage just fine." She laughed again.

"What's so funny?"

"Oh, nothing really. Michael is just a bit ... different is all. He makes me laugh."

I didn't quite know how to take what she said, but for the first time in weeks, I felt good.

14

ENEMIES IN OUR MIDST

P at appeared on the porch just as the first shafts of light broke the dawn. I jumped out of the chair in front of his door and placed my hat on my head. I clenched my sweaty hands within my gloves, then, realizing what I was doing, tried to relax my arms at my sides. I wanted to be useful to Pat and the others on the ranch. And I really did not want to fail this time.

Pat looked at me with a tilt of his head and a small grin on his lips. "Well, aren't you eager this mornin'?" He chuckled and ushered me in to grab breakfast before his brothers came outside. My stomach was twisted in nervous knots, so I didn't have much of an appetite. But knowing I'd need my strength, I grabbed some biscuits, cheese, and bacon. Pat followed and made himself a plate.

"Did you figure something out?" I made a small sandwich with my breakfast offerings and took a large bite.

"I reckon that depends on you."

"What do you mean?"

"I met with my brothers last night, and they agreed it'd be good for you to learn the ranch. We're happy to teach you," he said around a mouthful of food, "but I need a favor in return."

"What do you need?"

"Sarah told me that you were a teacher at a big university in Philadelphia," he continued. "I'd like you to teach here. As you probably know, we don't have a schoolteacher in this area. I'd like you to spend a few hours each day teachin' the little ones. I do the best I can, but I don't often have time with everything I gotta do around here, and teachin' isn't somethin' that comes naturally to me. Hell, Laura ends up takin' over half the time, and I'm supposed to be teachin' her."

Even though Pat said I didn't owe his family anything, I felt differently. I hadn't taught children before, but I was eager for the opportunity to finally give something back to the men who had helped me.

"Of course, Pat," I said excitedly. "It would be an honor."

He threw his head back and laughed. "You obviously haven't spent much time with the little ones here, but I'd be real obliged if you think you're up to it."

"Absolutely."

"All right, then." He looked out the window at the activity starting around the ranch. "It'll be my two oldest children, Laura and Eddie, along with one other. Sulley is one of my long-time ranch hands, and he's got a girl about Laura's age. We'll need to take a trip into Lone Tree for supplies— before the trail is blocked by snow. It'll take a few days to get what you need, so we'll get you started on the ranch, and then you can start teachin' next week."

"Great!"

"If the teachin' isn't what you expect, or you find you'd

rather not do it, I won't hold it against you." He looked at the ground and shook his head back and forth. "My children can try the patience of a saint."

"Well, I did teach adults in Philadelphia, but I can adjust." My mind was already racing with all the things I could do to help Pat, and my excitement was not easily contained. "Don't worry, Pat. I can handle it. So, what about today?" I slapped my hands together, rubbing them briskly in anticipation.

"Today we work." Pat's expression changed back to the serious man I was accustomed to. He picked up his coffee, and once we were outside, he started heading briskly toward the dairy shed, while I tried to keep up. "I'm gonna show you a few of the daily chores, and then we'll ride the ranch to get you acquainted with all the men and the land. I need to get supplies out to the line camps anyway, so you can help me this afternoon." Before I caught up with him, he was already going over my first duties.

"You'll start early each mornin' in the dairy shed. I know you think your arm is healed, but it might be best to start slowly at first, and milkin' will help build strength in your arms." I narrowed my eyes and gave him a look he must have been expecting, because he raised an eyebrow as if to say, *You asked for it.*

He looked at the horizon and took a long drink of his coffee before entering the shed and placing the mug on the post by the door. "All the cows need to be milked twice a day," he said. "Sarah usually does most of the milkin', but from now on, your first duty will be to come here and help out. Don't worry about the milkin' in the afternoon; we'll take care of it." Pat walked through the stalls and patted each cow as if they were old friends. Finally, at the end of the line, he picked up a pail and moved to the side of a cow.

"You'll need to sit on the left side of each cow. It helps 'em get used to you. Now sit on the pail." Pat gestured toward the upturned pail as he looked into the stall. I hesitated for a moment and then cautiously walked around the cow, to the metal pail, and sat down. When I'd offered to learn the ranching business, I hadn't thought of the dairy shed. I'd thought of roping and shooting and all the rough and tough work I had witnessed over the weeks. Looking at the bottom side of that cow made me wonder what I was doing. But then … I was determined to do whatever was needed around the ranch. I straightened my shoulders.

Pat handed me a small bowl of warm water and a cloth. He instructed me to wash the udder thoroughly before beginning. "If you're ready," he said, kneeling down next to me with another empty pail, "rest your head against the cow's flank and place the empty pail under the teats." Was this some horrible joke? When I looked up at him and saw that he was serious, I turned back to the cow and did as I was told.

"Now, gently take a teat into the palm of your hand. Start to squeeze the teat from the top with your thumb and forefinger." He demonstrated what he wanted me to do and then gestured for me to take over. He noticed the horrified expression on my face and began laughing when I touched the cow's bulging teat. "Continue to squeeze as you wrap the rest of your fingers, one at a time, around the teat, forcin' the milk into the pail. When all your fingers are around the teat, you let go and then do it again." When I began, Pat watched me closely and made a few adjustments. He warned me about being too rough, as the cow could kick if it became uncomfortable.

"When the teat becomes soft and only a little milk comes out, you move on to the next one," he said, patting me on the back. He stood and leaned against the wall. After he became comfortable with my progress, he told me to finish up and then take the milk to the main house, leaving it on the stoop by the kitchen door. Then I was to gather all the eggs from the chicken coop and bring them to the house as well. He left me alone in the shed and instructed me to meet up with him when I had finished with all the chores.

After the initial horror subsided, the action of milking the cows became quite soothing. It was a good opportunity to have some time alone and to reflect on the day ahead. The cows were actually sweet beasts once you got to know them. All it took was a soft hand and a soothing voice to move the process along quite nicely.

For the rest of the morning, Pat and I went over every aspect of riding a horse, from picking out the best one for the need at hand, to saddling and riding. I'd thought I'd known a lot about horses, but I found that most of what I thought I knew was wrong or unclear. After I'd saddled and unsaddled Ginger more than ten times, Pat finally took me on a tour of the ranch. We ambled through every building, and he explained what duties were performed. I met over twenty men who had stayed on to work for the winter.

Remembering Pat's privacy about Turner, I realized that the ranch could be harboring any number of unknown enemies. I watched the faces of all the men as I was introduced, knowing that Pat did the same. Most of the men seemed pleasant and helpful, with only a few exceptions. One of them was the man I had seen talking to Sarah on several occasions. His name was Josiah, a good-looking man in his early twenties, and he obviously disliked my presence. Others kept their distance and rarely spoke to me unless they had to. It was difficult to determine who was friend and who was enemy. The sooner I learned how to fight, the better.

Lori R. Hodges

We dropped off supplies to each of the line camps, and I met the men who were staffing them for the winter. Pat gave me the entire lay of the land, which was incredibly important if I was going to do any work away from the main house.

As the sun set over the mountains, Pat and I talked while we slowly rode our horses back to the ranch. Surprisingly, I found that Pat was highly educated due to many years of tutelage under his father. He was also deeply devoted to family and the people at the Lazy D Ranch. Out of all the men at the ranch, I trusted him the most.

He told me about his life, his wife and children, and growing up in Colorado. The only thing he wouldn't talk about was his wife's death. Whenever the subject would steer in that direction, he quickly spoke of something else. Our discussion remained deeply personal, however, and I felt that perhaps he had wanted to talk to me for some time but had not been given the opportunity.

"Can I ask you a somewhat personal question?" I asked. Pat raised an eyebrow and straightened in the saddle as if preparing for battle. I noticed the strain in his jaw as he clenched his teeth, waiting for some devastating blow. "Don't worry," I reassured him. "I may not understand your reasons, but I'll respect your wishes and not return to our unfinished conversation from yesterday."

As I expected, Pat's face instantly softened, and he settled back into his saddle. No one looked more natural than Pat riding a horse. "I know this is none of my concern," I continued, "but I was wondering why Sarah has never been married." I noticed the laughter in his eyes and hastily added, "Or Tommy or Will?"

Pat looked up at me and grinned widely. "I could probably ask the same of you," he said, waiting for a reply. "Why is it that you've never settled down and gotten hitched?"

"I suppose I have just never found the right woman," I said with a shrug, feeling somewhat awkward. "My aunt has tried for years to find a woman for me to marry. At first, it was probably just defiance on my part, against the whole affair, but even when I looked, I never found a woman that ... stirred me."

"So you aren't against marriage?" he asked.

"Not at all."

We rode in silence for a few moments, watching the sun disappear behind the hills. "Are you going to answer my question?" I finally asked.

"Well, as for my brothers, I imagine you've noticed the lack of women around these parts. I think Will would like to settle down, but Tommy is a born hell-raiser if I've ever seen one."

"And your sister?"

"Have you ever seen her when she's angry?" he asked with a laugh.

"Yes ... but ..."

"I'm kidding, Mike." There was a look in his eyes that I had trouble deciphering. He seemed pleased that I was asking about Sarah, and my face began to heat considerably. "Actually," he continued, "Sarah came close to gettin' hitched when she was a bit younger than your sister, but she found the son of a bitch courtin' another woman in town at the same time he was courtin' her. The only other man she allowed herself to get close to was a terribly jealous man, and in a fit of rage, he struck her." Pat's jaw clenched again at the memory, and I could feel my own anger rising at the thought of anyone abusing Sarah in such a way.

"Sarah wasn't always as strong and independent as she is now," he added, looking back in my direction. "But she won't stand for any man strikin' her. The bastard threatened more harm if she told anyone what he did, but that didn't keep her from tellin' me anyway." A wicked smile crossed Pat's lips as he leaned forward in the saddle.

"What did you do?" I chuckled, knowing Pat well enough to know the man did not go away unpunished.

"I made certain that he'd never darken Sarah's world again."

"You … killed him?" I gulped.

"No, I didn't kill him," he said, rolling his eyes just as Sarah would have. "Death would've been too good for the likes of him." He paused, deep in memory, and then just shrugged nonchalantly. "I simply made it impossible for him to use his hands in anger again."

Knowing he wouldn't elaborate, I merely nodded and muttered, "I see." I had hoped he might give me some key into Sarah's heart, but his answer didn't comfort me at all.

"At least now I understand why she greeted me with such disdain when we first met on the train," I said finally.

"Actually, that was because she'd been in the city for a bit. Sarah gets … out of sorts around city folk. Also, she had that run-in with Turner's men, which put her on edge for every other encounter."

Pat paused for a second and then unexpectedly smiled. "She doesn't hesitate to teach men proper manners when confronted, and she is *real* good at what she does. She's turned into quite a pistol over the years. Sarah deserves something special, and I fear all she's found is disappointment. And then after … " Pat's face changed suddenly. "Well … it doesn't matter."

I sensed another secret just beneath the surface, but I said nothing. I figured the only true way to understand the Donnelly clan and all the secrets that haunted them would be to gain their trust.

"It sounds as if Sarah talks to you about everything." I wanted more than anything for Pat to tell me it wasn't true, but I sensed I was wrong before he ever spoke.

The wrinkles around his eyes deepened as his face broke into a large grin. He started laughing—a big belly laugh I had never seen from Pat. "Yes," he choked. "Everything."

"Damn," I muttered, knowing why he was laughing and suddenly wanting to strangle Sarah.

"Don't fret, Mike," he sputtered. "We've all fallen off a horse a time or two." I shook my head, knowing he was just trying to keep me from feeling like the clumsiest man alive. "Of course," he added, rubbing his chin, "I did drink two bottles of whiskey first." His laughter intensified until he was holding his side to ward off the pain with each breath.

We stopped in front of the stable, and Pat swung off his horse. I was just moving my leg over Ginger's back when Pat held both hands out toward me. "Be careful," he said with a chuckle, "I wouldn't want you to hurt yourself." Then he doubled over in laugher again, totally incapacitated. I took a deep breath, trying to ignore his obvious joy in my inadequacies.

I'd completely forgotten how sore my backside could get after riding, but after spending the afternoon traveling around the ranch with Pat, the feeling was vivid in my memory. I knew that I would get used to it as the days went by, but I was also certain that it would be almost impossible to get out of bed once I got into it that night.

When I went to the stable to settle Ginger for the night, I realized again what a beautiful horse she was, standing tall and strong among the others. I talked to her as I removed the saddle and then went to get a brush. She had been very good to me since we'd gotten her in Fort Collins, so I came to the stable to talk to her often. Other than Lucy, Ginger knew more than anyone else did about my thoughts and feelings. It might sound absurd, but Ginger had become a trusted old friend who was always willing to listen.

I left Ginger in the middle of the stable and went to an empty stall in the corner, which was used for storage. I knelt to get the supplies to wash Ginger and brush her. Hearing heavy steps behind me, moving fast, my head screamed out a warning, but before I had a chance to turn around, something was thrust over my head, blocking my vision. I was forced to the ground, onto my stomach. I gasped for air, wondering what was happening.

A knee lodged firmly in my back, keeping me down. At least two men tied my hands behind my back. They even tied my feet together as if I were a steer.

Punches assaulted my body. I attempted to get to my feet several times, only to be knocked down again. There was no escape.

Each blow struck my stomach and my back. They kicked and punched me. The attack went on and on, and I doubled over in pain. An occasional punch was thrown to my face for good measure. A stabbing pain shot through my arm as they hit my old bullet wound near my shoulder, tearing the flesh from my body.

Every time I tried to catch my breath, I'd endure another blow. They were there to kill me.

It didn't make any sense. I had just started feeling human again. My arm was better, and Lucy and I were talking. I was looking forward to the future again. Why did someone want to cause me further harm?

The last thing I remember was a boot striking my face, causing black spots in my vision and the coppery taste of blood in my mouth.

15

A COWBOY IS BORN

"Michael?"

Several drops of moisture dripped on my forehead and neck, and I wondered where it could be coming from. I heard the voice but was having a difficult time deciphering the words.

"Michael?"

I tried to open my eyes, but they refused to budge.

"Can you hear me, Michael?"

I lifted my arm but only got a few inches before someone took my hand. The touch was soft and tender. The fog slowly cleared.

"Don't try to move, Michael." Lucy held my hand and spoke quietly near my face. "You're all right now. The doctor just left, and he said you would be fine with some rest and care."

A rush of memories flooded my mind. I wasn't in Philadelphia in my old bedchamber. I slowly remembered my journey to Colorado, the Donnelly ranch, the cabin, the bunkhouse, the stable, and … oh, yes … the stable. I was no longer lying on the ground in the horse stall where I was attacked. Trying to open my eyes again, I found that my left eye was swollen closed and my right seemed to be caked in dried blood.

"Lucy?" I rasped.

"I'm here, Michael," she said quietly. "Don't try to talk. Everything will be all right." Lucy had clearly been crying, and her hands and voice shook with worry for my condition. I felt warm water on my face again as someone used a cloth to remove the blood. Lucy continued to hold my hand and talk to me soothingly. "You broke a few ribs, but otherwise the doctor says you'll be fine. Do you understand?"

"You … okay?" I asked, gaining a little more of my voice. Every word caused pain to shoot into my side.

"I'm fine," she said. "Everything's going to be all right." Those words seemed to be the only ones I needed to hear for the time being, because I returned to sleep and the peaceful darkness without pain.

The next time I woke, I felt large quilts draped over my body and the warmth from within. The confusion I'd felt directly after the attack was gone, and without opening my eyes, I knew Lucy remained beside my bed. The pain quickly returned as I recalled the assault on me.

Who would do such a thing? Turner?

No. The men who attacked me were the worst sort of cowards. If Turner was responsible, he wouldn't have just beat me, he would have killed me. The men who cornered me in the stall did their very best to hurt me, but I couldn't imagine Turner wasting that kind of time.

The act of violence was something else entirely.

An alarming thought came to me. If I had been attacked, perhaps others had been as well. Lucy was all right but what about … "Sarah!" I sat upright in bed. A spiking pain shot through my body. I gasped for breath and could only manage one word at a time. "Find. Sarah!"

"It's all right," Sarah said, moving closer to the bed. "I'm here. Everything's fine." She placed a gentle hand on my shoulder and urged me to lie back down. I lay quietly for several minutes to let the pain subside. I concentrated on trying to slow my breathing to decrease the pain.

Lucy and Sarah were both safe. There was nothing I had to do right away, so I allowed the warm moisture and soothing touch of Sarah's hand across my forehead to lull me back to sleep.

———————————

"How's he doing?" Pat asked. The sound of his voice woke me. I attempted to open my eyes but could only open the right one. Sarah had removed all the blood from my face, allowing me to make out shapes at the door.

"He seems to be doing better," Sarah said quietly. "He's been moving more and talking in his sleep."

"Is he awake?" Pat asked. Both Lucy and Sarah shook their heads.

"Yes," I said, surprising everyone. It wasn't until then that I noticed all three brothers in the room.

"Hey, Mike, how're ya feelin'?" Tommy moved toward the bed.

"I've been better."

Pat grabbed a chair and sat down close to the bed. "Michael, who did this to you?" Pat wasn't one to waste time. And he only used my full name when something was very wrong.

Lucy's hands started to shake again, and she stared at Sarah in obvious discomfort. She still refused to talk to any man on the ranch, other than myself. I grabbed her hand and squeezed to reassure her.

"I never saw them." Whispering was the least painful way for me to communicate. "They put a bag over my head." I remembered the hands that had attempted to squeeze the life out of me. I took a good look at my wrists, which had been tied behind my back, and noticed the red, raw look of my skin. Everyone in the room remained quiet, watching me examine my wrists and wounds. "My hands were bound."

"Michael," Pat said, leaning close to me, "you said 'they.' How many were there?"

"I don't know."

"What do you remember?" he asked. "Did you see anything?"

I shook my head. Lucy stood and placed her hands on her hips. Even though she wouldn't speak, her meaning was clear. Sarah insisted that everyone leave to allow me to rest. Pat stood reluctantly. I knew he was disappointed that I could not provide him more information about the attack. I reached out and grabbed his arm. He sat back in the chair and put his head close to mine again.

"How did you find me?"

"Ginger," he said with a shake of his head and a smile. I raised my eyebrows. "When we were havin' supper, we saw that horse outside the house, stompin' and snortin'. When Tommy and I left the house, we noticed that she still had her bridle on, but the saddle was gone. So we took her back to the stable and tried to get her into her stall. She fought us with fury. Finally, she broke free and went straight to you." He cleared his throat and patted me on the shoulder. "If it weren't for that horse, we probably wouldn't have found you till mornin'."

I smiled weakly at the thought of Ginger saving my life. I knew she was a good horse. I needed to remember to bring her a carrot as soon as I could walk again.

Pat started to stand, but remembering something suddenly, I took his arm again. "One of the men said something. He told me to go home."

He leaned down and grasped my shoulder. I could feel the anger flow through him, but he kept his voice even for my sake. "Don't worry, Michael," he said sternly. "We'll find 'em." He straightened and walked out of the room.

His sense of responsibility for Lucy and me was apparent. He had reassured me repeatedly that she and I were safe on the ranch. Lucy had told me he'd stormed out of the room and interrogated everyone on the property when he found out I'd been beaten. He threatened the jobs and the lives of others. Knowing he was taking it personally, I felt incredibly uneasy about what he was going to do next.

Lucy's demeanor changed as soon as the Donnelly brothers left the room. The tension in her shoulders eased considerably, and she began to talk and laugh as if they were never there. Sarah left the room and came back with soup, insisting that I eat before I slept again. While Sarah and I argued about the food, Lucy sat in her chair, pretending to read, with a small smile on her face. I found it odd that she had no problem ushering the men out of the room to let me rest, yet she was perfectly content to allow Sarah to annoy me.

"Michael, just eat a few bites," Sarah said in an irritated tone.

"I don't feel like eating."

"You haven't eaten in two days." She slid the soup closer. "You need to start eating again.

"Two days?"

"Yes. You've been asleep most of the time. Now you need to eat!"

"I told you"—I pushed the bowl away again—"I don't feel like eating."

She lowered the tray and sighed in resignation, glaring at me. "Are you always such a horse's ass when you're hurt? First it was the porcupine, then the gunshot wound, and now this. You are the clumsiest person I have ever known—and an ingrate to boot!"

Amused by her comment, a smile spread across my mouth. I burst out laughing but had to hold my side to keep the pain down. The last time she'd tried to help me, I'd treated her the same way.

She lifted one side of her mouth in a smirk.

I tried to sit up, with my back supported by pillows, and noticed that I was naked under the blankets. I pulled them quickly to my chest.

"Do you mind telling me who undressed me?" Heat burned in my cheeks. I avoided Sarah's eyes. Lucy hid her face behind her book, but her shoulders shook with laughter. I took the cloth Sarah had given me as a handkerchief and tossed it at her. "Quit laughing at me," I said, quickly recovering from my embarrassment. "Can't you see I'm an injured man?"

She lowered her book just under her eyes. "Well, you sure seem to be getting better." Her eyebrows rose and she laughed again.

I scowled at her and readjusted myself on the bed. I then extended my hand toward Sarah. "Are you going to give me the soup, or am I going to have to starve to death?"

She and Lucy looked at each other and rolled their eyes; she then handed me the tray with soup and tea. I made sure once again that I was covered with the blanket before I began to eat. My head finally felt clear, and I thought again about the attack.

"Lucy," I said between bites, "doesn't it strike you as odd that you and I have so many enemies in a place we've never been before?"

She looked up from her book and stared at me for a few moments, all traces of humor gone. "I thought of that myself."

⸻ ⟨◎⟩ ⸻

Over the next few days, I was plagued with nightmares about Lucy, Sarah, the Donnelly family, and all the strangers that surrounded us. Lucy left my bedchamber door open at night to wake her if I shouted out, just as I had when she was injured.

It didn't take long for me to get back on my feet. Being inside all day had caused me great stress along with the night terrors. It was so much more comfortable when I was able to move around the ranch. Most of the men were pleased to see me up and around, but a few avoided any contact with me.

Despite the protests of Lucy and Sarah, I started work again as soon as I was able to walk around the ranch without losing my breath. I didn't have much time before spring, when Pat and his brothers planned to go after Turner. The assault merely increased my determination to go with them. The words of one of my attackers—"Go home"—stuck in my mind, but I would die before I'd give up and go back home. Besides, I no longer knew where home was.

Pat started me off slowly, even though I was eager to do more. I wrapped my ribs tightly with cloth for support each morning and tried my best not to show any pain while around the men. I noticed that I was rarely left alone until I finally retired to my cabin at night. I began to understand why Lucy hated to be chaperoned all those years in Philadelphia. I was grateful to everyone, but I sorely missed my privacy.

Lucy began to spend part of each day outside the cabin, on the bench on the porch, wrapped in a thick quilt. She'd silently watch everything that occurred around the ranch. Will came by the cabin regularly, rocking in the rocking chair next to the door, trying to engage her in conversation. At first, Lucy would go back into the cabin when Will came close, but after a time, she became comfortable enough to remain seated in silence. Sometimes Will would talk to Lucy, and other times he would just sit and whittle or hum.

I believe the humming is what finally put Lucy at ease in his presence. He never demanded anything from her and never became upset when she refused to answer his questions or reply to his comments. Will seemed like a man who was never in a hurry and never troubled. There was a definite air of serenity when he was near, and the humming became incredibly soothing to Lucy throughout the long days.

Another thing that decreased my anxiety about Lucy was finally receiving a letter from Aunt Olivia. Pat delivered the package to me one day after returning from Lone Tree. Inside we found a book, *The Odyssey* by Homer, and a letter from home. I laughed briefly, as I realized why she'd chosen the book.

Her letter confirmed my suspicions about Mr. Westley. He had stopped by once after Lucy's disappearance, but since that time, she had not heard from him. She learned later that he was courting another woman in town. He obviously felt less for Lucy than expected. I was relieved to learn his feelings before I had to tell him or anyone else about what had happened to her physically. Lucy and I lived day by day in a state of uncertainty, but my aunt's news would finally allow us to think seriously about the future.

As for my aunt, she decided to spend some time in the country with her sister. Without the two of us around, she craved companionship and wished to get out of the city for the winter. She related that Arthur remained anxious about our return, and she wanted me to tell Lucy she was in his thoughts and prayers.

When I returned to the cabin that night, I found Lucy at the table drinking tea. I set the book on the table and handed her the letter. At first, she seemed overjoyed to receive a letter from home, but as she read, her joy dimmed somewhat. When finished, she folded the letter and stared out the window. I learned that the window had become her comfort over the last several weeks, and that she sought the view of the snow-covered forest whenever uneasy or deep in thought.

"It's all for the best, really," she said quietly. Despite Lucy's outward indifference, I could see the pain in her eyes.

"How can you say that, Lucy?"

"I saw a lot of women at the hospital who went through something similar to what I've been through." She paused and looked down at her hands in her lap. "I have also seen their families. First there is horror and then pity, and after some time, I have seen husbands and fiancés turn away because they cannot bear the thought of it. I wouldn't expect any man to throw everything away to marry me out of obligation alone."

"Lucy—"

"This letter saves me from having to tell Aunt Olivia, Mr. Westley, or anyone else," she said with determination. "No one at home needs to know now."

"Was I right to show this to you?" I asked, sitting near her again.

"Of course." She offered a sad smile. She got up, poured two cups of tea, and brought them to the table. "I'd rather know than hope for something that will never be. Besides, I'm not the same woman I was in Philadelphia. I've changed, and I'm no longer sure I would want to return to being who I once was, or to a society that would so easily toss me aside. We cannot hold on to things from the past, Michael. It won't do either of us any good. We're both different now."

The sadness I had seen when she first read the letter had vanished. Lucy had the most amazing strength. I now understood what Will had been talking about when he'd stopped me on the porch. She had an inner strength that surpassed that of anyone I'd ever known.

Lucy blew on her tea to cool it, looking at me over her cup. She tilted her head and scrunched up her mouth in concentration.

"What are you looking at?" I asked, suddenly grinning.

"What about you, Michael?" she asked. "What are your plans now?"

"I'll go where you go, whether back to Philadelphia or somewhere else," I said, spreading my arms wide. "My life is in your hands."

"Oh, really." She slammed her cup down on the saucer and crossed her arms. "You'll just pack up and move wherever I ask, at a moment's notice?"

I couldn't understand her sudden annoyance. "Lucy, what—"

"What about Sarah?" She glared at me.

"What *about* Sarah?"

"Do you honestly believe that I want you to be alone just because I am?"

"Well, no," I said. "But that doesn't mean that Sarah and I ... I mean ..."

"You and I both know how much you care for Sarah. Don't even try to deny it. Are you planning on leaving her here and never thinking of her again?" Her face turned red as her agitation grew.

"Of course I care about Sarah," I said. "I greatly admire her and the life she lives." I hadn't recognized how deep my feelings had become for Sarah until Lucy mentioned it.

Could my admiration and infatuation have turned into something more?

"During all the years when our aunt was trying to find you a wife, I never saw the look I see in your eyes when Sarah is near," she continued. "Admit it … you love her."

"I don't think this is something we should discuss." I moved my chair away. I was a little uneasy about talking to Lucy about Sarah, and I frantically tried to find a quick way out of the conversation.

"Of course it is," she said with agitation. "We've always shared everything with each other."

"Things are different, Lucy."

"They don't have to be." She rested her hand gently on my cheek and looked into my eyes. "I know you think that you cannot be happy if I'm not, but the thought of you with Sarah makes me incredibly happy."

"We have both been through too much." I shook my head and tried to will the conversation away.

"I can see the burden you carry," she said. "You have to start making decisions for your own life—not mine." She glanced outside at the snow-covered trees and looked back into my eyes. "I'll make my own decisions from now on."

Back in Philadelphia, I used to marvel at the independence of my sister. But looking across the table, I saw what she meant about the two of us changing. I had underestimated her over the years. She had become an extraordinary woman.

"So," she said with a smirk, "are you going to tell me how you feel about Sarah, or will I have to beat it out of you?"

I laughed quietly and looked at her for a few moments. "I have had enough beatings, thank you." I glanced around the cabin and out the window, as if someone might be listening to our conversation. Finally, I sighed heavily, sat up straighter in my chair, and leaned in close to her. "Sarah is everything I could have hoped for in a woman."

Lucy squealed with delight and clapped her hands together, startling me. The cabin had been so quiet during our conversation, and I felt the whole world could hear her. Lucy loved to see me uncomfortable, so she began to dance around the room, laughing and carrying on.

I tried to shush her by placing my hand over her mouth, but it was useless, and we both ended up laughing hysterically as we struggled. I wanted to hold that moment forever just to hear her laughing.

"I think you should tell her," she said, recovering from her hilarity.

"You should mind your own business." I pointed a finger at her, instantly serious. "I will haunt you throughout eternity if you mention this to her, do you hear me?"

"I'd never do such a thing," she said. "I said that I think you should tell her."

I shook my head doubtfully. "I don't know, Lucy. I'm not so sure she would be pleased to be the recipient of my affection."

"What woman wouldn't be pleased to have you by her side?" She playfully pinched my cheek. I shooed her hand away and messed up her hair as I stood to go to my room. My days weren't getting any shorter, and I needed as much rest as I could get.

By my fourth day of work, I could not imagine having the time or the energy to begin teaching. Every muscle in my body felt as if it would tear in half with the slightest provocation, and my bones ached constantly. I stumbled back to the cabin at the end of each day, barely able to place one foot in front of the other.

Lucy laughed at me when I tried to climb the three measly steps up to the front door. "You look just pitiful." I shuffled my feet across the floor, unable to lift them, and collapsed onto the bed.

Lucy tugged off my boots. "Don't you want supper? You need to keep up your strength."

"I don't want supper," I mumbled. "I just want to die."

"If you died, I'd have to eat alone, and I just will not accept that." She poked me in the ribs to get my attention.

I shooed her hand away. "Fine, but you'll have to make supper, as I don't think I can move for at least a half hour."

"Don't worry, my brother. I will take care of everything." She left the room and I could hear her working in the kitchen, while I lay frozen on the bed. It wasn't so much the pain that kept me glued to the bed. I felt numb and had a difficult time getting my body to work. I knew from the previous couple of days, however, that the real pain would arrive sometime in the night as my body began to stiffen from lack of movement. The taunts launched from the men at the ranch had a whole new meaning for me, and I had to agree, after living their life for a few days, that I was indeed a tenderfoot.

Lucy came into the room some time later, and when I

opened my eyes, she stood over me with her hands on her hips, smirking. "Now, you cannot eat lying face down in bed so get up and come to the table." She didn't wait for me to answer; she just returned to the kitchen. "By the way," she said loudly, so that I could hear her from my room, "I've invited Sarah to supper."

I sat up abruptly. "You did what?" The news got my legs and arms working again. I cleaned up quickly with the water in the basin on my dresser and hastened into clean clothes.

Lucy grinned madly as I walked out of my room and sat down at the table. "Now there's the brother I know. Don't you feel better?"

I rested my head on the palm of one hand and mumbled, "I should have died when I had the chance."

At that moment, we heard a soft knock on the door, and Lucy opened it to invite Sarah inside. I managed to stand briefly to greet her, but then I fell back into my seat clumsily. I couldn't understand how someone who worked as hard as Sarah could look so wonderful at the end of each day. She wore a pale blue dress that brought out the beauty of her eyes and the bronze color of her skin from working in the sun. Her long hair was pulled back from her face, and it curled around her shoulders, down her back to her waist. A few strands dangled around her temples.

Lucy served us each a plate of food and then sat across from me. She was right about the food. The smell alone had the ability to make me feel whole again. I ate slowly, in silence, as I listened to Lucy and Sarah talk. It amazed me to see Lucy so animated and lively in Sarah's presence, while she remained silent amongst the others at the ranch.

"I was thinking," Lucy said. "I've been watching Michael working over the last few days, and now that my arm's almost healed, I'd like to help as well. Would you be willing to show me a few things?"

"Are you sure you're up to this, Lucy?" I asked with concern. Lucy had always been incredibly active in the city and worked hard as a volunteer at the hospital, but I was still surprised that she felt ready to begin working again. The doctor had taken the splint off a mere two days earlier.

"You and I are so much alike, Michael," she said. "I'm tired of sitting around all day. I know I'll need to take it easy at first, but I think it will help me gain my strength again."

Sarah placed her hand over Lucy's. "I think it's a fabulous idea."

Not having enough energy to argue the matter further, I fell into silence as I listened to them make plans as I finished my meal. Lucy had lost so much weight over the last few months, and she looked more frail than I'd ever thought possible. I couldn't imagine her doing the work Sarah did each day. In my heart, however, I knew that she was right. The sooner she became active again, the sooner her physical strength would return.

Resting my head on my palm, I continued to listen as Sarah devised a plan to ease Lucy into the work on the ranch. I knew Sarah would take things slow and make sure Lucy didn't injure herself.

I must have dozed off because the next thing I heard was Lucy say, "As long as I don't end up like Michael at the end of the day." I opened my eyes and found both of them still at the table with me, watching me with smiles on their faces. Supper had ended a little while earlier, as witnessed by the absence of plates on the table. Sarah and Lucy had warmed some tea to sip as they quietly talked.

I felt incredibly foolish knowing I had fallen asleep at the table. I smiled weakly and tried to straighten up in my chair, while removing my elbow from the table. Lucy got up to get a third cup, brought it to the table, and poured me some tea. When she handed it to me, she patted me on the head, which only increased my mortification.

"I apologize, ladies," I said sheepishly. "I guess I'm not very good company this evening."

"Don't worry about it, Michael." Lucy took a long look at my face. "Why don't you go to bed and get some sleep. Sarah and I have some things we still need to discuss."

Without arguing, I took my cup in my hand, stood slowly, and bowed to Sarah as I said good night, apologizing again for my rudeness. I went carefully to my room and fell asleep almost the instant I hit my pillow. The last thing I remembered was hearing Sarah say, "Poor Michael, he looks awful."

Perfect.

16

TENDERFOOT

The next morning, Pat and I went into town to get the supplies I needed to teach the children at the ranch. I was itching to return to Lone Tree to see what news I could find about Turner and his men. The knowledge that Pat felt the same way, and the fact that we brought four other men with us, was a comfort during our ride out of the valley.

Our first errand was a stop at the jail, which wasn't much more than a large shack with two small cells along one wall. Daniel and James were talking at the large desk in the corner. James's casual tone and easy laughter immediately transformed into tension and silence at my appearance. James stood when he saw us, but he remained in front of the desk. My appearance must have brought back his worst memories of his brother's death and the days following.

Daniel, on the other hand, noticed Pat and stood up immediately to greet us with a large warm smile. "Good to see you Pat," Daniel said cheerfully, keeping an eye on his son. "I'm surprised to see you in town this late in the season. I would've thought the trail would be buried too deep with snow by now."

"Well, it wasn't the easiest time to travel, but it couldn't be helped," Pat said with a smile. "We wanted to see how things are going in town, and we need to pick up some supplies to see us through the cold months ahead."

"Of course," Daniel replied. "I'm glad you came."

"Daniel, I want you to meet a friend of mine." Pat gestured toward me. "This is Mike Mullen from Philadelphia." Surely, Daniel had every reason already to know who I was, for my sister's condition was the reason his son had been killed. "Mike," Pat continued, "this is Daniel Morgan, our new town marshal."

"Good to meet you, sir," I said sincerely, deeply grateful for the chance to meet the man and to have the chance to make things right with James.

Daniel glanced over at his son, who stared at the wood-planked floor, and then looked toward Pat and me. "May I ask how your sister's doing?" he asked quietly.

"She's getting better by the day," I said, making sure James could hear me clearly. "I wanted to come by today to thank you and both your sons. My sister told me what John did for her, and I wanted you to know how deeply the two of us regret his death." I paused for a moment until I received a nod from Daniel. "And if it weren't for James," I continued, "I may not have found Lucy in time."

My last comment made James look up from the floor to meet my eyes. Daniel didn't say anything right away, and a long, tense silence ensued as James and I studied one another. Finally, Daniel nodded again and held out his hand for me to shake.

"Thank you, son," he said with a sad smile. "I'm just glad to hear your sister's doing well."

"Would you and Pat mind giving James and me a moment in private?" I asked.

"Sure," Daniel said, patting my shoulder. "Pat and I have some business of our own to discuss. We'll head to the Franklin Hotel. Join us when you're through." Daniel took one last worried look at his son before following Pat out the door.

When I turned to address James, I noticed he had taken several steps forward. "So your sister is really doin' better?" he asked.

I smiled. "Yes, she seems to be doing well ... considering. I am sure she'll heal with more time." I pulled a note out of my pocket and held it out for James. "Lucy wanted me to give this to you. She still won't speak to any of the men at the ranch, so I think it took a lot for her to write this to you."

James looked at the note for several moments and then placed it in his coat pocket, obviously wanting to read it in private.

"I also wanted to apologize for misjudging you," I said evenly. "After Lucy told me what really happened, I realized how poorly I treated you ... and how much I owe you for helping me find Lucy."

James suddenly looked pained. He shook his head back and forth and turned his face away, toward the jail cells on the opposite wall. "I never should have told you she died," he said with a hitch in his voice. "I keep thinkin' about what could've happened if you would've listened to me and not gone to the cabin to find her that night." He turned back toward me and shook his head again. "It's me who should be apologizing. I never thought anyone could live through somethin' like that."

"Don't blame yourself," I said, not wanting to relive the time in the cabin. "Only a brother could understand just how stubborn Lucy can be."

James laughed at that. It was nice to see his face relax

and to hear the gentle, easy laughter I had heard when we first arrived at the jail. "We're square then?"

I held out my hand to him in friendship. "We are most definitely square."

When we met Pat and Daniel at the hotel, they were deep in conversation, no doubt talking about the town and Turner's presence in the area. Pat and Daniel both looked up and pasted smiles back on their faces for our benefit.

"What's the latest news?" I asked without hesitation. "Where's Turner?" I'd noticed when we first arrived in town that the number of Turner's men had decreased. They were still there, of course, but the havoc they had created when I had first arrived in Colorado was gone, leaving a peaceful feel in the town.

It was easy to see who was part of his gang. They had an arrogance about them that caused my blood to boil. But it was Turner I wanted, and I was willing to wait to find him.

"Daniel and I were just discussin' the situation in town," Pat said as he adjusted himself in his chair. "Why don't the two of you join us for dinner?"

We moved to the dining room located in the hotel and ordered. The sun was at the highest point in the sky. It was a mild winter day, and the warmth of the sun melted the traces of snow on the roofs of the buildings and the splintered wood of the boardwalks. Miss Patterson, the owner of the hotel, was in a fine mood, laughing and joking with those in the room. I could hear the faint strands of classical music floating from the small parlor next to the dining area.

Pat chose a table in the corner so we were facing the other patrons. He liked to sit where he could see everyone and everything. Even while in conversation, Pat remained observant to the voices around him and the looks of the men who came and went. Other than a few wary looks, no one approached us.

After ordering, Daniel repeated to me what he had been discussing with Pat. Since our late-night raid of his cabin, Turner had disappeared again without a word. R. J. remained in town, however, confirming our belief that Turner would be back.

"Since Blake's death," Daniel said, "R. J.'s been keepin' to himself and rarely talks with the townspeople or the other members of Turner's gang. I know something is in the works, though. This peace we've had lately isn't gonna last long." He downed the last of his mug and leaned back in his chair.

While we ate, I reached into my coat pocket and withdrew another message from my sister. Seeing James again, and apologizing for my behavior when I met him, was the easy part of my journey into town. The second message was going to be much more uncomfortable for me to deliver.

"Well," Pat said with a chuckle, looking at me over his mug, "you'd better get to it. We need to get our supplies and start headin' back before it gets too late."

Daniel and James looked at the two of us and smiled. Neither knew of my problem, but seeing Pat's joy was enough to join in on the fun.

"Why did my sister have to do this?" I asked, frustrated, studying the folded correspondence again.

"Your sister is an exceptional woman," Pat replied. "Most would dismiss Belle, no matter what kindness she showed 'em. It's good of her to send that letter."

"I have no problem with my sister's intentions," I said, looking back up at Pat's face. "I just wish she wouldn't have made me deliver the message in person."

Finally understanding my hesitancy, Daniel's face broke out into a large grin. "Are you afraid to go to Belle's?"

"Of course not!"

"He's a scaredy-cat!" Pat said with a laugh. I turned and found Pat chuckling to himself behind his mug, obviously amused with my discomfort.

"I am not afraid," I said, taking a drink of my ale. "I'm just ... uncomfortable. Unlike the rest of you, I have not spent the majority of my adult years in a brothel."

The humor at the table escalated from soft giggling to outright howls of laughter. "I can understand why that would make you uncomfortable," Pat said with a snicker. "All those women!" Pat faked a cold chill and ran his hands up and down his arms. "Gives me the shivers just thinkin' about it. Do you want me to go with you? I think, between the two of us, we might just make it out alive."

"Stifle it!" I hissed, standing in exasperation. I dropped a few coins on the wood table and placed my hat back on my head. "Save my seat, wiseass. I'll be right back." One thing was for sure: my sense of propriety and my language had both taken a turn for the worse since coming to Colorado.

As I moved to the exit, I heard Daniel say, "Call out if you need help. We'll round up a posse to come save you."

I rolled my eyes and continued on, hearing the laughter that arose behind me. "A bunch of damned comedians, every last one of you," I said under my breath.

Men my age went into brothels all the time. Hell, it was expected! But I had never associated with a prostitute. More importantly, however, I kept remembering Sarah's face when I first saw Belle in the street—and her comments about my being a typical man. I didn't want to be just any other man when it came to Sarah, and even though I was just going there as a promise to my sister, I couldn't help but feel uneasy.

Before leaving the hotel, I walked through the parlor on

my way outside and once again heard the sad strands of music coming from the piano. I slowly turned to find a young woman, her head bowed, gracefully playing the instrument. The petite woman never took her eyes off the keys, and her hair hid most of her face. She was small and looked to be no more than sixteen or seventeen years old. She seemed sad and out of place in the loud, energetic hotel.

"Good-bye, Mr. Mullen," Miss Patterson said loudly as she reentered the dining room with a wave. The girl at the piano looked up abruptly at the mention of my name. At that moment, I realized who she must be. A large jagged scar, still red and healing, ran from her temple to the corner of her mouth and accounted for her reluctance to look at me when I'd first walked through the door. This quiet young woman—the prostitute we had heard about when first arriving in Lone Tree—was another victim of Jack Turner. It was the briefest of moments before she realized that I was staring, and she lowered her face again, moving her hair to cover the scar.

I shifted uncomfortably and finally placed my hat on my head before going outside. I remained troubled on the way down the boardwalk toward Belle's, and my head swam with new questions about the young woman at the piano. What could have possibly led a woman like her into a brothel? What circumstances existed in her life to create such a fate? Perhaps my visit to Belle's would be worthwhile after all.

I reached the doors at Belle's, took a calming breath, and walked inside. The sitting room was much more cheerful and elegant than I would have imagined. It was a soft yellow with tasteful paintings of people and landscapes hanging from the walls. Thick velvet drapes hung from the windows, and all the furniture looked as if it came straight out of one of the finest parlors in Rittenhouse Square. A few women talked softly by one of the windows, while another sat in a rocking chair by the fire, giving a tranquil quality to the room.

"Sorry, honey," a voice said from behind me. "We don't start entertainin' for another couple hours." I turned around to find a fourth, older woman, sitting by the window with a book in her lap.

"Now, now, Millie," another woman said, standing and moving toward me, "I'd be willin' to make an exception this once." Her hips swayed back and forth in an enticing manner. "It's not often we have the privilege of entertainin' such a handsome fella."

"You know the rules, Anne Marie," Millie admonished.

"Rules were meant to be broken," said the woman still lounging on the couch.

Suddenly, the room became terribly quiet. The women stopped teasing each other and turned to focus their attention behind me. I turned my head from the ladies in the room to find Belle standing in the doorway. She was exactly as I remembered her, elegant and beautiful. Belle wore a dark blue gown made of fine silk, with her red hair pulled up, adorned with pearls and ribbons.

"Ladies," she said softly, "I am sure that our visitor is here on business, not pleasure. Isn't that right, Mr. Mullen?"

"Y-yes, ma'am," I stammered, thankful for her interruption.

"Why don't we speak in my office?" She gestured for me to follow her down the hall through two large mahogany doors. Once inside, she motioned for me to sit in one of the two chairs placed in front of her desk. Instead of going behind the desk as I expected, she sat in the chair next to me, obviously curious about my visit.

Belle took a decanter from the corner of her desk and filled two glasses with whiskey, elegantly offering me a drink. "How may I help you?" she asked, sitting back in the chair casually.

I lifted the glass to my lips, took one smell of the strong liquor, and decided against the drink. The last thing I needed was to get intoxicated in Belle's presence, and I didn't have a good track record with whiskey so far. "I'm sorry to disturb you, ma'am," I said, setting the glass back on the desk. "I promise not to take too much of your time—"

"Please," she interrupted, "call me Belle."

"All right, Belle," I said uneasily.

I was alone with the madam of a large brothel. I wanted to leave as soon as possible.

"I have come here to deliver a message from my sister, Lucy."

"Your sister?" she asked with an astonished stare. Whiskey from her glass spilled onto the desk as she grasped the glass in her hand.

"Don't you remember treating a young woman over a month ago in your upstairs rooms?" She remembered my name—she had to remember treating Lucy's wounds.

"Of course I remember your sister," she said, regaining her composure. "It's just that I never expected her to know about me or my brothel. I thought you left so that she wouldn't know where she had been."

I shifted nervously in my chair and grinned at Belle. "I thought that was best at the time," I began, "but Lucy and I have no secrets from one another. She was curious and so I told her what happened." I reached into my pocket and held out the correspondence for Belle.

She hesitated, just as James had done, but eventually took the paper and placed it in her lap. Instead of waiting to read it in private, however, she gave me one more wary look and then opened the letter and began to read.

Before leaving, I couldn't help but ask her about the woman I had seen playing the piano at the Franklin Hotel. Belle confirmed that the woman, named Melissa, was in fact the one who was attacked by Turner before I arrived in Lone Tree.

"She never really belonged here anyway," she said. "Until something else can be figured out, she'll stay at the hotel and help Miss Patterson with the cooking and cleaning."

I thought once more about Melissa playing the piano and felt the weight fall heavily on my heart. For the rest of her days, she would carry the reminder of Turner on her face. The scar would fade, but it would never be completely gone. It would stare at her each day in the looking glass. I didn't know her past, or how she came to be at Belle's, but I knew she deserved better. It seemed as if reminders of Turner's poison lingered everywhere.

<hr/>

Pat and I returned to the ranch just after dark. As we led our horses to the stable, Red met up with Pat and pulled him aside. His face was tense, and he was obviously hesitant to speak to Pat. He stared at the ground as he spoke, making calming motions with his hands. I headed toward the cabin, knowing that Red was probably upset about some ranch business, but the sight of Tommy and Will as they passed made my stomach flip. By the look in their eyes, something was terribly wrong. I turned around and followed them, no longer worried about getting involved with their private business.

"No, I will not calm down!" I heard Pat holler when Red was done. "I won't let anyone ruin everything my pa worked so hard for. Someone has to stop him, and I don't plan on waitin' another day to see him six feet in the ground!" Pat's face turned a deep crimson, almost purple, as his temper too hold of him. I had seen Pat worried when he saw Sarah in the woods, happy when he returned to his children, and sad when he was thinking about the past. But for all the time I'd spent at the ranch and in Pat's company, I had never seen him so consumed with fury.

"Pat, we've been over this a thousand times," Tommy pleaded. "It'd be suicide to hunt the man now, with winter gettin' worse by the day. We agreed to wait until the snow breaks, and that's what we're gonna do!"

"Are you talking about Jack Turner?" I asked, joining them. I had argued with the brothers repeatedly about letting Turner out of our grasp, and I always heard the same argument that they gave Pat.

"He's killin' our men and stealin' our cattle!" Pat yelled at Tommy, disregarding my question. "You might not remember what Pa went through for this land, but I do! He worked day and night, tryin' to give us a better life, and I won't allow some son of a bitch to ruin his dreams. That man has already taken too much from all of us." He stopped kicking the dirt and looked up at the four of us standing near the side of the barn. "He has taken too much from me!"

Before giving his brothers the chance to argue with him further, he turned and stomped off into the woods, cursing with every breath.

"Can someone please tell me what's going on?" I asked after several moments of silence.

"We found out this mornin' that two of our men were shot and killed at one of the line camps," Will said angrily.

"Over one hundred head of cattle are now gone, and the shack was burned."

"Pat's right then," I said, with new hope that we could go after Turner. "We need to find Turner and stop him."

Tommy slapped his hat against his leg and kicked the dirt. "No, Mike," he said with irritation. "This changes nothin'! We can't stop winter from comin', and it gets colder every day. You just got back on your feet as well. Now is not the time to go off half-cocked and fight this fight. And besides, Turner will disappear before we even get to town—it's what he always does. He baits us and then makes us waste our time and energy hunting him. We need to find a better way."

"What about baiting him instead?"

Tommy stopped fidgeting and walked up to me. He stood about a foot away and stared into my eyes. "What's on your mind?"

"Well, if Turner is always one step ahead, and he finds pleasure in your pain, why not turn the tables on him? Bait him until he cannot stand it anymore and he makes a direct attack."

Tommy started pacing back and forth as I spoke. "You're sayin' we should make him come to us?"

"Yes, but not only that. I think you should get him so filled with rage that he forgets his little game."

"How can you be sure this'll work?"

"For a man like Turner, power is everything. Take away his power and control, and you will win. Part of my job involves studying people, and if there is one thing I know, it's that Turner craves power."

Tommy took several minutes to pace and think. He absently rubbed his bristled jaw. Occasionally, he would look in the direction Pat disappeared. "I think you're on to somethin', Mike," he said. "There's plenty we need do here at the ranch to make sure we're ready. We'll wait till the time is right to even the score."

"What about Pat?"

"Pat will understand all this when he cools off a bit. We just need to give him time."

17

SETTLING IN

By the next morning, Pat was back to working the ranch without a single mention of Turner and the poison he was spreading through the area. His mood remained solemn, however, and he tended to keep to himself. Tommy and Will left early in the morning to check on the rest of the camps and place more men on guard throughout the ranch. As for the rest of the people at the main house, life went on as normal, with the exception of a few more visible firearms.

I, on the other hand, started working on a plan. One that would draw Turner out into the open and cause him to make the mistakes that were needed to finish him for good. At first it felt strange to chart the demise of a man, but whenever a doubt crept into my head, I thought about everything Sarah had told me about what happened to Pat's wife, Lilly, and to my sister. The world would be a better place without a man like him. Good with details, I spent each night studying the facts and developing a way to get through the winter while also preparing for Turner.

I fell into a routine. I woke up each day and started in the dairy shed. This was probably my favorite part of the day, as

Sarah often worked beside me. After milking the cows and teaching for a few hours, I'd spend the afternoons mending fences, splitting wood, taking Ginger out to the line camps, or performing any other task that was needed. Each night, after everyone else had retired, I sat at my desk and outlined what still needed to be done.

As the weeks passed, I also learned how to shoot, use a knife, and fight with nothing but my fists for protection. My fatigue and pain turned into renewed energy, and I looked forward to each day's work, which was unlike anything I had ever experienced—raw and deeply physical. I just couldn't get enough. Looking into the mirror as the days passed, I also noticed changes in my physical appearance. My shoulders seemed broader and my chest and back were much more defined. The physical nature of the work worked wonders on my confidence and state of mind.

The weather became colder and wetter as the winter progressed, soon making it impossible to visit the men at the far reaches of the ranch. The trail to town was also covered in a few feet of snow, making me understand why Tommy was confident that we had time to work through a plan to lure Turner to the ranch during the spring thaw.

I learned quickly that there was really no right way of doing anything. It all involved technique and skill, developed over years of practice. Whenever one of the men would try to show me something new, such as roping or shooting, anyone else in earshot would come over and give me his two cents.

When Tommy was showing me a few things with the lariat, the other men said, "That ain't right; you should hold your hand like this," and "Use your shoulder more; it'll give you a better swing." For everything I learned, there was always someone with a new opinion about how it could be done better.

The men also found great joy in harassing me about my speech and my accent. If I said something that sounded too formal to their ears, they'd pounce on the opportunity to give me a hard time. They'd prance around like idiots and attempt to imitate the people back East.

"I say, ol' chap," a young man named Sean said one afternoon in a haughty manner, "I do believe my tea has gone cold. I must amend the situation posthaste." He stuck his pinkie high in the air as he pretended to sip the tea, grimacing at its taste.

Therefore, despite my best efforts after years of education, my accent began to change, and my language slipped considerably. The only time I checked myself was while teaching the young children. It was incredibly important to show them the proper way of speaking.

The men constantly practiced roping. Whenever there was a dull moment, I would see them get out their ropes and attempt to round up anything in sight, whether it was a barrel or one another. Seeing how fast some of them moved with the lariat, and the skill with which they roped a calf, made me confident that the men who'd assaulted me worked on the ranch. A small shiver went up my spine as I watched two men rope a calf's legs in mere seconds and then pounce on him to finish the job. I looked down at my arms again, as I often did, examining the marks of my attack still lingering in brown rings around my wrists.

Eventually, I regained some of my freedom and privacy. I never allowed myself to get into a position where I didn't have a way out, however, and the awareness of my surroundings was acute. I watched the men without raising too much attention, and I made mental notes whenever something didn't add up.

Shooting was the one thing that came rather naturally

for me. Even though the men would often argue about the best type of gun or how to hold it properly, I soon realized the pistol was my strength. With practice, I hit almost anything I aimed at, even from long distances. Even Will, the best shooter I had ever seen, seemed impressed. It came to me easily, without a struggle. After learning how to shoot, I strapped a gun to my right hip and kept it on me at all times.

While working near the corral, a cowpuncher approached me with his hat in his hands. "Mike ... I mean, Mr. Mullen, sir?" He came closer. I recognized him as Sulley from around the ranch and knew that Amanda, one of the girls I taught, was his little girl.

"Why don't you just call me Mike?" I asked. I still didn't like the name, but it had spread around the ranch like wildfire, so I had given up trying to get folks to change.

"Well, I'd like to talk to you about yer classes." He was shuffling back and forth nervously, as if he wanted to flee at the first opportunity. Sulley was one of the older hands on the ranch, and he was always kind. I knew his little girl meant more to him than anything else in the world.

"Is something the matter?" I asked, thinking there might be something wrong with Amanda, or that he was unhappy with my teaching methods.

"Oh, no," he said. "My little one sure does enjoy yer classes. It's just ... well ... I was wonderin' ... " He looked around cautiously and then stood closer to me. "I hoped maybe you'd help me the way you helped her."

"Why don't you come inside and tell me what you mean." I gestured toward the stable.

He followed me inside, but it took him several minutes to start talking again. I thought he'd changed his mind about asking me to help him, but he finally leaned closer and said, "It's just that I have kin I ain't seen in a long time, and I'd like to be able to write 'em and tell 'em how I'm doin'." He looked down and twirled his hat in his hands. "In the past, Sarah's helped me with the writin', but I thought maybe you could teach me to write so I could give my kin a letter written in my own hand."

"I see." I hadn't thought much of the possibility that some of the men on the ranch had little education. "Are you able to read," I asked cautiously, "or is it just the writing you would like help with?"

"I don't read neither," he said keeping his head low.

"I don't think it would be a problem if you started coming by in the evenings. I'm sure you'll learn quickly and soon be able to write your own letters home." I patted him on the shoulder and smiled to encourage him.

"D'ya think … I mean … will it be hard on my Amanda, knowing I need yer help?" His face wore a look of concern.

"Knowing Amanda, I'm sure she'll be delighted," I said reassuringly. "She is proud of you, and I think she'll be even more proud knowing that you want to improve your mind. I hope to see you tomorrow night."

"Well, that'd be great, Mike. Let me just run it past Pat and Red to make sure it's all right, and I'll maybe see ya tomorrow evenin'." He seemed much happier as he sauntered away with his shoulders straight and his gait confident.

Pat wholly supported the idea, and within two weeks, I was teaching Sulley and three other ranch hands after dinner. Since it was the winter, they had the time to end each day with a lesson; however, during the spring roundup and the summer, I doubted they'd be able to continue.

At the end of another incredibly long day, while sitting on the porch of the main house, Pat stood and watched the horizon. Several other men followed suit. The sound of horse hooves approaching the ranch reached my ears. Four of Pat's men had surrounded another man on a horse, and they all had their guns drawn. Hank, one of the men guarding the gate, rode ahead and told us that a man—a very large man—had been found on the road asking about Lucy and me.

I focused on the approaching horses again and realized that they weren't exaggerating when they'd described the man as large. He made the full-grown horse he wa,s riding look like a pony under his bulk. He wasn't so much heavy as he was large in build, tall with broad shoulders. He also looked as if he'd been to hell and back. His clothes were wet, and ice was crusted around his trousers near his boots. The snow on the trail was much too deep for anyone to be traveling, unless he had important business—or a death wish.

Hank told Pat that the stranger refused to answer any questions as soon as he saw their pistols. I looked him over as they rode up to the main house, studying him closely. His clothes were in rags, and his skin dark from days of travel and dirt from the trail. The man had a huge black beard, and his hair looked mangled under his large hat, with twigs and leaves buried in the tangled mass. Something familiar clicked in my brain, making me smile when he looked in my direction. The only man I knew that could claim that man's size was—

"Arthur!" Lucy hollered from the top of the steps of our small cabin, before crossing the lawn with her skirt hiked up as she ran. She threw her arms around him as he got off his horse. He picked her up as if she weighed no more than a feather and swung her around.

It was an unbelievable sight to witness my sister forgetting all her inhibitions and fears when she saw Arthur. It was as if she'd returned to the sister I knew in Philadelphia, full of joy and life. The Donnelly brothers all looked stunned as they watched the transformation. Will's face creased into a large grin when he heard Lucy speak for the first time.

"Arthur?" I walked toward them, examining him closer. "Is that really you?"

"Aye, lad, it is." He hadn't taken his eyes off Lucy, and even though he looked tired and beaten, his broad smile was unmistakable through his black beard. When I stepped closer to him, I shook his hand heartily and then gave him a great bear hug, which plainly surprised the hell out of him.

"You can't know the pleasure I'm feelin' to see you both safe again," he said in the deep Irish accent I'd missed so much.

"How about you, Arthur?" I asked. "Are you all right?"

"Aye, I'm feeling grand, I am." He glanced back at Lucy. "I met with a few ruffians in my travels, however, who found it necessary to attempt to shoot me and steal me horse."

"Who would be daft enough to cross you, Arthur?" None of us could stop grinning.

He gave me a look of disbelief. "While I did have the compassion to leave them alive, I'll guarantee you they won't be up to stealin' anything for quite some time. The marshal has them waiting in a cell in town." His smile returned, making his white teeth visible through his thick black beard.

Pat and his men remained frozen, standing nearby but not interrupting. They were obviously wary of the new stranger but kept their distance and let us catch up. The ranch hands, the Donnellys, and even Red, were clearly in awe over Arthur's size. I had told them he was a large man, but it took seeing to believe that I had not exaggerated. He was taller and outweighed every other man on the ranch. Red, who was closest in size to Arthur, leaned against the post and watched him closely, obviously attempting to size the man up and discern his temperament.

I finally turned around and introduced Arthur to everyone. Pat placed a hand on Arthur's back, welcomed him to the ranch, and led him to the house. Tommy followed and asked May to set up a room for Arthur, while Gus shuffled into the kitchen to put together a meal.

"Let's get you settled," Pat said. "You look like you could use some food and some rest."

"And a good long bath," I added with a laugh before Pat ushered him down the hall. Arthur looked at me with surprise, making me truly realize how much my demeanor must have changed since leaving the city.

After Arthur cleaned up and ate, Lucy and I refused to leave his side until he retired that night. His mere presence made each of us feel as comfortable and secure as we had while growing up. The family and ranch hands left us alone in the parlor while we talked late into the night, getting to know one another again.

He looked at Lucy often, as if to ascertain whether she'd really survived her capture. I could tell he felt guilt over her disappearance. The sadness caused his eyes to darken and worry lines to form on his brow.

"Sweet lass," he said softly, "I truly am sorry for failing you. I should've been more careful."

Lucy looked down and shook her head. "Michael and I have talked about this for a while now," she said. "No one is at fault but the men who took me. You aren't responsible, Arthur, and I don't want you to feel bad about anything that happened."

He looked at me warily, while I nodded in agreement

with my sister and patted him on the back. "We're just really glad to see you again."

"It seems you two are in a spot o' trouble—more than you led on." His tone had changed.

"What do you mean?"

"When I arrived in town, some lads tried to recruit me to join their gang. They're gatherin' supplies and men to come after you as soon as winter breaks. They were daft enough to share some of their plans with me since I was a newcomer to the area."

Lucy paled slightly, and I grasped her hand in reassurance before asking Arthur to continue.

"I finally got rid o' them by agreein' to meet up the next day," he said. "I took me horse and left in the wee hours of the morn. I wasn't certain you were both safe, and your letter hadn't mentioned any danger. So, despite warnings from town and me own better judgment, I left Lone Tree and made my way to this ranch as fast as that wee horse could move."

"How did you end up in this condition?" I asked, looking him over again. "You look like you've been to hell and back."

"Well, I have to admit I am unfamiliar with these thick woods, and I got a wee bit lost on my way here. I spent a few lonely nights in those woods, sleepin' in the mud and snow. Then I met a strange mountain man named Jules, who was travelin' on a white mule. I took it as a sign I had better ask for help before I starved or froze to death. He was a right good soul who led me back on the path to you."

Although he smiled warmly and looked relaxed, Arthur looked exhausted, even with clean clothes and a shave. His eyelids became heavy as we talked, and it was easy to see how desperately he needed rest. Lucy and I excused ourselves and told him to meet us at the cabin in the morning so we could all have a private breakfast together.

"Thank you, both," he said, standing slowly.

"Arthur," I said, "it's so good to have you here. I missed your Irish bones, old man!"

He chuckled. "'Tis good to see you as well, lad, and to hear that Western accent. 'Tis strange ... but good."

━━━━●《❉》●━━━━

Unlike me, Arthur seemed to take to the ranch like a bear in the woods. He was so easygoing and comfortable in his surroundings that the men took a liking to him right away.

The day after he arrived, Arthur began working head-to-head with the hardest workers at the ranch. More than anything, he loved working outdoors and with the horses. He had more life in his eyes than I had ever seen. It became hard to imagine him living in the city as he did with my father and our family for so many years.

Arthur joined me each night to discuss the trouble coming and how best to handle it. Arthur shared what he'd heard while in town, which helped the situation greatly. Pat, Tommy, and Will were soon involved, and our meetings were moved to the main house because there was more room. Pat was pleased with the idea of causing Turner pain by turning the tables on him, but he remained impatient for it all to end. He couldn't wait to face the bastard once and for all.

As for Arthur, he seemed to be at peace being near family again. He watched Lucy closely but it was clear that he soon realized we were among good men at the ranch, and that Lucy was well cared for.

"Arthur," I said as we worked side by side one day, "when did you decide to come to Colorado?"

"As soon as your aunt received your letter from the ranch, I knew it was time to leave," he replied. "She decided to leave and stay with her sister, and without you and Lucy, my services were no longer needed."

"But what made you decide to travel all the way out here?" I asked, still amazed that he was standing next to me again. "You could've gone anywhere, or done anything."

He paused in his work and motioned toward the small cabin where Lucy and I had lived for the past few months. "I needed to make sure the two of you were safe."

"Whatever the reason," I said with a smile, "I'm glad you're here, and I hope you decide to stay for a while."

"No need to worry about that," he said, grabbing a shovel. "I've no plans to leave." He swung the shovel over his shoulder and started heading toward the fence line near the back of the stable.

I picked up my step to try to keep up. "What do you mean? You want to live here?"

Arthur stopped and looked out at the forest and the valley surrounding the ranch. "Aye. I got a letter from your pa just before his death," Arthur said respectfully. "He'd asked me to protect you and Lucy at all costs. I didn't understand his anxiety until Lucy was taken from us. Now that the two of you are together again and safe, I intend to honor his last request."

"But what about you?" I asked. "Will you be happy here? I don't even know where Lucy and I will end up."

Arthur smiled as he kept his eyes on my worried face. "I am happy, lad," he said, "and you won't be goin' anywhere."

"Wha—"

"You and Lucy belong here as much as the Donnelly clan," he interrupted.

"How can you possibly know that?" I asked. "I've been

agonizing over our future for weeks now, and after spending a few days here, you know what I'll do?"

"Aye."

"Even if that's the case," I said, suddenly hoping he was right, "it doesn't mean you are obligated to stay here with us."

"You two kids are the only family I've ever had." He looked away.

Understanding finally dawned. He was right: we were a family. He had watched Lucy and me grow from children into adults. If anything, he was as much a father to me as my own had been.

As soon as Arthur stood up straight and turned around, I grabbed him and hugged him, swiftly choking up with emotion. Arthur's face was filled with emotion as well, but he tried to hide it by pushing me away.

"Enough standing around, old man," I said. "Let's get some work done." As I walked away, I turned around to find Arthur grinning at me and shaking his head.

18

CHRISTMAS GIVING

"Do you remember the last time we were to-gether like this?" Lucy asked as we prepared for Christmas dinner at the main house. "I was anxiously waiting to go downstairs to the party, while you were wallowing in your own self-pity."

I turned from the mirror and glared at Lucy. "Aunt Olivia's party?"

Lucy nodded, looking around the room. "Things are a bit different this time, though, aren't they?" Lucy's face brightened considerably at the memory. "Last time you were dreading going downstairs, and this time I see how excited you are."

"Our lives certainly are different now." I turned back to the mirror to finish dressing before going downstairs. Lucy was right. I had been excited about dinner since Pat first mentioned the large party they traditionally put together for the ranch hands and the family. I used to hate getting dressed up for social gatherings, but that was when I dreaded the people with whom I'd have to socialize.

"Michael," Lucy continued, stepping into her shoes, "I've been watching you closely, and I honestly can no longer imagine you in the city. You certainly have changed in the last few months."

I turned to look at her carefully. "It's strange, isn't it?" I said with a chuckle, slipping on my jacket. "I am completely awkward out here, but I somehow feel ... alive."

"I know what you mean," she replied. "I miss Aunt Olivia terribly, but I no longer miss the life I once led. I definitely miss working at the hospital, and the women's organizations I worked with, but all the rules and propriety somehow seem silly now."

I agreed completely, but unlike Lucy, I had always felt that way.

"None of that nonsense has a place out here," she continued. "The people work harder than I ever imagined possible, and they are some of the best people I've ever known."

"You amaze me, Lucy," I said, staring at her in the mirror. "You have more strength than ten women combined." I continued watching her, reviewing her words, and I noticed all the external differences in her as well. Instead of wearing a gown with that horrendous corset that made her sit unnaturally rigid, she wore a pale pink gown that flowed around her waist and ankles in a way that looked casual yet elegant.

Switching my gaze from Lucy to myself, I also remembered the hated starched cravat and the formal attire we had to wear on any outing. That Christmas evening, I wore navy trousers, my best boots, a clean white shirt, and a dark waistcoat under my jacket. While they considered it formal attire at the ranch, the clothes were much more casual than Lucy and I were used to.

Seeing Lucy across the room tapping her foot reaffirmed my belief that she was as excited as I was. No fear or uneasiness could be seen on her face, and her hands no longer fiddled nervously with her skirt. Her cheeks were slightly flushed, and her eyes shined with anticipation.

"One thing I definitely do not miss," I said, "is Aunt Olivia's constant matchmaking."

"Imagine if she were here now," Lucy said, moving to the door with a wicked grin on her face. "She'd have you and Sarah matched up in no time."

I raised my eyebrows and frowned at the mention of something going on between Sarah and me. "Lucy—"

"She'd see the look in your eyes when you watch Sarah," she interrupted, "and she'd know she finally achieved her goal."

I opened the door, suddenly wishing to end the conversation, and ushered her into the hallway with a warning glance. Before reaching the bottom of the stairs, I finally muttered, "I *do not* have a *look*." She stopped at the banister and turned with a knowing smile before she grasped my arm to lead me to the parlor.

The entire Donnelly clan was already assembled in the large room off the main hall, and Pat's children were running helter-skelter through the house. Pat's efforts to make them presentable were wasted in approximately ten minutes. One side of Eddie's shirt was hanging out of his trousers, and Little Bittie's hair had fallen down over one side of her head, leaving a blue ribbon dangling from a few neat strands. She also had a gaping hole in her stocking from running around barefoot, and Laura continued to chase her around, scolding her on her behavior and appearance. Good old Laura, always trying to help make everything perfect.

As we entered the parlor, I saw Pat and Tommy standing near the fireplace, talking about the work they needed to start in the morning, and Will was charming sweet May by the window, making her blush like a young girl. Then I heard the beginning strands of a song drift into the air, and I turned toward the piano. I thought my heart would stop at that moment.

"Oh ... holy ... Jesus," I muttered to myself, hearing a slight groan escape the back of my throat. I stood in the doorway, too stunned to move until Lucy let out a small yelp on my right side.

She leaned close to me and stood on her toes to whisper. "Michael, let go or you'll break my hand."

Snapping out of my stupor, I glanced down and noticed that I was squeezing Lucy's hand so tightly that her fingers had turned a deep scarlet. I quickly let go and muttered my apology before looking back at the piano.

Sarah sat on the piano stool in a shimmering ivory dress that cascaded down her body and onto the floor around her. A burgundy sash crisscrossed her waist, knotting in the back, hanging down to the hem of her skirt. The front of her hair had been pulled up on her head, but her brown locks glistened down her back to her waist. She was a vision.

Lucy leaned toward me again and whispered softly in my ear. "You most certainly do have a look when it comes to Sarah." Before I could respond, she giggled and moved into the room toward Arthur. Everyone exclaimed about how lovely she looked and how nicely I cleaned up, but nothing really registered. I entered the room and greeted everyone I saw. I picked up a cup of punch to keep my hands busy, but my mind remained focused on the corner where Sarah played Christmas songs on the piano.

I had just taken a drink of punch when Red entered the room. He slapped me on the back, causing me to choke on the liquid and spill some on the floor. The ranch hands followed him through the entryway, heading toward the drinks on the sideboard. Before long, the house was filled with people mingling, drinking, and laughing.

As the night wore on, Sarah's wholesome Christmas songs turned into raucous ranching and mining songs that all the men from the bunkhouse enjoyed thoroughly. They hooted and hollered as she sang one distasteful song after another. Leaning against the railing with a smile on my face, I could tell that Sarah enjoyed it as much as the men did. Her face shined with joy and enthusiasm every time she heard the men's happy laughter and loud whistles. I imagine it was her Christmas gift to all of them, so far from town and many far from home.

Dinner was served buffet style in the dining room, allowing each person to come and go as he or she wished. Gus busily rushed in and out, making sure every bowl remained filled and every dirty dish had been put away. After a while, however, Sarah insisted that Gus stop fussing over the food and the state of the kitchen and join the party.

A loud cheer sounded from one corner of the parlor, where Arthur entertained the young ranch hands with stories of his past and jokes about Ireland. Pat held Eddie by his waist upside down, making him beg for mercy as Tommy tortured him into eternal giggles. Laura and May sat on the sofa with their heads close, looking serious as they secretly conversed.

A small hand tugged on my trousers as I surveyed the room, and I looked down to find Bittie looking up at me expectantly. "Mikey?"

"Yes, sweetie?" I bent down, picked her up, and settled her on my hip.

"Where's Sarah?"

I looked toward the piano and around the room, realizing that Sarah had disappeared. "I don't know, but can I help you with something?"

"I lost my shoe."

Laughing quietly, I walked with her through the room to help her find it. After picking up a small pink slipper from behind the door, I moved to a chair and settled Bittie on my lap to help her put it back on.

"I like you, Mikey," she said sweetly, making no move to get off my lap once I was finished.

"Thank you," I returned. "You're not so bad yourself."

For the next half hour, she talked nonstop about everything under the moon. She asked me a million questions about my childhood, and about Lucy and my family. Finally, after wearing herself out, she rested her head on my chest and slowly drifted into a deep sleep.

⚓((◉))⚓

The ranch hands left the house, along with Red and Arthur, to go to the bunkhouse and begin their Christmas tradition of playing poker until dawn.

Will pulled out the checkerboard and ushered Lucy over to the window to begin another game. "You may think you can beat me, Lucy," Will said confidently, "but your beginner's luck is about to run out." Since he'd taught her the game, Lucy won much more than she lost, and Will had started to get more competitive.

Lucy shook her head back and forth, laughing. After moving into relative privacy, but before Will sat down behind the board, Lucy placed a hand on his arm and leaned over to him. "Thank you for looking out for me, Will."

He stared at her for a long moment with a blank look on his face and a visible lump in his throat. It was the first time she had ever spoken to him directly. He appeared delightfully stunned.

"Thank you for taking care of me after I was injured," she continued, while he remained speechless. "I wanted you to know how much it means to me, even if I don't always show it."

"Ahh, Lucy," he said quietly, showing off that charming smile while placing his hands on his heart. "You don't know what a great gift this is for me."

Lucy blushed slightly and sat next to him at the table, the checkerboard suddenly forgotten.

"Does this mean I've gained your trust after all this time?" he asked.

"I've always known I could trust you," she replied." "I just ... well, the person I haven't trusted is myself."

Will leaned in, resting his elbows on the wooden table to look closer into her eyes. "I don't reckon I understand."

"I don't expect you to," she said assertively, "and I don't think I can explain it right now, but I wanted to make sure you knew that it isn't a lack of trust in you that makes me hesitant to speak."

Will continued to watch her with a puzzled expression but didn't push her for more. They had made progress that night, and he clearly didn't want to risk ruining it. He clapped his hands together and rubbed them briskly. "So what do ya say we start this here game?" He started placing the pieces on the old board.

Lucy nodded and smiled. "You're on."

<hr/>

Sarah returned to the parlor several minutes later with a package in her hand. She noticed Bittie resting in my lap with her head on my chest, and she smiled. She moved over to Pat and motioned in my direction as she whispered in his ear. After seeing his daughter asleep in my arms, he motioned Eddie next to him and told Laura it was time for bed. May stood up to help, but he gestured for her to relax. Pat's final stop was to take Bittie gently from my arms before he went upstairs with all his kids.

As soon as Pat disappeared, Tommy escaped out the front door to join the other men in the bunkhouse. Sarah approached, sitting next to me on the couch near my chair.

"Have you liked the party, Michael?" she asked pleasantly. "I hope Bittie didn't bother you too much."

"No, she was very sweet," I replied, "and the party has been great. I don't remember ever being at a party where I felt this at ease. Your family really knows how to make others feel at home."

"What was Christmas like back home?"

I scrunched up my face and thought for the briefest of moments. "Elegant and classy … but most of all boring and uncomfortable."

Sarah tilted her head back and laughed. She had the most amazing laugh. It was soft and rich, and she never put a hand over her mouth to stifle it. I loved her for that.

"I wanted to talk to you before the party wound down and you and Lucy returned to your cabin." She handed me a small package, wrapped with blue silk. I looked at her suspiciously as I repositioned myself in my chair, the package in my lap. "I had something made for you in town for Christmas." She rested her chin on her forearms on the arm of the couch as she watched me open the package.

"You had something made?" I asked stupidly. I untied the twine, removing it and unfolding the silk. The last fold revealed a large leather journal with gold initials, *MWM*, in the corner. I fanned through the pages and ran my hand over the smooth leather cover, resting my thumb along the gold embossed letters.

"Is something wrong?" she asked, looking at my face. I had been silent for several minutes, staring at the gift. I had kept a journal back home, but I had forgotten it in my haste to leave the city.

"No," I said quietly, "nothing is wrong." I didn't tell her that the journal reminded me of my journey to Colorado and reading my father's journals. There was so little of his life I really knew about ... and so many questions still left unanswered.

"You look so sad," she said, resting her hand on my arm. "Was it a mistake to give you this?"

She was such a sweetheart. "Absolutely not," I said, standing up to sit next to her on the couch. "It's the best gift I could've hoped for. Thank you."

"Then why do you look so sad?" she asked, apparently not convinced.

Everyone else in the room was busy talking or playing checkers, and I didn't think anyone could overhear our conversation. I looked back down at the journal. "Did I ever tell you that my father kept a journal?" I asked quietly.

"No."

"When Lucy first disappeared, my aunt Olivia gave me his journals in hopes they would hold the answers to where she had been taken. I had never read them before; I didn't even know they existed until that day."

She shifted and turned in her seat in order to see my face better as I spoke. "When I read the first several journals, they were all about Joseph and your ranch. I wish he would have told me more when he was still alive—perhaps I could have come out here with him."

She smiled but didn't interrupt.

"Anyway, when I was on the train headed to Colorado, I read the rest of his journals, and I found something written in them that I have had a hard time accepting."

"What is it?" she asked.

"My father was gone from home most of the time, and I often resented his time away from the family. In all those years, however, I never doubted his love for my mother. They were perfect together, which was one of the reasons I found it so hard each time he would leave home again." I kept my eyes focused on the journal in my hands. "But when he returned, I'd see the love between my mother and father and quickly forgive his absence."

"He did love your mother very much," Sarah said quietly. "He talked about her all the time and couldn't wait to bring her here."

"You don't have to cover for him, Sarah," I said, looking back at her face. "I know now that he had a relationship with a woman at the ranch." I paused and lowered my eyes. "I believe now that she was the same woman Lucy mentioned when she told you about Turner ... and the woman Pat refuses to discuss. Everything leads back to Maggie, which means that it also leads to my father."

Sarah took a deep breath and placed her hand on my chin to make sure she had my complete attention. "Your father did not have an affair, Michael," she said seriously.

"How can you be so sure?" I asked. "I read the journals, and there's no other explanation."

"I promised Pat I would never speak of her again," she said in a whisper. "Your father was *not* unfaithful to your mother with Maggie."

A sudden irritation grew in my stomach as I remembered all the times I'd attempted to get information from one of the Donnelly brothers, especially about Maggie.

Thinking back to what I'd been through, my anger spiked. "So you and your family knew why Lucy was taken, but you didn't tell me?"

"Shush, Michael," Sarah said, placing a finger to her mouth. She took a long look around the room to make sure no one was listening. "All I know is that Turner wants to find Maggie. And that doesn't make sense because the last time we saw him, she was with him."

My anger faded, and I leaned in close. "Sarah, I have gone over this a thousand times in my head. If my father didn't have an affair, then what is his connection to Maggie? Who is she, and why won't Pat talk about her?" I grasped her hand. "Please ... I need to know."

"Maggie's mother died when she was young, and when her father died, she came to live here at the ranch with her sister ... Lilly. She knew my father and yours since she was a young girl. She's only a few years older than you are. Your father and Maggie were quite close—he was like a father to her as she grew up. What you read was most likely the love he felt for a woman that was as close to him as you or Lucy."

I remained silent for several minutes as I contemplated her words.

"Michael," Sarah murmured, "when did your father's journals end?"

"A few years before his death," I replied. "I imagine he had his last journal with him when he died."

"That explains a lot," she said. "If you read about his life here, and everything that happened in that last year, you would understand everything much better. Your father stayed at the ranch after your mother's death because he refused to give up his dream of the two of them living here together. He'd worked so hard to get everything ready for her, but your mother's illness became so advanced that she couldn't travel. She was always his focus, Michael."

"I don't understand." I rubbed my temples, which had started to pound. "If all this is true, then why did Pat get so angry when I mentioned Maggie's name ... and why did you hide her existence from me? Did you feel I wouldn't understand?"

Sarah was quiet for so long that I figured she wasn't going to answer my question. She took a deep breath and looked me directly in the eyes. "Maggie was married to Jack Turner—she was his wife."

She paused and waited for the shock of her statement to sink in before continuing. "Pat won't talk about Maggie because he thinks she betrayed her sister and our family. He believes she is the reason Turner killed Lilly."

"How could she be responsible for Lilly's death?"

"Lilly and Maggie spent several years on the Lazy D Ranch. When Lilly turned twenty, she married Pat," she said slowly. "Whenever your father came to the ranch, he made sure that he made time to spend with Maggie since she felt a bit displaced by her sister's marriage. Your father took her under his wing, so to speak, and helped to show her a new world, beyond the sadness from her past. But when he had to leave, she felt lonely. I think that she saw Pat and Lilly's relationship and wanted something similar in her own life."

"So Turner entered her life."

She rested her hand on my arm near my elbow. "Yes. She was young and naive when she first met Jack," she said slowly. "When he proposed, she jumped in with both feet. She later told me that everything changed on their wedding night. Turner started drinking heavily and began beating Maggie. The more he beat her, the harder she tried to please him. She would try to hide the bruises and scars, but we all knew what was happening. We tried to talk some sense into her and get her to leave while she had the chance, but she kept thinking he would change.

"Jack had always been extremely jealous of Pat and his relationship with Lilly. Pat had money, security, a family that loved him … and he had Lilly. Jack was obsessed with Pat and Lilly. More often than not, he would fly into a rage over something to do with Pat. His jealousy and anger continued to boil over with each passing day. Jack's ranch was struggling, and he began drinking more often."

"So she harmed her sister to please her husband? That doesn't make sense."

"I don't think that is what happened, but none of us will ever know unless she returns. Only your father knew what really happened, and he died before he could tell us." Sarah fidgeted more with her dress, and her hands shook a bit as she continued. "When Maggie found out she was pregnant, she decided to leave Jack. She knew that it was no longer just herself she needed to protect, and that seemed to make all the difference. She sent me a message asking if she could return, but Jack found out about it and beat her senseless. We found her there the next morning and took her to the ranch to heal."

I rubbed my chest over my heart, remembering how Lucy looked in that small cabin in the woods. I couldn't imagine a woman staying with a man like that.

"Lilly and I stayed with Maggie when she went into labor and gave birth to a beautiful baby girl. She named her Beth, after her mother." A tear ran gently down Sarah's cheek, without her seeming to notice. I reached up and gently removed it with my finger.

"That's the last time I saw her. Lilly went to the cabin one morning to check on her and never returned. When Pat went looking for her, he found Lilly dead in the house, and both Turner and Maggie were gone."

"Didn't anyone go looking for them?" I asked. "Maybe Maggie was taken against her will."

"Pat went after them, but he was found later in the forest, having been shot several times. He barely made it. He lived with Six Moons for some time while he recovered."

"What could have happened to Maggie?"

"No one knows. But when Pat returned, he was filled with hatred toward her and refused to have her name spoken in his presence. In his mind, Maggie is responsible for whatever happened that day."

"Thank you for talking to me, Sarah. This changes things."

The two of us sat in silence for some time, while I tried to absorb all the new information. I'd had everything wrong. My father wasn't having an affair. He was trying to help a woman in need. But why did she leave with Turner?

Sarah nudged me in the side with her finger to regain my attention. I glanced back in her direction to find her smiling at me. "So ... do you like your gift or should I send it back?" she asked, trying to lighten the mood. "Mr. Linton will be upset if he hears you don't like his work, so I'll just have to find someone else with your initials to befriend."

"No." I gripped the journal tighter. "You can tell Mr. Linton that I was incredibly pleased with my gift." I looked down sheepishly. "I wasn't sure if I should do this earlier, but now I think it will be all right."

I stood and went to the corner of the room where I had placed Sarah's gift earlier in the evening. "Sorry about the wrapping." It was wrapped in plain brown paper, not nearly as elegant as the silk wrap on Sarah's gift to me. I held out the package and placed it in Sarah's hands. "I can't take the credit," I continued. "Lucy made this in our cabin and insisted it would be perfect for you."

Feeling suddenly embarrassed about giving her the gift, I desperately wanted to snatch it back and pretend I'd never brought it to the party. I hadn't ever given a woman a gift before, unless she was a family member, but Lucy had assured me it would be all right.

"I am sure that whatever it is, it's lovely." Sarah smiled brightly and unwrapped the package. I sat nervously next to her. "And if Lucy made it, then ..." Sarah's voice trailed off as she pulled the dark purple and blue shawl from the wrapping and held it up. Her face lit up as she draped it over her shoulders. "It's lovely," she said softly. "Thank you."

That's when I noticed Lucy smiling my way. The expression on Sarah's face had clearly shown her that the shawl was perfect. I turned back toward Sarah and placed my hand over hers, pleased that I had listened to my sister.

"Merry Christmas, Sarah."

19

A WOMAN'S CHARMS

I left the corral after an hour of my daily punishment from Tommy. The man was as solid as a brick and showed no mercy during our fights. Even Arthur egged him on. I couldn't wait for the day when the crowd rooted for me to win instead of Tommy.

I had gotten better at dodging the devastating blows from his powerful punches, but rubbing my jaw, I could feel those few that had hit their mark. Each day it got a little better, and I even managed now and then to cause Tommy some pain, which gave me a great sense of joy.

On my way down the path, I noticed several of the ranch hands talking near the bunkhouse. Josiah, the one man I knew who disliked my presence at the ranch, stopped what he was doing and started to follow me as I passed. He approached me with a scowl on his face.

"I've seen you with Sarah," he said in a gruff voice.

I continued past the bunkhouse and toward the cabin.

"She ain't for you." He placed a hand on my shoulder to stop me. I turned to look him directly in the eye. After an hour of fighting, I was sore and tired, but I was more than willing to find the energy to fight this man.

"What do you want?" I stood close to him and made him look up at me as I spoke.

"Is yer hearin' bad? I said she ain't for you. Sarah's spoken for so just keep away from her, ya hear?" I could feel his breath on my face.

Anger boiled up inside me, and not just because the man in front of me could very well be one of the men who'd thrashed me in the stable. "I think I'll let Sarah decide when she is spoken for, sir. Now let me by!" I leaned over him in an intimidating manner, allowing my height to show the advantage.

"Hey, Mike!" I heard over my shoulder. I didn't take my eyes off the man in front of me until he looked away and took a few steps backward.

"I'll be watchin' you," he mumbled as he quickly walked away.

"Hey, Mike, come up to the house for a bit, will ya!" Tommy hollered again from behind me. I took a deep breath and turned around as Josiah joined his friends.

"What's goin' on?" Tommy asked, watching me closely as I approached the house.

"Just a slight disagreement." I could hear someone playing the piano inside, and I hoped it was Sarah, safely in the house.

The confrontation was disturbing, but I also felt a little relief. At least I finally understood what had happened. It wasn't about Lucy or Jack Turner. I no longer had any doubts in my mind about who had attacked me and why. The man was jealous.

The only thing I didn't know was where to go from there. Could I just allow the man to get away with treating me like that? If not, what were my options? I knew that as long as Josiah was at the ranch, he remained a threat, but I needed more time.

Another thing I needed to know was who else had helped Josiah in the stable that day. He wasn't alone, and even though I had my suspicions, I remained unsure about the other man. One thing I did know was that I was getting closer. I knew who to watch and why. Even though I wasn't sure of Sarah's affections, I had a feeling deep in my gut that she wasn't interested in the man who'd confronted me. I hadn't ever thought it would be about Sarah, but now that I did, I was determined to make sure she remained safe.

Tommy and I sat on the porch and listened to the sweet music from the parlor inside. The night was fair, and I felt at home talking with Sarah's brother. After some time, Pat and Will joined us outside. It was the first time all day we'd been allowed a few minutes of peace. I decided not to tell them right away about Josiah, as they would most definitely take the matter into their own hands. Instead, I would wait and watch. He wouldn't get the best of me again.

——— ((•)) ———

A few days later, as Will and I returned from the stable, we came around the corner to find Josiah talking to Sarah on the porch steps. He had his hat in his hands, and he shuffled his feet back and forth as he gazed at her.

"Come on now, Sarah," he said, in a much different tone than he used with me. "All I'm askin' for is a walk."

"I'm sorry, Josiah, but I really can't," she said, trying to move past him, broom in hand. He came closer to her and placed his hand on the post in a possessive manner, blocking Sarah's way off the porch.

"You and I were startin' somethin', I know it."

"I don't know what you thought was going on," she

said, looking at him sternly, "but I don't think of you that way. I thought we were friends. I'm sorry if you feel differently."

"It's 'cause of that tenderfoot, ain't it?" He took a step up, closer to Sarah. All the kindness was gone from his voice and eyes as he approached her.

I started to move forward to intervene, but Will stopped me with his arm. There was danger in his eyes as he watched Josiah threaten his only sister, but he stayed where he was.

"This has nothing to do with him," she said, raising her voice. "Now please leave me alone!"

"Yer a liar! This has everything to do with him. Ever since he came here, you spend all yer time with him. What makes him so darn better than the rest of us?"

Sarah backed up and clenched her fists as Josiah took his last step onto the porch. When he made his next move, a blade whipped through the air and struck the post, inches from his hand. In a split second, the man halted his pursuit and froze in place, staring at Will's knife.

We came out of the shadows and walked up the steps toward Sarah and her overzealous admirer. Will glared at Josiah and surely saw every bit of fear that existed within the man. "Leave," Will said. "If I find you near my sister again, I'll aim that knife at your heart. You're no longer welcome at this ranch."

Josiah removed his hand from the post and rubbed his hands together in front of him, obviously glad he still had all his extremities intact. "Come on, Will," he whined. "You know I ain't meanin' no harm."

Will removed his knife from the post and held it under Josiah's chin, silently daring him to continue. Without further argument, Josiah flew down the steps, glaring at me with fury and pure revulsion while heading toward the stable. I suspected things were far from over between the two of us.

"Are you all right?" I asked Sarah, watching Josiah disappear around the corner.

Her face was flushed and she seemed incredibly uncomfortable. Whether it was from the altercation with Josiah or the thought of us overhearing the conversation, I couldn't tell.

Will gave her an odd look. "How long has he been bothering you?" he asked, putting his knife away.

"Not long." Sarah's gaze remained lowered toward the wood planks of the deck, while she swept away the last of the dirt into Will's path.

"Sarah, I told you to let one of us know if anyone caused you trouble." He turned toward the stable and looked around the ranch. He kicked the post when he turned back toward Sarah. "You have to be careful, damn it!"

"I can handle myself with these men, Will," she said, raising her head to glare at Will.

"I know it, but not all men are like Josiah. Some are downright hateful creatures who could do you harm." He stood next to her and then began to speak softly. "Please, from now on, just let one of us know, if for no other reason than to watch you wallop him." He grinned and wiggled his eyebrows up and down, trying to get her to smile.

Finally, one corner of her mouth went up as she pushed him out of her way. "Fine," she said, "now will you get out of my way so I can get back to work?"

Will winked at me and headed back down the steps. I followed him toward the stable. "I'm glad you were here, Will," I said. "It's good to know Sarah has people looking out for her."

"Don't think for a moment Sarah couldn't handle Josiah,"

Will said. "Even though I didn't give her the chance, Sarah can be as ruthless as a man. I just never wanna put her in that position if I'm able to have the fun instead." Will suddenly snapped his fingers, as if remembering something, and returned to the porch.

"Sarah," he said, "Now'd be a good time to talk to Mike about our agreement with Lucy. We're pretty much done for the day." He turned back around and went to the stable without further explanation.

I stepped up onto the porch and waited. Sarah watched her brother leave and then invited me to sit down for a few minutes. "Is something wrong?" I asked, suddenly nervous.

"No, but Will and I want to ask you a favor for tomorrow," she said, sitting next to me.

"Of course … anything."

"We're planning on showing Lucy some ways in which she can defend herself, and we wanted to ask you to assist us." Sarah was grinning as she explained their plan. "I'm going to be the one who gets attacked, and Will needs to be free to show Lucy things, so he can't be the one who attacks me."

"What are you suggesting?"

Her grin widened considerably. "We want you to volunteer to have your butt kicked … by me."

I studied her for several moments before responding. At first, I thought she was joking, but I could see the seriousness in her eyes. Finally understanding what she was suggesting, I shook my head slowly. "I don't know if this is such a good idea, Sarah." As tempting as the thought of wrestling with Sarah was, I didn't want to put my sister in a position that may cause her additional pain. "My sister isn't like you. She's small and used to a more delicate life. I don't know if it's a good idea to get her hopes up."

"What are you saying?" Suddenly Sarah's smile disappeared and she stood. She looked about ready to spit nails. "You don't think your sister can learn to fight back?"

"I don't mean offense, but I just don't know," I said, standing. "I don't want to make her feel she can fight, and then if it comes to it, have her fail." I could see Sarah's face turning red with indignation as I continued to speak. "I'd rather she learn to defend herself before a physical confrontation arises."

"The world doesn't work that way, Michael," she said, balling her hands into fists. "Women don't always have the choice of staying clear of a fight. You should know that already because your sister was grabbed and pulled into an alley before she knew what was going on. Lucy must learn how to fight back!"

"I know you mean well, but I still don't think it's a good idea," I said with a shrug.

Sarah stared at me angrily for a moment, her hands on her hips. I couldn't understand why she was so upset, but she looked at me as if she wanted to tear me apart, slowly and methodically to prolong the pain.

"I thought you were different," she fumed, "but you are just like every other man I've ever met. You think you're so damn superior, but you're just an arrogant horse's ass!"

I took a quick step back with my hands up in surrender. "Whoa, what just happened here?" Our friendly conversation had taken a terrible turn.

"We'll just see how superior you are tomorrow, won't we?" she said with new determination and a gleam in her eye.

"What do you mean?"

"Regardless of how you feel, Will and I *are* going to help Lucy. Meet us in the morning if you want to assist." She started down the steps and then turned toward me again. "If you're not afraid, that is."

"Wait a minute," I said, slapping my gloves against my leg in frustration, and bounding down the steps after her. "I said it was a bad idea. I never said it was impossible or that I was afraid."

A smug grin formed on Sarah's lips, and she suddenly looked quite pleased with herself. She had me exactly where she wanted, and it was written all over her face. She leaned against the post. "Help us show Lucy a few things tomorrow, and if I cannot defend myself against you, then I'll give in, and you can find your own way to protect Lucy." She paused for a moment to gauge my reaction before continuing. "In addition, I'll make you a wager. If you beat me, I'll give you anything you want."

"Anything?" I asked, suddenly liking the conversation again. I stepped closer.

"That's right," she said, putting her hand up to stop me. "If you prove how mighty powerful you are as a man, then I'll give you anything you want."

The only thing I could think of that I wanted was Sarah. I knew that's not what she had in mind, but the thought of asking her made me smile. It would definitely take that smug grin off her face. She was the one who said I could ask for anything, after all, and many men would take advantage of an offer like that.

Contrary to what Sarah was beginning to believe, however, I was not like all other men, and I wanted a chance to prove it. Perhaps just a nice dinner for two? It would help show her my better side, which I had to admit was often lacking where she was concerned. Yes, dinner for two would be grand.

"You've got yourself a deal," I said, holding out my hand

to seal our agreement. I couldn't wait to see the look on Sarah's face when I won.

Instead of shaking my hand, Sarah crossed her arms and stared at me without moving. "We aren't done negotiating, Michael," she said. "We haven't discussed what happens if I win tomorrow."

I had to admit, reluctantly, that the thought of not winning had never crossed my mind. Perhaps I *was* just like every other man she had known. I hated that thought, but I had been too busy thinking about spending a whole evening alone with Sarah. She was just so sweet and wonderful ... and feisty and ornery. There was no way I'd miss the chance of getting a dinner alone with her. I refused to lose our wager.

"If I lose," I said, still not wanting to think about it, "then I will offer the same wager. I'll give you anything you want as well." Perhaps she'd want the same thing I did. Doubtful ... but perhaps. That'd definitely make losing worthwhile. Then again, there would be no way I would lose, so it didn't matter. After a few seconds, Sarah held out her hand and we shook on our new agreement.

As Sarah walked away, she turned back toward me with a large toothy smile on her face. "You'd better get some rest tonight, Michael. You're going to need it." She waved sweetly. "I'll see you in the morning."

I leaned against the railing and watched her leave. The sight of her made my heart beat faster and my breathing come quicker. She certainly had a way of getting under my skin.

20

PUNISHMENT

I hiked to the field near the corral the next morning. Looking up, I was pleased to see blue skies again. Even in the depth of winter, I had never seen bluer skies than in Colorado. The air was cool and fresh, but the chill from the previous few days had lessened, creating the impression of a warm spring day. The weather looked as if it might hold throughout the morning as the sun began its path across the sky.

I wore comfortable clothes for Sarah and Will's experiment. Even though I made it sound as if I thought the whole idea was silly, I had no doubts about Sarah's ability to do bodily harm. I had prepared for every eventuality.

Instead of meeting just the three of them, however, Little Bird and Two Dogs greeted me as well. Everyone seemed happy to watch the spectacle that was about to unfold. My queasiness increased, but I shook each man's hand firmly as I approached, doing my best to look confident.

"Hello, Michael," Lucy said enthusiastically. She was wearing men's pants tied with a large leather belt. She looked smaller than usual in the overly baggy jeans and Sarah's boots.

"Thank you for doing this," she said, giving me a hug and squeezing me tight. "You have no idea how excited I am."

"Oh, I can see how excited you are," I said. "You're about ready to burst out of your britches." I should have seen the need in her eyes before. I latched on to that excitement, suddenly glad that Will and Sarah had asked me to help.

Sarah greeted me pleasantly, but I sensed the fire and competition brewing in her eyes. She wore a shirt and pants as well, but hers fit her snugly, outlining every curve and enhancing every move.

I shook Will's outstretched hand and noticed the knowing grin plastered on his face. I was in for *big* trouble. I turned back to Sarah after assessing our audience one more time. "I thought you said you needed me to be your attacker," I said crossly. "I see several men here who could do the job."

"Little Bird and Two Dogs are here to help Lucy," Sarah replied, crossing her arms over her chest, challenging me to argue with her.

I took a step closer, for good measure. "So why am I here?"

"Because," she said, stepping closer, "there is no other man on this ranch I'd like to attack more than you." As soon as the words left her mouth, it was clear that she realized how they sounded, and before she turned away, a bright red blush shot up her neck and onto her face.

"Well, Miss Donnelly," I said with a chuckle, "I don't believe a woman has ever said that to me." I stretched out my arms and lifted my chin to the sky. "Please ... by all means, attack me."

Before I knew what was happening, Sarah twirled around and punched me hard in the gut. I doubled up in pain. "You'd better hope you're a better fighter than you are a cowboy."

I looked up from my crouched position to see all three men laughing. Lucy stuffed her hands in her pockets, stifling a giggle. I took my time straightening and looked at Sarah with a smug grin pasted on my face. I leaned in close to her, with our noses almost touching. "That's mighty confident talk ... for a girl!" I couldn't help myself. I loved to see Sarah riled, with the color rising in her cheeks and her neck, and the fire in her eyes. What a beautiful sight.

Will's eyes widened, and he stepped back, pretending to shield Lucy and the others from Sarah's oncoming wrath. After a few moments of Sarah and me staring, he laughed and gestured us forward.

"If you two are about ready," he said, clearing his throat, "we've got work to do." I smiled, waiting for the fun to begin.

———◦《◦》◦———

Over an hour later, I found myself lying on my back in the mud for the fifth time, staring up at the blue sky. A morning that had started out so promising had ended up incredibly humiliating. One attempt after another had failed, and I found my confidence from the morning plummet into oblivion. I slowly and painfully realized that Sarah would win our wager.

With Sarah, Will demonstrated a number of moves that would help Lucy get out of trouble, and then Lucy practiced each one until she felt comfortable. Sarah continued to slip out of my holds. I had one last try before I lost, and this time I wouldn't show a hint of mercy. Will instructed me to come up behind Sarah and wrap my arms around her, grabbing her arms so she wouldn't be able to use them. He chose a realistic stance, and she would have a difficult time getting free. Perhaps not all was lost.

I stood slowly and wiped the dirt from my face. Approaching Sarah, I took a deep breath and sent a prayer to the gods as I grabbed her around the middle, capturing her arms. Then I realized my true weakness. As soon as I pressed my chest against her back and rested my cheek against her head, I lost all thought of why we were there. She smelled like a wonderful mixture of soap and lavender water. I took in a deep breath through my nose to savor the scent. The heat of her body was intense, and my head swam. A moment later, I was lying flat on my back on the ground with a bloody nose. How in the hell had *that* happened?

Sarah had slammed the back of her head into my nose, causing me to lean backward. Then she'd moved to my side and swept my legs out from under me with one swift kick. I had to let go when I started falling backward. I should have been angry with myself for being so easily distracted, but only one thought crept into my mind: Sarah was an amazing woman!

After holding my nose and waiting for my eyes to stop watering, I opened one eye to find everyone peering down at me, with the exception of Little Bird and Two Dogs. They stood off to the side, shaking their heads.

Lucy nudged me in the side with her foot. "Get up, Nancy!" she said through her laughter. It was something we called each other when we showed weakness. She hadn't called me that since I was a schoolboy.

"Did you just call me … Nancy?" I asked, pulling myself into a seated position. My sister took a step back, but her grin merely widened. Boy, was I glad to see my sister getting lippy again, and from the smile on Arthur's face, he had noticed the change as well.

"That's right, Nancy. What're you going to do about it?"

As soon as I jumped to my feet, Lucy shrieked and

started running. It didn't take long to catch up with her and swing her around and into my arms. Before she could regain control, I whipped her around so that her head was hanging down my back, and I had a good grip on her legs so she couldn't kick and wouldn't fall. Her hair fell free, and her golden curls dangled down in her face. I headed slowly toward the horse trough, disclosing in detail how I would get retribution for her comment. She squealed and laughed so hard she could barely speak.

"I think you'd better apologize, Lucy," I said evenly. "That water looks mighty cold, and there's something … *unfamiliar* floating on top."

She pleaded with me and grabbed my back to straighten up. "I won't set you free until I hear those words come from your mouth." I looked down into the muck floating on top of the water. "What's it going to be? You can apologize or have nasty green stuff attach itself permanently to your lovely hair. I think green is a wonderful color for you—it goes with your eyes." I moved closer to the trough.

Finally, Lucy gave up. "Okay, fine. You win." She leaned toward me to get away from the water. "I apologize for calling you Nancy."

"And who's the best brother in the world?" I asked, loosening my grip suddenly, causing her to scream again.

"You are! Now let me go!"

I turned away from the horse trough and gently set her on the ground. She punched me in the arm, as if I hadn't had enough abuse for one day.

I brushed the dirt off my jacket and trousers as I walked over to Sarah to face my punishment. I couldn't delay it anymore, so I held out my hand in surrender. She hesitated when she saw my smile, but after a moment, she placed her hand in mine. I bowed as gallantly as I could while holding her hand. "Your servant, ma'am." I said. "I offer you whatever your heart desires, as agreed by our wager, and I apologize for ever doubting your ... superiority."

Sarah stiffened slightly upon hearing my words, and she removed her hand from mine. I looked up to see her face turning red. She seemed flustered. It struck me that Sarah was embarrassed by my praise. My words had affected her in the same way that her presence affected me. I was delighted. As I stepped closer, I found it impossible to hide my ever-increasing smile.

"So," I said, feeding off her tension, "what do I owe you?"

My question brought Sarah back to the conversation. She straightened her shoulders and smoothed her trousers. "Since you seem to think that women are inferior ...," she began.

"I never said—"

"I'm going to be easy on you," she interrupted. "Since men's work is so much harder, I'll be kind and only ask you to spend one day performing my work."

I took another couple of steps closer to Sarah. "Let's get a few things straight, once and for all," I said softly. "For one, I never said you were inferior, and two, I never said your work was anything less than a man's. On the contrary, I think you work incredibly hard, and I'd be honored to take that burden off your shoulders for a day."

Once again, I found Sarah too stunned to reply. I had removed her smug grin without winning after all. Lovely. She stared at me with her mouth slightly open. I saw Lucy, Will, and Arthur watching us closely.

I turned back toward Sarah and cleared my throat. "Now that I know the magnitude of your wager, I find that what I would've asked of you would've been far too small."

"What were you going to ask me to do?" she asked, suddenly curious.

I turned around so that she was unable to see my face. "Never mind, I'll save it for our next wager."

―――――――

I woke up before dawn with Sarah's words echoing in my head: *I thought you were different, but you are just like every other man I've ever met.* I decided to spend the day doing everything to prove to Sarah that I was nothing like the other men in her past. It was my chance to prove that I was, in fact, the man she wanted me to be.

Since it was Saturday, I didn't have to teach my classes, so I could devote my entire day to Sarah. I dressed in my best work clothes and sauntered to the main house in the predawn darkness to make sure the preparations Gus and I had discussed the night before were ready. Then I went to the dairy shed, where Sarah and I started work each morning. I knew Sarah would still insist on working, even though I was supposed to take that burden away. So I made sure the cows were milked before she got up, so she wouldn't argue about helping me.

The sun lit the sky as I carried the milk bucket to the kitchen. I was carrying a loaded egg basket from the chicken coop to the main house when I saw Sarah move down the steps and start toward the dairy shed. I followed her quietly and watched her prepare to milk the cows.

"Sarah."

She turned around to find me standing by the door, watching her closely. "Good morning, Michael."

"What are you doing?" I asked.

"What do you mean? I'm getting ready to milk the cows."
She looked at me with her brows knit in concentration.
"I've already taken care of the milking." I took her hand
in mine and led her out of the shed and back toward the
house.
"What are you doing?" she asked irritably.
"You asked me to do your work for the day." I leaned
closer. "And that is what I intend to do. Your only task for
the day is to relax."
"Michael, when I asked you to do my work for the day, I
didn't mean to take a day off."
I led Sarah into the dining room, where she stopped
abruptly. The table sported a clean new tablecloth, with
Sarah's favorite breakfast foods steaming in bowls on top.
My surprise clearly astounded Sarah. We usually rushed
through our morning meal as we got ready to begin our day.
I ushered her to the head of the table and pulled out a chair
for her to sit down.
"You won't be working today, Sarah," I said in her ear as
I moved her chair closer to the table. I noticed goose bumps
rise on her skin when she felt my breath on her neck. "For
once in your life, the work will get done without you. I lost
the bet, and I plan to fulfill my part of the bargain."
"I don't think I can be idle all day while others are working. Why can't we —"
I put my fingers to her mouth to quiet her objections,
and I placed a cloth napkin in her lap. "This is not subject
to negotiation so enjoy yourself. I've told everyone that you
are not to be disturbed, and you are not to lift a hand today." I picked up her plate and started placing various foods
on it as I circled the table.
"Don't worry," I added, "tomorrow will be here soon
enough. There will be plenty of work left for you to tackle

then." I straightened and sighed dramatically. "Gus went to a lot of trouble to make you the perfect breakfast, and I know he'll be disappointed if you don't take your time and enjoy the meal." I placed the plate in front of her. "So stop arguing and eat."

"Would you at least join me?" she asked as she picked up her fork and stared at her food.

"I wouldn't dare," I said with a smile. "Besides, I've already eaten, and I have a full day of work ahead of me."

"When did you get up this morning ... or did you just skip sleep all together?"

"I slept plenty. While you're eating, I'll be waiting for instructions on the work you would like done today." I stepped back against the wall and waited by the door.

Sarah took several bites of her breakfast, savoring each one, before she answered me. Despite her protests, it pleased me to see her enjoying the first surprise of the day.

"Saturday is usually wash day," she finally said, "but I just don't know about you doing it alone."

"Never fear. You can instruct me from the porch until I get the hang of it."

Despite Sarah's initial hesitation about skipping work for the day, it didn't take her long to warm to the idea. By noon, she was lounging comfortably on the porch with a blanket and a book, quietly reading and relaxing. Every now and then, she looked up and made a comment about the wash, but otherwise she enjoyed herself.

I had two more meals planned with all of Sarah's favorites, according to Gus. She, on the other hand, had a list of chores the length of her arm waiting for me between lulls in the wash. The downtime gave her the opportunity to organize her thoughts and determine all the things she would like accomplished. Many of them weren't things she'd normally do, but they needed to be done nonetheless, so I kept quiet and continued to work. I had to show her that I was the kind of man she could admire and trust. Every time a quick comeback or insult popped into my head, I squashed it and focused on pleasing Sarah. If that meant I had to mend socks and wash Pat's underwear, so be it.

Her brothers sabotaged my efforts at every turn. If I took my eyes off the laundry basket or the clothesline, I'd find sheets on the roof of the main house or long johns hanging from the corral. It suddenly seemed as if there was nothing but free time for them to torment me.

"You surprised me today," Sarah said with a grin as I started up the steps at the end of the day. "I expected you to grumble and whine about the work and losing our bet, but you took it like a gentleman."

"Aw, shucks, ma'am," I said, mocking her, while shoving my hands in my pockets and shuffling my feet.

"Don't make fun of me, Michael," she said. "I might be a mere woman, but I can still skin you like a pig." She spoke sternly, but I noticed that she was fighting back a smile. Even so, I figured I shouldn't push my luck. Instead, I moved closer to her on the steps and took her hand in mine. She stood on the porch, while I stood one step below, allowing us to look one another in the eye.

"You are truly a remarkable woman, Sarah," I said quietly, moving my thumb slowly across her knuckles. "I don't think I've ever met another quite like you."

I stepped back and moved toward the door, but before I could leave, she grasped my arm and swung me close. Without giving me a chance to regain my balance, she leaned in and kissed me soundly on the lips, while wrapping her arms around my shoulders.

Just as abruptly as the kiss had begun, however, it

ended. She forcefully pushed against me to release my grip, and as a grin slowly spread across my face, she wiped it off with a swift slap that jarred my teeth and caused my skin to tingle in pain.

"What the hell was that for?" I rubbed my jaw gingerly. Boy, did she pack a wallop in such a small frame.

She huffed out a breath. "You get me so damn confused I can't think straight." She turned around and placed her hand against her mouth. She smoothed her hair and turned back around with a tentative smile. "Sorry I slapped you." She straightened her dress, as she did whenever she was nervous.

"Of course." Seeing her flustered always brightened my day. After several seconds, I took a reluctant step away. "I'd better go. Pat wanted me to get up early tomorrow and ride out to a few of the line camps."

"Throughout all this mess," she said looking up at me, "we've both found a bit of luck as well." Without waiting for my reply, she turned and entered the house.

"I've never felt luckier," I said to myself as I watched the door close behind her.

21

THE FACE OF DEATH

I t was a fine day to spend away from the ranch—brisk but sunny. Pat had asked me to help him check on the men at the distant line camps and help round up stray or stranded cattle. Many of the herd would be weak after the winter, causing them to get into distress if they wandered too far.

I hurried toward the stable to get Ginger ready, thinking about everything that needed to be done that day. Most of all, we needed to solidify our plans for Turner. I needed to know what interested him so much about my family; and the only way to make that happen would be to find Turner and end his wrath upon the Donnellys, the townspeople, and my family. Lucy continued to have frequent nightmares. We needed to stop Turner so he could no longer haunt her dreams.

Unexpectedly, a piece of metal whirled past my head, inches from my nose, lodging itself into a nearby post. I stopped dead in my tracks and stared at the large knife sticking out of the wood, before turning around, with my hand on my gun, ready for another strike. I found Lucy standing next to Will, with her hand over her mouth in surprise.

"I am so sorry, Michael," she said with a nervous laugh. She walked by me to retrieve the blade and then returned to her position by Will.

"Christ, Lucy, what are you doing?"

"Will's teaching me to throw a knife," she said casually.

"*You* threw that knife?"

"I most certainly did," she replied, looking awfully pleased with herself.

"You almost took my head off!" I rubbed my nose, thankful it remained intact.

"I know. Isn't it wonderful?" She clapped her hands together and raised her arm for another throw.

I quickly removed myself from the line of fire and stepped behind the two of them. "Will, if you're going to arm my sister, could you at least teach her how to aim?"

"Oh, there's nothin' wrong with her aim, Mike. You just happened into her path."

I took one last look at Lucy as I walked away. A new sparkle shone in her eyes, a look filled with promise for the future. She threw the knife again, saw it hit its mark, and grinned at Will. Each day she spent learning new skills to defend herself, her confidence grew and her old fire ignited and flared.

Pat, Tommy, and I left the ranch less than a half hour later. At the end of the winter, much of the herd was weak and thin. The losses from the heavy storms were especially great, and the day proved that the winter had taken its toll. With the oncoming spring, however, the older ones would grow big and strong and be ready for sale by summer's end.

The day ended up being long and tiring as we gathered cattle from around the outskirts of the valley. At one point, Tommy and I had to rope a calf to remove her from a mud bog in which she had become stuck. Her strength nearly gone, she merely stood there, waiting for us to work to get her out.

Pat and Tommy left together over a hill to look out for other mud bogs and tricky terrain; it was a welcome break and the first time I had been alone all day. I took a deep breath, expanding my lungs to their fullest capacity. The sun started to sink in the sky, and the air began to cool with the onset of nightfall. I relaxed in my saddle and took in the snow-covered landscape. There was something inexplicably peaceful about the land and the trees blanketed in white. I felt a slight tightening of my chest at ever having to leave such an amazingly beautiful valley.

I knew at that moment that I couldn't return to the city. I thought that perhaps I'd find my own land and build a cabin for Lucy and me. She'd told me not to worry about her, that she would take care of herself, but I couldn't imagine staying here without her. I looked up at the mountains again and let out an easy breath. The peace of the day turned into a brief moment of happiness as I thought about the home I could one day have ... and perhaps a beautiful woman with whiskey-colored hair who would share it with me.

I pictured a small cabin sitting next to the meadow with the twisted trees and a view of the snow-capped peaks behind it. It would have a corral and stable, and people would see chickens running in the yard and a stubborn old mule hollering at us when they arrived. We'd have a garden with herbs and vegetables, and a cow or two for me to milk each day.

Leaning down close to Ginger's neck, I patted her gently. "I wouldn't forget about you, girl. I couldn't leave you behind, now could I?"

Just then, I heard a shot and felt something whiz past the back of my head. A second shot just missed me as I tumbled off Ginger's back. She lunged forward and took off in a run.

When I heard the first shot, I thought it a stray, but when the second and third bullets came my way, I realized that someone had deliberately shot at me. Would it ever end?

I flattened my body to the ground and frantically looked toward the origin of the gunshots. Two men on horseback were several hundred yards away, too far to recognize, heading quickly in my direction. Another shot hit the snow and dirt a foot away from my leg. I had to do something. I couldn't just lie there and allow the men to get close enough to fire the shot that would kill me.

A new fire burned in my belly as I felt the rage of being beaten in such a cowardly fashion in the stable. I felt the rage of Blake shooting me while I was unarmed, and I felt the rage of my sister's innocence being taken by a man like Turner. Feeling the surge of courage I needed, I got to my feet and swiftly pulled my gun from its holster. Standing there in the wide-open valley, I leveled my pistol and started shooting.

One man's horse reeled and turned to make a hasty retreat into the woods. The other man wasn't so smart. He continued to ride toward me, shooting until his pistol had emptied. As he reached for his other gun, I stood straight and tall with my feet planted firmly on the ground. I had one more shot to take before I'd have to reload. I aimed and pulled the trigger.

The shot hit the man in the chest, and he rolled off the back of his horse and landed with a thump on the snow-covered ground. The horse turned and continued running in the opposite direction.

The man lay more than a hundred yards away, but I wasn't taking any chances. I walked slowly forward as I reloaded my pistol, keeping my eyes glued on him every step of the way. After assuring myself that he wasn't going to move, I quickly glanced around the area to make sure his friend was in fact gone. Pat and Tommy were riding hard and fast in my direction.

I slowed as I got closer to the man on the ground. He rested on his right side with his face buried in the snow and both arms behind his back. His pistol was over twenty feet away, and I knew when I looked at the bloodstained snow that the man was no longer a threat. I knelt down and took hold of his shoulder to move him onto his back so I could see his face. I needed to know who he was.

After turning him over, I brushed the snow from his face. I stood abruptly and took several steps back. Blood had soaked through his jacket, just below his left collarbone, over his heart. Behind me, I heard Pat and Tommy halt their horses and run toward me. Unable to look at either of them, I continued to stare at the man lying dead at my feet. His eyes were closed, and his face held a peaceful expression, as if he were pleasantly dreaming. The realization that I had killed a man made me drop my pistol.

Tommy leaned down, picked up my gun, and tried to hand it to me. I stood motionless, watching the body on the ground. After holding out the gun for several moments, he finally placed it in his belt and glanced down. He checked the man's pulse and then looked toward Pat. "It's Josiah," Tommy said. "He's dead."

Pat gave me a long look. "What happened?"

Still in a state of shock, I didn't answer him right away. I continued to stand over the body and stare into the face of Josiah. He couldn't have been more than twenty-five years old, and seeing the peace on his face made me forget all the hateful stares and the days of pain following my attack. I only saw a young man, dead by my hand.

Pat came closer and shook my shoulder slightly. "Michael," he said, "tell me what happened."

I moved my eyes from Josiah to Pat. His face was filled with alarm as he examined me closer. I blinked a few times and finally broke the trance. "Two men started shooting at me ... so I shot back." It seemed as if so much more had occurred, but I couldn't think of anything else to say.

"What happened to the other man?" Pat asked. He straightened and tightened his grip on his pistol.

"He got away," I said.

Pat gave his brother a nervous look, and without hesitation, Tommy flung himself back onto his horse and rode away, following the tracks left by the horses. Pat also mounted his horse and rode away. A few minutes later, he returned, leading Ginger and Josiah's horse.

"I didn't mean to kill him," I said when Pat dismounted.

"Well, he meant to kill you. Be glad it's him lyin' there instead of you." Pat wore a stern look on his face, and he moved in a businesslike manner as he brought Josiah's horse closer. "I know he's been after you for some time. I never thought he'd try somethin' like this, though."

"Neither did I." It occurred to me that for the first time since coming out West, I had defended myself against an attack. Pride and guilt raged a battle in my chest, fighting to see which would win.

"I need your help getting him onto his horse, Mike," he said, shaking my arm again. "Will you grab his legs?"

He didn't wait for a response but knelt down and pulled Josiah's shoulders up so that he could reach around his chest. I took his legs, and we both lifted him onto his horse and draped him over his saddle.

Tommy returned without finding the man who'd fled, but he was certain they would find out his name when we returned to town because the tracks led in that direction. Pat and Tommy decided to take Josiah's body to the town marshal, and knowing he'd have questions, I insisted on going along. This was my struggle, and I couldn't leave Pat and Tommy to handle it.

When the two brothers stopped at the ranch on the way to town, I decided to stay with Josiah and his horse in the trees near the entrance. I was still conflicted and didn't want to face anyone I didn't have to.

We traveled in silence into Lone Tree and stopped at the Franklin Hotel to find Daniel Morgan. Pat was confident that Daniel would understand what had happened that day. In my mind, however, it wasn't so clear. On one hand, there should've been another way. Josiah was too young to be shot down, and I couldn't forgive myself for taking his life. On the other hand, I had no choice. Shoot or be shot.

Daniel and James came downstairs in a hurry. Pat stepped forward to talk to them, but I stopped him by placing a firm hand on his chest. "No, Pat," I said. "This is my responsibility." Pat relented and stepped back.

"What is it, Michael?" Daniel asked apprehensively.

"A man was killed on the Lazy D Ranch today," I said quickly. "His name was Josiah ... and I shot him."

A momentary look of surprise passed over Daniel's face before he schooled his expression. James stared at me in disbelief as I told them what had led to Josiah's death. By the end of my tale, both men nodded in comprehension. Contrary to my guilty protestations, both men agreed that, under the circumstances, there was nothing else I could've done.

"You sure did stir up a hornet's nest with Turner's men, though," Daniel said after we had talked for some time. "From all accounts, his men were only with him because he had promised them riches when this is all over. But the rumors about him have taken root, and more of his men leave each day."

"So they believe that Turner has nothing to give them?"

"With the constant talk around town and at Belle's, they have no choice. Only the most loyal to Turner remain, but even they are starting to turn. It seems that Turner isn't the same these days—a bit loco, if what I'm hearing is true. So be careful with this game you're playin'. It could backfire."

I thanked Daniel for the news about Turner. At least one side of this fight was starting to turn in our direction. We left the town and took Josiah to the graveyard on the hill. James and his father were kind enough to help, and we quickly went about the business of getting Josiah properly buried.

All the men left the graveyard after placing the last mound of dirt on Josiah's grave, giving me a few moments alone in the dark. I didn't say anything before turning to walk away, but the time alone was important nonetheless. I tried one last time to make sense of what Josiah had done, but I found no answers. I remembered the jealousy I'd felt when I first saw him talking to Sarah near the main house, and I thought about how that emotion had quickly gotten out of control. Now the young man lay buried beneath the ground.

A short while later, we said good-bye to Daniel and James, and the three of us returned to the ranch. We brought Josiah's horse back with us and put him in the stable. I took extra time with Ginger, lingering inside while brushing her and talking softly to her.

"Hey, Mike."

Turning, I noticed Eddie coming into the barn, heading in my direction. Pat's son was only twelve years old, but he definitely had Pat's build. He grabbed an extra brush and moved to the opposite side of Ginger.

"I hear you had trouble today," he said, looking as serious as his pa.

I considered not telling him, but I knew he'd figure it out eventually. "Yes, Josiah met us while we were working and tried to kill me. I didn't have a choice but to shoot him."

"That's good, Mike." He nodded his head firmly, never missing a stroke. "Men like that need to be stopped. I heard you and my pa talkin' about finding the man that killed Ma. We have to make sure the ranch is safe."

I was taken aback by his comments. "Eddie, you shouldn't be listening in on our conversations. You are too young to worry about such things."

"I ain't too young to know there are bad men out there, and that my Ma was killed by one of 'em." He set the brush down and cleaned off his hands with a rag. "If I had the chance, I'd stop Turner myself."

"Eddie ..." I turned to talk to him, but he was already walking quickly away. His comments made me uneasy. Hopefully, his talk was all bravado, and Eddie would stay out of trouble. Just in case, I made a note to talk to Pat in the morning. I also needed to make sure we were more careful about what we discussed when he was around.

I wasn't ready to go home, or to talk to anyone else about what happened, so I left the comfort of Ginger's stall and ducked into the darkness. Without forethought, I headed straight toward the downed pine tree Sarah and I had shared when I'd inadvertently spilled my soul to her regarding Lucy and my family.

I sat down on the log and silently listened to the trickle of water running underneath the ice. The forest was cool and peaceful. The sun peeked over the horizon, allowing a small amount of light to dance over the landscape.

The air had chilled considerably, making each exhalation visible. I listened to each breath closely, feeling my heart beating slowly in my chest. It was a strong, healthy heartbeat, keeping rhythm with the sounds of the morning. The heart is a truly marvelous creation. Even if the body is ready to give up the fight, and even when the spirit feels it cannot handle one more day, the heart decides if it's time to live or die.

If I hadn't killed Josiah, he would have killed me. I knew that, but I repeated it in my head over and over again. I also knew he most likely would have left me lying on the cold ground, alone, to slowly decay or be eaten by buzzards. He would not have taken the time to bury my body and mourn my death. He wanted nothing more than to see me dead. Yet, defending myself against another attack, I was left only with sadness and overwhelming guilt. My stomach was tied in knots, and a sick feeling lay heavily in my throat.

I noticed a flash of white on the trail near the house and figured it must be Sarah starting her day. My heart sank in my chest when she started down the trail toward me. The last person on earth I wished to see at that moment was Sarah. How would I explain to her what had happened?

Sarah was soon close enough that I could see her face. She'd clearly been told about what had happened. Her face was etched in concern, and her eyes held the same sadness as my own, but she managed a weak smile before she reached the tree.

I stood when she approached. "I'd really rather be alone, if you don't mind."

"I know," she said, proceeding to sit down on the log, swinging her legs. I let out a loud sigh and slumped down next to her.

"You have a habit of disappearing into the forest when you're upset."

"And you have a habit of finding me when I don't wish to be found," I replied, never taking my eyes off the ground. We sat for a long time without speaking.

"It's going to be a cool day, don't you think?" she asked, as if we had nothing to worry about but the weather.

"Sarah," I said quietly, "I appreciate your concern and your coming out here to find me, but I really just need to be alone for a while." I got up to walk away, but she followed behind me.

"No, you don't."

I turned around so fast that she ran into me. I glared at her. "How on earth do you know what I do or don't need? I told you I wanted to be left alone."

"No, you said you *needed* to be alone, and I disagreed with you," she said. "What you need is to talk to someone about what happened. What you want is not really a priority."

I stared back at her, dumbstruck. "A man I don't know attacks me—twice—and leaves me no choice but to shoot him and watch him die. I'd like to be left alone." Crossing my arms, I faced the river. Sarah went and sat back down on the log without saying a word. I waited for her to leave, but she refused to budge. Finally, I turned back toward her in frustration. "What do you want from me?" I asked, raising my arms in the air.

"I want you to tell me what happened yesterday."

"You already know what happened. I can see it in your eyes." I sat back down and placed my elbows on my knees, burying my head in my hands. "I killed Josiah."

She placed her hand on my arm. "Are you sorry that it happened?"

"Until today, I didn't think I'd be sorry to see him dead," I admitted to her. "I felt like throttling him when I saw him with you on the porch. But now ... yes, I am sorry it happened. I've never taken someone's life."

"Do you feel guilty?"

"A little."

She sighed heavily and leaned close. "So do I."

"Why would you feel guilty?" I asked, confused. "I'm the one who pulled the trigger."

"It might as well have been me. We both know he hated you because of me. I could've told him months ago that we weren't the right match, or I could've ignored him when he attempted to charm me."

"He cared about you, but it isn't your fault he came after me," I said. "He was confused and jealous, and he didn't deserve to die, but you didn't make him do what he did. He chose to do that on his own."

"Exactly," she said, nudging my shoulder, trying to get me to look up.

I turned my head to gaze at her, still confused, and saw a pained smile on her lips. I forced a smile in return. I felt a great amount of relief knowing that Sarah didn't judge me. She rested her head on my shoulder and slid her arm through mine. It wasn't until that moment that I felt her shivering.

"Are you cold?" I asked, looking down at her flushed skin.

"A little."

I pulled her up into a standing position and slid off my jacket so I could drape it across her shoulders. No wonder she was cold. She wore nothing but a shawl over the thin fabric of her dress. I rubbed her arms to try to warm her as we stood in the early morning light and, without thinking, pulled her close to me.

We were both shivering at that point, but I don't think I trembled from the cold. She felt soft and wonderful in my arms, and her hair smelled once again of perfumed soap and lavender. She leaned into me and wrapped her arms around my waist, pulling me closer.

"So, what about that dinner you promised me?" she asked with a chuckle. "Don't think you're getting out of making me a home-cooked meal."

I laughed and squeezed her tighter before letting go and taking her hand to walk with her back to the ranch. "I wouldn't dare disappoint you. I just hope Lucy doesn't have plans tonight, because I'm a lousy cook."

22

SECRETS REVEALED

March 1883

O ver the next few weeks, I worked harder than ever before in my life. My body changed a little with every new day, becoming leaner and stronger. Every time I thought about how tired I was, or how much my muscles ached, I forced myself to remember that Jack Turner was alive out there, waiting for me to find him.

I stopped asking the Donnelly brothers about him or about the past, resigning myself to the fact that some secrets would remain hidden until we found Turner. I knew enough to keep me focused on training my body and my mind for the battle to come. Jack Turner had caused my sister unbearable pain, and he had hurt the Donnellys, whom I now loved as much as my own family. He must be stopped. I knew the day of reckoning drew near.

One morning while I worked in the stable, thinking about my circumstances, Sarah approached me from behind. I'd recognize her sound anywhere. The rustle of her skirt and the sound of her footsteps made my heart skip a beat. I smiled to myself, knowing her arrival would remove all my dark thoughts.

Turning, I found her leaning against a rail with a frown on her face and her arms crossed. She tapped her foot impatiently and looked downright hostile. My pleasant thoughts vanished.

"Who the hell do you think you are?" She spoke through clenched teeth.

"Excuse me?" The last time I'd seen Sarah was in my cabin after having a nice dinner, and she'd left with a smile on her face. What could've gone wrong? I brushed the dirt from my knees as I stood to face her.

"I heard Pat talking to my brothers about your plans."

"I don't—"

"Don't play stupid with me!" she interrupted. "You plan on hunting Jack and his men, don't you?"

My shoulders sagged. I had been dreading this confrontation, hoping it wouldn't occur until the day we left to find Turner. Seeing Sarah's worried face, however, made me realize I could no longer put it off. "Yes, Sarah," I said quietly. "I do."

"Have you completely lost your mind?" In her anger, her face turned a deep scarlet. My own emotions also began to rise, but I tried to tame them.

Sarah took a deep breath, straightened her skirt, and clenched her hands into white-knuckled fists, obviously trying to control herself. "I know better than you what Jack Turner is capable of," she said. "You have no idea what you're getting yourself into. I've seen it. I know what will happen."

Her comment took me by surprise and made me take a quick step back. I studied her face and found pain in her eyes.

"I've tried to find out about Turner, but you all shut me out. Tell me what you know. What have you seen?" Suddenly, a terrible thought came to my mind as I recognized the fear and sadness on her face. My heart plummeted in my chest, and I was sure the color drained from my face. "Has he ... done something to you?"

Sarah was silent. Then she looked down and began to cry, covering her face with her hands. Alarmed, I took hold of her arm tightly and lifted her head with my other hand. "What has he done to you, Sarah?" Scenarios ran wild through my mind and made my blood boil.

Sarah moved her head to the side and shoved my other hand away, removing it from her arm as she turned away. "He took my sister away ... and changed Pat forever."

"You mean Lilly?"

"Pat told you he hunted Turner, right?" Sarah faced away from me, speaking so softly I could barely hear her. "Pat crossed him, and instead of going after my brother, Turner killed his wife—the only sister I have ever known. He killed her, and his men left Pat to die, shot and beaten in the woods." She turned around, with tears running down her cheeks. "That is what will happen to you if you go after them. They'll kill you and come after your sister again."

"None of us will be safe as long as that man walks this earth," I said angrily. "I cannot allow him to take my sister, treat her like a piece of garbage, and then walk away."

"And what about Lucy, since you mention her?" she asked. "Do you plan to leave her here alone? What will happen to her if you fail?"

"That isn't fair," I said with increasing frustration. "Lucy is safe here with Arthur." I started pacing back and forth, attempting to calm myself before continuing. I turned back toward Sarah and took her by the arms to look her directly in the eyes. Her face was still flushed with anger.

"Sarah," I said quietly, "Lucy's wounds are healing and getting better each and every day, thanks in large part … to you." Sarah's face softened slightly. "As for her spirit, recovery may be more gradual, but I see her old fire returning." Sarah was silent now. I wanted her to understand, so I continued.

"It is time for me to heal. I've also been wounded by this man's wrath, and there is only one thing that will make me whole again."

"But—"

I squeezed her hands to quiet her objections, finishing what I needed to tell her. "I will do whatever is necessary to ensure that evil bastard never harms another again. It's the only way I'll be able to live with myself."

Sarah's fire was briefly gone. Instead of rage, she looked incredibly sad, and it took every ounce of my energy not to grasp her body and hold it close.

"I told you before," she said quietly, "what happened to Lucy is not your fault. Why can't you understand that?"

"It may not have been my fault in the past, but it will be my fault if I allow anyone else to be injured because I decided to sit back and watch him continue to torment innocent people."

She sighed heavily, wiped her eyes with her sleeve, and then looked up at me with new determination. "If you insist on going, then I am going with you."

"No, absolutely not!" I said brusquely, releasing her arms. The thought of her anywhere near that man sent a chill up my spine.

"What makes you think you can tell me what to do?"

"Sarah, please!" I threw my hands up in the air and

turned away. I knew pleading wouldn't work, but I needed a way to quell my frustration, which was escalating rapidly.

"If you plan on carrying on with this foolish notion—and it is foolish—then you'll take me with you."

"I said no! This is not a task for a woman!" As soon as the words came out of my mouth, I wished desperately that I could snatch them back and destroy them so they could never be spoken again.

"What!" she exploded, making me flinch. At its peak, Sarah's anger was really something to see. Her rage would make the meanest bull on the ranch cower in fright.

"I'm sorry ... I didn't mean ... I ..."

"You arrogant bastard!" She closed in on me with her arm outstretched, fist clenched, obviously wishing she had a weapon. I silently thanked God that she didn't. "Not a job for a *woman*! Because of me, your ass isn't still sitting in Fort Collins. If it weren't for me, you'd be dead from an infection because you couldn't take care of yourself in the forest. Not a job for a *woman*! Well, you can't even handle a woman's work without help. What makes you think you can handle this, you ... you ... horse's ass!"

"That's not fair, Sarah!" I hollered back as we stood a foot away from each other, yelling face-to-face.

"What's not fair is you thinking you can order me around like a child!" She finished her argument with a hard push to my chest, forcing me back a few paces.

"Then stop acting like one."

"You have no right to judge me! You know nothing about my life before you arrived."

"You're right!" I yelled back. I took a few deep breaths before stepping away. I had no right to tell her where she could and could not go. If I ever tried that with my sister, she would have castrated me on the spot.

"Who do you think you are?" she continued, not backing down.

"Sarah, I said you're right. I'm sorry."

"What did you say?" She seemed suddenly deflated, and she stopped and lowered her arms to her sides.

"I said I'm sorry." I let my breath out slowly. "I was wrong, and I ask for your forgiveness."

"So I'm coming with you?"

"No, I didn't say that," I corrected. "I merely meant that it was wrong of me to say what I did. I still don't want you to go with us."

"Why?" Moisture gathered in her eyes.

Unable to think of a way to reason with her further, I quickly grabbed her by the waist and pulled her close. "Because somewhere in all this mess, I fell in love with you, damn it, and I won't see you in harm's way." Before she could respond, I leaned in and kissed her hard, stopping all further conversation. She quickly softened in my arms. Her smooth, warm mouth tasted of the sweet honey she'd been sampling in the kitchen.

She tentatively placed her hands on my shoulders and slowly put them around my neck, urging me closer. I squeezed her waist and deepened the kiss. My tongue moved over her lips, and without any encouragement, she opened her mouth and allowed me to dive within.

A small groan from the back of Sarah's throat temporarily brought me back to my senses. I ended the kiss and rested my head against hers, trying to gain control. Both of us were breathing heavily, and I could feel the flush of my cheeks from the inner fire that burned.

"You're not going to slap me again, are you?"

Sarah stood still in my arms for a moment before shaking her head and locking her eyes with mine. "I'm going with you," was all she said before pushing me forcefully away and stalking out of the stable.

Later that afternoon, I washed and went in search of Sarah. We'd both had time to calm down, and I had worked out everything I wanted to say. She wasn't doing laundry, so I went to the main house, where she usually spent time in the afternoons. May stood outside, swinging a broom at one of the hall rugs, scattering dust into the air.

"Excuse me. Have you seen Sarah this morning?" I asked, trying to act nonchalant.

"She left for Little Bird's first thing this morning with Will." She turned back to her work.

On my way home, I checked the stable one more time, but her horse was gone. I spent the rest of the afternoon in my cabin, unable to focus until she returned. I lay on my bed in contemplation until I finally drifted into sleep.

I woke before sunrise, to a knocking on the door. I hastily dressed and went to the door, hoping it would be Sarah. Instead, I found Pat and Tommy waiting on the porch.

"Get your things, Michael," Pat said quickly. "We're goin' hunting."

"What should I bring?" I asked reluctantly.

"Whatever you think you'll need for several days in the woods," Pat said. They headed back toward the main house.

I didn't like the idea of leaving while things were still so confused between Sarah and me, but the early morning visit from Pat and Tommy wasn't really an invitation. They expected me to go, and they were waiting. I hastily grabbed my clothes, a rifle, my father's pistol, and my knife before leaving the room. I wrote a quick note to Lucy and left to meet Pat and Tommy outside near the stable. Ginger waited, fully saddled, near the other horses. I put my belongings in the saddlebags and looked around one last time. Sarah was still nowhere to be found.

"Should I bring any food?" I asked, my stomach growling in anticipation of breakfast.

"I told you, Michael," Pat said. "We're goin' hunting."

"Of course." These men were seasoned hunters. We would surely find enough food on the trail. My stomach growled once more as I nudged Ginger forward, following Pat and Tommy away from the ranch.

23

LOST IN THE WOODS

T hroughout the day, the three of us spoke little, other than their giving me instructions on tracking methods and the sounds of the forest. One of them would suddenly become quiet, look around, find his target, and shoot, always coming back with an animal. During dinner, they instructed me on how to skin and cook animals. It seemed they were both extraordinarily careful to share every small detail about the wilderness and hunting.

When we returned to riding, we left the trail and forged into the immense forest. Tommy rode close to Ginger and reviewed proper shooting techniques. With confidence after weeks of practice, I rattled off answers to his quizzing without hesitation.

"Shootin' a moving object is much different than shootin' cans off a fence," Tommy said, as if sensing my arrogance. "Pat and I are leavin' it up to you to find us food for supper. If you don't kill anything, we don't eat!"

Tommy was true to his word. Even though he and Pat had seen several animals as we rode, neither of them tried to take a shot. Only after several misses did I finally admit that I might have been a bit hasty in my confidence with hunting. Pat gave me pointers and made some corrections to my shooting after his observations of me over the first few hours.

The sun lowered in the sky, creating dark shadows through the trees as I visualized my prey. A small deer was eating up ahead. I slowly stopped Ginger and leveled my rifle. If I didn't hit the deer, all three of us would go to bed hungry. Taking my time, I settled into a comfortable position and aimed carefully.

Just before I could shoot, Tommy's horse let out a loud grunt, frightening the deer and sending it running through the trees. Immediately, I nudged Ginger briskly in the sides and headed in the same direction. I didn't plan to go to bed hungry and look like a fool once again in front of Pat or Tommy. Ginger instinctively knew which way to go, dodging downed trees and boulders as she fearlessly chased our supper. With the deer in my vision again, I raised my rifle and fired a single shot before it could disappear into the safety of the oncoming darkness.

The deer fell heavily to the ground. I reined in and slowed Ginger to a stop. Pat and Tommy rode past me, heading straight for the downed animal. By the time I recovered from my shock and met up with them, they were off their horses, examining the deer.

"I can't believe it!" Pat said.

Looking down at the deer, I saw the bullet wound. The shot had struck it in the head, killing it instantly. Both men patted me on the back and congratulated me, making me feel immensely proud of my new abilities.

With a permanent grin attached to my face, I made camp, started a fire, skinned the deer, and prepared it for supper. All through our meal, I thought about how much fun the next day of hunting would be, now that I knew more about what to do.

"Michael?" Pat said, after taking his last bite. "Tommy and I need to talk to you about a few things."

He had a stern look on his face that made me pause for a moment. I grabbed my coffee and sat on a log next to the fire, waiting for him to continue.

"We wanted to get you away from the ranch to talk about our plans for Turner."

"Has anything changed?"

"We'll be leavin' the ranch in a few days," Pat answered. "We've gotten word from town about a possible place where Turner's been hidin'. A friend has been watching his movements, and he's preparin' for something big. I think he plans to hit us soon. We need to go after him before that happens and catch him off guard."

I nodded enthusiastically, knowing that once we left, we would not be returning to the ranch until Turner was found and brought to justice. Out of all the emotions I expected to feel, relief was the least expected but most appreciated.

"Is there a reason why we need to wait?" I asked. "Can't we go now, while we are away from the ranch?" It would be easier in many ways not to have to return and face Lucy or Sarah.

Tommy shook his head. "Don't worry, we'll be leavin' soon enough."

"Good." I rubbed my hands up and down over my trousers and stood to get ready for sleep. Just a few more days of waiting, and it would all be over.

"One more thing, Michael," Tommy said, looking at me across the fire. "It's about Sarah."

A large lump formed in my throat, and I accidentally dropped my cup when I heard Sarah's name. I slowly picked it up and looked at the two men. Neither was smiling.

"Sarah?" I said uneasily. "What about her?"

"We wanna know what's goin' on between the two of you." Tommy leaned closer to the fire, allowing the flames to light up his face.

I put my cup back down on the ground, knelt down, and placed my hands on my knees, trying to steady them before either man noticed my anxiety. I had rehearsed in my head a hundred times what I would say to Sarah the next time I saw her, but I hadn't yet thought about my conversation with her brothers.

"I don't think I understand," I said, knowing perfectly well what he meant.

Pat came closer to me and sat down again. He pointed back and forth between himself and Tommy. "Both of us have noticed a certain ... *look* you have whenever you glance at our sister."

"I don't have a—"

"Yes, you do," Tommy injected.

I scowled at them. Pat continued to stare at me, waiting for a reply in his usual patient way, while Tommy had his head cocked to one side as he examined me. It was quiet. Even the noises of the forest seemed to be awaiting my answer.

"Okay, so I do look at your sister with a certain ... regard," I blurted out, standing again. "I think she's beautiful and funny and kind, and I'd like nothing more than to have her by my side for the rest of my days." I walked away from the fire and paced back and forth.

"Michael," Pat said softly, "sit down."

"I think I would rather stand, thank you." I stopped pacing and crossed my arms across my chest, my feet braced apart.

"Please, Michael, sit down for just a minute," he said again. I walked back and forth a few more times, and then returned to the fire and sat down.

"Are you under the impression we're mad at you?" Pat asked.

"Of course you are." I waved my hands in the air, standing again. "That's why you brought me out here, isn't it? Hunting, my foot!" I kicked the dirt and jammed my hands deep into my pockets.

Pat scrutinized me. "We planned this hunting trip several weeks ago. Now, we think it is the best time to talk to you alone about Sarah."

"Oh," I muttered as I sat back down and took a deep breath. What the hell was wrong with me? I acted guilty but had done nothing wrong.

"Sarah is our only sister, and we're both a bit protective of her, as you've already noticed," Pat said, glancing at Tommy.

I nodded dumbly and waited for him to continue.

"It's important for us to know your intentions toward Sarah," he continued.

"Would it help if I tell you that I think your sister is an amazing woman, with a bright mind and incredible spirit?"

"It might." Pat leaned back. A small grin formed on his lips as he looked at me.

"Never before have I met a woman quite like her."

"Do you see my sister in your future?" Pat asked. "Do you intend to marry her?"

"As far as I'm concerned, there is no future without Sarah." I grinned sheepishly and looked from Pat to Tommy. They couldn't possibly doubt my sincerity, as I was sure the truth was written in my eyes.

"Good, I'm plum glad to hear it," Pat said.

"Seriously?" I asked stupidly. "I have your blessing?"

Pat placed his hand on my shoulder. "You're a good man, Michael," he said. "You've always treated Sarah with respect and kindness, even when she's bein' difficult. Of course you have my blessing."

I grinned as I looked at Tommy, who had taken his knife from his belt and was cleaning his fingernails with it.

"Treat her badly, Mike," he said, "and I'll cut off your nuts and feed 'em to my dog."

I smiled at him across the fire. "I wouldn't dare."

Tommy sheathed his knife. "Glad to hear it. I like you, and I'd feel awful bad about havin' to kill you."

———— ((O)) ————

I woke to a gentle snow falling on my face. Part of my shelter had come down during the night, causing a small opening above my head. I bundled up tightly and swept the snow from my clothes before crawling outside to fix my shelter. The leather strap I had tied around a tree branch had come undone, so I quickly refastened it tightly so it wouldn't come loose again.

The horizon began to lighten ever so slightly. I figured I had maybe an hour more of sleep before the day would begin. I pulled my coat close to my body and crouched to get back under my blanket. I believed winter was over, but in Colorado the snow often came as late as April or May. After shivering slightly, I curled up in my blankets. The snow created a cozy atmosphere under my lean-to, and I fell asleep wishing for summer.

I woke several hours later, with the sun high in the sky. The snow around my shelter had melted from the heat of its rays, and I could hear the soft *pfffmmt* of snow as it fell from trees and hit the ground. I had been lying under my blanket for a few moments before I realized that the forest was quiet. I couldn't hear Pat or Tommy. Without grabbing my coat, I plunged out of my shelter and looked around. Nothing. Tommy's bedroll was gone, as well as Pat's. I looked toward the horses and found only Ginger standing alone in the trees. The brothers and their horses were gone, as well as all traces of the deer I'd skinned the night before. Several inches of freshly fallen snow covered any sign of their departure. I looked at the sky to find the clouds parting.

Hurrying to my shelter, I removed my clothes and bedroll before taking my shelter down and rolling it tightly into a ball. I moved quickly over to Ginger to secure my belongings. She was waiting quietly under a tree, with a small piece of paper tied to her saddle. I dropped everything and unrolled the note:

If you are truly ready, you'll get back to the ranch as soon as you can. We go after Turner in two days—with or without you.

—Pat

"No, no, no, no, no!" I said, rereading the note. I swung around, studying the forest, hoping this was some bad joke, and then looked down at the paper again. "Dirty rotten bastards!" I crumpled up the paper and threw it into the trees.

I stomped around for quite some time before my anger finally subsided. I tried to remember as much as possible about the trip into the woods, but I had been so preoccupied with learning to hunt that I hadn't really paid close attention.

"Okay, so I've learned lesson one," I said aloud. "Always watch where you're going."

I thought of the disappointment the brothers would feel

if I failed to find my way home. I thought of Lucy and my need to get back safely for her sake. I thought of Sarah and how much I wanted the chance to tell her everything I had told her brothers. Finally, I thought about the possibility of missing the opportunity to go after the man who'd hurt my sister and my friends. I stood and straightened my shoulders with new determination. This wouldn't beat me. I'd make it back in time.

I went back to the horse and took one last look around. Then I placed my foot in the stirrup and lifted myself securely into the saddle. Leaning down, I patted Ginger's neck. "Sorry to get you into this, girl," I said sincerely, "but I'm glad you're here with me." I took a long, deep breath and then nudged Ginger into motion.

I figured it was almost noon by the time I finally headed out of camp. Even though I wasn't paying close attention the day before, I did know that we'd spent most of the day traveling uphill. Therefore, my brilliant plan consisted of heading downhill to see what it would bring. After guiding Ginger in the direction I wanted to go, I let her pick the path that best suited her needs, and we began to wind down the mountainside.

I knew almost immediately that the path we were on wouldn't lead to the trail we'd taken the previously. It was steeper and less traveled than I remembered. Several times I had to dismount and try to coax Ginger across an icy slope or a deep patch of snow. As the day wore on, I also realized I'd be spending another night in the cold wilderness. Nothing matched my memories of the day before, and the sun was beginning to sink in the sky.

Just before darkness enveloped the sky, I lost my footing while leading Ginger through steep terrain. The ground was muddy and slick, causing me to tumble and slide several hundred feet downhill. My clothing and skin caught on tree branches and rocks. I attempted to grab anything I could find to stop my fall, but my descent was too fast.

Finally, just as I began to think I would never stop falling, the ground leveled out. I rolled a few more times before hitting my head on a large tree and coming to an abrupt stop. Just before everything went black, I looked up into the branches to see a squirrel scampering up the trunk.

I woke to find Ginger standing over me, snorting and stomping in the mud. Darkness had fallen while I was unconscious, and a cold chill was in the air. If I didn't get up and start a fire soon, I'd freeze to death in the forest. All the fears I had over Pat or Tommy beating me bloody for my affections toward their sister were nothing compared to the thought of what my sister would do to them if I didn't return. Laughing to myself, I slowly rolled on my side so I could sit up. Every muscle in my body ached. It hurt to breathe. I checked over my limbs and body to make sure nothing was missing, and then I carefully got to my feet.

"Good to see you, girl," I told Ginger, patting her neck. "Maybe next time you can show me a better way to get down, okay?"

I quickly wiped away the blood on my face and limped around the area, gathering firewood and pine needles for a bed. It took over a half hour to get my fire started due to my painful movements and the wet wood, but finally I was able to sit and warm my cold bones.

Despite the fact that I had become the clumsiest man alive, unable to put one foot in front of the other without stumbling, I felt a deep connection to the surrounding land—the darkness, the woods, the sounds and the peace. Each day, my fascination grew, and I finally saw what had linked my father's heart to the land.

My stomach began to rumble from lack of food. Hearing the river to the east, I left Ginger to rest as I meandered through the forest and along the water, planning my route and wondering how I'd find supper. I came across an antelope, a raccoon, and a squirrel, all of which I missed with the rifle when I tried to shoot them. When I was about to give up completely, I managed to kill a small rabbit, which solved the most pressing problem of the evening.

I returned and sat down by my wonderful fire. I slowly turned the rabbit above the fire and tended to my injuries. Despite my fall and being left alone in the woods, my spirits were actually quite high. I had many scrapes and bruises, but everything was working, and Ginger was with me. Without her, I would have none of my belongings, my guns, my clothes, or my blankets, and my chances of making it through the night would have been slim. From the tracking techniques that Tommy had shown me, I was also certain that I had finally found the way home. All in all, I was quite lucky.

"Lesson two," I said to Ginger, "always bring a book when you travel, so that you have something to do when your friends desert you in the middle of nowhere."

I looked back at the fire, and my heart nearly stopped. A man dressed in assorted animal furs stood across the fire, partially hidden in the trees. He looked like a large bear, salivating at my future supper. Quickly standing, I reached for my pistol, which I realized too late was lying next to my bedroll.

"Lesson three," the man said quietly, moving out of the woods, "always have your gun within reach, in case of trouble." He grinned at me, showing his tobacco-stained teeth.

I watched in silence as he inched closer and closer to my fire. My heart pounded loudly in my chest, but I tried to keep my breathing slow and steady. If I showed any fear, the man could use it against me.

When he came into the light, I realized he wasn't as big as I'd originally thought. He was a foot shorter than I was, and he was quite broad, with tree trunks for arms and legs, but he looked bigger because he was covered in a bearskin cape and wolf and deer hides.

"Mind sharin' your fire?" he said, sitting down across from me. "I could start my own, but it'd be easier if we could share."

"Of course," I said apprehensively. The shock of finding someone in the woods with me was wearing off, but the uneasiness remained. Something about the man just seemed … off. He looked as if he could crush me with one hand, but what made me nervous was his face. He had several scars across his forehead and cheeks, and he chuckled to himself at random moments, obviously pleased about something. His smile didn't quite reach his eyes, however. They were blank, and certainly detached. The man was either mentally disturbed or had been alone for much too long.

Watching him closely, I continued cooking the rabbit. He occasionally talked to himself or sang, but otherwise we remained quiet, watching the fire and each other. When the rabbit was fully cooked, I noticed him licking his lips and looking at me expectantly. Not knowing what he would do if I refused, I offered him half my supper. Within minutes, he had finished his portion, leaving a trail of food on his shirt and pants. He wiped his mouth with his arm and settled close to the fire, obviously intending to stay.

"I'm sure surprised to find someone out here this early in the season," he finally said, after several awkward moments. "New to the area?"

"I was out hunting," I said quickly, "but I had an accident. I'll be on my way in the morning."

Over the next few minutes, he told me his name was Henry, and that he had lived as a trapper and mountain man in the woods for over a decade. His home was a two-day ride away, up in the mountains. I told him little, and what I did say was mostly untrue. My instincts had never failed me before, and I felt incredibly uneasy about the man sitting at my fire.

"So, where you headed?" he finally asked.

"I'll be going downstream, back toward Lone Tree." I cleared my throat.

"Would you know how I could find the Lazy D Ranch?" he asked, shifting his weight a bit.

The hair on the back of my neck stood on end. If he was truly a trapper who had lived in the mountains for years, he would know how to find the ranch. "Sorry, no," I said firmly. "I'm not from this area. Just headed toward town."

He watched me closely for a few moments and then pulled out a bottle of whiskey. After taking a large gulp of the amber liquid, he leaned over and stretched his arm out to offer me some. When I declined, he grinned again and took another large gulp before chuckling to himself. The man was in dire need of a bath and good oral hygiene. He smelled of stale liquor and body odor, and his teeth weren't just tobacco stained—they were also yellow and probably rotten. I could smell his stench across the fire.

"Are you headed to the ranch?" I asked carefully, afraid to give anything away, but horribly curious about the man.

"I'm an old friend of Pat's," he said. "There's just a little somethin' I need to pick up at his ranch." He took another large drink and then winked at me. Winked!

I had to get out of there. The man was trouble if I'd ever seen it, and I needed to get to Pat before he did.

He got up and spread out his blanket to go to sleep for

the night. I did the same, knowing that I wouldn't be able to sleep in his presence. Each time I glanced in his direction, he would quickly close his eyes and pretend to sleep, but when I looked away, I felt his eyes on me, watching and waiting. We seemed to be in a game to see who would sleep first.

Finally, with a little help from the whiskey, he drifted off to sleep. I waited until late in the night, listening to him snore loudly, before I quietly and quickly saddled Ginger, glanced back at camp once, and rode out of the area. I had to find the ranch before he did.

24

HOME SWEET HOME

It was late morning when I arrived back at the entrance to the Lazy D Ranch. I rode down the long trail toward home. Two cowpunchers met me on the trail and laughed heartily when they saw my ragged form. The Donnelly brothers were outside when I reached the stable, and I could see the relief on their faces.

"I'm pleased as punch to see you," Pat said enthusiastically, patting me on the back as I got off my horse. "If you weren't here by supper, we were gonna send out a search party."

"I thought you were planning on leaving before I returned," I said crossly.

"I told you we'd give you a few days." He looked up at the sky. "You made it just in time."

I shook my head, wanting to punch him for leaving me in the woods. "When do we leave?" I asked, hoping for at least a few hours of rest.

Pat looked me over closely. "We'll leave the day after tomorrow."

Arthur wrapped an arm around my shoulders and jostled my already sore muscles. When I flinched, he let me go, slapped my back, and smiled at me with his usual warmth. There was no man like Arthur.

I must have looked grotesque with my torn and bloody clothes and the gash across my head, because Lucy had a worried look on her face when she rushed up to me. I could feel her tension slip away when she saw my wide smile, however, and she hugged me tightly before letting go.

"I knew you'd come back," she said finally. "Don't you dare do that again!"

"As if I had a choice." I looked over at Pat and Tommy, who were still smiling broadly. I looked around at all those gathered around me and finally saw Sarah standing on the porch of the main house. When I caught her eye, she slowly moved down the steps and along the path until she stood directly in front of me. She put her hand up while examining the wound to my forehead, tracing it in the air without actually making contact. I saw tears in her eyes, and she covered her mouth and turned away. Without saying a word, she walked quickly toward the stable.

I looked at Pat with concern. "Is something wrong?"

"She was worried about you. She almost broke my arm when I told her what we did."

I looked in her direction, and as I wondered if I should follow her, she rode her horse out of the stable and galloped away.

"Don't worry about Sarah," Pat said. "She's relieved that you're back. She just needs some time alone. Let's get you something to eat."

"Someone should go after her." Remembering the grotesque man in the woods, I started for the stable to get my horse.

"Don't worry. She won't leave the ranch."

I turned briefly. "She can't be left alone. Someone needs to go with her."

"What's wrong, Michael?"

"I know this will sound strange, but I met a man in the woods who said he's on his way here. Something wasn't right about him, so I left in the middle of the night to get here before he did."

Pat looked at his brothers, who'd both heard what I said, and gestured for them to go to the stable to follow Sarah. Pat stopped my progress with a hand on my arm. "What did this man say?"

"He told me that he was a friend of yours and was coming to pick something up."

"Come inside and tell me everything." Giving me no choice, Pat led me inside with a hand gripping my shoulder. "What was the man's name?"

"He said his name is Henry, and that he's a close friend." I sat at the table, and May brought me some food from the kitchen. Pat stayed with me and continued to ask about the man in the woods. I described him in detail and tried to recall everything he had said.

"I don't know a mountain man named Henry." A muscle started to twitch in Pat's jaw, and his eyes took on a desperate look. He absentmindedly rubbed a spot near his ribs. "I only know Jules, who has lived in these parts since he was a boy. But from what you describe, this man definitely wasn't Jules. He doesn't go anywhere without his mule."

"Pat, this man wasn't right in the head. If you had met him, you'd know it."

Pat looked more uncomfortable than I had ever seen him. His face was flushed, and he had begun to sweat around his forehead and temples. It wasn't that he was nervous so much as that he seemed physically ill. He wiped the moisture away with his handkerchief and stood, ending our conversation. Pat told me he had to think for bit, so I left him alone and headed for my small cabin. The uneasiness in my stomach increased, and a headache formed behind my right eye.

Several hours later, I woke to a knock on my door. Before acknowledging it, Sarah entered my room and quietly closed the door. I sat up quickly, a bit disoriented, and stood to be near her. Now that she was there, I didn't plan to let her go without resolving everything between us. I leaned over to the table and lit the lantern. It suffused the room with a cool yellow glow.

Sarah had obviously ridden a great deal throughout the day, as her dress was lined with mud and her face was red from the sun. I found her appearance quite lovely.

"I'm sorry I woke you," she said quietly. "Should I leave and let you sleep?" She shifted her weight and turned the knob on the door.

I reached out quickly and grabbed her hand. "No, please don't go. I've wanted to speak with you all day."

"So have I," she said with a smile. I noticed that she didn't pull away from my touch. Instead, I felt a slight squeeze of my hand as she stepped forward. "Are you all right?" She looked worried about the bandage on my forehead.

"Actually, I'm quite well. Your brothers gave me an incredible gift."

She looked at me disbelievingly and shook her head. "I almost strangled Pat and Tommy when I found out what they did."

"Well, I learned some good lessons while in those woods." I glanced at her and then smiled mischievously. "The last of which was to never go hunting with your brothers." This comment caused Sarah to laugh, and her face shone with instant warmth and tenderness.

"Sarah," I said, after the quiet between us returned, "about the other day—"

"We were both upset," she interrupted, placing a hand on my chest. "The things you said were done so out of frustration. I understand that now."

"I meant what I said." I looked at her quizzically, not understanding what she meant. Perhaps she was trying to give me an easy way out—one I was not planning to take.

"You meant to insult me?" she asked, confused. She had moved away, back toward the door.

"How could my telling you I love you insult you?"

"Oh," she said with a small laugh. "I thought you were talking about when you told me your plan had no place for a woman."

I smiled at her in relief as well, moving closer. "In that case, I'm sorry to have offended you."

"Since you mention it, however," she said hesitantly, "did you mean it when you said you loved me ... or was that frustration as well?"

Without hesitation, I stepped close to her and kissed her gently. She didn't push me away or falter in any way. She wrapped her hands around my neck and pulled me close. "It was frustration, all right," I said when we separated, "but not the kind you think."

I watched the blush creep up her neck and into her cheeks as we held each other in the candlelight. Her eyes were moist with tears as she gazed up at me. "I was so worried for you," she said, eyeing the bandage on my forehead again.

"I was worried as well," I whispered. "When I found out you had left for Little Bird's, I wasn't sure if you were leaving because of me."

"Actually, I did leave in part because of you. I didn't mean to disappear with so many things left unsaid, however. And then when I came back and found you gone, I was terrified." She wiped a tear from her cheek.

"Why are you crying?" I swept another tear from her cheek with my thumb.

"I have waited a long time for you to tell me how you feel," she said, producing more tears.

I pulled out a handkerchief and dabbed away the moisture on her face. Holding her close, I kissed her neck. "I love you," I whispered in her ear. Then I pulled away to look into her eyes. "I love the way the candlelight strikes your hair, creating a beautiful glow, and I love the way your hair hangs around your face, no matter how much you pull it up." I lifted a long strand and tucked it behind her ear as I kissed her softly on the lips. "I thought I would go mad over the last few days, not being able to talk to you."

She stood on her toes and kissed me lightly. "How do you feel now?"

"Wonderful." I pulled her into my embrace. She wrapped her arms around my back and leaned against my body. A fire slowly built as we swayed together in the dim room.

"You didn't tell me why you left the other day," I said.

"Will wanted me to go with him to Little Bird's to pick up something for Lucy."

"What did you pick up?"

"I can't say. It's a surprise for her."

I looked into her wonderful stormy gray eyes and smiled. "Secrets, secrets."

My flippant comment about secrets seemed to stir something inside Sarah. She stepped out of my embrace and sat on the bed. "Michael," she said quietly, "do you still plan on going with my brothers to find Turner?"

I knelt in front of her and placed my hands on both

sides of her on the bed. "This is something I need to do. Please understand." I rested my head against hers, taking a deep breath, hoping to have a few more moments of peace together.

"I do," she said quietly. "Lucy and I talked about it, and I know now why you feel you have to do this. It doesn't mean I want you to go, but I understand why you feel you have to."

I sighed a great breath of relief. Fighting with Sarah was the last thing I wanted to do just before leaving with her brothers. I wished to make the most of every minute we had left together.

I led Sarah toward the corner of the room and sat down in the rocking chair next to the bed. After settling comfortably in the chair, I pulled her onto my lap so I could continue holding her close.

Sarah slowly lifted her head and stared sadly into my eyes. "Before you leave," she said, "I want to tell you about your pa's death."

"I already know how my father died. The railroad said he died of an infection."

"I realized while you were gone that you cannot possibly go searching for the man unless you understand all his sins," she said, not acknowledging my statement. She seemed a thousand miles away.

"When Maggie was found in her cabin after Turner beat her that last time, we sent a message to your father about her condition. She stayed at his cabin to recover." Sarah shifted to face me, and I noticed tears on her cheeks. "After Lilly died, Pat went after Turner in a fury. When he didn't return home, my brothers went looking for him, found Lilly, and raced toward town. They later found Pat lying in the forest, shot several times and barely alive."

The tears increased as Sarah recalled the pain the family had endured after Lilly's death. "Pat was lost in a world of grief and anger and was hell-bent on finding Turner. He never told us what happened that day. I don't know if he can't remember because he was in shock from his wounds ... or if he just can't bear to think about it." Sarah had curled up tighter next to me in the chair. I wrapped my arms tightly around her in hopes of shielding some of the pain.

"They ended up taking Pat to Six Moons', where he spent several months in bed. Red stayed at the ranch to make sure I was safe, while Tommy and Will left to find Turner. Your father returned to the ranch and found out what had happened. He joined the search for Maggie."

"So Turner was telling Lucy the truth, that he killed my father?"

"Yes. After hearing about the abuse Maggie endured, your father wouldn't accept Pat's notion that she would help Turner. He left the ranch in search of her—and hopefully to find the truth about what happened that terrible day. Your father ran into Turner in Fort Collins and shot him twice before Turner got away. Then he continued his search for Maggie."

She rested her head against my shoulder and closed her eyes. "When your father returned to town several weeks later, Turner and his men were waiting. Your father was shot in the back while riding toward the ranch. He hung on for five days before finally letting go. He never said a word about where he had gone, or whether he found Maggie. He never had the chance." Sarah sighed and slowly wiped the tears from her face with her hand.

When she rested her head back on my shoulder, she brushed her fingers along my neck. "I'm sorry I didn't tell you sooner," she said softly. "You deserved to know the truth about how your father died. It's just so difficult to re-live those years."

"Thank you, Sarah," I said softly into her ear. We re-mained together, rocking back and forth, watching out the window as the clouds slowly drifted across the moon. Unlike with most people, the silence was comfortable with Sarah. We could spend hours together, without ever making a sound, and be truly at ease.

After several minutes, I noticed that Sarah's breathing had changed to a slow, even rhythm. I looked down to find her peacefully sleeping against my chest, with moisture still lining her eyes. Her tenderness was inescapable, and the candlelight shimmered in her golden brown hair.

Placing my arm beneath her knees, I lifted her off the chair and settled her on the bed. I covered her with a blanket.

"Don't leave me," she said sleepily, without opening her eyes. She placed her hand on my arm to keep me close.

"Never," I whispered, bending to kiss her forehead. I reached for the extra blanket and settled next to Sarah on the bed. Any anxiety I'd once felt had been erased with her gentle, loving touch. Before drifting off to sleep, I held her close, feeling overwhelming joy fill my soul.

———————※((◉))※———————

I woke while it was still dark, entwined with Sarah peace-fully sleeping in my arms. I rested my head in my hand and watched her as she slept. The lantern had gone out during the night, leaving the room dark, with nothing but the moon to light it. Her face was sweet, and her lips were full and red. She looked positively blissful lying there in my arms, and I didn't want to move or disturb her sleep. I enjoyed watching the slight movement of her mouth and the curves of her body. She was truly amazing, a gift in my life. I lay my head back down and sighed deeply with contentment. Her hand moved gracefully up to my head, and she started running her fingers through my hair.

"You aren't worrying about the future, are you?" she asked quietly.

"As a matter of fact, I was just thinking about how I have never felt this peaceful." I raised my head to find her looking at me with pleasure. I rolled onto my side so I was facing her.

She gently traced the area around my old bullet wound and then kissed it softly. "I know I cannot stop you from going, but will you promise me you'll be careful?"

"Nothing could keep me from coming back here."

The memories of past terrors and pain reminded us both how precious our time was together, and we stayed up through the rest of the night, holding each other close, as if it would be the last time we were ever together.

I noticed the sun start to rise, creating a pink glow in the sky. Sarah seemed to have read my thoughts as she leaned into me. "I should probably leave before Lucy wakes," she whispered. "Do you think she would feel this was scandalous, my spending the night here?"

I grinned widely. "Actually, I think it would please her to no end." Sarah kicked me under the covers and pushed me away. Not wanting her to leave, I grasped her arm and pulled her back, hugging her tightly as we laughed. "As for your brothers, however, I think they'd be more than happy to tie me to a rope and have a horse drag me back to Philadelphia if they found out you spent the night in my room."

Sarah laughed. "You're probably right."

"Oh, so the thought of my being tortured brings you joy, does it?"

"No, but the thought that I have brothers who care so much does." She smiled and kissed me once more before getting up and straightening her clothes. I walked her to the door, not wanting the night to end, but knowing there wasn't a choice.

"Thank you for telling me about my father, Sarah. It's the first time I've been given a glimpse of the man he truly was."

She smiled sweetly, kissing me gently on the cheek. I kissed her once more and then watched her stroll down the path toward her house.

———— ◉ ————

Sarah met me in the stable later that morning. She stood in silence, watching me work. I finally looked up and noticed her casually leaning against the railing, assessing me. A shiver of excitement ran through me knowing that she'd been watching me work—knowing that she *liked* watching me work.

My future had changed dramatically the night before. Instead of uncertainty, I had woken that morning with a clear sense of my place in the world. With every motion and every bead of sweat on my brow, I knew I'd be staying in Colorado to begin a new life with Sarah.

I slowly stood, rested the shovel against the wall, and motioned Sarah forward with my finger. She looked lovely in a pale green skirt and crisp white shirt, with her hair pulled up into a loose knot. She wore a brilliant smile that widened when she placed her hands behind her back and sauntered forward. She took an awfully long time to reach me.

"It occurs to me," I said, grinning, "that you never told me how you felt about me last night. I was somewhat ... distracted ... and didn't think to ask."

"Oh, yes," she said, coming closer so that our bodies touched. "I seem to recall your ... distraction." She slid her hand slowly up my chest.

I took several steps backward, out of her reach. "Oh, no you don't," I said, pointing at her to stay put. "You keep your hands to yourself." She lowered her arm and frowned with disappointment.

Quickly changing my mind, I looked around the stable and took her hand in mine. "Well, at least until you answer my question."

She kissed me briefly. "I thought I showed you perfectly well how I feel."

"Yes, you did do that," I said quietly, "but I would still like to hear it."

She moved against me and placed her cheek next to mine. "Of course I love you, you big idiot."

I tilted my head back and laughed loudly. I would have expected nothing different from my sweet Sarah. "That will do."

"Would you be able to take a walk with me after you are finished here?" she asked, tightening her grip on my hand.

"Nothing could keep me away." I leaned down and kissed her tenderly. All ideas of work swiftly escaped my mind as I held her body next to mine, making me reluctant to let go. I wrapped my fingers around hers and kissed her hand as we parted.

Before letting go, I noticed a slight movement near the entrance to the stable, and when I turned, I found Pat leaning against the wall, watching us closely. Sarah jumped and started to move away, but I squeezed her hand tighter and kept her close. I wanted her to know that now that we were together, nothing would come between us again.

Pat straightened and came closer. I could feel Sarah's anxiety through her shaking hand, and I could see the apprehension on her face. After my conversations with Pat, however, I felt confident about his acceptance of what Sarah and I shared.

A grin spread across Pat's face, and he winked at Sarah. She looked confused, but her tension eased a little when she saw Pat smile.

"Well, I didn't mean to interrupt," he said, clearing his throat, "but Michael and I need to talk." Sarah looked at me and hesitated, obviously trying to figure out what was going on. Pat moved closer to her and kissed her on the cheek. "Don't worry, Sarah, I just want to talk with him for a few minutes alone. I promise to deliver him back to you in one piece."

I squeezed her hand again and let go. "I'll see you in a few minutes." I kissed her lightly on the cheek. The intimacy in front of her brother made her blush, and she lowered her head to hide her embarrassment.

As she walked away, Pat laughed at the increased color in her cheeks. It was so rare to see Sarah embarrassed, and Pat and I both enjoyed the novelty. She repaid his teasing by punching him in the stomach as she passed him. He bent over and held his ribs, still laughing as she left the stable.

Pat slowly recovered and stood up straight, rubbing his stomach. "Let's go for a walk." He motioned for me to follow him outside and down the path, away from the ranch. I noticed his expression change considerably the farther we got from the stable and from Sarah. His smile first disappeared, and then it slowly lowered into a fierce frown. He waited until he knew we were alone, and that no one could hear us, before he stopped walking.

He stood close to me and spoke quietly. "It's about Turner."

"What is it?"

"Tommy returned from town today. He found out that the man Josiah was with when they tried to shoot you was Frank, a ranch hand that's been workin' here for about a year."

"How did he find out?" I asked, stress beginning to build in my shoulders. "You said yourself that you've tried to find information about Josiah and couldn't find anything."

"Turner's been watchin' us for some time. Josiah and Frank have been passing him information about the ranch since you first got here." Pat's face was lined with tension and nervousness.

"How long was Josiah helping Turner? I was under the impression that he'd been on the ranch for some time."

"He just started workin' for him after you arrived at the ranch," Pat replied. "It seems you were right. When he realized he didn't have a chance with Sarah, he went to town to drown his sorrows, with Frank by his side. R. J. befriended him and told Josiah that you had arrived at the ranch to cause Sarah harm. Everything he did, he thought he was doin' for her. He helped deliver information to Turner and tried to kill you to win her favor. He was young and naive."

"Where is Frank now?"

"I don't know. He may have just left town after what happened to Josiah. No one has seen or heard from him."

"I'm so sorry, Pat," I said, shaking my head. Too much hardship had already been placed on his shoulders without having to deal with my family as well.

"Don't be," he said with a shrug. "Josiah never had a

chance with Sarah, and R. J. has a way of manipulating people, especially those as young as Josiah. He was weak and jealous. There is nothin' you could've done to stop his actions."

"What does this mean for us?" I asked, thinking about the dangers that lay hidden all around the ranch. "Do we still leave tomorrow morning?"

Pat slowly nodded and looked back toward the ranch. "He knows our plans, which means we need to leave right away, before he makes his next move." Pat scanned the horizon and raised his determined eyes to meet mine. "I can't let him get away again."

"Do you know where he is?"

"That's the worst part, Mike." He hesitated a moment. "I am rather certain Turner was the man you met in the woods."

25

THE LONG GOOD-BYE

"**A**re you telling me that I may have sat across a fire and shared a meal with the man who raped and tried to kill my sister?" All the blood drained from my face, and my anger caught hold.

"You couldn't have known, Mike," Pat said, seeing my horrified expression. "You knew he wasn't right when you locked eyes on him, and you came home to warn us. That's all you could do."

"I could have killed him!"

"You'll still have your chance."

Why couldn't I have known? This would all be over now instead of just beginning. I thought about everything that had happened, and everything that needed to be done. I knew Pat wouldn't be leaving without knowing for sure that we could find Turner. He was a thinker, a ruminator. He took his time to make sure his actions were appropriate. After I learned about his wife's death, I also understood that he wanted nothing more than to find Turner and remove him from decent society.

"Mike," he said, after watching me in silence, "with Turner this close, the ranch is in great danger. I don't know if he's alone or meetin' up with some of his men, and I'm no longer sure who I can trust on the ranch. This puts Sarah, Lucy, and the little ones in danger if we leave."

"I understand. I've been worried about leaving the ranch as well." This new information about Turner and how close he was to Lucy made me cringe. How could we leave with that man in the woods, waiting to strike again? But we couldn't stay and just wait for the worst to happen. It was time for action.

"I sent Red to town yesterday for help. There are men comin' to the ranch this afternoon, and they'll stay till we return. They'll also keep an eye out for anything out of sorts. I trust these men like family. They won't let me down."

"Who knows about our departure?"

"Only my brothers, Red, and Sarah. Even my children don't know yet. It's important to leave without anyone's notice."

"I have to tell Lucy," I said, "but I'll wait until this evening. I also want Arthur to stay here at the ranch. He will ensure her safety."

"I reckon you're right." Pat turned and walked back toward the main house with me following close behind. Even though I felt great anxiety about leaving Sarah, and would feel even more if she insisted upon going, my goals hadn't changed. I supported Pat and would help him in every way I could. I had Lucy to think about as well. Even though she'd hate the fact that I was leaving, there had to be an accounting. Turner had hurt too many people to let him slip by once again.

Killing Josiah had originally given me doubts as to whether I could kill again. He was a confused and jealous young man who had made bad decisions in his life. I regretted having killed him, but after learning about his ties with Turner, I figured his death might have saved the Donnelly family and the ranch. Some of the guilt I had been feeling since the day of the shooting was relieved with this new information.

When I thought of killing Turner, I didn't feel the same reluctance as I did about the death of Josiah. I felt no hesitation at all. He was pure evil and needed to be stopped before causing further harm.

"Pat." I stopped him before we left the path. "There is one more thing I want to talk to you about before we leave."

"What is it?"

"I plan to ask Sarah to marry me," I said carefully, "but I don't plan to ask her until after our return. I wouldn't want to put that kind of strain on her if something happens."

He nodded and placed his arm around my shoulders, leading me toward the house. "I guess we'll just have to make sure you come back on home, then, won't we?"

"I'd appreciate that."

"Sarah has an awful temper, Mike," he said. "If you don't come home, I reckon we're all in trouble."

I laughed with him at the thought of Sarah's fiery spirit and knew he was probably right. He told me the family would all be having dinner together that night, and that he expected Lucy and me to be there.

———— «◉» ————

I rode up the hill as the sun was beginning to stretch its fingers toward dusk. There was nothing in the world more beautiful than a Colorado sunset. I could find more colors in the spring sky than I ever imagined existing in one place, and each moment created a change so glorious it took my breath away.

It was no wonder I chose dusk to begin the long ride up the hill and through the valley to the edge of the trees to complete my task. I had thought about it since first speaking to Pat, and as the moments lingered closer to the time I'd have to leave with the Donnelly men, I knew I couldn't leave without finishing what I'd set out to do.

I stopped near a grove of aspens and took a deep breath before dismounting and hobbling Ginger nearby. I headed slowly toward the trees, stopping next to a pile of rocks gathered together on the ground. I hadn't returned to that spot since I'd first marked it with stones after Josiah's death. Even though he was buried deep in the ground in the cemetery in town, I'd felt a need to mark the area where he died as a reminder. I had found a group of small white rocks that were piled high near the clearing in the trees.

Pat had attempted to find Josiah's family, but after a long search, he couldn't find a single person to mourn the loss of the young man. It seemed he'd lived most of his life utterly and completely alone. In a way, I couldn't blame Josiah for his alliance with Turner, or for his hasty judgment where I was concerned. He was desperate to belong to something or someone in this world, and perhaps he thought Turner's gang could give him comfort or a sense of family. Instead, it led to his ruin.

If I felt anything for the young man, it was pity. I continued to focus all my anger and hurt toward Jack Turner. Josiah turned to that dark man while his emotions were raw and dangerous, and Turner exploited those feelings for his own benefit.

I knelt down in the wet grass and stared at the rocks for a few minutes before speaking. "Josiah," I said aloud, "I've come here to let you know that I forgive you." I pulled several weeds away from the rocks and tended to the surrounding area. "I haven't forgotten that you are the man responsible for beating me within an inch of my life. I haven't forgotten that you frightened Sarah on more than one occasion. And I haven't forgotten that when I shot you, you were trying your damnedest to end my life." By the time I was done speaking, I found that I was violently yanking the weeds from the area.

Standing, I took another long, deep breath before continuing. "Despite all your actions, I feel I know a little more about you now. I know more about Turner and his methods for getting what he wants from innocent people. I know that you were lured by promises he made you, and the thought that you were doing the right thing.

"I also sympathize with you with regard to Sarah. God knows I haven't been able to resist her charms. For that fact alone, knowing that you thought you were saving her from evil, I forgive everything you did to me. Sarah is worth all the protection in the world. I have no doubt that you genuinely cared a great deal for her.

"Whether it will bring you any sense of peace, I intend to leave this ranch tomorrow and search out the man whose lies caused your death as much as the bullet fired from my gun. I seek vengeance for both of us, and perhaps peace will follow. As for Sarah, the only thing I can offer you is the promise that I will spend all my living days ensuring her safety and happiness."

I turned and readied Ginger to ride back to the ranch. I took one last look at the marker on the ground before continuing forward. "God keep you, Josiah," I said, placing my hat back on my head. "Hopefully you can find some peace."

I spent the rest of the afternoon preparing for our travels. None of us knew how long we'd be gone, but I packed only necessities, other than the journal Sarah had given me. No matter what happened, I would carry that journal with me everywhere.

When I finished and felt there was nothing more I could do, I stepped outside to search for Lucy. She was sitting on the bench and wringing a cloth in her hands. As soon as she saw me, she stood and embraced me tightly. Her anxiety was overflowing, and she refused to let me go.

"What is it, Lucy?"

"You're leaving, aren't you?" I could see that she had been crying, and the tension had left its mark on her beautiful face.

"How did you know?" I wiped her hair from her face.

"I always know what's going on with you." She continued to hug me tightly, with both arms wrapped around my chest.

I pulled away to look at her. "We leave at sunrise tomorrow morning, but before I can leave, I need to know that you'll be all right."

She finally let go and placed her fists on my chest, tightly wrapping the fabric of my shirt in her fingers. "I'll be all right when you come back home," she said, shaking me.

"Lucy, I will be coming back." I looked into her eyes and noticed the fear and the worry hidden behind those long lashes. "I promise to return to you in one piece."

"You cannot make such a promise, Michael," she said with irritation.

"Of course I can. I have to come home if I plan to get married."

Lucy took a quick step back and stared at me with astonishment. Her eyes were wide and her jaw gaped open. "You asked Sarah?"

"She loves me, Lucy," I said with a schoolboy smile, "and I love her. I plan to ask for her hand on the day I return."

Her hands flew up to her mouth as she laughed, bouncing up and down. "Oh, Michael, I am so happy for you." She hugged me again, much tighter, and jiggled back and forth. The thought of my marriage had completely erased her concern.

I glanced over her shoulder and noticed Sarah and Will heading toward our cabin. As soon as Lucy turned and caught sight of Sarah, she bounded off the porch and ran toward her. She wasted no time in swinging her arms outward, hugging Sarah tightly as well.

"I am so happy," she said with a squeeze. Sarah had a puzzled look on her face as she looked over Lucy's shoulder, but she hugged her back nonetheless. It wasn't often that people saw Lucy so happy.

Catching up to them, I laughed at Lucy while keeping my eyes on Sarah. "I'll explain later," I told Sarah, taking her hand in mine to lead her toward the path away from the ranch. Before leaving, I leaned toward Lucy. "Pat wants us to have dinner with his family tonight, but I promise to talk to you more when we return to the cabin."

She smiled up at me and quickly kissed me on the cheek. She then led Will to the porch. Sarah and I paused in front of the cabin, watching Lucy walk away. It was so nice to see Lucy and Will so comfortable together. Her lessons had continued almost every day, and she now had a confidence about her that could be seen in her walk, her posture, and especially her smile. Will had given her back her freedom and her sense of peace.

I glanced to my left and found Sarah watching me with a knowing smile on her face. I placed her hand in the crook of my elbow and finally led her down the path toward the river, hoping to escape the watchful eyes of those around us.

As we walked quietly toward the trees, Sarah clung to my arm, trembling slightly. The expression on her face had changed as well, showing me for the first time how terribly afraid she was for her brothers and me. She had lived through all the hard times at the ranch and had already faced Turner on many occasions. Through the tough exterior that she usually portrayed, I could see the fear of loss that she already had to endure. It would be hard to wake up tomorrow and leave her at the ranch to wait for our return. It would be difficult, but still necessary.

"Sarah?" I said quietly, squeezing her hand slightly as it rested on my arm. "What are you thinking?"

Arriving at the large downed tree, we sat facing one another. There was never a point in our walk or conversation where we didn't have some physical contact, as if by her keeping a hold on me, I wouldn't be able to leave. There was the brushing of her leg against mine, the holding of hands, her foot wrapped around mine, or her hand on my leg. I believe she was doing her best to keep it together, but the stress was overwhelming. It wasn't only me leaving her, but all her brothers as well.

"I don't want today to end," she said finally, after a long silence.

"Sarah, I have to leave," I replied, pleading with her to understand. "But I promise you that I'll return as soon as possible."

"You can't make that promise, Michael."

"You sound more like my sister every day," I said with a sigh. I ran my fingers through my hair and grasped her hands. "Should a man like Turner just be allowed to continue tormenting decent folk? Should we just wait until he hurts another person?"

"Of course not."

"His men will be back, Sarah," I continued. "They know where we are and will come after us. They've already taken too much from this family and this ranch. We must do something. I think it's about time he learned not to mess with innocent people."

I tried to convince her that it wasn't a choice but a matter of time before a confrontation occurred. I smiled at her and raised my eyebrows as I leaned close. "Who better to teach him proper manners than a dandy from the good city of Philadelphia?"

With that, I finally got a slight smile from her lips. "You're impossible," she said, sliding her arm through mine while laying her head on my shoulder. "Absolutely impossible." In a silent gesture, she'd finally told me she understood.

———— ❦ ————

As soon as Lucy sat down on the bench on the porch, Will took his usual seat in the rocking chair and carelessly threw a package onto her lap. "I know I taught you to defend yourself," he said, "and I know you will if you have to, but I wanted you to have this anyway."

Lucy remained silent as she unwrapped the cloth to find a pearl-handled derringer pistol, small enough to put in her pocket. She placed the light pistol in her hand, testing the weight and feeling it before she looked back up at Will. The expression on his face was surprising. His usual casual nature and kind smile had been replaced with unease and lines of worry around his eyes.

When he realized that Lucy was watching him, he schooled his expression back to the calm pleasantness she had become accustomed to. Lucy realized at that moment that Will and her brother might not return.

Lucy didn't want to be left alone again, but she knew that no matter how hard she pleaded, it was bound to happen. So instead of ranting or screaming, she thanked Will for the pistol and bravely told him she would be waiting at the ranch for his return.

"Don't you dawdle now," she said, her chin tilted up. "You take care of business and get back to the ranch. There's a lot of work that needs to be done."

Will smiled as if knowing well the anxiety Lucy had to be hiding. "Yes, ma'am," he teased. "And promise me that if any man approaches you that you don't know, you aim that gun at his heart and fire. Ask questions later ... understand?"

"Don't worry," she said, straightening her shoulders. "I won't let you down."

"We'll come home soon," he added, "and don't worry none about Mike. We may give him a hard time, and Tommy enjoys tormentin' him, but he's a strong man, and he's ready. There's no man I'd rather have on my side than your brother."

"Me either."

"Speakin' of Mike," he said, looking toward the path, "here he comes. I should help him and my brothers get ready."

She turned to see Sarah and her brother coming out of the woods hand in hand, laughing happily. Lucy stood and brushed off her skirt with her hands. "Thank you again, Will ... for everything." She took his hand and squeezed it gently. "You have given me more that I can ever repay, but I'd still like the chance to try. You had better come back in one piece."

"I'll do what I can, Lucy."

———◦《◉》◦———

I caught up with Arthur before we all were scheduled to meet for dinner. While Pat and I had become as close as brothers, there was no one I trusted more than Arthur.

"I wanted to talk to you before we all leave tomorrow," I said quietly. "Would you come with me to the stable so I can check on Ginger?"

"Aye."

"I need to ask you a favor, Arthur."

"Aye, lad."

We stopped when we reached the stable, and I reached into my inner coat pocket to retrieve three letters I had written that morning after Sarah left the cabin. One was addressed to Lucy, another to Sarah, and the last was for Arthur. "I would like you to keep these letters safe for me until I return."

The letters were intended to be read if I didn't return from the fight with Turner. We had already agreed that Arthur would remain at the ranch to watch over Lucy and Sarah, while Red continued to run the ranch in our absence. I hoped to be able to burn the letters upon my return to the ranch, but there were still too many unknowns. I didn't want to die with too many words left unsaid.

Arthur understood immediately. He took the letters from my hand and placed them in his pocket. "I'd rather not have to face either of them with such a task, lad, but I'll keep them safe while you're gone." His expression was sad as he patted his pocket. I thanked him with a heavy heart as I entered the stable and he headed to the main house.

26

THE FIGHT BEGINS

I woke and bolted upright. The sun hadn't come up yet, and I found nothing but darkness outside my window. Then I heard it. I focused on the room and the early morning darkness, realizing that someone was knocking on the cabin door.

With the sense of dread that often settled in my stomach, I quickly dressed before leaving the room to answer the insistent pounding. Before I could answer, however, Pat burst into the cabin, sending slivers of wood flying as he broke the lock on the door. Arthur came in behind him, eyes ablaze. He pushed Pat aside and went toward Lucy's room. I could see the relief on Arthur's face as soon as he saw Lucy standing in the hallway.

"What's going on?" she asked.

"Have either of you seen Eddie?" Pat asked hastily, looking around the cabin and out the door.

"Why would he be here?" I asked nervously. I remembered the conversation I'd had with Eddie in the stable about Turner and realized I never told Pat. "What's going on?"

"Eddie's gone! I can't find him anywhere. I thought—I

hoped—maybe he was here with you and Lucy." He cleared his throat awkwardly and regained his composure, searching the cabin from room to room. "I've told him again and again not to leave the area, but he's been restless and fidgety for days."

Tommy and Will rushed into the cabin a few minutes later, informing Pat that they had searched the outbuildings and found Eddie's horse missing, with a fresh set of tracks heading toward town.

"Pat, his tracks weren't the only ones," Tommy continued, stress in his voice. "A trail of tracks met up with Eddie's horse and, as far as we can tell, followed him toward town.

I ran to my bedroom and grabbed my pistols and my packed saddlebags. I turned to Lucy, who was holding on to Arthur's arm. "I'm sorry Lucy, but—"

"Go with them, Michael," she said with confidence. "Pat needs your help. I'll be all right."

I nodded and shoved a rifle at Arthur. I then checked my guns to make sure they were loaded. Before leaving, I kissed Lucy on the cheek and looked at Arthur. "If anyone comes anywhere near you or my sister, shoot him!"

Arthur straightened his shoulders. "No problem."

Thoughts of Pat's anguish and all the possibilities of Eddie's capture raced through my mind. I had to get to the stable and saddle Ginger before the men caught up to Eddie. Will and Tommy saddled up and raced toward Little Bird's homestead to get reinforcements before meeting Pat and me in town. After we'd quickly saddled our horses, I jumped on Ginger's back and rode away from the ranch with Pat in front of me. I don't think he even knew I was there. He plainly had a single-minded determination to destroy those who were a threat to his son.

Not too far from the ranch, we came upon a man walking near the tracks. He held his right arm close to his body. He had no chance of raising his pistol before Pat jumped off his horse and wrapped his hands around the man's throat. It took every bit of strength I had to remove him from the injured man.

"Where is my son, you bastard!" he shouted, trying to go after the man again. Tears of fury were in his eyes as he lunged forward. I held him back again, while trying to get information from the man who now lay on the ground.

Realizing Pat would gladly kill him, the man finally volunteered that when they'd caught up with Eddie and tried to grab his horse, the animal had kicked the man in the chest, causing him to fall and break his arm. Eddie tried to ride away but was quickly intercepted by Turner's men. They were taking him to town.

We leapt on our horses and continued our race toward town, leaving the man to find his way on his own. I pushed Ginger faster and harder than ever, trying to keep up with Pat in his pursuit. I'd never forgive myself if anything happened to Eddie or any other member of the Donnelly clan. The very man I had been hunting had given me a warning that night in the woods, but it didn't fully make sense until Eddie disappeared. I should have known Turner from Lucy's description—especially after seeing his horrible teeth. And I should've taken Eddie's comments more seriously. My mind kept circling around as the mountain of guilt weighed me down.

I heard gunshots in the streets before we even arrived

in town. People were scattering for cover, and screams were heard as men on horseback entered the town. We couldn't see Eddie, but I knew from all the commotion that Turner must be near. The town had filled with armed strangers. The rest of Turner's men had arrived.

After tying our horses to the corral at the livery on the outskirts of town, we drew our weapons and crept along the inside of the building to get a closer look. The men on horses continued to shoot at any face they could see from doorways or windows. Before we were able to reach the front door, gunshots were fired into the stalls, splintering the wood and ricocheting off metal that hung from the ceiling.

We ducked near the entrance to the livery and peered outside to find out where the shots were coming from. A horse grunted and fell when a stray bullet hit him in the neck. The other horses kicked and thrashed in their stalls, unable to get out of the line of fire.

I glanced out of the livery again, and the first person I noticed was a man standing against the side of the mercantile, shooting directly at us. I shot his gun out of his hand, and the second bullet caught him in the chest. He fell to the ground.

Pat left the livery along one side of the building as I moved along the other. Most of the men on horses were preoccupied, so I crept quietly around the building to get a better view of the chaos in the street. A man was leaning against the outer wall of the jail, peering inside. Walking quietly behind him, I tapped him on the shoulder. Before he could turn around, I broke his arm and disarmed him in one swift motion. I pinned him up against the wall and elbowed him powerfully in the nose, causing him to fall to the ground, unconscious. I grabbed his guns and the knife strapped to his leg before continuing around the building toward the front of the brothel.

I glanced around again and found Pat on one side of the mercantile, gesturing toward me with his arm. He waved and pointed toward the roof across the street. I looked in that direction but saw nothing.

As I started to walk toward him, I finally saw what Pat had seen, and I stopped in my tracks, flat against the wall. A man lay on the roof with a rifle perched in his arms. He aimed at Pat, who was cornered behind a wagon. The man hadn't seen me, and I had a clear shot.

I leveled my pistol and aimed at the roof of the house. I fired two shots in succession, causing the man to plunge off the roof and onto the hard ground below. I watched the motionless body for a few moments and then signaled to Pat that it was clear. Pat was instantly in a dead run toward the center of town.

The noise had intensified as more people entered the fight in the street. Tommy, Will, and the men from Little Bird's family had arrived and entered the gunfight. The townspeople were mostly hidden in their homes and businesses, waiting for it to end.

Tommy was in the street. His left upper arm was bleeding, but he didn't seem to notice. He had a gun in each hand as he searched ahead of him for trouble. A man approached him from behind with a rifle near his shoulder. The man came into full view and lifted the rifle to aim it at Tommy. Before I could raise my gun, I heard a shot ring out above me and saw the villain plunge to the ground with blood dripping from his head.

I looked up to find Belle on the balcony with a smoking rifle in her arms. She bowed gracefully to me before reloading the weapon and resting it on the railing, waiting for someone else to challenge her.

Daniel glanced out the front door of Pate's Place and

waved me inside before disappearing again. I slipped in the front door to find James lying on the ground with a bullet wound to his leg—the same leg where he'd been shot the day we met. Sweat lined his brow as he hastily tied off the bleeding wound. Daniel reloaded his pistol.

"I just saw Tommy," I said. "Is Will all right?"

"As far as I can tell," Daniel replied, scanning the street again. "What the hell happened this mornin'?"

"Turner's gang took Pat's boy, Eddie, and they led us here," I said. "He has to be hiding him somewhere in town."

James slammed his fist into the floor. "That no-good goddamn son of a bitch!"

"I'm going to keep looking." I reloaded my pistol.

"I think I saw R. J. going into Buck's Saloon," James said, trying to get to his feet. "Start there."

"I think we should find the Donnelly brothers and surround the saloon," Daniel said, nodding. "We can go in as a group and draw Turner out."

"We have to check everywhere," I argued. "There's no way to know if Eddie's with him. I need your help searching the rest of the buildings in town."

"No." James shook his head violently. "If Turner is in that room, we should go together."

I looked down at James, knowing he wouldn't be moving anytime soon with such a horrible wound. "We can't take a chance with Eddie's life," I said. "We have to find him before Turner hurts him."

James and Daniel shared a knowing glance and then nodded in unison. "All right, Michael," Daniel said. "I'll check the other side of the street, while you check this side. If either of us finds Eddie, we'll meet back here."

I reached the front door and checked both my pistols, noticing Pat creeping along the wall of Belle's, slowly moving toward the back of Buck's. James was able to get Tommy's attention and lure him into Pate's Place, as Daniel moved in the shadows, from one building to the next.

There were fewer riders in the streets. Some lay dead in the dirt and mud, while others had undoubtedly fled the area when the gunfight became too heavy. Little Bird and his family had chased several men out of town, in an attempt to even the odds. I hadn't seen R. J. yet, but I knew he was still in town. He'd be the last to abandon Jack Turner for the safety of the woods.

I checked the few buildings on my side of the street before reaching the front of Buck's. Knowing I was about to face the biggest challenge of my life, I took a long, deep breath and entered the dark saloon. The bar had been destroyed, and most of the furniture had been removed. The large room was nearly empty. Feet shuffled above my head as people moved around upstairs, but no one waited to greet me as I went through the room toward the stairs.

When I placed my boot on the first step, I heard a creak and saw a quick flash from the back room. Before I could turn around, the butt of a gun struck the back of my head, causing me to stumble forward. Luckily, I wasn't knocked unconscious by the blow and managed to remain on my feet. I reeled around to face my attacker.

Three men entered the room. The man I had met in the woods stood in the middle, holding Eddie by the neck in front of him, his pistol pointed at Eddie's temple. His eyes had a crazed look, and I knew without any doubt that I was looking at the face of Jack Turner.

Moments later, Pat stormed into the saloon from the back door. As soon as he saw his son, Pat slowed, never taking his eyes off Eddie's face.

"Welcome to the party, Pat," Turner said coldly, that

crazy look in his eyes. "Drop yer guns." He kept his pistol poised at Eddie's temple, his finger on the trigger.

Pat composed himself quickly and lowered his guns to the floor. "How're you doin', son?" He was calm and methodical in his movements. He gestured for me to remove my weapons as well, and I rested them on the ground.

It was clear that Eddie was trying to be brave, but his lower lip quivered as he answered. "I'm fine, sir. But I'd be better if you'd shoot this man so I could go home."

Pat winked at his son, smiled, and faced Turner. "What do you want?"

"You know damn well what I want. Where's Maggie?"

"Maggie left the ranch the day you killed my wife," Pat said calmly. I could see a muscle jumping in his jaw as he stared at Turner. "Last I knew, you two were together."

"Well, you'd better find her quick," Turner said, disbelievingly. "Your boy's life depends on it. He stays with me as long as you hide my wife."

"I ain't stayin' with you," Eddie said defiantly. "My pa's gonna shoot you dead, mister."

Turner's grip around Eddie's neck tightened, cutting off his air. Tears sprang to Eddie's eyes as he struggled to breathe.

"I don't know where she is." Pat kept an eye on Eddie as he inched slowly forward. I couldn't tell what Pat was thinking, but I knew something was in the air. The room was quiet, and Pat spoke softly while watching his son. The two men standing near Turner seemed relaxed and confident about their situation, and the noise from outside faded.

"You won't be leaving with my son," Pat said softly. "He'll be coming home with me."

"The hell he will."

Eddie obviously knew his cue. As soon as Turner shifted

slightly and lowered the gun, Eddie fell limp in his arms, creating dead weight. When Turner looked down to try to catch him, Pat and I lunged forward. I grabbed the arm with his pistol, while Pat punched Turner in the face and took hold of his son. Eddie scurried out of the way toward the door. "Get out of here, Pat!" I yelled as Turner's men came forward. "Get Eddie to safety." Pat hesitated a moment, knowing he was leaving me alone with Turner, but he finally grabbed his son by the arm and dragged him outside.

With my knife in hand, I attempted to fight off the two still standing before me. One wrenched the knife from my grasp; the other pummeled me in the stomach. They were relentless in their punishment, never allowing me to get close enough to turn the tables.

Both my arms were restrained by the time Turner rejoined the fight. He hit me in the face and stomach, while his men held me back. The man had hands like rocks, and they assaulted my senses and rattled my bones with each devastating strike. He came after me with searing fury, blow after blow, knowing he'd lost his leverage again when Pat took Eddie away.

"All you had to do was tell me where you hid Maggie, and this would've ended long ago!" he shouted.

"I don't know Maggie, you bastard!" I hollered, getting back on my feet. "Neither does my sister, Lucy. Remember her? You used and abused her and then left her to die alone!"

Ignoring my remarks about Lucy, Turner threw a chair against the wall. "You lie!" he screamed, red in the face. "Yer pa never woulda left Maggie with all that money!"

The men on the sides of me gripped my arms, holding me up but rendering me helpless. "Like I said, I don't know Maggie, and I don't know anything about your damned money," I said evenly. "What I do know is that you are nothing but a coward, preying on defenseless people."

Turner clenched his hands into fists and started slowly toward me as I continued. "You killed my father. You killed Pat's wife. You're responsible for every nightmare and sleepless night my sister has had to endure since being beaten and raped by you."

"Yer forgettin' one thing," he said, regaining some of his control. "Once I kill you, I'll be able to do whatever I like to your little sister. I'll make her suffer more than you ever thought possible. My one night with that little bitch will seem like a holiday by the time I'm done with her."

Even though his words made me feel edgy, I maintained my composure and kept my eyes glued to his. I straightened my shoulders and focused on controlling my breathing. "You will never harm Lucy again," I responded. "She is no longer the innocent she once was. You did that to her, but you'll find she'll no longer take your abuse. If I don't kill you, she will."

Turner laughed, such an evil sound that it made my skin crawl. "That whore couldn't hurt me any more than that little girlfriend of yers." My eyes flashed, and my mouth formed into a scowl as Turner talked of Sarah. "That's right," he continued, "I know all about you and Sarah. I'll make her my prized piece when I'm done with you."

"Your days on this earth are over," I said calmly, knowing he was just trying to get me angry. "You are a worthless human," I continued, using his own strategy against him. "Women find you so disgusting you have to force them into your bed."

Turner's eyes flashed with fire as he backhanded me with his fist. The grip on my arms lessened slightly, giving me the chance I needed. "No wonder your wife left you,

you piece of shit." I slammed one man's head against the bar and pushed the other into Turner as he leapt forward. Before he could strike, I heard a door slam open, and Pat and his brothers entered the saloon.

Turner's rage kept him from taking his eyes off me, and we both lunged at the same time, striking each other brutally in the middle of the room. Turner clearly no longer cared about the money, Maggie, or anything but killing me.

Men came down the stairs, and others came from the back room. A fight broke out around us and on the stairway. Shots were fired, and furniture was broken. Pat had taken care of the men who'd held my arms, and his brothers started the brawl upstairs just as Turner's reinforcements started to arrive.

Without paying attention to anything else around us, Turner and I wrestled and punched, ultimately breaking the front window and ending up in the street outside. We fell to the ground, stunned, and then resumed the fight. Before I could rise, Turner leaned over me and grabbed my collar. "I'm gonna take great pleasure in killin' you and watchin' the last breath escape from yer filthy stinkin' corpse."

He'd made a serious mistake. He thought I was already beaten. The words no longer affected me. His days of torment were over.

I swept my left leg up and around, causing him to lose his balance and fall heavily onto his back in the mud. I scrambled to my feet and crashed into him as he tried to rise. We slipped as we wrestled on the ground. Turner pulled out his knife and slashed it across my arm. I punched him in the jaw and slapped the knife from his grasp.

All my rage was unleashed as Turner and I fought. I knocked his head into the dirt as he pummeled my chest and face. When it seemed the fight would never end, Turner planted his fist into my gut, and I doubled over. He swiftly crawled toward a pistol lying less than ten feet away.

I lunged toward a man lying dead on the ground near us and grasped his pistol firmly in my hand. I got to my feet just as Turner latched onto his gun and turned to face me. He aimed and pulled the trigger, but it only clicked in his hand. The chamber was empty. I noticed the fear in his eyes, along with the realization that he would die that day.

Unlike with Josiah, I felt nothing—no fear, no anger, no guilt, and especially no pity. For the first time, I welcomed back the vision of my sister lying naked on the floor, curled up in a ball and bleeding, her entire body bruised and beaten. I remembered her silent wish as she'd waited in that room. She had prayed to die because of what he had done to her. I leveled my pistol and aimed it at his head, thinking he had no heart, so shooting him in the chest would be a waste of time.

"Wait!" he pleaded, raising his hands in surrender.

"I'm tired of waiting," I said coldly, pulling the trigger without hesitation.

I kept my pistol aimed at him, even though I knew he was dead. The color had faded from his skin, and a glaze passed over his eyes. After a few moments, I stepped back and lowered my gun to my side. A nearby shot made me blink and look away. Pat was holding his own against a man in the street, and the others began to pour out of the saloon and surrounding buildings. Tommy and Will were close enough to lend help to their brother, while the townspeople found the courage to join the fight.

Taking a deep breath, I backed up a few more steps. That's when I felt the blinding pain. The first bullet struck my back, and the second cracked a rib on my side. I turned and fired blindly as one last shot pierced my abdomen, and

I fell to my knees on the ground. I had been shot in the back—just like my father.

I attempted to get up but found no strength to support me. Several more shots were fired in succession, but I didn't think they were aimed at me, as none came anywhere near where I was lying. The last of Turner's men hastily gathered their horses and rode away.

I turned my head to find R. J. standing several feet away, clutching his chest. He seemed suspended in time, staring down the long street through town. As the blood began to show along the left side of his gray shirt, he collapsed and fell face-first into the dirt.

With what little energy I had left, I followed the path R. J.'s eyes had taken before he died. A lone woman stood in the middle of the gunfight. She stood tall with flaming red hair blowing in the wind, her pistol still pointed in R. J.'s direction. I had the strange feeling I knew the woman who'd joined our battle. Even though I had never met her, it could be no other than the elusive Maggie.

The gunshots stopped, and silence crept across the town. I couldn't even hear the wind blow or the people in the street. Relaxing my head on the ground, my eyes shifted to the sky, with its glorious shades of yellow and pink. I closed my eyes. It was going to be a beautiful day.

27

REDEMPTION

A knock came upon Lucy's door as she was preparing her things to move to the main house until the men returned to the ranch. Thinking it was Arthur returning to help, she opened the door without hesitation—but stopped abruptly as she recognized the man in front of her.

"Hello, my dear," he said with a warm smile.

"Mr. Westley?" Lucy was stunned at the sudden appearance of a man from her past, and her hands began to shake. "Is it really you?"

"Of course, Miss Mullen. I've been searching everywhere for you since you disappeared." He took both of her hands in his to steady them. "I spoke to your aunt and she told me what happened."

"You've spoken to Olivia?"

"Yes," he said. "She has been very worried about you."

"I had hoped after I wrote her that she'd no longer worry."

"Miss Mullen." Mr. Westley squeezed her hands. "Are you going to keep me outside all day, or are you going to invite me in?"

"Actually," she said, "why don't we sit out here on the

bench? I enjoy the fresh air." Lucy did enjoy the fresh air, but she had other reasons for staying outside. She hadn't seen Mr. Westley in several months. He seemed like a stranger to her, and she didn't want to be alone with him until she felt more comfortable. Also, a thought nagged at her from the back of her mind. How had Mr. Westley gotten on the ranch without anyone stopping him?

He was hesitant at first but then consented to talk outside on the porch. He continued to hold Lucy's hands as he talked to her about the past. "Lucy, I would like you to come back to Philadelphia with me."

"Mr. Westley, there is something you need to know." Lucy stood, separating herself from his touch. She didn't want to feel his reaction when she told him about the rape. "When I was taken—"

"I already know, my dear," he interrupted, standing next to her.

She looked him directly in the eye. "What do you mean?"

"I mean that I already know all about what has happened to you since you were first taken from Philadelphia. Your aunt told me everything."

"Well, how do you feel about it?" she asked, stunned to realize he knew her past but was willing to come to Colorado anyway.

"It was quite a shock at first. But I've had time to think about it, and I don't want anyone but you."

"You honestly want me ... to go with you ... to be with you?"

"There is nothing I would like more," he said softly. "I've come to take you back with me. Aren't you ready to leave this godforsaken place and get your life back?"

She studied him closely but could no longer imagine the affection they'd once shared. She had changed too much to return to her old life. Looking longingly around the ranch, she realized for the first time that she considered it home. The people she met were so genuine and kind, never passing judgment over her or her situation. And then there was Will. She didn't know if her admiration of him was because of the help and kindness he had shown, or just because of the man he was. He had become her truest friend, someone she could be completely honest with, and Lucy realized she felt none of those feelings for the man standing before her.

As she looked at his face closely, she saw something in his eyes that sent a chill down her spine. The hair on the back of her neck stood up, and her breathing quickened. She couldn't explain it, but she knew that Mr. Westley was not all he claimed to be. Lucy was suddenly on guard, and she lowered her hand into the folds of her skirt, wrapping her fingers around the handle of her knife.

"Well, get your things. If we leave now, we can make it to town for the night and start our new lives in the morning." He started toward the stairs, but she stopped him.

"I cannot leave without telling Michael."

Mr. Westley started fidgeting with his hat nervously, which made Lucy take a step back as the truth dawned on her. She knew that her brother had never mentioned to a soul that she had been raped, and Lucy had never told her aunt Olivia. Westley couldn't possibly know what had happened … and yet … he did. Lucy shuddered at the sudden realization of what she saw in his eyes. She had seen that evil look in Turner's eyes when he sat across from her in that small room in the cabin. Lucy took another involuntary step back and kept a tight grip on the knife hidden in her skirt.

She took a deep breath, suddenly feeling confident, and smiled at Mr. Westley. "I think we should have supper here first," she said. "You must be tired from your journey."

She moved down the steps, managing not to run. "Let me just tell the cook." When Lucy stepped off the porch, out into the open, she noticed Arthur walking toward her, and several riders were coming down the road toward the cabins. She recognized Will immediately.

Will jumped off his horse to run to Lucy. As soon as he and Mr. Westley locked eyes, Westley drew his pistol and grabbed Lucy by the arm to hold her close against his chest as a shield. He kept the barrel of the pistol firmly against Lucy's temple. Will had drawn his gun as well, and he was moving toward them with concern etched across his face.

Arthur ambled slowly forward, towering over everyone. His eyes never left Westley's. It was obvious he remembered all the times the man had been in the Mullens' home and eaten their food. His anger was palpable.

"Lucy is coming with me," Westley said coldly.

"Over my dead body." Arthur took another step forward.

Westley pointed his gun toward Arthur with a smile on his face, clearly more than happy to oblige.

"No!" Lucy said quickly, placing her hand on Westley's arm. She raised her other arm to stop Arthur from coming closer. Lucy still felt guilt over the men who had died to save her, and it would have destroyed her if anything happened to Arthur.

"What's going on, Mr. Westley?" Arthur asked loudly, staring at the man who had courted Lucy for several months in Philadelphia. Will's nervousness and Lucy's fear showed on their faces.

"It's Jim Turner," Will said quietly. "This man is Jack Turner's brother." Will kept his pistol pointed at the man, cocked and ready to shoot.

Lucy's face paled and filled with terror at the thought of Turner's brother breathing the same air as she did.

Memories of all the time they'd spent together in the city, and of the possibility of her marriage to such a man, swam through her head. Memories of her captivity came rushing back as well, causing her to become dizzy. Her knees buckled, but Jim Turner kept her upright with his stern grip around her neck.

"I don't understand," Arthur said in shock, raising his own pistol. "How could you be Turner's brother?"

"I've been living in Philadelphia for over a year, watching the three of you. God, what a boring place that is!" he said, shaking his head. "But Jack was sure you could lead him to Maggie, so I stayed. Finally, Jack got tired of waiting and decided to take little Miss Mullen here. He was sure it would lead him to our money."

Jim Turner finally took his eyes off Will and looked down at Lucy. "But Jack messed up, as usual," he said, ignoring Arthur's stream of questions. "He tainted and damaged my future bride." His jaw clenched and unclenched angrily.

Will stepped forward, making Jim Turner focus his attention on him instead of Arthur or Lucy, although he still held her by the neck against the front of his body, trying to use her as a shield against the guns pointed at him from all directions. Will was calm and spoke softly, never talking his eyes off Lucy. Her face took on a drastic change, from one of fear to one of gentle calm. The corner of one side of her mouth curved upward as she kept her eyes on Will.

Lucy looked up at Jim Turner and told him she would take him to Maggie. He looked down for a second in surprise. She continued to talk to him about how she wanted an end to the violence. She described the place where Maggie had been hiding for the last several months, and she told him she could take him there. Jim became so involved in the details of the story that his gun lowered slightly so that it was pointing toward the ground. He was just as greedy as his brother was.

Without a moment's hesitation, Lucy lifted the knife from her skirt and stabbed him in the leg, causing him to release his grip on her neck. Lucy removed the knife and thrust the blade into his stomach.

"Rot in hell," she hissed.

He stared at her face with a mixture of surprise and anger. When he raised his hands toward her in one last act of defiance, Will shot him in the head, and he fell backward onto the ground. As Lucy kept the man occupied, Will had plainly been waiting for the right opportunity to shoot. As it turned out, however, Lucy had another plan in mind.

As he died in front of her, she looked down at the man she had known as Mr. Westley. She felt numb. She moved backward a few steps and turned to find Will watching her, calm as always. She quickened her pace as she walked into his waiting arms. Will had given Lucy the ability to protect herself against Turner's brother. He had given her freedom.

After several minutes, when Will was certain Lucy could stand alone, he placed his hands on her shoulders and pulled her away to look at her face. "Are you all right?"

"Yes," she said confidently. "He didn't hurt me. I'm fine." Before Will could ask her another question, Arthur stepped up and swept Lucy into a big hug.

"I know I'm rushing you, Lucy," Will said, anxiety building on his face, "but we need to leave—right now."

Lucy tore herself away from Arthur, and they both stared at Will. It seemed to dawn on all of them at once that Will had come back without his brothers. "Where is everyone, Will?" she asked. "Where's Michael?"

Sarah had been running toward them, and she arrived just as Lucy asked her last question. She slowed in front of

Will, waiting for his answer. Arthur placed his arm around Lucy for support, and Will took Sarah's hand. "Mike's been injured," he said cautiously. "He's in pretty bad shape, but he's been asking about both of you. We need to leave right away and get to town."

Sarah just stared blankly at Will, clearly waiting for him to tell her more. As if expecting Lucy to fall apart, Arthur had remained standing by her side, holding onto her shoulders. Instead of breaking down, Lucy understood exactly what he was telling her, and she took a step back.

"I won't be but a minute," she said steadily, although her eyes showed that she knew how bad it was. "I'll just grab a few things and meet you by the horses." She glanced at Arthur as she hurried away. "Arthur, I'm sure he would want you there as well. Please get your horse ready."

28

THE COST OF REVENGE

Before I knew it, Pat and Tommy were kneeling by my side, along with Daniel and Little Bird. They all looked at each other cautiously after seeing the blood on my shirt. The abdominal wound would most definitely kill me.

"Is Eddie all right?" I whispered.

"He's fine, Michael," Pat said, taking hold of my shoulder. "But he won't be able to sit for a month when we get back home." He grinned down at me.

I nodded slowly and rested my head back on the ground. "Don't be too hard on him," I said. "At least now it's over." I could see the pity and sadness on their faces as each told me to hang in there, and that everything would be all right. It was at that point that I realized how bad my situation had become.

———◦((◦))◦———

I don't remember being carried to Doc Boylen's door outside of town. I must have lost consciousness between being carried to the wagon and the pain caused by the bumpy ride out of town. Pat was by my side each time I woke. He was covered in my blood and fighting hard to tend my wounds. My body felt as if it were on fire by the time we rode up to the doctor's house and they carried me through the front door to the exam room in the back. Doc took one look at me and shook his head, showing the same sorrow on his face that I had seen from the Donnelly brothers.

After he stripped off my shirt to expose the wound to my abdomen, I heard the air escape from his clenched teeth as he examined the wound a little closer. He finally left the room to speak to Pat and Tommy outside.

They decided to perform the surgery as soon as possible due to my worsening condition, but I insisted he wait until Sarah and Lucy arrived. I was unsure if I would make it through the surgery, and I wasn't willing to go without talking to them first. After several minutes of arguing with the doctor, I asked to speak privately with Pat.

"Pat," I said, holding out my arm to grasp his sleeve. "I need to be awake when Sarah gets here."

"Michael, Doc says if you don't have the operation now, you'll die." He leaned down next to me, speaking softly in my ear.

"If you had one more chance to talk to your wife, wouldn't you take it?" I whispered. He hesitated and stood to think about my question. He knew the answer as well as I did. "Please, Pat, I need your help. You can't let him give me anything to sleep. I cannot have surgery before Sarah and Lucy get here." I gripped his shirt tighter as I spoke, trying to bear the pain as best I could. "Promise me."

He leaned back down and placed his hand around mine on his arm. He removed my grip but grasped my hand firmly. "I promise," he said with a nod and a new look of determination. "I promise."

He let go of my hand and placed it on my chest. He paced around the room a few times before swearing and opening the door. "I have given this man my word," he said, squaring his shoulders and raising his head as he spoke outside the room. "We'll wait until our sisters arrive."

"But Pat—"

"I told you," Pat said again, "I've given him my word." Through the open door, I saw him look around at all the people in the front room of Doc's house. Little Bird and his family stood by the door, while Tommy, Daniel, and James sat in silence.

"You can do whatever is necessary to stop his bleeding or to make him comfortable," he continued, "but he says he won't take any medicine that'll make him sleep until after he sees Lucy and Sarah."

The doctor lowered his head and shook it back and forth in disbelief. "You understand that if we leave him, he is likely to die?"

Pat shrugged slightly and ran his hand across his face. "We have to respect his wishes, Doc."

Clearly knowing that the matter was closed, Doc came back into the room and prepared to clean my wounds. He said he was going to get as much done as possible so that he could start the surgery immediately after the women arrived. He used thick padding in an attempt to stop the bleeding, and he methodically cleaned each wound. I refused laudanum, only taking small sips of whiskey to take the edge off the pain. I lost consciousness a few times during those first hours when the doctor tended to my wounds, but Pat kept his promise since I was unable to speak for myself.

In the late hours of the night, when darkness settled over the landscape, I woke to a commotion on the other side of my door. I was too weak to move my head, but I recognized Sarah's walk as soon as she stepped into the room. She leaned over me and kissed me gently on the forehead, allowing her tears to fall upon my face. I opened my eyes and gazed at her as she took a cloth and carefully wiped my cheeks.

When she saw that I was awake, she smiled warmly and kissed me again on the lips. I couldn't raise my arms to hold her, which caused me a great deal of frustration, so I merely watched her as she sat silently next to me, brushing my hair away from my forehead.

"I'm sorry, Sarah," I whispered as a tear escaped from the corner of my eye and slid down into my hair. "I don't think I'm going to be able to keep my promise."

"That is hogwash," she said, wiping her face and grabbing my hand. "Don't you dare say that to me. We've been through far too much for you to just quit now."

"Will you stay here with me?" I asked with a crack in my voice.

"Of course, but you need an operation as soon as possible. You have already waited far too long."

"In case I don't wake up after surgery, I want to tell you how much I love you."

"Michael, please." Sarah had her hands wrapped around my arm as she sat next to my bed. Feeling her soft skin against my chest and arm, I wished to be able to hold her next to me.

"I want you to know," I said continuing my thought, "that I never loved another before I met you. Even with everything that has happened, I thank God for the gift of you in my life. I needed you to know that."

"I love you too, Michael," she said tearfully. "But you're going to have to wait until after the surgery to find out how much. Now stop being such a quitter and begin fighting like the man I fell in love with." I laughed weakly, causing pain to shoot through my body. Sarah smiled at me and kissed my hand before getting up to go get the doctor.

As soon as she opened the door, I heard Doc finishing his explanation of my injuries to Lucy. He told her, very gently, the same thing he had presumably told the men earlier. He mentioned the possibility of bleeding to death and the ever-present danger of infection from the wound being open so long. He also made sure that she knew my chances of survival were slim.

Lucy's raised voice startled me, causing my eyes to open again as I listened. "Don't you *dare* give up on my brother like that!" she hollered. "You have no idea if he'll survive or not until you try. Now move!" Unable to laugh, I lay smiling at the ceiling, listening to her berate the physician. That was the Lucy I knew and loved.

Even though I remembered nothing of the surgery, Pat later told me that Sarah stayed with me throughout the entire procedure. Lucy was there as well, refusing to leave and assisting the doctor in removing the bullets. She knew what needed to be done to help me, and she also knew how serious my injuries were. After working in the hospital, there was little Lucy hadn't seen, especially with regard to gunshot wounds.

The last thing I remembered before slipping into unconsciousness was the doctor telling everyone waiting in the other room that recovery was unlikely due to the loss of blood and the high probability of infection taking hold of my body.

I didn't wake again for three days. When I finally did, Sarah was sitting next to me with her head resting on my arm. She was talking in a low voice, and it took several minutes for me to figure out that she was praying. "Please," I heard her say, "I've waited all my life to find him. Please don't make me a widow before I've had the chance to be married. Don't let him go—I love him too much."

It was at that moment that I turned the corner. I started believing that the infection would subside and my wounds would heal. I listened to Sarah late into the night, talking to some invisible force, willing me to stay with her. I felt the strength within me build, and my breathing became more even.

Just before dawn, I felt my fever break. Sarah must have run out of nice things to say, because I woke to hear her voice again, but her words had changed. "Stupid dumb-ass man," I heard her say. "Won't take my advice ... thinking you're invincible ... You'd better wake up, or I'll never forgive you ... stupid man ..."

Her ramblings continued until she finally noticed my chest shaking with silent laughter. She was shocked into silence and sat there for a long moment, trying to comprehend what was going on. "Don't let me stop you," I said in a hoarse voice. "I want to hear more."

Lucy stood from the chair next to Sarah and ran to get the doctor, while Sarah placed her hands on both sides of my face, kissing me repeatedly. I opened my eyes to see that she was grinning from ear to ear, but tears remained in her eyes. I smiled back at her as I lifted my hand to touch her face. For several days, I had hoped for the strength to touch her, and now that I was able to, my body trembled as I felt the soft skin of her face and neck.

29

MAGGIE

They moved me to the Franklin Hotel after I was out of danger but not well enough to return to the Lazy D. I had to spend several days in bed, which was horribly annoying. The only saving grace was the fact that Sarah visited me each and every day. No matter how monstrous I became, or how many times I complained about wasting away in bed, Sarah stayed by my side.

We got into a routine of playing chess and reading each day. While I would much rather have spent time with her in more productive ways, I looked forward to our visits more and more. The two of us would talk for hours, about anything that came to mind. She told me about her fears concerning men, and the relationships she had in the past that had destroyed her trust. I told her about my doubts and fears, and about finally letting go of the resentment I felt for my father. No matter what happened in the past, the two of us agreed to start fresh, with a clean slate, and look toward a bright new future.

One morning, I woke to the sound of the door slowly opening. Thinking it was Sarah, I smiled and rolled over, opening my eyes. Luckily, I hadn't make a crude comment, because the woman standing in my doorway wasn't Sarah. She merely stood at the door and stared at me, without making a sound, for several long minutes. The look of shock on her face must have matched my own. She took a few steps forward, turned, and closed the door. Then she took a chair and sat next to the bed. I straightened as best I could, waiting for her to speak.

"Hello, Michael," she said. "I've wanted to meet you for a very long time." Sadness filled her eyes, and a single tear ran down her cheek. "My name is Maggie Graham."

No longer feeling the pain of my healing wounds, I sat straighter in bed and watched her closely. She couldn't have been more than thirty years old, and despite everything I had heard, the hardness of her face held an innocence and sweetness I hadn't expected. After so many months of thinking about the woman, I no longer knew how to feel.

"How did you know I was here?" I asked, when my ability to speak returned.

"Belle sent me a letter and told me what happened to Lucy," she said quietly, so quietly it was barely a whisper. "I've been traveling, so it took a while for it to reach me. I took the first train I could manage."

"How did Belle know where you were?" I asked. "No one around here seemed to know anything about your whereabouts—either that or they just refused to speak of it." After all my searching and fights with Pat and his brothers, I found it hard to believe that the answers to my questions lay in Belle's hands all along.

"I guess that's understandable after everything that happened when I left here." She seemed incredibly nervous, as if unsure whether I would accept her or try to throw her out my window. "To answer your question, however, Belle sent me money not long after your father died. It seems your father wrote to her after he left me in Nebraska, asking her to transfer money into a bank account in my name. He knew she would be the last person anyone would expect to know anything about me. I don't know what I would've done without you father's generosity."

"I was told that my father went to find you," I said, "but he died before he was able to let anyone know what happened."

She sighed deeply and looked down again, the same sadness returning to her face. "That's why I'm here, Michael," she said at last. "I came to put an end to Turner's fight against your family. When I arrived in Fort Collins, I heard about Turner's presence in Lone Tree. I bought a horse and rode to town as fast as I could. I wanted to face Turner and find out what happened to my daughter. When you killed him, I lost the last link I had to her whereabouts."

"I didn't know."

"It isn't your fault, Michael," she said. "I never would have gotten what I wanted from that man anyway. If you hadn't killed him, I would have. I have never hated anyone the way I hate him."

"Why are you here now?"

"I almost rode out of town after you were shot. I still have to find my girl, after all. But I figured you still may have some questions, such as how your father died and why Lucy was taken, and I owe it to you to answer all I can."

She lifted her head and looked directly in my eyes with new resolve on her face. Even though her breathing was still slightly ragged, she kept it together.

"Why *was* Lucy taken?" I couldn't help my curiosity after so many months of questions.

"She was taken because of me," she said. "My sister, Lilly, died because of me, and your father was killed because of me. Before I tell you my story, I need you to know that I am the reason all this pain has happened. I never should've brought that monster into any of your lives."

"I don't think—"

She held up her small hand and shook her head as if thoughts had begun to swarm in her head. When she continued, her eyes were glazed over, and she seemed lost in memories.

"After Jack beat me, I woke up at the Lazy D with Lilly at my bedside. The Donnelly family nursed me back to health, and my baby miraculously lived. I prayed that Jack had left me for dead and would never come for me. I feared his return each day, but I managed to go through the remainder of my pregnancy in peace. I moved to your father's house, since it was empty at the time, and spent most days trying to figure out how to piece together my life.

"I should have known Jack would find me. He always seemed to know everything a day before anyone else. Two days after Beth was born, Lilly and I came back to the cabin with Beth … to find Jack standing on the other side of the door. He had a big smile on his face, and he told me he'd finally hit the jackpot. He said that we were rich and could have anything we wanted.

I slowly made my way over to the crib in the corner and lay Beth down, safe in her bed, before Jack had a chance to hurt her. I pleaded with him to let Lilly leave, but he was drunk and wouldn't listen. Something had changed in his eyes, and I felt as if I were looking at a stranger.

"He continued to talk excitedly about his newfound wealth and all the things the three of us could do when we left Colorado. It was as if he felt all his problems were solved by finally having money. He talked about how envious Pat would be when he found out, and how he had finally gotten the best of all of them.

"Maggie," I said, "you don't have to tell me the rest. I understand."

She shook her head and returned to the chair next to the bed. "I have never told anyone what happened that day."

"All right," I said. "Tell me."

"Lilly tried to reason with Jack, but he insisted that she come with us. She then told him that she needed to be with her children. Jack pointed the gun at Beth's sweet face and asked Lilly again what she felt was important. He threatened to kill our little girl." She was sobbing at the reminder of her precious daughter.

I straightened in bed, reluctantly nodding for her to continue. It was extremely difficult to sit back and watch someone in such torment.

"Lilly lost her temper and told Jack he could never be the man Pat was. Without warning, he stormed over and backhanded Lilly, sending her sprawling onto the floor. At that moment, he became the monster you came to know. He tied me up and made me watch as he beat my sister on the floor of that cabin. The last thing Lilly said before she died was how much she loved her husband—and how Jack could never take that away." A sob escaped her throat.

"Jack never wanted to kill Lilly. But he finally just ... snapped. Jack put his hands around her throat to silence her talk about Pat, and he slowly squeezed the life out of her. Afterward, when he realized what he had done, he sat on the floor and cried like a baby. She was the one thing he'd wanted that he could never have.

"After what seemed like an eternity, he got up, untied me, grabbed Beth, and yanked me out the door. Four of his men waited outside, scanning the landscape, as Jack pushed me into the wagon. He threw Beth into my arms, as if she were a bag of flour, and jammed his pistol into my ribs. He told me that if I made a sound or moved an inch, he'd kill Beth. At that point, I couldn't have spoken if I wanted to. Something had tripped in my mind when Lilly died at the hands of my ... husband. I merely continued to breathe and go through the motions of living.

"Pat must have shown up at the cabin shortly after we left, because Jack saw him riding toward us in a blind fury before we reached town. I now realize how it must have looked to him—me sitting quietly and calmly on the bench in the wagon, smiling down at the bundle in my arms. I had blocked everything else out of my mind. Beth was the only thing real in my world anymore. I didn't even look up at Pat as he rode closer and Jack's men went after him.

"Jack and I continued into town, never seeing Pat again, and boarded the first available train. After a day's ride, Jack finally found a town he liked in Kansas called Spring Creek. He rented a room at the local hotel. He talked to himself non-stop in fragmented sentences that I couldn't understand. I tried not to acknowledge his presence. I went through the motions of caring for my child as if nothing had happened.

"He'd disappear each morning and return in the evening, always with another bag of stolen money or jewelry. Finally, one night while I slept, Jack took Beth and disappeared. When he returned, Beth wasn't with him. He woke me as he packed our bags and told me it was time to leave. Beth's absence pulled me back to reality, allowing horrible memories to flood my brain and my senses. I started shaking violently, and I couldn't stop the tears from pouring down my face. I asked Jack what he did with Beth, but he just shrugged and said, "'I got rid of her. She was useless.'

"Black spots swam in my vision, and I became dizzy with

fear and dread. I could barely stand, let alone fight, so Jack grabbed me by the arm and wrenched me out of the hotel. He threw me into a new wagon and started out again. I knew that Beth's only chance was if I held my temper and found a way to return to her as soon as possible. So, once again, I remained silent and waited. As soon as Jack let his guard down and left our new room, I disappeared. I had no idea where I was. I only knew I needed to return to Spring Creek to find my little girl."

"Did Jack find you?" I asked.

"No," she said. "Jack never found me."

"I know you blame yourself for Turner," I said, "but I cannot see how his actions are your fault."

"The reason Jack never found me was that your father came looking for me and found me living on the streets in Spring Creek, barely alive. He took me to Nebraska, to a small farm belonging to your family, and nursed me back to health. Your pa knew that the farm was secluded enough to not draw suspicion. He left me in the care of incredibly kind people and promised to return to Spring Creek to search for Beth. When he arrived back in Fort Collins, Jack was waiting. He ... he shot your father several times in the back after he'd asked questions about Jack in a saloon. I'm the reason your pa was shot and killed." Maggie paused to take a deep breath.

I looked at her closely and noticed the worry lines near her temples and the dark circles around her eyes. She looked incredibly tired and emotionally drained. I reached out and gently took her hand in mine. "Perhaps we should talk more tomorrow," I said gently.

"I haven't told you the worst part," she said sadly. "I haven't told you why Lucy was taken."

"It doesn't matter anymore." I straightened in bed and

moved my legs off the side to sit up straight. "Turner is dead."

Maggie leaned down and lifted her bag onto her lap. She removed a book from its depths and held it out toward me. I knew immediately that what she held in her hand was my father's last journal, the last thoughts of a man I was just beginning to know.

"When I left Jack, I wanted to hurt him in the way that he had hurt me when he took away my daughter," she said fiercely. "Out of anger, I told your father about Jack's involvement in a train robbery that caused the train to derail, killing several people. No one ever knew who was responsible for the blocking of the tracks, which caused so many deaths, but Jack told me all about it one night while he was drunk, bragging about the money he made that night. He never really cared about the people whose lives he stole."

"I don't understand," I said as my face tensed.

As the book was placed into my hands, she'd opened it and thumbed to the end. One of the last entries explained in detail the train robbery and the investigation that had followed. My father was a part of the investigation, but he had never been able to find the men who were guilty. The journal described everything Maggie had just told me and how they finally had the proof that was necessary to make Jack hang for those deaths. On the next page was a handwritten map, showing the location where Turner had hidden the money from the robbery.

"I just wanted to make him pay for everything he had done. I hoped he would be arrested and convicted so that we could all live in peace."

The final pieces of the puzzle finally slid into place. "So he took Lucy to find you and silence you."

Maggie kept her eyes glued to mine. "Your father must have removed the money from its hiding place, because Turner has been hunting me ever since his death. If I had known he was after anyone but me, I would've come out of hiding. After he killed your father, however, I knew that no one else knew where I was. I thought as long as I remained in hiding, everyone I loved would remain safe. I was horribly wrong. I should have known he wouldn't give up that easily." Maggie looked down into her lap. "I'm so sorry."

"Maggie," I said, taking her hand again, "I know I just met you, but I don't think you have a mean bone in your body. A series of events caused Lucy to be taken and brought here, but I still don't blame you. I haven't changed my mind. Jack Turner is the one to blame for all the harm caused to our families and those on the train."

She looked up into my eyes with tearstained cheeks, red eyes, and a sad smile. "Thank you," she said softly, "but you're wrong. When I find the man who has my daughter, I won't hesitate to put a bullet in his heart." Her eyes held a fury I hadn't seen before over the loss of her child. "I'm not the innocent you believe me to be."

We sat in silence for several minutes as Maggie regained control of her emotions. A weight that she had carried for far too long had been lifted from her shoulders. I leaned forward and squeezed her hand.

"Maggie, would you mind telling me what you know about Beth?"

"I pray daily that Jack gave her away, and that she is alive and well out there somewhere, with a family that loves her. But knowing him as I do, I doubt he would have been so kind. I took the money Belle gave me and continued to search for her, but I never found her. Now that Jack is finally dead, however, I'll have access to places I didn't before. I haven't given up on the thought of seeing her again, and I won't give up until I know what happened."

We both heard the door creak and turned to find Sarah standing in the room, staring. Maggie stood slowly and unsteadily, hanging on to the back of the chair with her shaking fingers. "Oh my ..." She looked as if she would faint dead away from the shock of seeing Sarah again. I realized that she had most likely intended to leave the area without any of the Donnelly clan knowing she had ever been there.

"Maggie?" Sarah said. "Is it really you?" Without waiting for a response, Sarah approached the young woman and placed a hand on her cheek as if to make sure she was real. Then, without warning, she wrapped her arms around Maggie, holding her in a tight embrace. Both women cried as they held onto each other. Because Sarah had been certain she would never see Maggie again, she was clearly overwhelmed that her old friend had returned.

By the time they remembered I was in the room and let go, they found me grinning like a fool. It was a healing time for all of us, and Sarah had just taken the first step in allowing Maggie the chance at a fresh beginning. I hadn't felt that happy in a long time.

"Don't you worry," Sarah said, grabbing both of Maggie's hands. "We'll do everything we can to help you find Beth."

"You little eavesdropper," I said teasingly. Sarah smacked my shoulder playfully. I placed my hand over hers on my shoulder and held it there.

"Sarah's right, Maggie," I said more seriously. "We'll help you in any way we can."

Sarah sat down next to me, and Maggie returned to her chair. "There is so much I want to talk to you about," Sarah said happily. "I'm so glad you're back. Will you be staying long?"

"I wasn't really planning on it, but I guess I can stay for a few days."

"Oh, you must stay longer than that. We'll be taking Michael home to the ranch in just a few days, and I would love for you to join us." Sarah was so excited that she rambled, and Maggie smiled as she did so. "I have so many questions. I cannot wait to talk to Pat and have the past resolved once and for all."

Maggie's face went through a dramatic change at the mention of Pat's name. Her face paled and her eyes were as wide as saucers. She stood abruptly and backed toward the wall. "P-Pat is ... alive?" She placed a hand over her mouth, and her eyes once again filled with tears. "Oh my God ... Oh my ..." She leaned against the wall before sinking to the floor.

Sarah rushed toward her, kneeling down beside her to steady her. "What is it, Maggie? What's wrong?"

"I thought Pat was dead," she said anxiously. "I thought Jack killed him the day Lilly died. He's really alive?"

"Yes," Sarah said, helping Maggie back to her chair. "He was terribly hurt that day, and it took him several months, but he pulled through. You know Pat—he's too stubborn to die." Sarah was trying to lighten the mood for Maggie's sake, and I wanted to grab her and hug her for it. Neither of us was sure how Pat would react to the news that Maggie was back in Lone Tree, but it was time for the two of them to air everything between them. Pat held so much anger about what happened to Lilly, as well as Maggie's possible involvement in her death, that I didn't want another day to go by with any misunderstandings between them.

"I think you need to speak with Pat," I said carefully. "There are several misunderstandings about your disappearance, and I'm sure the truth would help Pat heal."

"He blames me, doesn't he?"

Sarah broke in and put her hand on Maggie's knee. "Pat's confused. Even though I don't know the whole story of what happened that awful day, I think you owe it to him to tell him the truth."

"I agree," I said somberly. "After hearing everything, I know the truth will bring him a peace he hasn't felt in a long time. Would you please think about it?"

"Of course," she said with a slight frown. "I'd like some time, though. Don't worry; we'll see each other again." She hugged Sarah and left quietly.

After a few moments, Sarah turned back toward the bed. Even though my recovery was going to take much longer, I felt a brief moment of peace. The Donnellys were out of danger, my sister was safe, and I had Sarah by my side. I took Sarah's hand and softly kissed her palm as she settled next to me on the bed again.

"So you know the whole story?" she asked.

I nodded. "I imagine so. It feels so strange to finally learn what my father sacrificed for everyone, and how good a man he truly was."

"Do you think she'll come to the ranch?"

I looked attentively at Sarah and pulled her close, until our bodies were touching head to toe, with Sarah's head nestled into my shoulder. "I'm sure of it," I said. "I think she wants to resolve everything as much as the rest of us, and I think she knows that she owes it to Pat."

"What about her little girl?"

"She told me she'll continue the search as soon as she can, so I don't expect her to stay in town long," I said, absently moving my hand up and down her back. "Hopefully she comes to the ranch when you arrange to move these old bones back to the cabin."

I felt Sarah chuckle against my chest. "You'd better hurry and recover, old man," she said. "We have an enormous party to plan for the spring roundup, and I want to dance with you."

"Since you're planning a party anyway," I said, clearing my throat, "how about we make it an engagement party?"

Sarah sat up abruptly and smiled. "Is that some kind of pathetic proposal?"

"It's as good as I can manage in my ravaged state," I replied, coughing and trying to look weak and feeble.

She laughed aloud and hugged me tightly. "Of course I'll marry you. Who else could take care of someone as clumsy as you?"

"Trust me, love," I said with a kiss. "I feel my body healing more every minute you're with me. By the time we have the party, the two of us will be dancing circles around all the young bucks at the ranch."

"I do love you, Michael," she said through her giggles.

EPILOGUE

nstead of dancing circles around the other couples in the room, I was relegated to spending most of our engagement party sitting or standing off to the side. So many days in bed had taken a toll on my body, along with all my strength and energy. I was just happy to be able to walk into the room and greet the guests with Sarah on my arm. But at least I was definitely on the road to recovery, and each day was getting better.

The party ended up being a large barn dance that was held each year as a way to kick off the new season. Everyone from miles around came to the ranch for a night of fun and socialization. The townspeople all felt the same great weight lifted off their shoulders when Turner died and his men fled town. Even Pat, who had spent so much time consumed by anger and sorrow, had a lighter step and brightness in his eyes. He no longer seemed haunted by memories of the past, and he spent more time with his children than ever before. I think with the absence of Turner in the world, Pat could finally look at the future with some kind of hope.

A few days after I had returned to the ranch, Maggie finally came to talk to Pat. Sarah and I had told him everything

Lori R. Hodges

---

that Maggie had shared, but the meeting was still awkward for both of them. Maggie was blatantly afraid that Pat would still see her as an enemy to his family, and Pat still had so many questions. He accepted that she was a victim as much as his wife was, however, and after they spent a couple of evenings talking alone, I knew their lives would be bright again, given time.

Maggie ended up staying at the ranch for a few weeks as I continued my recovery, and Pat urged her to stay until at least after the big dance. Other townspeople didn't know quite what to make of Maggie at first, after so much time away, but when Pat took her hand and led her in the first dance, the rest of the town welcomed her warmly.

She still insisted on leaving after the dance to continue her search for her daughter, but at least she knew that she'd have a home to return to if she ever needed it. I offered her funds to help in her search, but she reminded me once again that my father had provided for her, leaving her with all she would need to move forward.

Several of the ranch hands, including Red, were fiddlers, and they gathered on the small stage they'd constructed for the party, keeping the crowd entertained. Arthur was deeply intrigued with the fiddle and made Red promise to teach him how to play. Similar in age and size, the two men were becoming fast friends.

Shortly after the dancing began, I looked toward the fields to find Tommy practically dragging Belle from the wagon toward the party. We had invited her over a week earlier, and she had graciously declined, saying she wasn't acceptable company in the presence of decent folk. After all she did to help us, however, and her quick shooting in town, I had told her that was hogwash. She'd earned the respect of more than a few people in town that day, and

356

she deserved to celebrate our engagement as much as any of the others did.

Still, she had refused, and Tommy had taken it upon himself to go and get her from town and bring her to the ranch. By the looks of him, it had been quite a task. And Belle, God bless her, looked ready to spit nails, she was so angry. By the time they reached the door, however, Belle slapped Tommy's hands away, straightened her spine, and walked inside alone, with all the dignity she could muster. I had always liked Belle.

Chuckling, I glanced across the room at all the people dancing and laughing. Sarah was among them, surrounded by friends and neighbors. She tipped her head back and laughed loudly at something one of them said, making my heart skip a beat. I picked up two glasses of champagne and moved slowly in her direction. I had only one wish for the evening and that was to harness enough energy to be able to dance with Sarah at least once. I couldn't give her the party she deserved, but I would be damned if I'd go the entire evening without holding her close. For me, there had always been something about dancing—so intimate, so sensual. It took me forever to cross that dance floor.

I finally reached her and placed a glass in her hand. Before I could ask her to dance, however, I looked across the room at all the couples and found my eyes focusing on my sister, standing alone by the door. She was smiling, but I could see all the old signs of nervousness and anxiety. From the crease on her brow and the smile that didn't quite reach her eyes, to her hands clenched in the material of her dress, I could see that she was tense from head to toe. She looked much as she had at the last party of Aunt Olivia's, when she met R. J. for the first time.

I realized that the dance was the first time since arriving

in Colorado that Lucy had been at a social gathering in the company of strangers. It was the first time she was in a room with men who may wish to dance with her or court her, and who may or may not know her history. She was trying to keep up a brave appearance, but I could tell she was incredibly uncomfortable.

Setting my glass down, I leaned to whisper in Sarah's ear that I would be back. I had a feeling that if something wasn't done quickly, Lucy would bolt out the door and run away as fast as possible. When I had taken only a few steps, however, I stopped. It seemed that Will had seen the same distress as I did in Lucy's eyes and had decided to remedy the situation himself.

<hr />

"Good evenin', Miss Mullen," Will said, taking Lucy's shaking hand. "Would you do me the honor of a dance?"

She stared at his hand for a moment, with glistening sad eyes, and then shook her head as she tried to move away, closer toward the door. "I think I'll just go back to the cabin. I'm a little tired."

"Now, that just won't do, darlin'." He led her away from the safety of the exit. "My night just won't be complete unless you give me at least one dance." Without waiting for her to answer, Will led Lucy onto the dance floor. "I must confess that I'm not much of a dancer," he added, "but I was hopin' you could help me."

"Will, I appreciate the thought. I honestly do," she said, looking nervously around the room. "But I really think it would be better if you found another partner. Besides ..." She was shaking so much that Will cupped both hands in his

own and looked down at her anxious face. "I just ... I feel ..."
Will moved her close to his chest and wrapped one arm
around her waist as he slowly started to move his feet. He
leaned his head down and put his mouth close to her ear,
while his cheek rested on her temple. "What is it, Lucy?" he
whispered.

"I feel like everyone is staring at me," she said with a
shaky voice. "I just feel so ... I don't belong here. You should
find someone else to dance with. There are many lovely
women here tonight. I know they'd be pleased to dance
with you." Lucy started to move away, but Will tightened his
grasp on her waist and pulled her close again.

"Didn't you hear what I said?" she asked, pulling her
face away to look into his eyes. "I don't think I belong here."

"You really are a lovely dancer, Lucy," he said as he continued leading her around the room.

"Will?"

He moved his head so that he was leaning against her
temple again, and he sighed heavily. "All right," he said quietly, "the first thing I'd like to say is that my night would be
plum ruined if you leave the party, and since I'm one selfish
bastard, I can't let that happen. Second, you're right about
everyone staring at you." He could feel her tense in his arms.
"But it isn't for the reasons you think."

"What do you mean?"

"I mean that everyone is watchin' you," he continued,
"because you are the loveliest lady in the room. The men
are standing in awe of your beauty, as they try to gather the
courage to ask you to dance, and the women are just green
with envy."

"You, sir, are a flatterer," she said, laughing, "and I do
not believe a word you say." Without seeming to realize it,
Lucy had stopped shaking and was dancing gracefully across

the floor.

"I am an honest man, darlin'," he said. "Besides, the women aren't just envious of your beauty. Not only are you lovely, but you are also dancin' with the most handsome man in the entire county. Heck, I wouldn't be surprised if there was a fight later. You'd better watch your back."

Lucy laughed louder, and her face suddenly brightened. She looked up at him with a beautiful ear-to-ear smile.

Will placed his hand on her cheek. "Now, that's what I've been waitin' to see all night."

They stayed on the dance floor after the end of the song and didn't move until a handsome blond man tapped Will on the shoulder. "Could I have the next dance?"

Will looked at Lucy and winked, nudging her in the side. "See, I told you everyone wanted a dance with you. This is Monty from the Triple L Ranch near Fort Collins."

Even though Lucy's smile remained, she squeezed Will's hand with renewed anxiety. She felt comfortable with Will, but she wasn't so sure about dancing with a stranger. Will wasn't about to let Lucy run away, however. Instead, he leaned down and whispered in her ear.

"What happened to that courage you spoke so much about?" he asked, chuckling. "You deserve to have a little fun tonight." He bowed in front of her, kissed her hand, and placed it in the other gentleman's grasp before heading off the dance floor. He grinned as she scowled at him.

Will walked over to the side of the room with a smile on his face. He watched Lucy closely and noticed her comfort level increasing. She glided across the dance floor as if she were floating. He could hear her laughing as she continued to dance throughout the evening. One by one, men asked her to dance all night long.

Will remained within view at all times during the

evening. Lucy would often look around until she caught his eye, then she'd smile and continue dancing. Will didn't dance again, even though he was asked, until the end of the evening, when he danced the last dance with Lucy.

◆◄◈►◆

Sarah and I remained near the refreshment table while the party continued in high fashion. Red and several of the ranch hands sauntered over to Sarah and me after their set was completed. Their faces were flushed from playing, and they seemed to be well on their way to drinking the entire refreshment table.

"I never knew you could play, Red," I told him, watching as he took a long drink from his flask.

He held his fiddle lovingly next to his body as if it was the most precious thing in the world to him. "Yeah, well, we've been together a long time, the two of us." He smiled brightly and took another drink. "The boys and I wanted to tell you we thought of an excellent wedding present for the two of you. I thought I'd run it past ya."

"That's awfully nice, Red," Sarah said.

"What we decided is that we're gonna build you a fine house, just as soon as you tell us where to start." Red nodded his head and winked at Sarah before taking another drink. If he kept that pace up, he wouldn't be standing for more than another few minutes.

"I appreciate the offer," I said, "but there won't be time to build a house with the roundup coming."

"You're right about that, Mike," he agreed, "but we'll find time just as soon as the roundup is over." He held his hand up in the air, swaying slightly. "I promise."

I glanced at Sarah's happy face and then back at Red and the other ranch hands with him. "We'll think about it," I said finally, thinking it was too much to ask of them.

Red leaned in close so the boys couldn't hear him. "Actually, Mike, I'd like to have my cabin back." He glanced around again and moved even closer. "I don't mind stayin' with the boys, but I miss my privacy. I'm an old man, and I just can't keep up with these young bucks anymore. Trust me, the work'll be worth it."

After six months, I had forgotten the cabin once belonged to Red. The poor man had been living in the bunkhouse all winter with the rowdiest bunch of men I had ever laid eyes upon.

"In that case," I said, "we would be honored by your gift."

Red stood up straight and drank the remainder of the liquor in his flask. "I'm glad we could do somethin' for the two of ya." He said this loudly so the guys would hear him. He winked at Sarah again, adding, "It's the least we could do."

I laughed softly and took Sarah's hand in mine. "Thanks again, boys," I said, "but you will now have to excuse us, as I want to dance at least one dance with my Sarah." I started to move toward the floor but felt Sarah tug my arm and body back away from the dancers.

"What?" I asked, confused.

"Are you sure this is a good idea? Doc told you to take it easy."

I pulled her onto the floor with me, despite her protests, and wrapped my arm around her waist. "I guess that means you'll just have to hold me up, then, won't you?"

"Michael!"

I sighed heavily, knowing that in a stubborn contest with

Sarah, I would most definitely lose. I looked around the room quickly until I spotted Doc Boylen in the crowd. "Doc!" I yelled. "Doc!" He began to approach us where we had frozen in the middle of the dance floor.

I quickly looked away from Sarah when I saw the fire in her eyes. "Doc," I said again as he got closer, "do you think it would hurt if I danced one itty-bitty little dance, very slowly, with my beloved Sarah?"

Doc studied us both closely, seeing the obvious worry on Sarah's face and the anticipation on mine. "Oh, I think it would be fine," he said carefully, "as long as you promise to take it easy."

Without another word, I twirled Sarah around and joined the others dancing. Sarah smiled up at me and leaned close to whisper in my ear as I laughed and twirled her faster. "If you don't slow down," she said through clenched teeth, "I'll kill you myself."

I continued chuckling but slowed to a mere shuffle, away from the crowd on the floor. Sarah immediately relaxed, and her smile turned into genuine enjoyment. We silently glided, in a slow beat, across the floor. Dancing slow was a much-preferred activity anyway.

"It's good to have you looking out for me, sweetheart," I said after a few minutes together, smiling against her ear.

"Someone has to."

I had to laugh. "I'm just glad you volunteered for the job."

"God help me!"

Before dawn the next morning, I went to the main house and woke Sarah quietly to see if she would meet me in the stable. As I was leading Ginger out of the barn, fully saddled, with a basket tied to the horn, I noticed Sarah on her way. She looked half-asleep as she stumbled out of the house in fresh clothes, while trying to pull her hair out of her face. The party had lasted until the wee hours of the morning, and the fiddlers had just packed it in a few hours before I got out of bed.

"What on earth are you doing up so early, Michael?" Sarah asked quietly.

"I thought today would be a good day for a picnic," I replied, patting the saddle. "Hop on!"

"Now?" she said in a hushed voice so as not to wake the revelers. "It isn't even morning yet."

I took her hand gently in mine and kissed her palm the way I did the first night I held her. "I have something I want to show you."

Without another word of protest, Sarah and I mounted Ginger and rode slowly and quietly away from the ranch, toward the valley below. After about a half hour of easy riding, we passed the remains of the cabin my father had built, entering the edge of the clearing. The sun was just starting to shoot dark orange rays across the sky, lighting the darkness of night in the beautiful shades of blue before sunrise. I stopped Ginger and dismounted, helping Sarah to the ground.

I led her into the trees, and we walked for several minutes—until a lake came into view, along with a large field of grass surrounded by trees. I set the basket down when I found the perfect spot, spreading the blanket across the grass. The air still held a slight chill, but it looked as if it would warm quickly as the sun began its ascent into the sky.

I settled next to Sarah on the blanket, lying on my back,

with my elbows supporting me. "I found this place while I was out exploring one day."

She remained silent and got comfortable on the blanket beside me. We watched the sunrise through the trees, and we each breathed in the peace of the morning. Finally, when there was enough light in the clearing, I raised my hand and pointed to our left. "Have you noticed something strange about the trees?"

"The trees that circle around each other?"

"Yes," I said, a smile forming on my lips. "They look as if they're embracing, do they not?"

She tilted her head and examined the clearing. "Actually, yes," she finally said.

"When you and I first met, I dreamt of this place." Surprise flashed across her face, and then she flashed me her lovely smile. "After the dream, I just couldn't let go of the feeling that this meadow really existed somewhere in these mountains. I'd never been to Colorado before, but I dreamt of this clearing in the woods, I dreamt of the trees twining around each other, and I dreamt of the two of us here … alone."

I rested my head in her lap and gazed through the branches of the aspen trees, imagining what the clearing would look like in the summer and fall. "I think we were meant to be here together, Sarah," I whispered. "I think this is where we should live."

Sarah slowly raked her fingers through my hair as I closed my eyes. When I opened them again, she was looking around the clearing. Her eyes rested on the twisted trees. "I don't think I've ever been anywhere this beautiful," she said softly, nearly lulling me to sleep with the rhythmic motion of her fingers in my hair. "Let's move in today."

I chuckled softly, pleased that she felt the way I had

when I'd first found the clearing. For once, I knew I was no longer asleep, dreaming of a place that didn't exist. When I opened my eyes, Sarah would still be there, and for the first time in years, I felt as if I had come home. From that moment forward, we could begin each day with new hopes and dreams, in our clearing in the valley, next to the loving trees.

CPSIA information can be obtained
at www.ICGtesting.com
Printed in the USA
FSHW011547240819
61391FS